## THE EXCA[...]

# THE
# PENDRAGON
# MURDERS

## A MERLIN INVESTIGATION

## J.M.C. BLAIR

BERKLEY PRIME CRIME, NEW YORK

**THE BERKLEY PUBLISHING GROUP**
**Published by the Penguin Group**
**Penguin Group (USA) Inc.**
**375 Hudson Street, New York, New York 10014, USA**
Penguin Group (Canada), 90 Eglinton Avenue East, Suite 700, Toronto, Ontario M4P 2Y3, Canada
(a division of Pearson Penguin Canada Inc.)
Penguin Books Ltd., 80 Strand, London WC2R 0RL, England
Penguin Group Ireland, 25 St. Stephen's Green, Dublin 2, Ireland (a division of Penguin Books Ltd.)
Penguin Group (Australia), 250 Camberwell Road, Camberwell, Victoria 3124, Australia
(a division of Pearson Australia Group Pty. Ltd.)
Penguin Books India Pvt. Ltd., 11 Community Centre, Panchsheel Park, New Delhi—110 017, India
Penguin Group (NZ), 67 Apollo Drive, Rosedale, North Shore 0632, New Zealand
(a division of Pearson New Zealand Ltd.)
Penguin Books (South Africa) (Pty.) Ltd., 24 Sturdee Avenue, Rosebank, Johannesburg 2196,
South Africa

Penguin Books Ltd., Registered Offices: 80 Strand, London WC2R 0RL, England

This is a work of fiction. Names, characters, places, and incidents either are the product of the author's imagination or are used fictitiously, and any resemblance to actual persons, living or dead, business establishments, events, or locales is entirely coincidental. The publisher does not have any control over and does not assume any responsibility for author or third-party websites or their content.

THE PENDRAGON MURDERS

A Berkley Prime Crime Book / published by arrangement with the author

PRINTING HISTORY
Berkley Prime Crime mass-market edition / February 2010

Copyright © 2010 by John Curlovich.
Cover illustration by Dan Craig.
Cover design by Annette Fiore Defex.
Interior text design by Kristin del Rosario.

ISBN: 978-0-425-23312-2

BERKLEY® PRIME CRIME
Berkley Prime Crime Books are published by The Berkley Publishing Group,
a division of Penguin Group (USA) Inc.,
375 Hudson Street, New York, New York 10014.
BERKLEY® PRIME CRIME and the PRIME CRIME logo are trademarks of Penguin Group (USA) Inc.

PRINTED IN THE UNITED STATES OF AMERICA

10   9   8   7   6   5   4   3   2   1

# ONE

England was at peace, at least superficially, and King Arthur was enjoying his kingship for the first time in memory. "My kingdom is quiet," he told Merlin, astonished at his own words. "Can you believe it? For once there are no insurrections and the nobles are quiet. No one in England is scheming against me."

"The barons are always scheming."

"Always, perhaps. But not now. You are such a killjoy, Merlin. Let me enjoy it while it lasts, will you?"

There were no foreign intrigues for him to concern himself with. Since the deaths of Leodegrance and Leonilla, France had been fragmented and posed no threat to the British. The Byzantine Empire had been distracted by wars on its eastern and northern frontiers; thus preoccupied, Justinian had evidently forgotten his interest in the British Isles. The only foreign concerns arose from Scandinavian raiders who plundered the northeast coast from time to time. But that was a military matter, and a relatively minor one, not a concern of Merlin's. Britomart had organized defenses and the situation seemed to be well in hand.

Domestically things were even calmer. Arthur's treacherous wife, Guenevere, was safely imprisoned in the far north of Scotland and showed no signs of hatching any new schemes against her husband's kingship. Her erstwhile lover and bigamous husband, the French knight Lancelot, was likewise securely held at a nearly inaccessible castle on an island off the Welsh coast. They had had no communication with each other, though they had tried. Although it was a given that they would find a way to make more trouble sooner or later, for the moment they were quiet.

Arthur's barons, who enjoyed the peace and prosperity of his reign, were showing signs of restlessness; submission to an overlord did not come easily to them, not even to an overlord as beneficent as Arthur. Now and then their discontent erupted into something approaching rebellion, but Arthur, aided by his minister of state, Merlin, and his military commander, Britomart, always managed to quell the unrest without bloodshed. For the moment things were calm even though England was far from unified.

That summer had been long and unusually temperate; when it rained, the rains were warm and nurturing, not cold and sterile. Now signs of autumn were everywhere. Trees turned color and shed their leaves. Unusual numbers of butterflies flitted about the countryside. Small game abounded. The coming winter would not be too hard on the people.

Merlin kept a watchful eye on all of the country. Arthur fretted occasionally about his royal security and the future, but for the most part he was pleasingly content. And Merlin was happy to leave him that way.

But Arthur could never resist goading him. "You worry too much, Merlin. You should learn to relax."

"Do not be lulled into thinking the world is well, Arthur. You do not worry enough."

"I wish you could stop being such a fussbudget."

"It is the fussbudgets and the worrywarts who always see approaching storms first."

"What storms?" The king was growing testy. "There are no storms. Do you think a swarm of cabbage moths will commit treason? Look around, Merlin. See the pastoral calm, see the beauty. Should we be alarmed by all the glow-worms?"

"There are worms that do not advertise their presence, Arthur. We have encountered enough of them. The seeds of war are always sown in peace. Crime is hatched in tranquility."

"You don't drink enough, Merlin. There are times when I wish you did."

"A lot of good I would be to you, drunk as a knight."

"A lot of good you are, fretting like an old woman."

They were at loggerheads, but then, they often were. When something happened, they would focus on it and not on their bickering. Merlin knew that. Arthur seemed not to want to.


"You should try and relax, Merlin." His assistant Nimue, who lived her life as a boy called Colin, was even more amused than the king by Merlin's constant watchfulness. "You're like a vain queen, always expecting a blemish to appear on her pure white skin."

"More like a physician, Colin, monitoring a healthy body for signs of disease." He smiled at her, pleased with his simile. "England is my patient."

"You must learn to take life easy, Merlin. England is at peace. Enjoy it." She gestured at the serene landscape outside the tower at Camelot where they lived and worked.

•

"While it lasts. Peace never does. Storms brew over calm seas. Wars erupt among nations in harmony. The country is too quiet for my taste. I would feel better if we had a few treasonous dukes to deal with. You and Arthur—" He snorted and left the sentence unfinished.

She put a foot up on the windowsill, gestured at Petronus, the French boy who was Merlin's other assistant, and said breezily, "We should make a trip to Dover. Petronus and I think it would be fun."

Merlin was busily heating some glass pellets over an open flame; with one hand he pumped a small bellows and with the other he turned the glass slowly till it was molten and ready to be blown. Without looking up from his work at Nimue, he said, "Dover? Have you developed a sudden passion for fish?"

The door opened and Simon of York, Arthur's majordomo, stepped into the room. He was breathing heavily. "Good Lord, Merlin, why don't you move to a decent part of the castle? Or at least to a lower level of this tower? I exhaust myself every time I come up here."

"Stay below, then." Merlin was gruff.

"The king sent me."

"Then stop grumbling. Or use the lift I installed."

"That thing? Only a madman would trust it."

"You could use a little madness, Simon. You spend too much time worrying about protocol. Try concerning yourself with something the rest of us care about."

Simon bristled. "When my king sends me, I come. He wants *you*."

"So help me, if he wants me to give him still another opinion about those bloody portraits of his . . ."

"He does."

"Then let him wait. Perhaps he will get bored and find something productive to worry over."

"Shall I tell him you said so?"

"If you like. Now leave me. I am blowing glass."

Simon stiffened; he was the very picture of a bureaucrat whose dignity had been offended. "That is your final word?"

"It is. I will join Arthur shortly. Now, go."

The man turned and left.

After him Merlin shouted, "Ride the lift down. You will enjoy it."

He stood and listened for a moment; there was no sound of the lift mechanism. Merlin chuckled softly. "Oh, the pleasure I get from needling that fool."

"There are times when you act like an adolescent boy." Nimue laughed. "Now about Dover."

"I have been there more than often enough, thank you."

"You know perfectly well Dover is not only a fishing town. It's one of our most important ports. Ships from all over the Mediterranean put in there."

"Yes, and sailors. And half the whores in England, to keep them happy. I hardly need you to tell me that. Be quiet while I blow these globes."

Quickly, carefully, he blew the glass into a series of small globes and placed them on a cooling rack. As he was working, one of his pet ravens flew into the room and perched on his shoulder; the bird nuzzled his ear in an attempt to get his attention, but he continued working without missing a beat. Vexed, the bird pecked him lightly, and he shushed it gently. "Be still, Roc."

Nimue smirked at him. "You expect us to be still but you permit that bird to behave in that unruly way."

"Human beings are governed by reason—or ought to be. Birds have only their instincts." Merlin continued his glass blowing.

"You're changing your tune, Merlin. You never stop complaining about how irrational human beings are."

"Be quiet." The operation was completed in a surprisingly short time. When he had set the last of the globes aside to cool, Nimue picked up where she'd left off. "Petronus and I haven't been anywhere for months, Merlin.

I'm feeling stale. And I'd like to take a trip somewhere before winter sets in."

"There have been reports of raids on the Scottish coast by Norsemen." He smiled at her ironically. "Would you like to go there? You could gather intelligence."

"Don't be difficult about this, Merlin. You know Dover will have a huge autumn market festival in two weeks. People from all over the southeast will be there, and probably visitors from around the Mediterranean, and Petronus and I want to go. And you should come, too. Who knows? We might pick up some interesting news."

"In Dover? The only news we could possibly pick up there is the price of mackerel." He turned to look at Petronus and asked him, in inquisitorial tones, "You wish to go there, too?"

The boy had been silent for the longest time, listening, amused, at their exchange. Now he nodded energetically and said in strongly accented English, "I love fairs. The ones at home used to have roundabouts. I love rides."

"You are too old for that sort of thing."

"I am not. Besides, if the weather is good, you can see France from Dover. I'm feeling a little bit homesick."

Merlin picked up the first globe he'd blown and inspected it. "No flaws. I believe I am getting better." To Petronus he said, "Dover attracts—what would the word be?—*eccentrics* from far and near. You might be shocked at some of the behavior."

"I am French, remember, not an English prude. Nothing shocks me." He tried to sound worldly, not quite successfully. "I attended a fair at Mendola once, in the Pyrenees, and there were young women there dressed as boys. I found it very exciting."

Merlin glanced at Nimue, who was keeping her features carefully neutral. Then to Petronus he said, "You are too young to be excited."

"Stop saying things like that. I turn sixteen in a few months."

"A man of the world, then." Merlin grinned at the boy; Nimue laughed openly.

Petronus sulked. "Why are both of you so determined to think of me as a child? You act as if you were my parents."

"Heaven forbid." Nimue had not stopped chuckling. "But Merlin, we really should make this trip. We all need a change. And for once there are no crises demanding our attention. Let's go."

He sighed. "I will raise the subject with Arthur. If he consents . . ."

"Yes?"

"If he consents, I will give it some serious thought."

"We can bring you around. We always do."

The bird Roc flapped onto the worktable and scrambled around, pecking at everything it thought might be food.

Suddenly a thought seemed to hit Merlin and he turned to Petronus. "Should you not be in school now?"

The school Merlin had established for the squires and pages at Camelot had grown with remarkable speed. Two teachers had been imported, one each from France and Germany, to take the teaching burden off Merlin and Nimue. The students, required to attend by royal order, grumbled but learned. The knights they served complained to Arthur constantly; books were for clerks and women, not knights and squires. It was a source of constant friction. But over time Arthur had begun to see the advantages of having men who were educated, not just skillful in combat. Camelot would be richer for it.

Petronus sulked again. "We're doing Sophocles today. I already know his writing—from you."

"Even so, you should go. Truancy is never a good idea. Run along, now."

The boy moped. "Yes, *maman*."

"And do not be sarcastic. Oh—when you reach the top of the staircase, would you check and see if the water is boiling?"

Nimue chimed in, "I started the fire half an hour ago."

"Even so. Now will you go, Petronus?"

Petronus jumped to his feet and ran to the door. "I'll be back after I've dazzled the class with my erudition."

"We'll wait. It may take a while."

Petronus left quickly. Once he was gone, Nimue's mood turned more serious. "That boy is onto me. You heard him."

"Sooner or later, it was inevitable. Do you not trust him?"

"After what he tried to do to Arthur last year? What do you think?"

"He was under duress. You know that. He has been tireless in helping me."

"Besides, it isn't that, Merlin. It's just that it feels odd, having someone know."

"Britomart knows. She has for ages."

"Yes, and I'm always ill at ease around her. Having someone else in on the secret . . ."

"And his interest is erotic." Merlin was amused by the situation. "You heard what he said. Women who dress as men excite him. And he likes you older women." His eyes twinkled. "Imagine, having a youthful admirer at your tender age."

"Be quiet. I want to go to the fair at Dover."

"You are relentless, Nimue."

"That is something else I've learned from you."

From outside the room Petronus called, "Everything is ready, Merlin."

"Thank you, Petronus. Now get to class."

He turned back to Nimue. "I don't know whether to be flattered by what you said. At any rate, if we are to go, I will have to get Arthur's permission."

She turned and pushed the window shutter open wide.

"It's going to be a lovely day, Merlin. And a lovely autumn, I think. Let's not waste it shut up in Camelot."

"It is too cool for my taste. Besides, the king—"

"You can handle Arthur. You always do."

"He has this little crisis right now."

"Is Guenevere on the loose again?"

"Nothing so dramatic, I am afraid." He extinguished the flame he had worked over. "We are planning to issue new coins. He is fretting about which portrait of himself to use on them. He wants to show himself to best advantage."

"Ah, the male ego."

"Women, of course, are all quite modest. At any rate, if he is happy with his final decision, he will be in a good mood. That will be the time to ask him."

"Do it, then."

"Yes, my lady."


Merlin's study-cum-laboratory was on the top floor of what everyone called, to his annoyance, the Wizard's Tower. When he reached the landing outside the door he stopped and looked down the stairway; more than a hundred fifty steps wound down to the main floor of the castle.

A steam boiler bubbled busily nearby; above it was an assemblage of wheels, gears and chains. One long chain hung down to ground level, connected directly to the mechanism, so that he could operate it from there. Merlin stopped to check a valve on the boiler. "Yes, perfect." Then he walked to the spot where a metal chair hung suspended precariously. "Time to go down." He smiled at Nimue. "Will you start the mechanism for me?"

He moved to the very edge of the stairwell and climbed gingerly into the chair. It swung giddily over the long drop, and he took tight hold of the chains to try to steady it.

"You're going to kill yourself in that thing someday, Merlin."

"I am feeling my arthritis today. The stairs would be . . . Besides, you know perfectly well this is safe if used with due caution."

"Of course." She did not try to hide her skepticism.

She pulled a third chain, and slowly the chair descended. Nimue followed along on the steps, chatting with Merlin as they went down. When finally the chair reached the main level, he stood, arranged his robes, stretched and headed off to see Arthur.

"Don't forget Dover," she prodded.

"Be careful. No one likes a nagging woman."

"I am a boy, remember?"

Merlin had built his "lifting machine" from plans by the legendary Hero of Alexandria. His friend Germanicus Genentius, the Byzantine governor of Egypt, had found them in the Library of Alexandria and sent precise copies to Merlin. Everyone at Camelot thought it was a marvel, some for its ingenuity, some for what they took as its folly. Arthur and most of his knights had insisted on taking rides in it, and most of them were duly terrified; one of them, the French knight Sir Accolon, shrieked like a terrified girl.

"I hope," Merlin had told Arthur dryly, "you will remember where the real courage at Camelot resides—among the scholars and teachers, not the knights."

"It might do you well to think about the difference between being brave and being foolhardy. You'll kill yourself in that thing. You'll fall, or one of the chains will break, or—"

"Then Camelot will enjoy the pageantry of a state funeral."

"You're hopeless." Arthur snorted and stomped away.


And so Merlin made his way to the King's Tower, the tallest in Camelot.

The halls were, as usual, alive with activity. Servants and

knights came and went. Women from the kitchen carried trays of food or packs of fresh provisions. Women carrying fresh linens for the living quarters smiled and greeted him.

At the foot of the King's Tower he gaped up at the scores of steps and sighed. He wanted to build another lifting machine there but so far Arthur had not been willing to permit it.

The guards at their posts saluted him as he ascended the winding staircase, each of them in turn as Merlin reached their stations on the successive landings, and offered him a helping hand. At the top, quite out of wind, he found Simon of York. Simon grinned at him, plainly enjoying his fatigue. "You made it."

"Do I not always?"

"Those steps are difficult, Merlin. I tend to come up here first thing every morning and then try and stay the whole day. When I'm lucky, Arthur doesn't have anything for me to do anywhere else in the castle. You should have that boy of yours come along to help you up."

"Petronus is in the schoolroom. He has lessons to learn. But I am surprised these stairs give you so much trouble. You are a generation younger than me."

"My parents are both arthritic. As a result, so am I." He rubbed his back. "I'm moving them here from Yorkshire, into a little room at the back of Camelot. I'm afraid wolves would get them otherwise. You know how bitter Yorkshire winters can get."

"Indeed, what could be worse than a wolf from York?" The none-too-subtle barb was lost on Simon, but he narrowed his eyes, plainly suspecting he was the butt of Merlin's sarcasm.

Merlin was slowly getting his wind back. Before Simon could decide how to react, he gestured at the king's suite of rooms. "How is he today, Simon?"

"Still worried about which profile to use. It's been a week, Merlin, and that is all he thinks about. We've gotten virtually nothing accomplished. Can't you prod him to make a decision?"

"Just be happy things are so calm for the moment. And that he is not drinking. Is anyone with him?"

Simon shook his head. "Go in. He's in the study, with those confounded portraits."


Arthur's study was large but simply furnished. There was a table and four wooden chairs, a few low stools, tapestries on the walls to kill drafts and enough torches to light the room but not terribly well. On stands were three large portraits of Arthur, one in left profile, one in right and one full face. The king stood before one of them, looking serious, rubbing his chin, when he noticed his advisor. "Merlin. Good morning. I think I like this one best."

"You said that yesterday, Arthur. Then five minutes later you preferred another one." He smiled. "Good morning."

"This is an important decision. I want to make the right impression."

"Most of your subjects have never seen you and never will."

"Exactly the point. I want them to know me, at least to the extent they can through a portrait."

"A miniature portrait. On a coin." Merlin sat down and arranged his robes. "I keep trying to learn how the Romans managed such excellent portraiture on their currency, but there is nothing about it in any of the libraries. But why worry about it? You could issue coins with a hunchbacked dwarf on them and it would hardly matter."

"Now you know that isn't true. My image must inspire confidence."

"Then use a portrait of Emperor Justinian."

Arthur snorted. "You think I'm being vain and foolish. I know that. But a king has a right to a certain amount of vanity."

"A king has a right to rule, not to dither. Besides, this business of kings having some sort of inherent rights is an idea left over from ancient Egypt—a culture you always scoff at. I am not at all certain it has a place in the modern world. You are king because you made yourself king, because you fought for it. Excalibur gives you such rights as you have." He sighed. "Simon is complaining. I know you think he is a fussy old woman, and if it comes down to it, I suppose he is, but he says you are neglecting your other duties. The kingdom is grinding to a halt, it seems."

"We've had this kind of discussion too many times. Villains have swords, too. If we are to have order, there must be something higher we're answerable to. The Christian Church is promoting the idea that kings rule by divine right."

"Bosh. If you are going to listen to that fool of a bishop, Gildas, I will not be responsible for what happens."

"Is this Merlin speaking? The architect of our new England, land of justice and equality? Do you really wish all of that to rest on nothing but my sword?"

"This is Merlin the pragmatist. Julius Caesar married Cleopatra because the Egyptian religion said that divinity rested in her. By marrying her, he acquired that divinity, that so-called divine right to rule. And Europe has been saddled with it ever since." He looked down at the floor. "*You* married Guenevere."

"Perhaps he loved her. They say Cleopatra was quite a beauty, Merlin. A fabulous woman. Legendary."

"Have you ever seen the coins she minted? Some of them still circulate in Egypt, believe it or not. She was plain, even matronly. But her legend trumps that, it seems."

Arthur grinned. "Then the image on a monarch's coins does matter after all. Is that what you're admitting?" He paused. "I've asked some of the knights which one to use. Sir Kay prefers the middle one. So does his squire, Jumonet."

"So you are letting squires advise you now?" Merlin sighed deeply. "I surrender. You are a handsome man, Arthur. Any of those three would make a striking impression on a penny, if that is what you want. For heaven's sake choose one."

Arthur walked from one of the portraits to the next. His tone turned unexpectedly somber. "I find myself," he said heavily, "thinking about my legacy. Do you know what I found last week?" He pointed to his temple. "A gray hair."

"Shocking. A silver hair among all those bright golden ones. You must be on your last legs."

"I'm serious, Merlin. How will I be remembered? Who will succeed me?"

"You are still in your thirties, Arthur."

"My *late* thirties."

"Even so. Talk like this is wildly premature."

He peered at Merlin. "Shall I make you my heir?"

"Horrors, no!"

"You will outlive me, Merlin. Wizards always live to enormous age."

"Do not be preposterous. Arthur, you are good for years. Decades, most likely."

"What if my loving wife breaks out of her prison and starts another war against me?"

"You will defeat her. You always have. She never wins."

"The old Count of Darrowfield never died—until last week."

"He was eighty-three. And he was one of the dreariest men I have ever known. He may actually have bored himself to death."

"Even so. His son is succeeding him. His legacy is intact."

"His son is two decades older than you." He lowered his voice slightly. "And rumor has always had it he was a bastard." Suddenly he seemed to realize where the king's thought was heading. He frowned deeply. "Arthur, what do you have in mind?"

"I must select an heir. England's stability depends on it."

"What a pity you did not marry more wisely. You would have sons now."

"I have sons. Probably more than I know. But would anyone recognize them as legitimate heirs?"

"Ah yes, the royal prerogative. How many bastards have you fathered?"

"Memory fails. If every country girl or chambermaid who has succumbed to me had given birth, I could be the strongest king in Europe."

"Or the weakest. Sons have a way of disrespecting their fathers. Look at you and yours."

"Uther is a foul old bastard. You know perfectly well that he all but disowned me when I was a boy."

"My point exactly."

"You think because Uther behaved so horribly toward me, that I would do the same to my boys?"

"It has been known. What about the French knight Accolon? Everyone suspects he is really your son."

"Accolon is still young. And he is too impulsive to be king, I think."

"So the rumors are correct? He really is yours? Granted, he is impulsive. But is he ambitious?"

Arthur brushed the question aside. "I want you to give some thought to this idea of succession, Merlin. I'd like to announce that I'm considering it when all the barons gather here for Midwinter Court. There has to be a way of doing it that will not set them at one another's throats."

Merlin was wry. "Despite my reputation, I am not really a wizard, remember?"

"There are wizards, Merlin, and then there are wizards. Do it for me." His mood turned suddenly bright and he pointed to one of the trio of portraits. "This one, then." Arthur turned to face Merlin. "Support me in this, Merlin. You'll stand there and pretend not to grasp the most obvious points rather than admit I might have a valid concern. But you are always several thoughts ahead of me and we both know it."

"Arthur, an heir—"

"And you'll keep it up for hours on end, if you have to. But this is one time you will not wear me down. Merlin, suppose we build the brilliant new England we both want to see. Suppose we make it as stable as any country in Europe. How long will it last? I have to know who my successor will be. I have to know he will continue our policies. Without that, everything we do is for nothing."

"Everything, ultimately, *is* for nothing, Arthur. The philosophers all agree that—"

"Oh dear." The king put on an air of long-suffering patience. "Not that 'sad wisdom of the ages' again. Please, Merlin, anything but that."

"In the name of everything human, Arthur, think. Suppose you live for another fifty years. Old Darrowfield did. Suppose you choose the wisest, kindest successor in England. Then suppose he goes mad a year after your death. Caligula did. Will you ever know? Will the worms tell you the political gossip?"

"Point taken. But I want to leave a stable England. Guenevere will outlive me, damn her. She'll do it to spite me, like everything else she does. Can you imagine what this country would be like with a gorgon like her on the throne?" Merlin started to say something but Arthur cut him off, "And don't remind me that I was the one who chose her."

"For the sake of your nerves, Arthur, and my sanity, why will you not stop obsessing about Guenevere? She is hardly the only villain in England."

"She was—is—my wife. Her betrayal never stops hurting. It's horrible enough when a friend does it. But a wife . . ."

"It will pass in time, Arthur. Everything does. In the meantime—"

"More philosophy?" Arthur narrowed his eyes suspiciously. "Yes?"

Merlin took a deep breath. "I would like to leave for a few weeks."

Suddenly the king broke into a smile. "Leave? To go where?"

"To Dover. My aides want to attend the autumn festival there. Do you mind?"

"No, not at all. If you don't mind making a detour, that is."

"A detour?" It was Merlin's turn to be suspicious. "To where?"

"To give our royal condolences to the new Lord Darrowfield."

"Young Darrowfield?! He's the biggest bore in England. He makes his father seem charismatic."

"Even so. Our rulership depends on the goodwill of the barons. He has a great many friends. Tell him we intend to formalize his title at Midwinter Court. Take him presents. A ring or something. Better still, tell him we'll send him a cohort of servants for his installation feast. He's invited me, of course, but I have no intention of going. Life is dull enough here at court. But butter him up, and do a good job of it. Another conspiracy is bound to be hatched sooner or later; I want him friendly to us."

"I was hoping for a vacation, Arthur, not a work outing."

"And you will have one—as soon as you do this for me."

Merlin slumped a bit in his chair. "I should have expected something like this. You always smile at me before you unload some nasty obligation on me. Give me two weeks' holiday, then I'll take a third for Darrowfield."

"Do this first. Then go and play for a month, if you like." He hesitated. "By the way, I've been meaning to mention, I've decided Camelot should have a court jester. Like every other court in Europe."

Merlin didn't blink. "You are promoting one of the knights?"

"For once, Merlin, restrain your sarcastic tongue. He is a young man named John of Paintonbury. I met him on my last tour about the countryside."

"A bumpkin, Arthur? Do you not think we have enough of those here already?"

"Stop it. He is a bright young man, witty and very verbal. When he gets here, I'd like you to do everything you can to make him comfortable here."

"A jester. From Paintonbury." Merlin was deadpan. "As if Darrowfield were not awful enough. Are you certain there is nothing else I can do? Climb to the top of this tower and stand on my head, for instance?"

"It isn't that bad, Merlin. If nothing else, Darrowfield lays a good table. He has the most skilled chef in the south of England."

"Really? I'm very fond of good food, and so are Colin and Petronus."

"I thought you might fancy the idea."

"Very well, Arthur. Done. But if Darrowfield does not provide some excellent dinners, I will complain to you, not him."

That was Merlin's worry. England was at peace. What else did he have to fret about? Yet just over the horizon lurked death.

# TWO

There was miscellaneous business for Merlin to finish before they could leave on their trip, minor bits of government business and two seriously ill patients he was reluctant to abandon; but they finally left Camelot on horseback several mornings after Merlin's interview with Arthur. The autumn weather was bright with sunshine for the first day of the journey. Wildflowers grew everywhere; butterflies flitted cheerfully from plant to plant; young foxes played in the fields. Merlin's young aides seemed to savor everything in the world. And the festival would be the cream of it all.

Merlin himself did not enjoy the weather. "I should have had Arthur provide us with a coach. My hip is aching quite fiercely."

"Why didn't you?"

"Britomart wanted to send a military escort with us, 'for security.' It was difficult enough to talk the two of them out of that. A carriage would have made us much too obvious a target for unwanted attention. Or for thieves."

Nimue sounded doubtful. "We're fairly conspicuous on horseback. But I'm glad you talked them out of that carriage. This weather is too lovely to ride inside."

Petronus added, "England is mostly peaceful. Why would we need security?"

"I am afraid you will have to ask Britomart about that. She seems to see threats and menace everywhere."

"It's her job, Merlin."

"I suppose so. I wish she would take some time off now and then, that is all. The soldiers of the Dover garrison will almost certainly keep track of us and report our doings to her. We will have to remain on our best behavior every moment. Government. I am not at all certain this will be much of a holiday."

"Do we have to stay at the garrison?"

"I hope not. But even so . . ." He made a show of scanning the landscape. "And that is not to mention this visit to Lord Darrowfield. His father did not die for long decades, even though everyone kept expecting him to."

"Are you saying this one may go soon, to make up for it?" Nimue was wry.

"We are entitled to some good luck sometime, are we not?"

"Don't be morbid, Merlin."

"Besides," Petronus added, "might the king not then send you as his envoy to the funeral? We'd get another trip." He grinned. "In a carriage."

"Keep your attention on the road, Petronus, and be quiet."


Merlin, Nimue and Petronus were accompanied by a pair of armed soldiers. This was at Britomart's insistence. It was only with difficulty Merlin had talked her out of a full military escort.

"You are important agents of the state," she had claimed. "You must be protected."

"So crucial to the national good that Arthur is sending us to Darrowfield to congratulate a new minor lord on his new minor lordship. How could England go on without us?"

"Don't be difficult, Merlin. I want to send a full squad, but Arthur knew how you'd bristle at that. Be grateful I'm in an accommodating mood."

"Fine, Brit. We are grateful. Does that make you happy?"

"There are times I wish you weren't quite so clever, do you know that?"

He was mordant. "You prefer that 'important agents of the state' be dull-witted?"

"Go to Dover." She turned her back and stomped away.

Happily the soldiers rode unobtrusively behind them. Petronus tried a few times to engage them in conversation, but they seemed as unhappy to be on this journey as Merlin was to have them.

The morning was cool but the sun promised warmth as well as brilliant light. Trees were just beginning to take on their autumn colors. Late wildflowers bloomed everywhere, it seemed; some even grew in the highway itself. Wayfarers on the road all seemed happy and content. Nimue leaned close to Petronus and whispered, "We couldn't have better weather for this trip. But don't say so to Merlin. He'd only take it as a challenge and try to find some reason why we'd be better off back at Camelot."

An hour after they set out a huge black cloud drifted across the face of the sun, plunging the world into a brief twilight. Petronus said it must be a bad omen for their journey.

"A bad omen?" Nimue scolded him. "Haven't you learned anything at all from Merlin? There is no such thing as an omen. If there are any gods, they are much too kind to grant us a glimpse of what our futures hold."

Merlin had been riding in silence, apparently lost in thought. Now he spoke up. "Too kind, or much too cruel. That would be much more in character for such gods as may exist."

Petronus found this thought chilling. "You always paint everything in the darkest tones possible."

"I have lived a long life in the company of other human beings. The more I see, the darker the world looks to me. Never mind the dark clouds that sometimes hide the sun. It is the dark clouds inside ourselves that should concern you. They are the one great constant in human affairs."

The boy found this line of talk disquieting and decided not to pursue it any further. "I have never been to Darrow-field. To be honest, I haven't even heard of it. Where is it?"

Merlin glanced at Nimue; he wanted no more talking, and he immediately fell back into his pensive silence. It fell to Nimue to play instructor to Petronus. "You know of Salisbury, don't you? In Wiltshire?"

"Yes, of course. I passed through there once, with Lancelot, and I have always wanted to go back. It was on a morning much like this one. I was only a boy then." He glanced at her nervously, but she refrained from any sarcasm. "We could see Stonehenge in the distance on Salisbury Plain. I would love to go again and see it close-to."

"Well, you may have the chance. Darrowfield adjoins Salisbury. But I'm afraid you might find that Stonehenge does not live up to your expectations. It is much smaller than it seems from a distance. Up close, it always disappoints."

"Even so, I would like to see it. Merlin, may we go there to see the monument?"

Merlin roused himself from his daydreams. "Darrow-field Castle is a forbidding sort of place in its own right. You may find it sufficient."

"Even so. I—"

"We will have to stay at Darrowfield long enough for protocol. After that . . . I suppose we will have to see. Will the two of you mind the detour to Darrowfield?"

"We'll be fine, Merlin."

When they had been riding for a time, Petronus broke their silence yet again. "Have you noticed that we are being followed?"

"Followed?" Merlin roused himself. "Tell the soldiers, quickly."

Petronus laughed. "Our pursuer is not likely to do much harm. Look."

He pointed upward and to their left. Above a stand of trees, a black bird circled. "It is one of your ravens, Merlin. It has been following us since we left Camelot."

They slowed their pace. Merlin shaded his eyes, then cupped his hands and shouted, "Roc!"

The bird circled the trees once more, then flapped directly toward the party of travelers. When it reached them, it perched on Merlin's shoulder and squawked shrilly. Merlin stroked its head and cooed, "Good boy, Roc. But you should not be here. Go home, now."

The bird cocked its head and stared at him, clearly puzzled.

"Go home, I said. Go back to Camelot."

And Roc lifted into the air and flew swiftly back the way they had come. In only a moment he was out of sight.

Nimue had watched it all without saying a word. Now she spoke up. "Do you really wonder why people think you're a wizard? Only a man with otherworldly powers could do that."

"Nonsense. Ravens are intelligent birds. It is merely a matter of learning to channel that intelligence in a desirable way."

"Ravens are scavengers." Petronus could not manage to keep an unpleasant tone out of his voice. "They eat the dead."

"They keep the world clean, Petronus. Much as I do, or as I try to. I never knew that you find my pets objectionable."

"I have never liked birds. They are cold, inhuman creatures."

"The fact they are so alien, so completely unlike us, is what draws me to them. You will never see a bird commit murder."

"Birds of prey kill all the time."

"Yes, but they kill for food. Out of necessity, not greed or jealousy, not ambition, not any of the thousand other petty motives that drive our kind to do mad things."

"You should get a dog or a cat."

"And put my ravens at risk? Never."

As they rode onward, Petronus let his horse lag slightly behind, midway between Merlin and the soldiers. At one point Nimue reined her horse beside his. "Is anything wrong?"

"No. It's just that sometimes Merlin frightens me. Sometimes he does not seem quite human."

She glanced forward at their master. "Or more than human, maybe?"

"Do you think he really is a sorcerer?"

"Of course not. Don't be foolish. If you go spreading word about what happened with Roc, and if you tell it so as to make it seem magical, he will be angry."

"I wish I had stayed in France. I wish my family had wanted me."

To Petronus's surprise, Merlin had heard this. He looked back, over his shoulder, and said in soft, reassuring tones, "Birds never abandon their young. And neither will I."

There was no more talk for a long time. When eventually they passed by Salisbury Plain and saw Stonehenge lit by the late-afternoon sun, no one said much.

The monoliths showed golden in the dying sunlight and cast long shadows. Petronus asked if they might stop and inspect the monument, but Merlin wanted to press on. "Two weeks from today will be the autumn equinox. Strict adherents of the old religion will be here in numbers to celebrate. Arthur's sister Morgan le Fay will be here, too, most likely, to officiate. We should be returning from Dover about that time, and we may stop here then. It is always quite a spectacle. This fair at Dover which you are so anxious to see will seem like nothing."

"But, sir—"

"Not tonight, Petronus, please. My back is aching terribly from this horse. I want to reach the castle and get some rest."

Glumly Petronus rode along. There was very little talk. Nimue whispered to Petronus that she was disappointed, too. "But Merlin never fails us in the end, does he?"

It was just after sunset when Darrowfield Castle came into sight. It rose up out of the ground, a massive square tower of black stone. It looked ancient, and Petronus said so. Merlin explained that it had been built less than two generations previously. "By one of those dull, literal-minded warlords England is ridden with," he added. "He was made a lord by Arthur's father, Uther, and he immediately went about demonstrating his new magnificence to the countryside." As they approached, they could see candles or torches being lit in a few of the windows.

"What is this new Lord Darrowfield like?" Nimue asked. "I don't believe I've met him."

"Even duller than his father was." Merlin did not try to disguise the fact that he was not happy to be there. "A hapless warrior, an inept scholar, a tone-deaf politician . . . a British lord, in fact." He smirked. "I would not like to guess how delighted he must be at his father's death. The old man survived wounds and illnesses that should have put him in his grave years ago. He showed signs of living forever. Now he is out of his son's hair."

"They never stop, do they?" Nimue narrowed her eyes. "All the intrigues, plots, secret grudges nursed for years . . . Remember last year when the Duke of Gloucester tried to kill the Duke of Cambridge over a drinking cup? All these supposed noblemen should try living like ordinary people for a change, and scrambling for their livelihoods." She paused. "How long are you planning to stay here?"

"The sooner we can get away, the happier I will be. I have not much been looking forward to this festival at Dover. But now that we are here, Dover has become a paradise in my imagination. I cannot wait till we leave for there."

They reached a line of guards a half mile or so from the castle. Merlin presented letters from Arthur by way of identification. But none of the sentries could read. One of them rode off to the castle for instructions.

Merlin and his companions idled till he returned. Petronus got a small chessboard from his luggage, and he and Nimue played; he was annoyed when she beat him in fewer than twenty moves. Their soldiers produced a wineskin and cheese, and they ate and drank happily, evidently pleased to be off the road and free of their protective duties.

Finally the rider returned. "Lord Darrowfield extends his warmest welcome to the envoys of King Arthur, and he anticipates your visit with the keenest pleasure. You may ride on at once. This road will take you straight to the castle."

They mounted their horses and proceeded. It took them longer to reach the castle than they'd expected. It was huge, massive, and its great size had fooled them into thinking they were closer to it than they proved to be. Lord Darrowfield himself was waiting for them at the main gate accompanied by a half dozen servants. A thin, pale, unenergetic man in his fifties, he waved listlessly but made himself smile. "Merlin. How splendid of Arthur to send you."

Merlin reined his horse to a stop and dismounted, handing the reins to a servant. "His Majesty sends his deepest condolences on the death of your father. And of course his felicitations on your inheriting the title. He sends you these presents as signs of his favor." He took three small ceremonial daggers from his saddlebag and handed them to Darrowfield; the handles were inlaid with precious stones.

Darrowfield inspected them as if he had no clue what to make of them. His manner suggested that he thought they might be poisoned. Finally he remembered this was a political situation and smiled. "Arthur always knows the right thing to do. You must convey my deep gratitude to him."

"You may do that yourself soon enough. He plans to confer the title on you formally at Midwinter Court. You will become Lord Darrowfield officially in front of all the nobles in England."

Darrowfield blinked. "I already am."

His obtuseness caught Merlin off guard. "Yes, of course you are. But surely you want the recognition of your liege lord and your peers, do you not?"

"Oh, yes, of course, of course. But—I have invited Arthur to the feast I'm throwing for myself. Isn't he coming to that?"

Merlin put on a sad expression. "I fear his other duties . . ."

"Oh. Well, perhaps it's just as well. At any rate, you are more than welcome at Darrowfield."

"Excellent." He introduced "Colin" and Petronus, and Darrowfield put an arm around his shoulder and ushered them all inside. "I've been getting letters from a lot of the other lords, you know. Congratulating me."

"And of course you have a staff of clerks to read them all for you and to compose replies." Nimue was dry.

"Of course. Men who can read are among a baron's most valuable servants."

"And I'm sure they are very fortunate to be in your service." Her sarcasm was apparent to Merlin and Petronus but lost on Darrowfield.

The interior of the castle was a maze. As plain, square and forthright a structure as it was on the outside, the inside was hopelessly convoluted. Corridors wound and wandered, turning back on themselves, twisting in unexpected directions, crossing one another as if they had been planned by a madman. Petronus made a polite, tactful comment about it. "Even if raiders were to breach your defenses and penetrate the castle, they'd be lost in no time at all."

"I believe that was my grandfather's plan. He designed the place himself, on the model of some maze in some old myth."

"The labyrinth at Crete? The one where the minotaur was kept?" Nimue was feeling a bit dizzy from all the convolutions. "But surely all these winding, meandering corridors must thwart your guests as well."

Darrowfield was unfazed. "You aren't the only one to think so. My other guests have said much the same thing."

"You have other guests? Who?"

Before he could answer, they turned a corner and came face-to-face with a blank stone wall. Without missing a beat, Darrowfield snapped his fingers and said, "Oh, yes, we should have gone the other way."

"Confounded by your own castle." Merlin glanced at Nimue and tried not to sound too ironic. "You must feel so very secure here."

"I do." Darrowfield beamed with pride.

They turned another bend in the corridor and came unexpectedly face-to-face with a woman in dark blue robes. Her face, in contrast with her clothing, was pale white; her hair was black as one of Merlin's ravens and her eyes were brilliant blue. Only a slightly hooked nose detracted from her cold beauty. She stood tall and imperious, glaring at them, as if their mere presence there was a terrible affront. And she held the leashes of two large dogs in her right hand. They were hounds, pure white except for reddish ears. They barked, snarled and strained at their leads, lunging at the newcomers.

Merlin recognized the woman at once. Carefully he backed away from the dogs and said, "Morgan le Fay. How interesting to meet you here, of all places. Have you brought your famous chest of poisons, or are you not here for pleasure?"

She ignored this, tugged at the leashes, and the dogs calmed down. "Merlin. And what brings you to Darrowfield?"

"Diplomatic business. Arthur's government never rests. You know that."

"Indeed." Her tone was far from cordial.

Darrowfield appeared shaken by her sudden appearance. He worked to recover his composure. "Morgan, I have asked you to keep those beasts outside. There are kennels at the rear of the castle, for my hunting dogs. I'm certain there must be room there for your . . . pets as well."

"My pets are not used to being kept 'outside.' They are descendants of the hounds bred by the first Great Queen of this country." She stroked the ears of one of them.

"Even so. They have a way of unnerving people." It was clear that by "people" he meant himself.

"You will get used to them." That seemed to settle the matter in her mind. She turned back to the others. "So. You say that my brother Arthur sent you here?"

"Of course. He has sent presents to Lord Darrowfield." He had been speaking to Morgan but turned back to their host and smiled. "Oh—and he will be sending some of his household staff to assist here when you host the other barons to celebrate your elevation. They should be here soon, perhaps even tomorrow. His Majesty has been pleased to send them as well as us." He remember his official manners. "Not that we require a royal order to visit you, of course."

Darrowfield seemed taken aback by what Merlin had said. "Servants? Cooks? I have my own. Why would Arthur—"

"Yes, and I understand they are excellent. But surely they can use help feeding all those additional mouths."

"I suppose." He sounded doubtful, as if he suspected there might be a veiled insult in Arthur's gesture.

"When, may I ask, are you actually planning the feast for? The autumn equinox is approaching. Will that be the date?"

"It will not." Darrowfield made an unpleasant face. "At each equinox, hordes of intoxicated, religious-minded revelers gather in the neighborhood, drunkenly convinced that that heap of stones out on the plain is mystical or some such. My feast will be in the following week.

"Aside from that, I have been thinking of attending the autumn festival at Dover. There will almost certainly be a slave market there. I am planning to increase the height of this castle; extra hands would be most welcome. In fact, it occurs to me that if you are planning on going there, I might attend with you."

Merlin was deadpan. "The festival at Dover? Why, the thought never occurred to us. But could you not ask Morgan, here, to postpone their revels?" He bowed slightly and gestured at her. "She is the high priestess of Britain, after all."

"As high priestess," Morgan answered for Darrowfield, "I am invested with a great many powers. The ability to postpone the equinox is not among them, I'm afraid."

"I see." Merlin smiled, pleased at himself for having ruffled her dignity, however slightly. "Might you not simply instruct your followers to remain sober this year, then?"

"Our feast is Dionysiac in nature," she intoned solemnly. "Sobriety would hardly set the proper tone for the manifestation of the god."

"Of course." He turned back to Darrowfield. "Naturally

Arthur's servants will return to Camelot as soon as your feast is over."

"I hope so."

"Do not worry, Lord Darrowfield, they will not steal any recipes."

Morgan put on a tight grin. "And of course they will do no spying. That would hardly be consonant with the 'new' England Arthur is trying to make, would it, Merlin?"

Merlin smiled and bowed slightly again without saying a word.

"And you have brought your assistants." Morgan looked Nimue up and down as if she were examining an art forgery, then turned to Petronus and gave him the same treatment. "What an interesting trinity you make."

Merlin was unfazed. "More than merely interesting, I hope. Challenging, perhaps? Provocative?"

She brushed it aside and spoke to Darrowfield. "Father is still unwell. Mordred is tending to him. I am not certain either of them will be joining us for dinner. Can you perhaps arrange for their meals to be taken to them?"

"Yes, of course."

"By those servants you are so proud of," Merlin added. The irony was lost on Darrowfield though a slight smile appeared at the corners of Morgan's mouth. Merlin glanced knowingly at Nimue: so old Uther Pendragon was in residence as well as Morgan's son Mordred. Nimue took his meaning and winked.

Darrowfield called for servants. In quick order a half dozen of them appeared, and he instructed them to get Merlin's party installed in a suite of guest rooms. "Let us show you how pleasing and efficient Darrowfield hospitality can be," he told his new guests.

"I am certain we will find it quite overwhelming," Merlin poured on the unction. He was not a government official for nothing. "Returning to Camelot will seem a true hardship."

"Exactly." Darrowfield gave more orders to the servants, clapped his hands, and at once everyone was in motion or seemed to be. Morgan's hounds barked and growled. Darrowfield kept clapping his hands together; he seemed to enjoy it; no one could fathom why.

"Should we notify Lady Darrowfield that there are new visitors, sir?" one of them asked.

"No." He said it in a firm, flat tone.

Merlin found it odd. The lord's wife ordinarily managed the household. But he was discreet enough to say nothing.

When they were alone in their rooms, Petronus asked Merlin about Arthur's father. "It has never occurred to me before, but I have never seen him, never even heard mention of him. I'd have expected him to reside at Camelot. So I think I took it for granted he was dead."

"As far as Arthur is concerned, he is." Merlin was offhand. "Look around and make certain no one is eavesdropping, will you?"

Petronus got to his feet and began checking behind tapestries. "But they are father and son."

"It would not do to remind either of them of the fact. To say there is bad blood between them would be understating the case."

"But—"

"When Arthur set out to become King of England and unite the country, he was not a great deal older than you are now. The essence of the challenge facing him was to conquer all the various petty kings and warlords. Uther was one of the first he went to war against."

Petronus puckered his lips and whistled softly. "I see."

"None of them were pleased to be crushed by Arthur's superior strategy and forces. That goes without saying. Uther took it harder than most. He had all but disowned Arthur when he was still a boy, you see, on the ground that Arthur was too much a dreamer, unfit to succeed him and assume power in their little fief. So to be bested by his own dream-ridden son in combat . . . to have been so publicly and humiliatingly wrong about him . . . You can imagine how he must have felt."

Nimue added, "You've told us that your relations with your own parents were never close, Petronus. This can't seem so odd to you."

"Yes. But—but surely they ought to have reconciled by now. In the interest of peace, if nothing else. I mean, look at old King Pellenore. Arthur defeated him, too; and took his castle of Camelot for his own seat of power. Yet Pellenore · lives at Arthur's court and supports him."

Nimue answered. "Remember, Pellenore is out of his wits. There are people who say that is Arthur's fault, but for whatever reason—"

"Yes, Colin, exactly, but Uther is not mad." Merlin seemed almost lost in reminiscence. "At least not to appearances. He sided with Guenevere and Lancelot in their first war against Arthur. No one has ever been certain why he did it, except out of fatherly venom. But that did not help the cause of family harmony. Now he is old and feeble—virtually an invalid. But Arthur still carries a grudge."

"You should mediate between them." Petronus sounded perfectly grave. "Fathers and sons . . . I wish I could make peace with my own father."

Merlin shrugged. "I have enough duties. And that particular war is, I suspect, unwinnable. Now if you both will excuse me, I would like to take a nap before dinner."

He retired to his bed, as did Nimue to hers. Petronus was left on his own, with uncomfortable memories of his home life back in France.


Two hours later a young serving woman knocked at the door of their suite. "Dinner will be served shortly, your honors."

"Thank you." Nimue yawned and smiled at her. "May we know your name?"

"Martha, sir."

"If you will give us a moment to collect ourselves, you may escort us to the dining hall."

Martha curtsied. "Yes, sir. I'll just wait outside the door here."

"Who else will be joining us for dinner?"

"Only the family. Oh, and Queen Morgan and Prince Mordred and King Uther, sir. Oh—and I almost forgot—his lordship's new sheriff."

She stepped out into the corridor to wait for the three of them to ready themselves. Nimue looked to Merlin. In hushed tones she asked, "Did you hear her? *Queen* Morgan? *Prince* Mordred? *King* Uther? Arthur will not be pleased to hear that they are styling themselves that way."

Merlin arranged his robes. "No, he will not. I would have thought Morgan would know better. Arthur has been flirting with the idea of 'converting' to Christianity, as they say. This kind of arrogance will hardly help Morgan's case for the traditional English gods."

Petronus looked thoughtful. "Are you serious, Merlin? Arthur, one of the Christians? I grew up in a Christian society. There was intrigue, murder, bloodletting, treachery, hypocrisy . . ." He wrinkled his nose as if there was a foul smell in the air.

"Christians are human beings, Petronus, and human beings are corrupt. I have taught you enough history for you to know what Greece and Rome were like, centuries before the man Christ. Besides, I said Arthur has been toying with the idea. Like the emperor Constantine two centuries ago, he sees the advantages of the Christian Church as a unifying, stabilizing force. Bishop Gildas has been making the case quite forcefully."

Moments later they joined Martha in the corridor and followed her to the dining hall. Very softly Petronus whispered to Nimue, "What do you know about the rumor that Mordred is Arthur's son, not merely his nephew? That Arthur and Morgan committed—"

Despite his whispering, Merlin heard him. He rounded on the boy and said fiercely, "That is not a topic to be broached. Not ever. Not if you wish to remain in Arthur's service. We can return you to Lancelot, remember; you can serve him in his prison. Or to France."

Petronus had never seen the old man so angry; he trembled. "Yes, sir. I'm sorry, sir."

"That is not a subject open for discussion. *Not ever.* Do you understand?" Without another word Merlin turned and resumed following Martha, who gave no sign of having heard what Petronus had said or of understanding Merlin's anger. But a moment later Merlin softened. He turned back to look at Petronus and told him, "There is a long tradition of kings . . . taking pleasure where they will. There is even a name for it. People call it 'royal privilege.' Arthur is human. But it is not wise policy to remind him of it."

"But I only asked—"

"Come on. Let us eat."

Martha moved quickly and with certainty through the winding hallways; her companions were disoriented and kept slowing down. The fact that the corridors were lit quite dimly didn't help matters.

Finally they reached the dining hall, which, unlike the castle's other chambers and corridors, and unlike the hallways, was ablaze with light. Scores of candles burned in candelabras; torches blazed along the walls. A dozen servants, all in uniforms bearing the Darrowfield crest, waited around the table, and Martha joined them.

Several guests were already seated at table, Darrowfield himself, a sad-looking woman Nimue thought must be his wife, two boys in their mid-teenage years, and a middle-aged man dressed in the robes of a scholar.

Entering, Merlin made himself the soul of heartiness; there

was no trace of his earlier ferocity, and Petronus sighed in relief.

"Good evening, all." He scanned the table, which was already set with a huge tureen of soup and a number of silver plates.

Darrowfield announced, "I would like to present my good lady wife and my two sons, Geoffrey and Freelander." The other Darrowfields smiled and uttered brief greetings to their visitors from Camelot.

The older of Darrowfield's sons, Geoffrey, said languidly, "I'm told that people at Camelot look down at those of us who live about the countryside. That you think of us as provincial." Like his brother, he was a handsome boy; but Merlin noticed a slight curvature to his back.

"Never!" Merlin feigned shock. "I am certain no one at Camelot holds such an ungracious opinion."

Just at that instant Mordred entered, leading an elderly man who walked slowly and leaned on his grandson heavily. He was obviously Uther Pendragon. Nimue remarked to herself that even kings must in time come to old age and weakness—those of them that survive long enough. Uther seemed the feeblest man she'd ever seen.

Nimue looked them up and down and decided that Uther must be blind or nearly so, in addition to his more obvious infirmities, and that Mordred was clearly quite fond of him. Introductions were made and Mordred selected a seat and held the chair for his grandfather. Then he took his own seat, which was between Uther and Nimue.

He recognized her with a start. "You are Colin, aren't you? Merlin's assistant?"

"Yes, I am. I'm quite flattered that you remember me. We've only met the once."

Mordred smiled. "I like scholarly men."

"So do I, but—"

Merlin interrupted. "You are looking fit, Prince Mordred." He leaned on the word *prince* with the heaviest possible irony.

"Prince? Oh, that. That was mother's idea, I'm afraid. You mustn't take it too seriously."

"I assure you I do not. And I hardly think your uncle the king will do so either."

The scholarly man at the table had not said a word. Now he spoke up. "So you are that Merlin who is counselor to King Arthur? I am Peter of Darrowfield, the new sheriff here. Only recently appointed by Lord Darrowfield." He beamed with pride. "I have known you by reputation for years. To actually meet you is a great joy for me."

Peter was a plain-looking man of about forty. They exchanged pleasantries for a few moments. Finally Merlin said, "You appear to be something of a scholar, Peter. You interest me. Most of the sheriffs in England are bumpkins, to say the least."

"And corrupt bumpkins, at that." Peter grinned. "But England under King Arthur is changing. There is a new breed of men engaging in law enforcement. I am far from the only one. Hanibert of London is one of the most brilliant men I know."

Merlin picked up a goblet, held it out and a servant filled it with wine. He raised it to Peter and sipped. "May England's criminals beware."

"It is your influence, sir. Everyone knows how brilliant you have been at solving crimes against Arthur's majesty. It has inspired some of us, who might otherwise be breeding dust in libraries, to become actively engaged in the detection and solution of crime."

"It is a promising development, Peter, and I could not be more grateful, nor more flattered, to hear about it."

"Of course most people still regard us as dull-witted fools. But that will change soon enough."

"I would not be certain. Reputations, even if they are

unearned, do not die easily. Large numbers of people still believe I am a magician, despite the obvious absurdity."

Freelander, the younger son, chimed in. "They say that Merlin himself created Stonehenge with his mystical powers. He brought the stones to life and ordered them to march to Salisbury and arrange themselves into a circle. Or that it was built by a race of giants, at Merlin's command. It is so exciting to live so close to it."

"You see what I mean? Stonehenge has been there on the plain for generations. No, for centuries. It may actually be as old as time itself. Yet the myth persists that a living man constructed it." Annoyed, Merlin set his wine cup down and turned to face the young man. "Or am I supposed to be immortal as well?" Cowed, the boy fell silent.

Merlin turned back to Peter. "No, I fear that centuries from now, when we are all long dead and buried, the myth of the town sheriff as a cloddish dimwit will still be alive."

"For once I hope you are mistaken, sir." Peter held out his own cup for wine.

Then with a sudden flourish Morgan le Fay swept into the room, black robes swirling around her as if the wind might be blowing them. "Cloddish dimwit?" She put on a huge artificial smile. "You are talking about my brother?"

Alarmed by her treasonous wit, Peter drank deeply. "Please, Morgan. We must be respectful of authority."

"Spoken like a man in a position of authority." She brushed him aside. "Mordred. Father." She nodded to each of them. "I was not certain whether to expect you here."

"Even the old get hungry, Daughter." Uther's voice sounded as if speaking might be painful for him.

"So they do." Lady Darrowfield, who had been oddly quiet in a melancholy way, got to her feet. "I believe everyone is here? Excellent." She gestured to the servants and they instantly sprang into motion. In a matter of moments the table was spread with a rich feast, ham, roast beef, eel, and an array of vegetables, breads and pastries. Despite all the animation the hostess still looked unhappy. Merlin wondered why. Was there trouble in the new lord's household?

The guests all tucked into their dinner, which was excellent. Petronus gobbled his food like the teenage boy he was. In only moments all the sweets had been eaten and Lady Darrowfield sent servants to the kitchen for more.

"Now." She scanned the table and, apparently satisfied that her guests were all eating contentedly, she began her own meal. "What shall be the topic of our dinner conversation?"

The guests all looked at one another but no one replied.

"Shall we discuss family relations among the nobility of England?" She asked the question in a wry tone.

"Miriam, please." Darrowfield was looking extraordinarily uncomfortable.

But his wife seemed unable to stop herself. "Shall we perhaps discuss the problems created by a lord who rides about his fiefdom, siring bastard children?"

"Miriam! Stop this at once."

The woman was trembling. "I am not the one who must be told to stop." She looked at Merlin. "What is the official line at Camelot on this shameful behavior? Does Arthur not expect more integrity from his barons?"

Merlin turned to stone. He looked down at the table, not at Lady Darrowfield. "I fear it is not my place to say."

Suddenly on the verge of tears, she got to her feet and rushed from the room. Everyone else looked at one another nervously, groping for appropriate comments. Finally Morgan found her voice and complimented Darrowfield on the roast beef. "It is the most succulent I've had in months. Isn't it delicious, Mordred?"

Mordred looked awkwardly away from her and muttered, "Yes, Mother. I mean, yes, Lord Darrowfield."

For a time there was no more conversation; everyone ate in silence. Then gradually people began to talk again. Con-

versation was thankfully light. The weather, news from the
Continent, reports of energetic jousting matches around the
countryside . . . There was gossip of outbreaks of plague in
parts of Europe, but no one knew any details. At one point
Lady Darrowfield reappeared at the door of the dining hall,
then seemed to reconsider and left quickly. Geoffrey and
Freelander kept pumping Merlin with questions about magic
and the black arts, much to his annoyance and the amusement of Nimue.

When finally the company dispersed, Merlin paused to
ask Darrowfield whether he had arranged for any entertainment to fill the rest of the evening. They walked together
through the maze of hallways.

"I beg your indulgence, Merlin. You will perhaps have
noticed that this is not the happiest of households. Do you
honestly think entertainment of any kind would be appropriate? Please let me apologize for my wife's childish outburst."

"Childish? Yes, of course. If there is anything I might do
to help the situation . . ."

"No, no, please don't give it a thought. It is merely a
domestic falling-out, nothing more. It will pass. She never
remains angry for long."

Turning a bend in the winding corridor, Darrowfield
walked smack into a wall. He recoiled, and his nose bled.
There was a sound of muffled footsteps, retreating away
from them along the corridors. Merlin tried to see who it
was, but whoever had been there had vanished.

Merlin fumbled through his pockets and found a kerchief. "Here, use this."

Darrowfield took it and covered his bloody nose with it.
It made his voice unpleasantly nasal as he said, "Damn my
grandfather and his damned building scheme. We've been
building castles in England for centuries, good, solid, simple plans. But no, he had to be novel. Damn him."

Merlin chuckled. "So the unpleasantness in your family extends across generations."

"Damned right, it does. How would you like to live in a foul rat's nest like this? No one in his right mind would. But I get to be Lord Darrowfield, so I have to live here. I'd be happier in the country, raising wheat and pigs."

"If you knew how many times I have seen Arthur in just exactly this mood."

"He is a wise king, then. Thank you for the kerchief. I'll have it laundered and returned to you. Can you find your way back to your rooms?"

"I believe so."

"I'll say good night, then." He made a sour face. "Back to my wife. Good night."

Back at his rooms, Merlin found Morgan waiting for him. She was, to appearances, in a jovial mood. When he entered she did not stand but sat regally, like a queen on her throne. "Merlin. What took you so long? Did you get lost in this absurd labyrinth of a castle?"

"Not at all." He made himself smile. "I was chatting with our host, that is all."

"Poor Darrowfield. He is not the first lord to have his wife resent his infidelities."

"And he certainly will not be the last. Extramarital copulation is what barons do. I have spoken to Arthur several times about regularizing and regulating the institution of marriage, at least for the nobility. But you know Arthur."

"Yes, believe me, I know him." She didn't try to hide her disdain.

"Of course. You know as well as anyone his attitude toward casual liaisons."

The dart hit home; Morgan stiffened. "That subject is not open to discussion. I am here to talk about Darrowfield."

Merlin had begun to feel absurd, standing while Morgan sat and acted grand. He found a stool and made himself comfortable. "Darrowfield? There would not seem to be much to say. It is odd, but someone seemed to be following us just now, out in the corridor from the dining hall."

"Perhaps someone could not sleep and wished to be bored into slumber."

Merlin chuckled. "The noblemen of England are all wise and magnificent."

"Of course. About Darrowfield's religious affiliation."

He narrowed his eyes. "You speak in riddles, Morgan. I know you are a priestess, and cryptic flummery is your job, but really—"

"It is rumored that he may convert to Christianity. That must not be permitted. We have lost several barons to this upstart faith already."

"And how would you propose I stop it?"

"England has thrived for thousands of years on the worship of the traditional gods. The true gods. We must stop this erosion now."

"I am afraid I cannot help you, Morgan. Even Arthur himself is—"

"I am quite aware of it. He has been meeting with that fool Bishop Gildas. It must be stopped."

"I am Arthur's advisor, not his nanny."

"Do you find there is much difference?"

Merlin sighed deeply. "I am so weary of superstition in all its forms. As if it mattered which gods a man sends perfumed smoke to."

"It does. It matters enormously."

"If the barons stop giving you tribute and begin donating it to Gildas . . ." He grinned at her, and she glared. "Christianity has stabilized half of Europe, Morgan. The tatters of the Roman Empire are beginning to coalesce in a coherent way. Such a vast historical process can hardly be stopped—not even if it were desirable. Progress, or at any rate movement, cannot be stopped. I doubt it can even be slowed by much."

She was stiff. "You will not assist me, then, in preserving sacred England?"

"I am afraid I am powerless."

"If you can persuade Arthur—"

"Morgan, this is out of my hands. I doubt I could even get Darrowfield to listen to me, much less Arthur."

She got to her feet and struck an imperious pose. "Very well, then. Saving England falls to me. As it has fallen to many a high priestess in the past. Good night, Merlin."

"We are fortunate to have had you. All of you." He smiled what he hoped was an ingratiating smile.

Then he stood and escorted her to the door. Darrowfield Castle had proved a much more interesting place than he had expected, and a much more turbulent one.

Late that night Lady Darrowfield came to Merlin's rooms. She had evidently been crying, and she was still trying to regain her composure. In her hand she clutched a kerchief.

"Lady Darrowfield." He yawned and frowned at her; the last thing he wanted was to become entangled in his host's domestic affairs. But she seemed not to notice. "What brings you to my chambers at this awful hour?"

"I wanted—I wanted to apologize for my unseemly behavior at dinner. I am so ashamed. I had liked to think I outgrew that sort of tantrum when I was still a girl."

"Everyone suffers weak moments, milady."

"It is not simply a matter of weakness. You have no idea what it's like, living with someone who says he loves only you, but in fact distributes his love freely, far and wide. Belief—*trust* becomes impossible."

"I can only imagine." He put a hand on her shoulder and tried to sound as sad and concerned as he could. "But it is not uncommon."

"I mean, I know that copulating with women far and wide is what lords do. All of them, or nearly so. What is the polite term they use? 'Baronial privilege,' I believe." She glanced at him with some mixture of hope and fear in her eyes. "But Merlin, he has been threatening to disinherit my sons and bring some of his bastards to live here as his heirs." She looked away from him, clearly abashed. "Might you—is there any chance you might ask King Arthur to intervene?"

"Arthur?"

"Yes. Surely it must be of interest to the crown to see that England's noble bloodlines are kept as pure as can be."

He wanted to ask her *Why? What makes you think they are pure at all?* Instead he said softly, "I will mention the matter to him."

"Do I have your promise?"

"You do." The situation was making him increasingly uncomfortable. He yawned an exaggerated yawn, hoping she would take the hint and leave.

But she seemed unable to move. "I may consider you a friend, then?"

"Yes, of course."

"My boys are good boys. I mean, they are boys, they get into mischief. But they deserve their birthright."

"Of course they do."

"Will you call me Miriam, please? 'Lady Darrowfield'— that is hardly the way friends address one another."

"Of course. Miriam." He wanted her gone. The last thing he needed was to get caught up in the domestic troubles of a minor lord. Not able to think of anything else, he yawned again.

This time she took the hint. Impulsively she threw her arms around him, squeezed him tightly, then kissed him hard on the cheek. "Good night, Merlin."

"Sleep well, Miriam." *But please go*, he thought.

"I will, knowing that you will have Arthur bring my errant husband into line."

She walked off down the corridor quickly, made a wrong

turn, stopped and waved to Merlin, then hastened down the correct hallway. Merlin sighed heavily, glad she was gone, and went into his room and crawled into bed. He realized he had forgotten to extinguish the candles and decided not to. Let them burn themselves out.

In the morning he told Nimue about the nocturnal visit of Miriam Darrowfield. Petronus was still at his morning bath, which was just as well; a boy that young would be unlikely to grasp the implications of the situation or have anything useful to contribute.

Nimue was unsurprised at his account. "You're right, Merlin. All the barons do it. And every woman in England knows it. Our 'lords and masters' expect us to let them have their way with us, then leave. Pity the woman who makes any fuss. And the woman unfortunate enough to conceive a child is left quite on her own. It is understood she is not ever to name the father."

Merlin listened and furrowed his brow. "And so she has had a night of pleasure, same as the man, and it has ended. What has changed for her?"

"You assume that the men trouble to give the women full pleasure."

"Full or partial—does it matter?"

"Perhaps to the woman. And if she is left with child? No man would marry a woman in such a plight, or at least very few would. Have you never suspected that your and Arthur's 'new' England must look quite different to a woman than it does to a knight, say, or a lord?"

"Nature has decreed that—"

"That men take vows and then shatter them? That men use women the way they use their horses or their hunting dogs?" Her tone was growing heated.

Merlin tried to calm her down. "You must not take this so personally. I told you, Darrowfield is renowned for his dullness. It is hardly fair to judge all men by that uninspiring standard."

"Hogwash. Other men may not be quite as callous to their wives as Darrowfield, but they all behave like him. I never realized how crass the average lord is till I started living among them as a man myself. You should hear the knights sometime. You and Pellenore are the only male members of the ruling order who don't regard women as chattel. Or so I thought."

He hesitated. "Thank you for exempting me."

"I exempt you, personally. I indict your sex."

"Sex?" Petronus breezed into the room, toweling his hair. "Did someone mention sex?"

"There—you see?" Nimue was exultant. "That completes the indictment, *milord*." She stuck her tongue out at Merlin and walked jauntily out of the room.

"What on earth was that about?" Petronus scratched his head.

"You would never understand, you *man*, you."

"But—I—"

"Never mind, Petronus. Do you know how soon breakfast will be served?"

The boy shook his head. "But there are some people to see you."

"People? What people?"

"From Camelot."

Merlin was bewildered.

"The servants," Petronus prompted. "The ones Arthur promised to send."

"Oh. But what do they want with me? They should be reporting to Lady Darrowfield for their instructions. She runs the household."

At a loss, Petronus shrugged. "Shall I show them in?"

"I suppose. Slowly, though. I am not awake yet. And the morning has already been too eventful."

Petronus left and Merlin pulled up a chair. Servants. He

would tell them to report to the lady of the castle and get rid of them. He was finding Darrowfield Castle and its inhabitants more and more tedious.

When Petronus returned, he was followed by a woman who looked to be in her late thirties and two teenage boys who looked startlingly alike. He had seen them around Camelot; he was certain of it. But he could not place them.

The woman curtsied to him and introduced herself as Marian of Bath. The boys, she explained, were her twin sons, Robert and Wayne.

Merlin smiled and made himself cordial. "And what can I do for you?"

"The king told us to report to you," one of the twins explained.

"He wanted you to know we've arrived," said the other. "Actually we arrived last night, but we were told you were engaged."

"Engaged? Who told you that?"

The boy shrugged. "One of the people here."

"But you were here last night?"

Both boys nodded.

For a moment there was an awkward silence, as if they were expecting someone to add something to what they'd said. Finally their mother added, "The king's instructions were rather vague, I'm afraid. What exactly are we to do here?"

"Lord Darrowfield has only recently been elevated to that rank, by the unfortunate death of his father, the old lord. He will shortly host a feast here for a number of his peers, in celebration of his new status. You are to assist the household staff, then return to Camelot. It is as uncomplicated as that." He narrowed his eyes and peered at the woman. "You work in the kitchen, do you not? I believe you are the cook who makes those heavenly honey cakes Arthur is so fond of."

She giggled with pleasure at his recognition. "Yes, sir. The king has shown me his favor from time to time."

"And you boys—you wait tables for us, do you not?"

They nodded but did not smile or give any indication of the kind of enjoyment their mother had displayed.

"Well, all of you, off to Lady Darrowfield now. I haven't time for any more small talk."

The boys turned and left quickly, leaving their mother to thank Merlin for his attention. "And . . . do you know if Lady Darrowfield has an herb garden I may have access to? The secret of my baking is in the herbs." She wrinkled her nose. "Camelot's herb garden is so large, so marvelous. I can always find anything I need there. But here . . ."

"I am sure there must be one. But you will have to ask someone who knows better than I." It was time to dismiss her. "But I am certain Lord Darrowfield's feast will be more successful for the contribution you can make."

"Yes, sir. Thank you. Sir." She followed her sons in an uncertain way, as if she was not certain where she was or what to expect.

"And be careful of this castle," Merlin called after her. "The corridors can be quite tricky. I have seen Lord Darrowfield himself become disoriented. Have one of his servants show you the way."

The Darrowfields showed no sign of having reconciled overnight. They studiously avoided looking at or speaking to each other. When on occasion at breakfast their arms brushed against each other, they stiffened like dictators expecting an assassin. The atmosphere in the dining hall was palpably uncomfortable, not to say hostile. Marian of Bath's sons, who helped serve the meal, seemed baffled by it, and no one bothered to explain.

This continued all day long. Merlin confronted each of the Darrowfields and hinted that it might be wise for them to make up their differences before the other peers arrived; neither would countenance the idea. After a time, he stopped trying. "The king would wish me to make an attempt at bringing harmony," he told Nimue. "I have made it. They want no part of it."

"How long do we have to stay here?"

"No longer. I intend to thank Darrowfield for his hospitality, such as it has been, and inform him we will be leaving tomorrow morning. However unpleasant Dover might be, I will find it quite cordial after this place."

She laughed. "I always enjoy it when your expectations are confounded."

"I had no expectations, except that this would not be a pleasant place to visit. It is worse than that. Will you find our soldiers and tell them to be ready to leave in the morning?"

"Yes. I think they're looking forward to Dover, too. It will be a holiday for them."

"Excellent. I will tell Petronus myself."

Over dinner that night the lord and lady of the castle threw all discretion to the winds and fought openly, about the same thing as before. Their sons shifted awkwardly and finally made excuses to leave the room. The twins from Camelot, who were again serving the meal, worked quickly and kept as much distance as possible between themselves and their temporary masters. Their mother kept to the kitchen; Merlin wondered whether it was by design.

During a lull in the combat Merlin announced his party's imminent departure. Darrowfield glared at him. "Why? Do you not like it here?"

"We are on holiday, Lord Darrowfield. All of us are anxious to reach Dover and the festival there."

Darrowfield frowned and continued questioning them, even turning on Nimue and Petronus. "You told me you weren't going there."

"It was your suggestion that gave us the idea." Merlin lied freely, like the courtier he was.

Darrowfield seemed determined to find some cause to

take offense. But Merlin was a more skillful conversationalist, or debater, than that; he salved every objection Darrowfield had.

At one point Lady Darrowfield asked him, "You will not forget your promise to me?"

"Promise?" Darrowfield roared. "What promise? Who do you think you are, making promises to a woman—and another man's wife?"

"If promises to wives were of any moment to you, husband," she scolded him, "we would hardly be at this impasse."

He raised a hand to strike her; the elder of their sons jumped to his feet and caught his arm. Darrowfield stomped angrily out of the room, muttering about "enemies everywhere—even in my own house."

When the rest of the party finally broke up, no one was in good spirits. But Merlin had his host's leave to depart.


"I hear you're leaving." Mordred encountered Nimue at the entrance to the dining hall, just before breakfast.

"I'm afraid we have to. We're expected at Dover." She told the convenient lie easily. "The king sent us as his representatives to their festival."

"I envy you. We'll be here till the equinox, so Mother can preside at the rituals at Stonehenge."

"I imagine I'll see you there, then. Our companion Petronus wants to see the monument. I can't imagine why." She wrinkled her nose in an exaggerated way. "He's French."

"Listening to our host and hostess fight all the time will be so unpleasant. And there are no signs of them being reconciled—or wanting to."

"Why don't you come with us?"

"Mother wouldn't approve. She can be so demanding. And she's angry at Darrowfield. He's flirting with Christianity, like half the nobles in England. She means to dissuade him. I want to try and maintain the peace, to the extent I can."

"And from what I hear, your mother can be so very vindictive when her demands are ignored. I hope you don't mind my saying so, but I pity Darrowfield if he defies her. But at least you'll survive, Mordred. You're young."

"So are you. So is Petro—Pet— What is his name again?"

"Petronus."

"Well, we should go in and have breakfast." He smiled a sardonic smile. "The condemned man ate a hearty meal."

"Cheer up. Arthur sent his pastry chef. You'll have the most wonderful cakes while you're here."

"If Mother doesn't poison them."

Breakfast was made into an ordeal by the Darrowfields' stony disagreements. When Merlin began saying his farewells, they both reacted unhappily. Then, when each of them realized the other wanted him to stay, they both made a show of bidding their guests good-bye.

Through it all, Morgan sat without saying much; Uther slept at the table; and Mordred sulked. Peter of Darrowfield came to table late and kept yawning. When everyone was finished with breakfast, Merlin, his aides and their soldier-escorts went directly to the stables, saddled their horses and made ready to leave.

At the last moment Lord Darrowfield approached Merlin. "I have changed my mind. I should like you to stay."

Merlin forced himself to smile. "May I ask why you have had such a dramatic change of heart?"

"Someone has been following me. Like a shadow. I can never see who it is—these damned winding corridors make it impossible. But someone is always there. You are famous for exposing villains. I—"

"I am certain it is nothing to be concerned about. Your

castle is so easy to become lost in. It could be anyone, for any reason. Just because someone is behind you does not mean you are being threatened. Besides, your new sheriff seems a capable man. I expect he can give you any protection you might need."

"But—"

"We must be off to Dover. The king's business, you know."

Plainly unhappy, Darrowfield bid them good-bye once again.

When they finally departed, just after the morning meal, their going seemed to come as a relief to everyone involved, except Lord Darrowfield himself. As he watched them go, a look of increasing concern crossed his features.

On the road, Merlin was lost in thought. When Nimue asked what was bothering him, he told her, "There is a line in the Christian holy book which I cannot get out of my mind. 'A man's enemies are the men of his own house.'"

"You mean Lord Darrowfield, don't you?"

"Yes, I suppose I do." Ruefully he added, "But Darrowfield seems to have enemies enough for three houses. It has all left me so uneasy."

# THREE

The weather was good for traveling, though clouds loomed in the west. Petronus commented, hoping they would make it to Dover before any storms might strike.

"This is England, Petronus," Merlin lectured softly. "There are always storms coming. If they do not strike now, they will hit us in Dover."

On the road from Darrowfield, heading for the main highway, they passed Stonehenge once again; they saw it in the distance to their left. It was still early morning; the monoliths cast long, strange shadows across the fields. Petronus asked if they might make at least a brief stop to inspect the monument.

"On our way home, Petronus." Merlin wanted no part of the suggestion. He hardly needed to explain that the place's association with religion, or superstition as he called it, was the reason why. "The celebration of the autumn equinox will be occurring. Even with Morgan there, doing her high priestess act and wielding her battery of poisons, it should be an entertaining festival."

"She seems so different from the king. How can they be brother and sister?"

Merlin lowered his voice. "They did not have the same mother. That accounts for so much in our so-called nobles. Have you not been paying attention these last few days?"

"I thought you like Arthur."

"So I do. He is one of my very few true friends."

For the first time Nimue spoke up. "If that is true of the nobles, how much more so must it be true of the common people? We are a mongrel nation, Merlin. Can such a race really engender the shining society—the peace and truth and justice—you envision?"

"Englishmen are human beings, Nimue, no more or less. You know I am not a religious man, but every religion I know of teaches that human nature is corrupt. It is precisely that corruptness that we must overcome. They also preach that we can attain the sublime."

He spurred his horse ahead, as if the conversation or perhaps the sight of the ancient stones in the distance unsettled him. The others spurred their mounts to keep up with him.

Dover was bustling with people when their party arrived, in late afternoon. The autumn fair was already getting under way. They reined their horses at the top of a hill, where the road began to wind down to the town, the harbor, the beach and the famous chalk cliffs. The harbor was crowded with ships from all parts of the Mediterranean, even as far away as Egypt and Palestine; a surprising number of them had painted sails.

From his pack Merlin produced a set of his "viewing lenses" and they all took turns inspecting the scene that spread before them. Petronus tried to count off as many national flags as he could recognize on the ships' masts, and he counted more than thirty. There were still others unknown to him.

"The Hebrew holy books tell of an attempt to build a tower to the sun." Merlin slipped into his best schoolteacher mode. "But the effort was undone and thrown into chaos by the huge confusion of languages. Dover must be like that now."

"Trust you to find some dark old myth for every situation." Nimue was in no mood for his cynicism. She held the lenses to her eye again. "Look at it all. I find it very exciting. I don't believe I've ever seen so many people gathered in one place."

From their position at the top of the hill, she scanned Dover and beamed at it all. "We are making progress, Merlin. The rest of the world is beginning to recognize England as a valuable venue for trade. Perhaps even a vital one." She was careful to add, "You and Arthur have a great deal to be proud of."

Merlin's mood changed quickly as they descended the road to Dover. Slowly a smile crept across his face. All the people and activity were affecting him despite himself. Nimue enjoyed his mood; it was rare for him to relax and enjoy himself.

"And a lot of the ships down there look prosperous," she added. "Look at how low they are riding in the water. They are heavy with goods. The Mediterranean economy must be strong."

Merlin smiled a satisfied smile. "We should all be proud, Nimue. Someday—soon, I hope—this country will be of international importance. I would like to think my life will last at least long enough to see that. We have spent far too long in the shadow of the European powers. The only time the historians ever even mention us is to note that the Romans invaded us."

"And Hadrian built that wall of his." Petronus was grateful for the chance to show off his learning.

They spurred their horses to move quickly down the road, and before long they reached the town's outskirts.

Vendors' booths began to appear along the road. Nimue bought a little cake from the first baker's stand they came to, bit into it and made an unpleasant face. "If we do gain international stature, it will not be for our cooking, I presume. How can you ruin something as simple as a poppy seed cake? The reputation of the French as superb pastry chefs is quite secure."

"It has nothing to do with nationality. The French hold no monopoly on culinary talent."

"We do." Petronus sulked defensively. "Everyone knows it."

"If Arthur is wise in nothing else, he always selects the best cooks. Take Marian of Bath, for example. She could do very well by striking out on her own. Arthur treats her more than well enough to keep her at Camelot."

Nimue spurred her horse. "Come on. Let's find our way to the garrison."

Merlin stiffened. "Garrison? We are on holiday. I want nothing with any scent of government. Let us find a nice warm inn."

"With the festival in progress, won't that be expensive?"

He pulled a little purse out of his pocket and jingled it. It was plainly filled with coin. "A gift to us from the king. As I said, he likes to keep his people content. A nice inn with a roaring fire and a good supply of wine will be just the thing."

Vendors and merchants were in the process of setting up kiosks in every street. Performers—minstrels, troubadours, acrobats, actors—were everywhere. Ordinary people crowded around them and the merchants. Dover was a huge press of people, all of them in a buoyant mood, all of them eating, drinking, singing off-key, applauding the performers . . . There were visitors who were easily identifiable by their clothing, Turks, Egyptians, North Africans, Byzantines; and others dressed in a more homogeneous European style.

Nimue and Petronus took it all in with relish. They seemed determined to try every kind of food on offer. After a few minutes, the boy disappeared into the crowd. Merlin grumped to Nimue, "Where is he? My hip is beginning to hurt. And the two of you are making yourselves fat. I want to find an inn and rest."

"This is a festival, Merlin. Eat."

Petronus rejoined them more exuberant than before. "There are Frenchmen here. I talked with one, and he says this is the liveliest festival he's ever seen. I am so proud to be an Englishman now." The boy looked slightly abashed. He lowered his voice. "I am one, am I not?"

A fat merchant pushed his way past them, stepping on Nimue's foot, and disappeared into the crowd. She glowered after him. "Are you really certain that's what you want to be?"

"Who do they represent, these Frenchmen you met?" Merlin made his inquiry with a smile. "What part of France do they hail from?"

"I don't know. I didn't think to ask." Petronus was mildly embarrassed.

"You do not have the makings of an intelligence officer. I wonder if you are really suited to any kind of government service—except possibly the military."

A look of alarm spread across the boy's face; he seemed to have no idea he was being kidded. "Please, Merlin, do not give me to the knights. Service with Lancelot was enough to convince me that—"

"I am only joking, Petronus. You have already made yourself so helpful to me."

Relief showed. "Thank you, sir. Can I buy some more cakes?"

Merlin sighed. "Perhaps I spoke too soon. But I am hungry, too."

This amused Nimue. "We already have some. Here." She handed him a bun. "That carefully constructed public image of yours—the wise man impatient with human weakness—always vanishes when your appetites take over, doesn't it?"

"Be quiet."

"Look. There's a nice inn in the next street. Why don't we try there?"

"Yes. But first I want another cake."

Nimue was about to make another wisecrack about Merlin's appetites, but he shot her a warning glance and she kept quiet.

To Merlin's disappointment, all the inns in Dover were full to capacity. After they tried five of them, he announced, "Not even the king's gold can open their doors to us. I suppose we will have to stay at the garrison after all."

Petronus was still eating breads and cakes. "Suppose they're full up, too?"

"We are high officials of the king. They will have to make room for us. If need be, some of the soldiers can double up."

"Two soldiers to a bed." Nimue was wry. "Like ancient Sparta."

"It may not come to that. There may be sufficient room. Still, I would prefer not to stop there. That will make it too easy for Arthur and Britomart to find me, for whatever crisis may arise this week. But it seems we have no choice." A passing juggler bumped against him, and he winced in pain, then scowled. "At least the soldiers will be disciplined enough to behave properly."

"Oh, yes." She could not hide her amusement. "No place bespeaks manners and decorum like a barracks room."

"Stop being disagreeable, Colin."

Petronus was eating his seventh cake. "The commander here is named Captain—Captain—?"

"Commander Larkin. I have met him at court but I do not know him at all well. Colin has corresponded with him a number of times." He looked at her. "What is your impression of him?"

She shrugged. "Solid. A military officer. A bureaucrat. There has never been the least flash of wit or irony in any of his communiqués, and certainly no imagination. So he is either very discreet or very dull."

"Splendid." Petronus wrinkled his nose. "The weather is so gorgeous. Why don't we sleep out of doors?"

"Are you joking?" Merlin was tart. "If I spend the night on the ground and waken wet with dew, I will be so stiff you will have to carry me home on a litter."

And so they made their way to the fort. It sat at the edge of one of the cliffs, overlooking the harbor and commanding a magnificent view of the English Channel. Merlin handed Petronus one of his ingenious viewing devices, a set of lenses supported in a wooden tube. "There." He pointed. "Your homeland, Petronus."

The boy took the device and held it to his eye. "I can't honestly see a great deal. It's a pity you haven't been able to make these any more powerful."

"In time, Petronus. Science and knowledge tend to advance slowly." He stumbled on a small rock and winced with pain. "Like myself."

In a few minutes they reached the gate of the fort and knocked. A sentry admitted them and asked them to wait there.

As it turned out, Commander Larkin was away on "official business"; Merlin did not bother to inquire what that meant. They were greeted by his lieutenant, an Irish sergeant named Ewan McGovern. "Merlin. We've heard so much about you here. And Colin. We all know your names so well. It's wonderful to meet you."

Merlin introduced Petronus and explained that they needed a place to stay for the duration of the festival.

"I'm afraid we're rather crowded in here." Ewan smiled, apparently embarrassed. "But I think we can find you rooms. If you'll only be patient for a few moments while we rearrange the living quarters . . . ?"

"Of course. Please, take your time. We do not wish to be more of a burden than is avoidable."

He vanished, then a few minutes later reappeared to install them in a suite of rooms against the back wall of the garrison. A window overlooked cliffs and the Channel; and a huge fire roared in the hearth. Then he proceeded, happily for everyone concerned, to leave them on their own.

Nimue sighed deeply. "I was afraid he'd feel obligated to entertain us. Which would have meant telling us all his soldier's stories. You know how the Irish are."

"Indeed. But as long as he keeps us warm, dry and well fed, I see no reason to complain."

Petronus ignored all this. "I wonder if I might meet some nice girls here," he chirped.

"Nice girls?" Merlin sounded incredulous. "In Dover? Like every port town everywhere, it is ridden with whores. And the ones here are notorious for leaving their clients with unexpected souvenirs of their coupling. Britomart always calls them 'fire ships.' She insists the men of the garrison be lectured about avoiding them once every month by a physician who is also charged with examining them."

"The women are earning a living, Merlin." Nimue was quite serious. "And a poor enough living, at that, I imagine. In a city this full of people, all interacting merrily, the spread of disease is inevitable. Singling out one segment of the population—"

"That is enough." Merlin turned uncharacteristically stern. "I was not attempting to 'single anyone out.' I merely want to warn Petronus that the friendly girls he meets here might have ulterior motives."

His enthusiasm punctured, Petronus sulked. "According to you, sir, everyone has ulterior motives."

"And so they do, Petronus. So they do."

The festival continued for two weeks. Every day more and more revelers arrived, and more and more vendors sprang up—"like toadstools," Merlin said—to sell them food, drink, clothing and everything else conceivable. Wine and ale were everywhere. The press of the crowds in the streets was increasingly unpleasant for Merlin, and exhilarating for his young companions.

An engineer from London came and set up a mechanical roundabout, and people lined up in large numbers to take a ride. Petronus stood in line for hours and did not want to ride alone, but he was not able to convince either Merlin or Nimue to join him. "I am dizzy enough, from the crowds and the wine," Merlin told him. "Apparently you are not."

"You ride that mechanical lift of yours often enough." Petronus sulked; his fun was being cramped.

"And if this contraption could help me bypass a long flight of stairs, I would ride it, too."

Nimue complained that she was gaining weight as a result of all the food at the festival.

Merlin told her in a low voice, "Relax, *Colin*, no one cares how fit or otherwise a scholarly boy may be. If you start acting like a vain girl, you will give the game away."

As the days passed, Merlin spent more and more time in their quarters, reading and avoiding the crowds quite pointedly.

"Come out with us," Nimue implored him on the festival's next-to-last day. "This will be over soon. You won't have another chance."

"I am quite content here, thank you. I have procured a lovely manuscript of poems by Catullus, Theocritus and Tibullus from a bookseller in town."

"Romans and their lovers—both girls and boys." She clucked her tongue and teased, "An important figure like you, reading such objectionable poetry?"

"Object all you like." He smiled and sat in a stuffed chair beside the fire to enjoy his reading. "I shall be passing my time among the finest minds Rome produced."

So Petronus and Nimue went out without their mentor, as they had been doing for days.

Petronus enjoyed passing time at the waterfront, where sailors from all over the Mediterranean could be found, drinking, wenching and spinning exotic tales of faraway lands. He was mesmerized by accounts of knights in Arabia and the djinn, demons and other spirits they encountered and frequently fought.

On that afternoon he managed to meet a group of sailors from a French ship, the *Mal de Mer*. One of them took a fancy to Petronus and "Colin," and the three of them went into town to explore the delights on offer.

His name was Jean-Gaston. He was tall, olive-skinned, athletic, he was second mate on the ship, and he exuded the easy charm the French were famous for. Nimue found herself regretting her male disguise; she would have liked to meet Jean-Gaston as her true self. He spoke no English, and she had very little French, so Petronus translated. Being the center of the threesome pleased him. At one point he stammered and refused to translate something Jean-Gaston had said. "It is quite improper," he explained. "Quite lewd."

"Good." She put on an impish grin. "Translate, then."

He did so, and the two of them giggled and followed the sailor through the crowd.

Late in the day Nimue decided their new friend should meet Merlin. Petronus explained this to him and they headed back in the direction of the garrison. Just as they reached the edge of the festival, Jean-Gaston began to cough uncontrollably. They stopped; Nimue put an arm around him and asked him, through Petronus, if he needed help.

But he could not stop the coughing. His face turned bright red, and blotches of a darker red, mingled with black, began to appear on his hands, his arms, his face, on every area of exposed skin. A moment later he fell to the ground, clutching his throat. In alarm, Nimue told Petronus to run and fetch Merlin. "And make sure he brings his medical kit."

She bent over the fallen sailor. The dark red blotches had begun to swell into large blisters; his complexion, other than the blotches, turned ghostly white. His skin was hot and feverish. Not knowing what else to do, she took his hand in hers, hoping it might calm him. He kept muttering in French, softly, almost inaudibly. Finally she saw Petronus coming back along the path, with Merlin in tow.

Merlin looked down at the man on the ground and asked, "What is the problem? What has happened?"

Nimue described the course of events.

"It happened that quickly?"

"Yes. He was fine only moments before the coughing began."

Merlin got down on a knee and felt his wrist. "The pulse is slow and weak." He looked up. "Very weak. Both of you, back away. Has either of you touched him?"

Nimue said that she had.

"Then quickly, find a clean cloth and wipe your hands. Wipe vigorously. Make sure every trace of him is gone from your skin." He swabbed his own hands with the hem of his robe.

"What is wrong with him?" Petronus asked.

"I cannot be quite certain, but those reddish-black swellings on his skin . . . I can only think that they are buboes." He got to his feet and wiped his hands on his robes once again. "I am afraid that this is plague."

"No!"

"I have never seen plague before. But this must be it. It conforms to all the descriptions in the medical texts. Let us hope he recovers. Then he will be able to tell us where he might have contracted this. And where he might have spread it. Petronus, run and fetch Sergeant Ewan. Tell him to come at once. *At once*, do you hear? We must send men into town to learn what may be happening there. There will be other men on his ship who are also infected."

Petronus was frozen, a look of horror on his face.

"Run, I said!"

"Yes, sir."

A moment after the boy left, Jean-Gaston heaved a loud sigh. He coughed up a huge quantity of blood. His body shuddered, and he was still.

Merlin took a step slowly, carefully, away from his body. "So much for that hope."

Nimue impulsively moved to the corpse, plainly wanting to do something to help.

"Do not touch him. He is dead, Colin. Nothing will do any good. We must keep our wits about us. How long were you with him?"

She explained.

"And this struck so quickly? It has all the symptoms of plague, but I have never heard of symptoms developing so rapidly. If plague is what we are actually facing—if he did not have some odd form of the pox or whatever—this may turn into a major crisis." They both stood over the body, to warn passersby not to touch it and risk contagion. Fortunately, no one seemed to want to. There were a few curious glances, and one woman suggested consulting the local priestess of Bran, "for your sick friend."

Petronus returned with Sergeant Ewan. Merlin explained what had happened, and what he suspected was the cause. "Have some men come and take the body away and burn it. Caution them not to touch it."

"Should they wear armor, sir?"

"No, I do not think that will be necessary. But have them wear gloves, and warn them not to come into contact with any exposed skin. Most physicians who have known the plague think it is probably airborne, but precautions will not hurt."

"Yes, sir. And I will send more men into town to warn everyone that there may be plague here. We cannot keep the populace in ignorance of the danger they may be facing."

"They will panic, Ewan. That will not be good."

"Let them. If nothing else, it will clear them all out of Dover."

"But if some of them are already infected with plague, they will spread it to every corner of southern England. No, it would be better to cordon off the town and quarantine everyone here."

"That would take more men than I have. There are seven major roads out of town, and any number of small footpaths."

"You will have to find the men to staff inspection points on all of them. Erect roadblocks."

"And you think that will not cause a panic?"

Merlin sighed. "We must take the chance, I suppose. We have never had to deal with a thing like this before. Every precaution must be taken."

Merlin looked at the dead sailor, then back at Ewan. "We cannot be certain this is plague until . . . well, until it becomes a plague. But we can hardly afford to take any risks. We do not want the whole country infected. I will write a message to the king. You must send one of your men to Camelot to deliver it to him. He will instruct Britomart that we need more soldiers here."

"And if my men panic?"

"We will have to hope they do not. England's future may depend on what we do here. Enforce whatever discipline is necessary. Colin, here, has some experience at planning large-scale operations. He will give you whatever assistance he can." Merlin nodded to Nimue, indicating that she should go with Ewan.

"Will you be staying to direct all our operations, sir?"

"I must return to Camelot as quickly as possible. If plague actually does break out, Arthur will need my counsel." Again he looked at the body. "More than ever."

Ewan and Nimue prepared plans for the soldiers of the garrison to place a cordon around the town and not permit anyone to leave. It was a larger operation than either of them had anticipated. The roadblocks required would be substantial—otherwise people could simply either walk or ride around them—and the manpower daunting. They planned shifts of men to rotate at the checkpoints. The garrison was stretched very thin. With luck, all plans would be in place by sunrise; with more luck, Britomart would post more men to Dover quickly.

A small group of men was attached to Merlin who, assisted by Petronus, monitored news from the town. The least indication of unusual illness, or of civil unrest fueled by alarming rumor, was to be reported to them. Merlin instructed them to ask discreet questions to try to determine what other ports the French ship had visited before coming to Dover. These soldiers were also to work in shifts. A small detachment of men was assigned to build a pyre and burn Jean-Gaston's body.

Then that night another sailor from the *Mal de Mer* died, in exactly the same way as Jean-Gaston. Not much later a third man died, this one from a Greek ship, the *Sophia*, that had come to Dover after a trading stop in North Africa.

Rumor spread quickly among all the festival-goers in the town. The word *plague* was bandied about freely, and the town and its visitors were palpably edgy. Then, when a fourth sailor, from still another ship, took ill, complete hysteria erupted. Foreign visitors flocked back to their ships. English visitors hastened to pack and leave for their hometowns; residents of Dover took to the countryside. Merlin and Ewan scarcely had time to react; in a startlingly short time—before midnight struck—Dover was nearly deserted. The roadblocks did little good to halt the exodus or even to slow it. And the plague, if plague it really was, was loose in England.

Next afternoon, with Dover quite empty of people, Merlin decided he would be of most use back at Camelot.

Ewan was alarmed. "You can't leave me, sir, not with all this happening. Remember, I am only a sergeant."

"With the people gone, there is not much for you to do. Is Captain Larkin not due back shortly?"

"On the day of the equinox, sir. Tomorrow."

"There should be no problem, then. You have done a first-class job, Sergeant, and I will make certain to tell Britomart and the king. Do you have a carriage you could spare for us?"

"Yes, sir. I'll make the arrangements. When do you wish to leave? First thing in the morning?"

"No, now, I think. There is no time to be lost. We must travel all night to reach Camelot, if need be."

"Yes, sir. I'll send a spare driver along, then, so you will lose as little time as possible."

"Excellent. We will leave our two soldiers with you. And you will of course brief Captain Larkin on all that has happened in Dover?"

"Naturally, sir."

"Splendid. We will get our things together and leave as soon as possible, then. Our two soldiers will remain here, to replace them and give what help they can.

"Please instruct Captain Larkin that we will expect daily communications from Dover, advising us on the situation here. The residents will have to return, eventually. There may be further outbreaks of illness or, worse, riots. We will need to know what is happening here. And of course you

must include any news you may hear of things in the surrounding countryside."

"Yes, sir. Of course."

It took little over an hour for Merlin and his aides to pack
for the journey back to Camelot. By that time, Ewan had
their carriage prepared. The three of them climbed in and
braced themselves for the long ride home.

Nimue was in a glum mood. "I've never lived through
anything like this."

"No one has. No one here, at any rate."

"It's going to rain."

"This is England. It is always going to rain."

No one laughed at Merlin's little joke, not even Merlin
himself. The carriage moved forward with a considerable
jolt, and they were off. Petronus asked still again if they
could stop at Stonehenge to witness sunrise on the morning
of the equinox. "I think we should get there just about at
the right time."

"We are facing a national emergency, Petronus." Merlin
looked out the window, not at the boy. "There is hardly
time for sightseeing. Besides, see those clouds building up?
I doubt there will be a sunrise for anyone to see."

"The ceremony, then? Surely a few minutes cannot
make such a big difference?"

"When this is all behind us, I will bring you to Stonehenge myself and give you a tour."

Nimue could not resist. "And what better tour guide than
the wizard who built it with his magical powers?"

Merlin snorted and shifted so his back was to them.

The first leg of their route took them directly through the
heart of Dover. Streets were deserted; abandoned animals
looked in vain for their owners; one lone ship remained in
the harbor, its crew seemingly frozen into immobility; it all

had the eeriest air. Nimue said she had never seen a place so melancholy.

"Hell may be coming to England, Colin. It may already have arrived. None of us will survive if we do not learn to love one another. Willful cruelty is the usual pastime of the human race. Let us hope this will change that. Arthur and I want to make a world where—" Unexpectedly he broke off. "No, this is no time for a speech. I am the greatest fool the world has known."

She put her hand on top of his, hoping the gesture reassured him, and they rode on in silence. Before long the rhythmic motion of the carriage and the clatter of the horses' hooves had lulled them all into a gentle sleep.


Not long after dark the rain began, a fierce, driving downpour. The noise of it woke the passengers. They shuttered the windows and rode on, quite safely encapsulated, without much conversation. Nimue offered blankets to the drivers, to help keep them dry, but it was useless. The blankets were soaked through in no time at all.

After a time, they slept again, all but Merlin, who was preoccupied wondering if the natural calamity he feared would be the undoing of the England he and Arthur had made. In time, he slept, too.


Early the next morning, well before dawn, the carriage's pace slowed almost to a stop. It woke Merlin and Petronus. The others slept on.

"What's wrong?" Petronus asked softly.

Merlin held a finger to his lips and said quietly, "There is no sense disturbing Colin." Then he leaned out the window and called softly to the driver, "What is happening? Why have we slowed?"

The rain had slowed to a steady drizzle that showed no signs of letting up. The sky was still overcast, almost black, though occasional breaks in the cloud cover could be seen. The driver, himself drowsing, did not hear him. On the seat beside him the second man, his relief, was fast asleep. "How they can sleep in this rain—" Merlin muttered.

He repeated his question a bit more loudly, and this time the man responded. "The rain, sir, has turned the road to mud. We can only go so fast. On top of that, the road is clogged with travelers. Most of them are on foot."

Merlin squinted and looked up the road ahead of them. Through the rain and the darkness he could see that there were enormous numbers of people on the road. They progressed in silence and in darkness; the rain had extinguished whatever lights they might have had. "Travelers? In such huge numbers? Who on earth can they be?"

The man shrugged. "People fleeing from Dover. We've finally caught up with them."

"Has everyone from Dover taken the same road, then?"

"And I think a lot of them must be pilgrims, heading to the shrine."

"Shrine? Oh. Stonehenge."

"Yes, sir. It's too bad. They won't see the sunrise."

"They will face worse disappointments soon enough."

Before long the press of people forced the carriage to slow to the pace of a man walking. Merlin suggested trying to find a way around the crowd.

"Look at them, sir. They are all around us. Everywhere."

And so they were. Hundreds of them, perhaps even thousands, as far as Merlin could see. They crossed the plain, clogged the road, made further progress excruciatingly slow. Soon enough, Merlin realized, it might be necessary to stop altogether. He said so to Petronus, who did not try to disguise his delight. "Then I will be able to see the monument after all!"

"Yes, I suppose so. Assuming the plague is not spreading through this crowd even as we speak."

The carriage inched forward. The driver woke his companion, and they tried shouting, "Make way for the king's advisor!" It had no effect.

"Tell me what it's like, sir. What should I expect?" Anticipation showed in Petronus's face.

But Merlin's mood was growing darker by the minute. "Expect a crowd of superstitious fools."

"But—"

"You have seen sketches of Stonehenge, surely."

"Yes, sir, but—"

"Expect to be disappointed, then. For all its reputation, Stonehenge is not all that large or imposing. People always expect something on a titanic scale, like the Pyramids or the Colosseum in Rome. This is nowhere near so massive. There is a stone circle, uprights with stone lintels connecting them. Inside, there are five more of these 'trilithons' as they are called, uprights and lintels, forming a rough horseshoe. Then near the center is a huge stone used as an altar. And there are a few other bits of debris; they have been given fanciful names like the Heel Stone and the Slaughter Stone. But for all the whimsy, they are only rock. It is nothing to be excited about."

"I'm excited, sir."

"Don't be."

"I can't help it. Wouldn't you have been, when you were my age?"

"I was never your age. And even when I was, I would never have admitted it."

In the distance ahead Stonehenge appeared, lit by scores of torches. The great stone circle glowed eerily, almost preternaturally. Merlin wondered why the rain did not put them out.

But the rain was easing; within a few moments it almost

stopped. It had done its job; the plain was a sea of mud. They would be lucky if the carriage wheels did not become mired in it.

Then there was the sound of another carriage behind them. Merlin leaned out the window to look. It was an enormous thing, painted jet-black, drawn by a team of six black horses. On either side of the driver torches burned brilliantly. "Morgan," he whispered softly to himself. Then to Petronus he said, "Apparently the high priestess of England is not daunted by terrible weather."

"They say she can control it, sir. Maybe that's why the rain is stopping now."

"Do not be preposterous." To the driver Merlin suggested, "The crowd will part for Morgan. Follow her carriage and we will make quick progress as far as the monument, at least."

And the crowd did indeed part for their priestess. Merlin's driver steered their coach behind hers. The quick forward jolt woke Nimue. She rubbed her eyes and asked what was happening.

Petronus excitedly told her, "We're going to see Stonehenge and the equinox rites."

Merlin grumped and kept his gaze outside.

Hordes of people surrounded the great stone monument, all of them seemingly with torches; they passed the fire one to another. The great stones glowed and shimmered in the predawn. They might have been fired by lightning. But he noticed that all the torches were outside the stone circle. Presumably the worshippers were waiting outside, away from the altar stone, in deference to their priestess.

Morgan's coach drew to a halt just at the paved pathway that led into the heart of Stonehenge. Merlin's stopped just behind it.

The crowd fell silent with anticipation. Slowly the door of Morgan's carriage opened and she descended. She was dressed magnificently, in voluminous black robes embroidered with silver. Just behind her, her son Mordred emerged from the carriage, looking self-conscious, dressed like her in black and silver.

When she saw Merlin and the others get out of their carriage, she crossed to him. "What are you doing here?"

Merlin resented her tone. He put on a sarcastic grin and said, "Why, Morgan. How nice to see you."

"I asked you what you are doing here. I can't recall a time when you were not disdainful of the ancient, solemn rites that made England what she is."

He was all sweet innocence. "We've come to see the monument. My assistant never has, you know. Surely you do not object to our visiting this sacred place?" He did not mean a word of it, and they both knew it.

"You are a sacrilegious old fool, Merlin. I will not have the equinox defiled by your presence. The ritual must be postponed."

"Postpone the movement of the sun? Really, Morgan, I had no idea even you had that kind of power."

"Do not be sarcastic, Merlin. You said yourself this is a holy place."

"Please, Morgan, do go on with what you came for." He made a sweeping gesture at the crowd. "I give you my word I will not interfere in any way. Look at the audience you have."

"Congregation," she corrected him.

"Congregation, then. These people have come from all over England to hear you invoke the sun god. My assistant Petronus is especially eager to witness the rites. It would be terrible of you to disappoint them all."

She stiffened and said nothing; she was obviously turning over the options in her mind. After a moment she turned to Mordred and told him, "Signal the celebrants that we are about to begin."

"Yes, Mother." In a flash he disappeared into the crowd.

She clapped her hands, and from her carriage an attendant produced a high stool. He placed it in front of her. Then she held out a hand and he helped her climb up onto it. Thus towering over the crowd, she intoned, "People of England!"

Her voice thundered, quite uncharacteristically. Merlin wondered who had coached her in the way to project it.

From seemingly nowhere, a band of musicians appeared out of the throng and played a low, mournful fanfare. And the vast crowd fell silent.

"The sun is dying." Morgan intoned the words solemnly, and they echoed across the plain.

To Nimue, Merlin whispered, "It is doing no such thing. It is merely following a course lower in the sky. It does so every year."

"Soon enough," Morgan went on, "it will be gone from us, only to be gloriously resurrected come springtime." Her voice echoed across the plain. The people were rapt.

Merlin glanced at Petronus. The boy was quite caught up in the moment. He watched Morgan wide-eyed, as if her flummery made any sense. Merlin shook his head and whispered to Nimue, "I really must teach the boy more firmly."

"And while you're at it, why don't you teach all the rest of them? You will never cure humanity of this, Merlin. It means too much to them."

Morgan went on and on about the sun, the gods, the promise of a resurrected life after death, as demonstrated each year by the sun itself. Merlin wanted her to get on with it; she showed no inclination to do so.

Overhead there were occasional breaks in the clouds. They grew more and more numerous, more and more frequent, and Merlin realized that Morgan was extemporizing to kill time in hope that the sun itself might become visible.

Finally a few shafts of sunlight broke through the clouds. Morgan continued her oration. But when the sun began to disappear once again, she ended it quickly and clapped her hands another time. "Let the autumn rites begin."

The musicians, who had obviously been rehearsed, formed themselves into a column and began to play a mournful march. Young girls with torches made a column behind them. Morgan, followed by her son, fell into place at the rear. And slowly, stately, the processional advanced into the heart of Stonehenge.

Merlin, Petronus and Nimue joined the ceremonial march. Petronus was plainly excited by the crowd, the music, the hundreds of flaming torches and the air of solemnity. Nimue's face reflected casual interest, no more. Merlin leaned close to her and whispered, "Our young friend is almost quivering with expectation. Why aren't you?"

"I grew up in Morgan's household, remember? Back when I was still living as Nimue, not Colin. I have seen her preside over this sort of thing before. When I was a child, it was all very exciting. Now . . ."

"Are you trying to imply that Petronus is still a child?"

"Stop trying to stir up trouble, Merlin."

The torches still shone brightly in the half-light. Glowing patterns danced on the monument's stones as the procession moved in to the heart of the monument. The clouds overhead closed up again; the sun, which they were there to celebrate, was lost completely behind them.

Then suddenly, abruptly, all forward motion halted. The people at the front of the march broke ranks and began to mill about in the most disorganized manner. There were shouts. The music petered out and stopped.

Morgan bellowed, "What is the problem up there? Why have you all stopped?" She turned to Mordred and told him to run ahead and see what the problem was.

Merlin took his two young companions each by the hand. "Let us go and see."

The orderly procession was quickly dissolving into a disorganized mob. But Merlin was determined to enter the monument and see what the problem was. He, Nimue and Petronus forced their way through the throng just behind Mordred.

Inside the stone circle, Mordred stopped and seemed to freeze. Merlin pushed past him.

The horseshoe of trilithons loomed around them, each formed by a pair of massive stone uprights topped by a stone lintel. The space at the center was empty of people; they were backing away.

Then he saw what was alarming them. Lashed to the altar stone at the monument's center were three men. One was prone on the top of the stone; the other two were lashed securely to its sides. A web of leather thongs held them in place.

The throat of each man was slashed. The altar stone and the earth around it were covered in dried blood.

And then he recognized them. "In the name of everything human." The dead men were Lord Darrowfield and his sons.

# FOUR

"Plague? You can't be serious, Merlin." Arthur paced and glared at Merlin. "Yes, of course I got your message from Dover. But I assumed you were joking."

"Joking! Arthur, sometimes I feel you don't know me at all."

They were in the king's study. As always, there was not enough light. The three portraits of Arthur were still there, on their easels. Pacing, Arthur stumbled over one of them. "Simon!" he bellowed. "Get these damned things out of here!"

"Calm down, Arthur." Merlin presented his soberest manner. "I am perfectly serious. Do you really think I would joke about such a thing?"

"Yes, I told you, I got the bloody message." He rubbed his shin where it had struck the easel. Then he took the letter from the table and shook it at Merlin. "I thought it had to be a joke. Or a mistake. Something brought on by

too much wine—or too much whatever—at the festival. So
did Britomart."

"It is hardly a thing I would joke about. Four men died,
all sailors. As near as we were able to determine, their ships
had all stopped in Algiers to take on cargo. Arthur, it will
spread."

Arthur stopped moving about the room and glared at
him. "You can't possibly be certain of that. This is England.
No Englishmen have died from this thing, have they?"

"Do you hold the opinion that the human body in England is different, in some way?"

"Algerian plague." He snorted.

Simon of York appeared with an assistant. "You are
finished with these, Your Majesty?" He indicated the portraits, one of which was now on the floor.

"Yes, get them out of here. They take up too much
room."

"As I have been telling you for weeks, Sire."

"Don't you start, too. It's bad enough that I've got him
picking at me." He made a vague gesture in Merlin's direction. "You know which one I want?"

"Yes, sir."

"Good. Put the artists to work on it right away. I want
those new coins in circulation as soon as possible."

"Yes, sir." He hesitated and looked from the king to
Merlin and back again. "Is—is everything all right?"

"No, everything is not all right." Arthur mocked his conciliatory tone.

"If I can be of any help, sir . . ."

"You can be of help by doing what I asked you to do."

"Yes, sir." Simon clapped his hands, and his assistant
gathered up the portraits and their stands. "Oh, and Your
Majesty?"

"What? What else?"

"That jester person is here." He frowned in obvious disapproval of the "jester person."

But Arthur suddenly, unexpectedly broke into an enormous grin. "John of Paintonbury?"

"I believe that is his name, sir."

"Excellent. Tell him I'll be with him shortly."

"Yes, sir." With that, Simon bowed and he and his assistant left.

There was a moment's silence between Merlin and the king. Merlin looked unhappy. Finally he asked, "A jester?"

"Yes." Arthur rubbed his hands together. "I told you about him."

"Memory fails. There has been so much else—"

"A very clever fellow. I met him on that visit to Coventry last month."

"And you decided to bring him here—to admit him to our court—without consulting anyone."

"This is not 'our court.' It is mine." Arthur sighed. "Do me a favor and don't pick at me today. I have too much on my mind. Including this plague of yours from Algiers, it seems. I don't even know for certain where Algiers is."

Merlin stood and stared at him.

And Arthur wilted under it. "All right, fine. This plague of *ours*, then. Is that better?"

"Thank you, Arthur. We do not know, yet, if it really is a plague. I suggest you contact your sheriffs in every part of southeast England and have them send daily reports. If there is an outbreak someplace other than Dover—"

"What can we do?"

For a long moment Merlin said nothing. Then finally, "Hope. That is all."

"Hope is not a commodity in long supply, in my life."

"Even so. If I were a superstitious man, I would say *pray*."

"Should I summon my sister Morgan to Camelot? Should I have her conduct some kind of public rite? It might reassure people, if nothing else."

Merlin smiled faintly. "The way she reassured Lord Darrowfield?"

Arthur frowned. "Poor Darrowfield. Tell me what happened."

"I told you the basic facts." Merlin shrugged slightly. "We found him and his sons at Stonehenge. Their throats were cut."

"But surely you investigated. I know you. You could never have resisted."

"I was on holiday, Arthur, remember? And this disease is a much more urgent matter. Besides, Peter of Darrowfield, the new sheriff there, took matters into his hands. He seems an able enough man. I did not want to tread on his authority."

Arthur narrowed his eyes. "But you know who did it. Or think you do. You always do, Merlin."

"Not in this case. The obvious suspect would be Lady Darrowfield. There was nothing but unpleasantness between her and her husband. And she would hardly be the first vindictive wife in England."

Arthur stiffened at this. "Leave Guenevere out of this. Leave her out of everything."

"Of course. I'm not at all certain I see Lady Darrowfield in that mold, anyway. If it was only her husband who had been killed . . ." He made a vague gesture. "But the boys were slaughtered as well. She hardly seems like the type of woman to play Medea."

"Then . . . ?"

He hesitated. "Your sister was there."

"Morgan?"

"Yes, with her son Mordred in tow. Nominally she was there in preparation for the equinox. But word has it that Darrowfield was flirting with conversion to the Christian religion. And Morgan was none too happy about it."

"You don't think she killed him, surely?"

"It would hardly be her first time removing an, er, inconvenient opponent. We both know her history. And she had Mordred there to do her dirty work."

"He was the only attendant she brought?"

"She had others, but they were at Stonehenge, preparing for the festival there." He paused uncertainly, then decided to go on. "But they could easily have gotten to Darrowfield Castle to help Mordred with any . . . business."

Arthur brooded. "I know Morgan's bloody reputation. I've never quite convinced myself she could be so lethal."

Merlin hesitated again, but decided to lay out all his suspicions. "She can be. And your father was there with her, Arthur."

"Uther? England's famous hero Uther Pendragon?" He laughed. "How badly is he decaying?"

"Rather badly, I'd say. I can't remember ever seeing anyone more feeble."

"Good. What on earth was he doing there? He ought to be in a basket on a shelf somewhere. But you're not suggesting—I mean, he could hardly have been the killer."

"Hardly. But your family's history raises, shall we say, so many suspicions."

"There. You see?" Suddenly Arthur was animated. "You've put your finger on precisely why I need to find the right heir. The one who is truly worthy. Thank you for making my point."

"In the name of everything human, you are relentless, Arthur. People look at your golden hair and call you the Sun King. But you are more like a storm of driving rain and wind."

"You're not the first to say so. But you taught me, Merlin. There is no other way to be king." His smile disappeared. "But do you really mean to say that one of my family must have killed Darrowfield? Are there no other possible suspects?"

"Wherever there is humanity, there are possible suspects. But I was hardly there long enough to know everyone who might have had a motive."

Suddenly there was a young man at the door, rapping at the lintel impatiently. "How long do you plan to keep me waiting?" Despite his brusque manner he was grinning. He was in his early twenties, to appearances. Short, thin, with unruly black hair and startlingly blue eyes. "I *could* be off taking care of my geese now."

For a moment Arthur stiffened; then, seeming to recognize the young man, he relaxed. "John. I'm glad you're here."

"You might act like it, then. Cooling my heels out here is hardly the reception I—"

"I'm sorry, John. Really I am." Arthur seemed to remember himself. "Ah, but the two of you haven't met. John of Paintonbury, this is my friend and trusted advisor Merlin."

Merlin gaped, uncertain of the protocol. Slowly he extended a hand. "Arthur tells me you are to be his jester."

"Satirist," John corrected him.

"Satirist, then." Merlin made himself smile as he shook the young man's hand. "You will be living here at Camelot? On the royal bounty?"

John's eyes flashed. "You needn't sound so disapproving. None of this is my idea. I was quite content raising geese. It is a modest living, but an honest one." A mischievous smile crossed his lips. "Unlike being a wizard."

"You are suggesting," Arthur interjected, "that those of us who administer England's affairs are not earning our livings honestly?"

"My geese, Your Majesty, permit themselves to be fattened. And slaughtered, by those who need their meat the most. Perhaps Camelot's residents might take a lesson from them." He frowned. "Of course, fattening themselves—that, they are already doing. Every time I turn a corner, there is a table of cakes."

"The king is terribly fond of cakes." Merlin was not amused by the young man. "Yet I have seen him go without them altogether, when he needed to. *You* might take a lesson from that."

Arthur grinned and turned to Merlin. "There—you see? He will be perfect."

Merlin was increasingly put off. And puzzled—it was not in character for Arthur to take such insults with such cordiality. He nodded to John, mock-deferentially. "With all the swords here, and with a slew of hotheaded knights wielding them, I suspect I will be earning an honest living soon enough, investigating a murder."

"Now, now, Merlin, don't be so touchy." Arthur wanted peace between them.

"I am not being touchy, Your Majesty." When he became formal with the king, he always emphasized titles like *Your Majesty* with strong irony. "Simply realistic. Your knights are hardly known for self-restraint. Or for having a sense of humor about themselves."

"John will soon cure them of that." Arthur put an arm around his new jester's shoulder. "Won't you, John?"

"If it pleases the king." John smiled with unconvincing modesty. "I would do anything in my power to please *Your Majesty*." His tone mimicked Merlin's perfectly.

"Yes. Of course you would." Merlin put on a tight smile. "As would we all. Now if you will excuse me, Arthur, there is a national crisis brewing. Or would you prefer that I remain here and listen to your new court comedian as he babbles more affronts?"

"There will be plenty of time for that, Merlin. John will be here permanently, remember?"

"Thank you for reminding me." To John he said, "You should be careful, young man. There is always the danger that living with geese may have turned you into one."

John laughed at him. "Honk, honk."

Exasperated, Merlin turned to go. "If you want me, Arthur, I will be in my tower."


Every day for the next week dispatches arrived from Captain Larkin at Dover, who had returned from his trip and was grappling with the situation there. Slowly, most of the town's citizens had returned. There had been several more deaths, all in the same manner as the first ones—rapid onset of symptoms, followed by stillness. Additionally, three more people had been stricken with the disease and then recovered almost as quickly as they had fallen ill. A low-grade fever seemed to be spreading through the town, as well. To date, none of the garrison's soldiers had been stricken, but that seemed only a matter of time.

Merlin wrote back as frequently as he received the letters. He requested Larkin to gather as much information as he could about the victims—occupations, families, any contact they may have had with the visiting mariners. He advised that their close friends and relatives be watched carefully. And he asked for detailed accounts from the three survivors of what they had experienced, their feelings, and any possible contacts they may have had with the foreigners.

On the tenth day the missive from Dover was signed by Sergeant Ewan. Captain Larkin had fallen ill in the same way as the others and died soon after. He was the first man of the garrison to be afflicted, and Merlin conjectured that he may have contracted the infection elsewhere. "He must have passed among a great many people on his travels, some of them infected."

Merlin consulted with Arthur and Britomart and arranged for Ewan to be appointed temporary commander of the fort. His dispatches continued, sometimes two or even three per day. The disease was spreading slowly but quite inexorably through the town. Reports began to reach Camelot of deaths in the surrounding countryside as well.

Then further reports, sent by local officials, arrived from nearby towns and villages. Two people had died at Folkestone. A whole family of pig farmers expired at Frogham. And there were unconfirmed reports of people dying of a mysterious disease at Sandwich and even Canterbury. The reports of what killed them, and descriptions of the disease's progress, never varied. The officials at Canterbury were quite perplexed; but they had heard rumors of a mysterious disease, possibly the plague, at Dover. Did Camelot have any reliable information, they asked, about what it was? Merlin wrote and told them there was no definite information about the nature of the disease, while admitting it was spreading. "There is no cause for panic," he assured them. "You may trust that Camelot will keep you posted as the situation develops."


"Marian, Robert, Wayne."

The three of them had returned from Darrowfield Castle. Merlin met with them in a small room at Camelot. It was seldom used and sparsely furnished; there were only a few chairs, nothing else. No tapestries hung on the walls, so the room was drafty. Marian of Bath and her sons were seated, waiting for Merlin.

"You asked to see us, sir." Marian looked uncomfortable but stood as he entered the chamber. Her twin sons were expressionless.

"Yes. Please relax, all of you. I hope your time at Darrowfield Castle was not unpleasant—given the awful events there, I mean."

"It was fine, sir." She was plainly nervous. "There never was a party or celebration, as you might guess. But Lady Darrowfield wanted us to stay and help provide for the

mourners at the funeral. There were not many of them, sir."
She looked uncomfortable saying it. "I don't think he was
well liked."

Marian's twin sons were seated just behind her, side by
side, quite close to each other. Their expressions were
completely vacant; they stared at Merlin without any evident interest or engagement. He found them slightly dis-
concerting.

He forced a smile. "Well, we are all quite happy to have
you back here." The smile grew even wider. "And to have
your cakes again. They have been missed by so many people. The ones we had while you were gone were nowhere
near so good. Only this morning Sir Bors was saying—"

"The Sheriff of Darrowfield questioned us, sir. As if we
might be criminals."

"Sheriff Peter? I'm sure he was only doing his duty,
Marian. He had to gather as much information as he could.
I would not be concerned."

"How can we not be concerned, sir? A lord was killed,
and the sheriff questioned us."

"Please, do not give it another thought. I will write to
Peter myself, vouching for you."

"Thank you, sir." She relaxed a bit.

He took a seat and stretched his legs out. "I would like
to ask you about your experience there. Nothing deep—
please believe that I do not suspect you of any villainy."

She thanked him for saying so; her sons shifted uncomfortably.

"Now." He paused slightly, then decided that being di-
rect with her would be the most effective way to proceed.
"What was the atmosphere like at Darrowfield? After I left,
I mean."

She looked directly at him. "Tense, sir. You saw how
they fought."

"The lord and lady, you mean?"

"Yes."

"And what about Morgan le Fay? And her son Mordred? And Uther?"

"They were there, too, sir."

"Yes, I know it. How did they cope with the tense atmosphere?"

"They—they—I'm not at all certain I should say, sir."

"Say it." He realized he had been acting the professional interrogator and made his tone softer. A reassuring smile crept across his lips. "You understand, this is not an official inquiry into the murders. That was Peter's job, and he seems to have done it well enough. My interest is— well, more personal. You know how we politicians love gossip."

"Yes, and the more malicious, the better." For the first time one of Marian's sons spoke up; he was not certain which it was, Robert or Wayne.

Merlin stiffened slightly. "Not necessarily. But the Prussians have a term, schadenfreude. It means a delight at the misfortunes and suffering of others. I am afraid too many of us are guilty of it. But I do not mind telling you, I felt supremely uncomfortable in Lord Darrowfield's house. I would enjoy hearing the worst."

The other son laughed. "You never stop assassinating one another, do you? Sometimes literally, sometimes not. But I mean—"

This was not going at all the way Merlin wanted. He interrupted forcefully. "I would appreciate it if you would not—"

The first son got to his feet. "What do you want to know? We don't know who killed the old bastard, any more than you do."

"I am not suggesting that you—"

An instant later the second son was on his feet. "You will not find a way to make us responsible for what happened."

"But I only—"

Finally Marian spoke up. "Boys! Stop this at once! Merlin is a friend. This is Camelot, not Darrowfield. We are home now."

The twins calmed down and resumed their seats. Sulking, one of them said, "Sorry, sir." The tone of his apology was not convincing, to Merlin's ear.

"It is quite all right. I know how stressful it was, having been in that castle for a day or two myself. Being there for an extended period, as you were, must have been unpleasant in the extreme.

"But we are avoiding the real issue. What I want to talk to you about is what you may have seen and heard while you were there. From the other servants. You know very well that they have a different reaction to persons and events than those of us who are higher up."

"We saw nothing," said one of the twins. "We heard even less."

"Come now." Merlin did his best to sound cordial and conciliatory. "Lord Darrowfield's staff must at least have expressed sympathy for either him or his wife."

"We don't know a thing about that."

The interview was not going at all the way Merlin had hoped. He found the boys' attitude difficult to comprehend. He made a mental note to discuss it with Nimue; she so often had an insight into people that was beyond him, especially when it came to the lower orders. And she was a shrewd judge of character.

Suddenly Simon of York rushed into the room. "Merlin! So this is where you've been." His tone was vaguely accusatory. "We've scoured the castle looking for you."

Mildly baffled by Simon's urgent tone, Merlin told him, "The four of us have been getting better acquainted, that is all. Is something wrong?"

"There is an emergency. A medical emergency. Fedora wants you."

It caught him quite off guard. He got to his feet. "Fedora, the old midwife? She must be ninety—a walking medical emergency herself. What on earth can she want me for?"

An expression of concern crossed Marian's face. "Fedora the midwife?"

Simon ignored her. "Come along. Hurry. Sir Dinadan's wife is giving birth. It is not going well."

"Oh. I see." To Marian and the boys he said, "Thank you for meeting with me. We must continue this at a more opportune moment."

One of the twins smiled; the other did not. Marian stood and caught at Merlin's sleeve. "You will not forget to write to the sheriff about us?"

"I will do it the moment I am free. You have my word."

"Thank you, sir."

Merlin followed Simon to the wing of the castle where most of the knights resided. Before very long they had reached Sir Dinadan's rooms. The knight was standing in the hallway, pacing, looking more than mildly alarmed. "Merlin. Thank God you've come."

"What is happening?"

"They are inside."

"I would have assumed. But what—"

Suddenly the air was cut by a low, piercing wail. A woman, presumably Lady Dinadan, was in severe pain. The sound actually made Merlin shudder.

Dinadan grabbed him by the arm. "For God's sake, you have to save my son. And my wife."

"Son? How do you know it is a boy?"

"My family always produces boys. I wouldn't have it otherwise."

"Of course."

Simon interrupted this. "Perhaps you should step inside, Merlin, to evaluate the situation for yourself."

"Yes, you are right. There may be little time to spare. Step in with me; I will need an assistant."

"Me? Merlin. This is childbirth." Simon was flabbergasted at the suggestion. "I don't know a thing about women. Or about delivering babies. I would be worse than useless."

Merlin glared at him, snorted and rushed inside the chamber.

Lady Dinadan was on her bed, undressed. Her body was shuddering; it was clear she was in pain. The top of the infant's head showed. The woman moaned again; she seemed not to recognize Merlin.

Bending over her was an elderly woman, stoop-backed, dressed in black, incredibly wrinkled. She was telling the lady, "Push. Push. You must keep pushing."

"Fedora." Merlin kept his voice hushed. "What is the problem?"

The old woman looked up at him. "Thank the goddess you've come, sir. The baby's head is too large for the birth canal. It is stuck there and won't come out."

"I see." He bent down to examine the woman on the bed. Softly he said to her, "Do not keep pushing. It will not come out, and you will only cause yourself more suffering. The infant, too, most likely."

"I am not pushing." The woman's face was wet with tears. "The contractions—" She let out a low, horrible shriek.

Merlin rushed back out to the hallway. "Simon, go and find my assistant Petronus. He will likely be in the classroom at this time. Tell him to bring my surgical tools. As quickly as he can. If you cannot find him, get Colin."

Simon looked on the verge of panic. He trembled, and he seemed rooted to the floor.

"Go!" Merlin bellowed. "Waste no time!"

Simon finally found his legs and ran off down the corridor. Merlin turned to Sir Dinadan and explained what was happening. "The situation could not be more grave."

"Merlin, you have to save them."

"I will do everything I can, believe me."

"But—but what *can* you do?"

"Difficult childbirth is so— There are several—" He paused and took a deep breath. "When a child's head is too large, sometimes we can pull it out with forceps. But the child is often damaged in the process. Mentally, I mean, if not physically. If it is too large for even that to work, the usual procedure is to use a speculum to shatter its skull. Once the infant's skull has been reduced to fragments, it will emerge from the birth canal easily. It will die, of course. But the mother's life will be preserved."

"That cannot happen. This is my son."

"Or daughter."

"Son." He said it with force. "What about— There must be another way."

Merlin sighed deeply. "In rare cases it is possible to cut open the womb and bring the child out that way. It is an extreme procedure, and there are grave risks. For both mother and child."

"Then do not do that."

"It may be our only hope. If you are so determined to have the child survive, that is. And it can be an effective procedure. It is the way Julius Caesar was born."

For the first time Dinadan's expression changed. "Caesar? Julius Caesar?" He seemed to derive pleasure from saying the name. "My son could be born the same way as Julius Caesar?"

"It is a medical procedure, Dinadan. It confers no pedigree."

But Dinadan was lost in reverie. "Julius Caesar. My son."

"Dinadan!" He caught the knight by the shoulders and shook him.

This snapped him out of it. "Yes, yes, you must do that. Do whatever you can to preserve both their lives."

Relief showed in Merlin's features. He had brought the man to reality, at least for the moment. He forced himself not to wonder what kind of life the child might face if its mind and character turned out less than imperial. Or if it was female.

An instant later Simon returned with Nimue in tow; she was carrying Merlin's surgical kit.

"You could not find Petronus?"

"He was nowhere to be found."

"Well, Colin is more than able. It is time he learned the facts about human reproduction and women's anatomy." He smiled at Nimue, and she returned it. Merlin never missed an opportunity to promote "Colin's" cover.

He took her aside and quickly explained what was happening. "Dinadan wants me to cut open the womb and deliver the child in that unnatural way."

"But what does *she*—?"

"It is our only hope for delivering the child whole and healthy." He lowered his voice to a whisper. "Dinadan wants it to be male, and to be another Caesar."

"And if it isn't?"

"Let us concentrate on saving it, for the moment, and worry about that later."

The two of them went back into the birth room. Fedora was there, on her knees beside Lady Dinadan's bed. She looked up at them. "Thank the goddess you're back."

"You must stay here to assist us if we need you, Fedora."

She showed him a scrap of cloth she had been holding to her chest. "I tied a strip of cloth into tight knots. It delayed the contractions."

"Yes, of course it did." He turned to Nimue and told her which surgical instruments he would need. "And send someone for more cloths. There is apt to be a great deal of blood. Fedora, you must be prepared to hold the lady down. This will be painful for her."

Nimue went, found a servant, explained what was needed and was back beside him in only moments. Merlin took his

sharpest surgical knife and went to work. A salve helped
dull the pain she felt, but it did not do the job completely.
Lady Dinadan cried out, shuddered, wailed almost unbeara-
bly. But, held down by Nimue and Fedora, she maintained
as much composure as she could manage.

Thirty minutes later, Merlin was finished. The baby was
indeed a boy; his father was happy. Fedora went off to find
a wet nurse. Merlin attended his patients at their bedside.
The infant, weakened by its difficult birth, had not cried
once during or after the delivery; now it slept soundly at its
mother's breast. Merlin thought the child was still at peril,
but he refrained from saying so. To Lady Dinadan he said,
"You have done well. But you lost a great deal of blood.
You must rest in bed for at least a week."

"May I see my husband?" Her voice was weak, almost
inaudible.

"Yes, of course. But not for long. Remember, you must
rest."

His job finished, he returned to his tower. There was no
one above, to fire the boiler for the lift, so slowly, painfully,
he made his way up the stairs. Reading Greek philosophy
would relax him; it always did. He sat and pulled out a favorite manuscript—Plotinus. His raven Roc flew into the
room, perched on his shoulder and rubbed his cheek with
the top of its head. Before long, philosophy or no philosophy, he nodded off.

Then later, just before sunset, there came a knock at his
door. It was Fedora, the midwife.

Merlin roused himself. "Fedora. You should not be here.
Climbing all these stairs cannot be good for you."

She smiled; most of her teeth were gone. "You climb
them."

"I live here. I have to. Besides, I have my lift. You should
have ridden it."

"Modern things." She made a sour face and mimicked
spitting.

He chuckled. "That is right. You believe in the old superstitions, do you not?"

"The babies I deliver all live."

"Would this one have, do you think? If I had not come?"

"It died."

"Oh."

"When I got back with the wet nurse we found it lying quite still at its mother's nipple."

For a moment he sat silently, digesting this. "Well. It was such a difficult delivery . . . It was amazing that it was not stillborn. Or that we did not have to kill it to save its mother's life."

"The babies I deliver all live." Her smile was gone. "Learn that lesson."

"Superstition . . ." He let his voice trail off. For the first time in as long as he could remember, he felt inadequate. "At least we saved the mother."

"She died, too. Not much later."

"Oh."

"I could have worked more charms. You wouldn't let me."

"Is that what you came to tell me? That scattering wolfbane and sacrificing puppies would have saved them?"

"I am more than twenty years older than you. I know so much more. How can you have learned so little?" Suddenly, explosively, she laughed.

"What do you know, Fedora?"

"A midwife learns many secrets. We deal with birth. Next to death it is the one great fact in human affairs. I leave death to you and the king."

"Do not bother me with this rubbish. Charms. Tying knots in strips of cloth. The human race is mired in rot like that. Hopelessly. Look at how Europe has declined. Can you do anything to stop this plague?"

Again she laughed at him. "I will go now. I am a tired old woman."

"You are a perverse old woman. Leave me alone."

"I tell you, Merlin, I know so many things that you don't. Not for all your books and philosophers." She pointed at the scroll in his hand.

"Of course. Get out of here, will you? Take the lift down. It should be ready; I had Colin fire the boiler."

"I had rather walk."

"Fine, but do not complain to me about your aching, arthritic knees."

"The child is dead, Merlin, and its mother as well. Sleep soundly."

The old woman left. Merlin stroked Roc's head, and it cooed softly. Where was Nimue? Death. Plague. Murder. This night, of all nights, he needed company.

•

# FIVE

Plague. The word, quite justifiably, caused panic.

More and more reports reached Camelot, often multiple ones in the same day. Dover was devastated; the disease spread more quickly there than seemed quite possible. Not everyone who was infected died; but the survivors, on the assumption they could not be reinfected, were pressed into service collecting and burying the dead in mass graves. In Canterbury, once it became inescapable that plague had arrived, there were riots. People hoarded food; robbers attacked the well-to-do and took their gold and their supplies of household goods, against the coming food shortages. The wealthy barricaded themselves in their houses, partly for protection from the mobs, partly in hopes of avoiding the disease.

Rumors of what was happening spread more quickly than the disease itself. There were riots in London days before any cases manifested there. Merlin and Britomart put up a map of southern England and kept careful note of outbreaks, riots and the other attendant horrors.

"Look," Merlin said to her. "It is following the main trade routes—the roads. Spreading like a living thing, like a carpet of flowers."

"Odd analogy, Merlin. But then, you always look at things in the most perverse way possible."

"Perverse? If you say so, Britomart. But no one has yet found a way to combat this awful disease. It strikes so quickly, its victims are often dead before the physician can arrive."

She pounded her fist. "We must have Arthur issue an edict. Have it proclaimed in every town and village in the country. No unnecessary public gatherings. Markets must be canceled. No festivals of any kind, not even religious ones. The people will want religion, for comfort, but they must pray at home, with their families, to whatever gods they choose to believe in."

"Yes, Brit, of course. Those are all very sensible precautions. But . . ."

"Yes?"

"There are physicians in every town of any importance."

"You've seen the reports. A lot of them have fled to the hills, Merlin." She made a sour face. "Doctors."

"Still, a great many remain. A network of communication among them must be set up, so that they can share information. If we can discover why it is that some people die of this disease while others survive and still others never get sick at all, it may give us a clue how to fight it. We must have Arthur send out riders to help establish the kind of communication this will take."

"So the riders can bring the plague back to Camelot?"

He frowned. "It will come here anyway. We have sealed off the castle from unnecessary contact with the outside world, but it will come here anyway. It is as inevitable as sunset." He sat down wearily. "So much for Arthur's new England."

"That is hardly the observation of a scientist, Merlin."

"It is. Everything we have tried to do here—fairness, social justice, all of it—depends on a calm, prosperous society. This disease will undo that. Petty kings and warlords will reassert themselves. Central government will count for next to nothing."

"It won't be that bad. It can't be."

He looked at her. "*Hope* is not a word I use often. But Brit, I hope you are right." He shifted his gaze to the window. "I keep wishing for rain. Not merely a shower but the kind of massive rainstorm we have had in the past. If nothing else, it would keep people indoors." He sighed. "It will be winter soon enough. That may save us, if anything can."

This was all too theoretical for Britomart. "I'll meet with my senior officers. We'll find a way to keep the plague out of Camelot, at least."

"If it can be done, I am certain you are the one to do it. But I have my doubts."

"It must be done. We are fighting for our lives. That's when knights are at their best."


The next morning Arthur summoned his closest advisors to a council on the crisis. Merlin was there, of course, with Nimue assisting him and taking notes, along with Britomart, Simon of York, and the most experienced of his knights, Sir Bedivere, Sir Bors and Sir Kay. Sir Dinadan would normally have been included, but he was in deep mourning over the deaths of this wife and son. Nimue and Petronus stood against a wall and listened, in case Merlin should need them.

Arthur was terse. "We all know the crisis we are facing. The question is what to do. I want to hear every idea you have."

Merlin as usual took the lead. He laid out everything that was known about the plague—the symptoms, the rapidity with which it spread and the social fallout from it. "We do not know how this disease is transmitted from person to person. It may be airborne, as we believe malaria to be. It may be passed from one victim to the next by physical contact. We have no way of knowing. But not everyone who becomes ill dies. And not everyone becomes ill at all. That is our one hope. Both Colin and Petronus had close contact with the first victim, for instance. If we can discover what makes the difference . . ." He looked around the table, from one of them to the next. "That is the only faint hope I can see."

Brit explained what was known about the riots, the food hoarding, the widespread panic. "Rumors of the plague," she told them all, "seem to have reached as far west as the Welsh border and as far north as Hadrian's Wall. We English have always been a taciturn people. Not now; not in the face of this. People seem unable to stop talking, and the talk is all alarming."

Various suggestions were made for imposing martial law. The knights seemed to like the idea. "We station troops in all the cities," Bedivere proposed with enthusiasm. "Then we can control the situation. There will be no riots then."

"And what will you do when the plague strikes the troops themselves?" Merlin asked.

"It will not. Our soldiers are all in splendid physical condition."

"More so than the rough sailors who died at Dover?"

Bedivere glared at him, but before he could say anything in response, Brit interjected, "We hardly have enough men to do that, anyway, Bed. How many men does it take to hold a city? And how many cities do we have?"

The discussion grew more and more heated. Merlin kept insisting there was no effective way to combat the disease, absent any real understanding of it; the knights kept countering that military force was the only recourse to prevent social disintegration.

Then suddenly the door of the council chamber flew open. A strong gust of wind extinguished all the candles. And in the doorway loomed a figure in swirling black robes. Once the initial surprise wore off, they realized who it was.

For a moment, no one spoke. Then Arthur said, "Morgan. You certainly do know how to make an entrance."

"Or, at the very least," Merlin added, "you know how to use the castle's drafts to dramatic advantage."

Arthur went on. "I wish you could enter a room like a normal human being. We already know you are the high priestess." There was uneasy laughter. "But what are you doing here? This is a private council."

"I have," she announced grandly and mysteriously, "determined what has brought this plague."

Merlin was deadpan. "You have."

"Yes. And I—and I alone—know what will stop it."

He rolled his eyes. "And I suppose it is a matter of worship. With you in charge, of course."

She brushed Merlin aside. "It is a foolish king," she intoned, "who ignores the gods."

But Merlin was not done with her. "Yes, of course."

Arthur got between them. "Merlin, let Morgan tell us what she knows. You have already confessed that you do not know what to do. Perhaps she does."

Merlin snorted and waved a hand. "Fine. Let her talk, then."

Morgan moved to the council table, but instead of taking a seat she stood there, dominating everyone else. "I can hardly be troubled to explain the situation to a roomful of doubters."

"No one doubts you," Arthur told her. "It is only that we are so frustrated by this awful situation."

Simon added, "You are our priestess. You are the chosen of the gods. How could we be anything but respectful of what you say?"

Merlin shifted in his chair and shot Simon a withering glance. "How, indeed?"

Morgan, still standing, still imperious, looked slowly around the table, from one person to the next. Her silence was glacial. Then finally she spoke. "It is," she said slowly and solemnly, "the Stone."

Everyone in the room, plainly baffled, looked first to Arthur, then to Merlin. Finally, after what seemed an eternity, Merlin asked her, "The stone?"

She nodded solemnly.

"What stone? What the devil are you talking about?"

"Now, now, Merlin." Arthur wanted peace. "That is hardly the tone to take." He turned to his sister. "But Morgan, might you please clarify what you just told us? Precisely what 'stone' are you referring to?"

"You ought to know well enough, Arthur. You spent years trying to find it. You sent one knight after another questing for it. Even now, it sits in that cabinet with your precious Excalibur and your other treasures."

Nimue, hearing this, could not contain herself. "You mean the Stone of Bran?!"

A faint smile crossed Morgan's lips. "You take my meaning precisely."

For the second time the council members looked at one another in obvious bewilderment. Arthur seemed most puzzled of all. He groped for something to say. "The—the—but Morgan, you are the one who prodded me to find it. You told me that having it in my possession would bring uncounted blessings to England. Now you claim that what it has brought is death."

Merlin snorted derisively. "Might we get back to discussing practical matters? People are dying."

Before Arthur could respond, Morgan went on. "The god Bran is angry. His sacred Stone has been removed from its resting place. The plague is the expression of his, shall we say, displeasure?"

"But—but—" Arthur was trying to wrap his mind around what she'd said. "But Perceval found it in an abandoned barn in Wales, near a place called Grosfalcon. In a cattle stall. It was buried in three feet of dirt and mud. Now it rests in a place of honor in the most splendid castle in England. What could the god be unhappy about?"

"Nevertheless," she said smugly. "You have had reports enough of the devastation. And," she intoned menacingly, "there is worse to come."

"And I suppose," Merlin interjected, "the remedy for the god's displeasure would be to give you more power or more treasure? Or both?"

Once again she ignored him. "This land is under a curse. Cursed of the gods. Deny their influence all you like. But this I promise you. England will know nothing but death until the Stone is returned to its proper place."

"To the mud, beneath the cow droppings," Merlin added unhelpfully.

"You have been warned. Ignore the gods at your peril—and at England's." With that she turned and swept out of the room, robes swirling, as abruptly as she had entered.

It took a moment for the tension to ease. Finally Merlin said, "And that is the woman who has charge of all our 'spiritual lives.'"

Arthur sat back. "I wish you'd stop picking at her, Merlin. As you said, she is the high priestess of England. She may be on to something. Things have been bad here ever since the Stone was recovered. Remember the murders of my so—squires. And the killing of the French king Leodegrance on our soil."

"Are you seriously suggesting that they would be alive today if the Stone had not been dug up?"

"Merlin, my sister is a difficult woman. Even an evil one, some people say. But she does understand these things. You keep telling me that you don't know what brought this plague, or how it is spread."

"I keep telling you we do not understand, yes. But Arthur, diseases are natural phenomena. They can be dealt with—if not immediately, then ultimately—by using reason. Logic. Science. Morgan's arcane flummery will accomplish nothing. But then when, in due time, the plague runs its natural course, she will take credit. She will claim to have ended it with incense or cat's blood or eye of newt."

Arthur fell silent for a moment. "No, I think Morgan may be on to something."

"Arthur, no. This is too serious a situation for—"

"I want to consult my other spiritual advisor. If he agrees with her—"

"Bishop Gildas? The 'Christian Bishop of England'? The day he and Morgan agree on anything will be the day pigs stop hunting truffles."

"You concur, then. If Gildas agrees with Morgan about the cause of the plague, we may be certain. Thank you, Merlin."

"In the name of everything human, Arthur, that is not what I said, and you know it perfectly well."

"I believe that is as much as we can accomplish here today. You may all go."

"But, Arthur—"

"Go, I said."

"Yes, Arthur."

And so the council meeting ended. Inconclusive as it was, it left no one feeling optimistic.


"The—the Stone of Bran." Nimue was still incredulous. "So Arthur really thinks that may have brought this pestilence."

Merlin nodded. "I demonstrated clearly enough that the thing is a fraud when I used its so-called magic to unmask the squires' killer. But Arthur and most of the court cling to their belief that it is a talisman of unimaginable power. Why does superstition always die so hard?"

Calmly practical as she nearly always was, she told him,

"I wouldn't worry about that too much. Bishop Gildas is certain to tell the king Morgan is wrong. With luck, that will put an end to the matter."

"But not to the plague. How many people will die while Arthur is shilly-shallying with these fools? But at least Gildas will have the chance to prove that he's good for something other than passing his collection plate."

"You are too harsh, Merlin. People's beliefs bring them comfort."

"The death toll from the plague has topped three hundred. How much comfort do you think the dead took from Morgan's spells and charms?"

"They might have died at peace with themselves. We have no way of knowing."

He sighed. "That is more than I will do, in all probability. I wish my mind was not so restless. So impatient of foolishness."

Nimue kissed him on the cheek. "Then you wouldn't be Merlin."

"Is that supposed to reassure me, in some way?"

"It's supposed to tell you that I love you, old man. My own father was distant, cold—to say the least. You have never been anything but encouraging to me."

"You are worth encouraging."

"So are you, Merlin. So are you."

"Fine, Nimue. But so is Arthur. Every time I think I've managed to persuade him that our laws, our government, our society should be based on reason, he reverts to this preposterous belief in gods and curses and whatnot. I'm surprised he's not seeking advice from old Pellenore."

"Pellenore? He's mad."

"My point exactly."

Old King Pellenore was indeed mad, and getting madder, and everyone in Camelot knew it. He never stopped fight-

ing the imaginary dragons, griffins, manticores he encountered on his various imaginary quests through the halls of
the castle. That afternoon he was doing battle with a sphinx
in the castle refectory, waving his sword wildly at the thin
air, when John of Paintonbury came upon him.

In his brief time at Camelot, John had managed to alien-
ate virtually everyone he'd met. The knights, he learned
quickly, did not appreciate being the objects of his "satire"
and tended to react to it with undisguised hostility. The
castle functionaries, up to and including Simon of York, re-
garded him with overt disdain. Several of the servants had spit
on him. But Arthur stood by him firmly. Since the king was
not noted for having a strong sense of humor, this generated
a great deal of puzzlement and not a little resentment.

The young man, now dressed in jester's motley except
for the usual cap and bells, paused to watch the spectacle of
Pellenore sparring with empty air for an instant, then asked
the old king, amused, "May I inquire what you're doing?"

Pellenore, breathlessly fighting his nonexistent beast, in-
haled deeply and explained, "Protecting you."

"Me? I don't believe we've met. Why should you feel
bound to protect me from—from—whatever it is you're
protecting me from?"

Not missing a beat in his swordfight with his sphinx,
Pellenore explained, "They are most ravenous beasts. They
devour humans, you know. I am protecting everyone in the
castle. I am the only one who can see her, you see."

"I see." John took a step back away from the old man.
"I'd be careful with that sword, though. You could do a lot
of damage to those of us you want to protect."

"Pellenore," said the old king.

"I beg your pardon?"

"I am King Pellenore. I live here."

"Oh. I see. And I am John of Paintonbury, King Arthur's
satirist."

"Satirist? Why are you dressed as a court fool?"

John stiffened. "It appears to me that that position may already be filled."

"Where is your cap and bells?"

"The ringing gives me headaches."

"And what does Arthur need with a 'satirist' when there are so many fools here already?"

"I am to mock pretension. Puncture false pride. Ridicule the power hungry. Belittle the arrogant."

"Watch out! Duck!" Pellenore caught John by the arm and threw him to the floor, where he struck his elbow.

Rubbing it, he got back to this feet. "What on earth did you do that for? If you weren't an old man, I'd—"

"She almost slashed you with her tail. They have venomous barbs in them, you know."

"They—meaning sphinxes?"

Just at that moment Merlin entered the refectory. "Paintonbury, we've been looking for you everywhere."

In his best ironic manner, John said, "I've been helping this old madman fight off a dragon."

"Sphinx," Pellenore corrected.

"Yes, sphinx."

"And you are *not* helping me." Pellenore thrust again at the nonexistent monster. "I'm protecting you."

Merlin, amused that John seemed to be in over his head, told him, "Arthur wants you."

"The king?" The jester stepped aside to avoid another of Pellenore's stabs.

"The king is the only Arthur we have." Merlin could not hide the fact that he found the scene entertaining. "He wants you. He is having a meeting with Bishop Gildas and myself, and he wants you there. I cannot imagine why, but for once I will enjoy having you around. You can have at Gildas all you want, with my blessing. Arthur says it is time for you to start learning how things are done at Camelot."

Watching Pellenore warily, John answered, "I can see how things are done here."

"Do not be too hasty to judge, John. Madness is in the eye of the beholder."

John was lost. "Do you mean to say there really is a beast here?"

"No. There is none." Pellenore produced a kerchief and mopped his brow. "I have driven it off."

Merlin took John by the hand and adopted a mock-friendly manner. "Come along, jester. You are plainly out of your depth here, and Arthur wants you."

Numbly, dumbly, John went with him.

They walked silently for a few moments. Then Painton-bury couldn't resist asking, "Who is that old fool?"

"Do you mean my friend Pellenore?"

"What other old fool would I mean?"

Merlin sighed. "You would do well to tone down your professional derision until you learn your way around better. From what I hear, you have made some powerful enemies already."

"There is at least one kitchen girl who likes me." Painton-bury put on a lascivious leer.

"The kitchen servants won't keep you alive. Do you not understand the difference between satire and schoolboy nastiness?"

This seemed to be a new thought. "You are saying I should tone down my ridicule."

"It might not be a bad idea. You might last longer."

"Do you mean last as Arthur's jester, or simply last?"

They reached Arthur's tower and began the ascent to the king's chambers. Merlin decided to change the subject. "Have you met Bishop Gildas yet?"

"No, I haven't had that privilege."

"He is a peculiar man. Some would even say delusional. He seems actually to believe he can unseat Morgan le Fay as England's spiritual leader."

"And what do you think? Will he do it?"

"I think," Merlin said slowly and deliberately, "that you

may find him the ideal object of satire." He couldn't resist adding, "Assuming that what you do actually qualifies as satire."

John bristled at this. "I know you think I'm a country bumpkin. Everyone does. But I can read. That is more than most of these knights and nobles can say. And we had a first-rate schoolmaster in our town. I've studied the Greek and Roman classics. Juvenal was more harsh on his subjects than I am. So was Martial. They didn't hesitate to mock the imperial court."

"You surprise me, John." Merlin looked at him with new eyes. "There is more to you than I thought."

"Merlin, I know it. You judged me much too quickly. So much for your reputation for wisdom."

"For once, I deserve your ridicule. But here we are. Arthur and Gildas will be in the king's study. If you think *I* merit your barbs, just wait till you meet Gildas."

"I thought you didn't want to encourage me."

"Whatever else I may be, I am a practical man, John."

Arthur and Gildas were seated at the table in Arthur's study, waiting impatiently for Merlin and John to join them. Gildas, looking more thin and gaunt than usual, was dressed in flowing robes of crimson silk. When they entered, Gildas barked at them, "Here you are at last. You should know better than to keep the king waiting."

"The king?" Merlin's eyes twinkled. "How nice of you to be concerned for him. Or—is it possible you are more concerned over being kept waiting yourself?" Then, not waiting for an answer, he turned to the king. "I have written to Peter of Darrowfield, Arthur. I have not heard from him in days, and I want to know what progress he has made in his investigation of the murders."

"We can discuss that later, Merlin."

"Surely you do not want the slaying of a peer to be ignored?"

"Later. We have other things to discuss." He smiled at

John. "Have a seat, jester. Welcome to your first private meeting of state. Have you met Bishop Gildas?"

"No, I haven't had the . . . *honor*." His voice dripped with sarcasm.

Arthur made a show of introducing them and of explaining to Gildas that John was to become a permanent resident at Camelot. "Like yourself," he added.

Gildas stiffened. "Are you comparing me to a mere court fool? And a boy, at that?"

Merlin laughed; he couldn't help it.

John, unruffled, said, "I have heard about your belief system, Bishop. And it must all be true. What startling honesty."

Gildas narrowed his eyes suspiciously. "What do you mean?"

John grinned. "You wear robes of the color associated with whores."

Merlin laughed again, out loud. Even Arthur chuckled at this. Gildas was fuming but it was obvious to him that he was expected to put up with the jester's barbs.

Struggling to control his pique—and it showed—he turned to Arthur. "Your Majesty, you have summoned me here to discuss this plague we are facing."

All the amusement disappeared from Arthur's face. "How do you know what I want?"

"I do not know it, sire. I divine it. This visitation is all anyone is talking about. I have heard that Morgan le Fay thinks the plague has been brought about by a certain pagan relic in your possession. A certain stone, carved in the shape of a human skull. Is this not correct?"

Uncertainly, thrown off balance by what the bishop knew, Arthur told him, "It is."

Merlin added, "You have assembled a remarkably efficient intelligence machine in your time here, Gildas."

Gildas was serene. "The Lord enlightens me."

"Yes, I'm sure he does. The Lord, plus a few paid operatives. Who do you have on your payroll?"

John interjected, "Don't be absurd, Merlin. Just look at him. It is clear that Bishop Gildas spends all his money on silk from China."

Gildas stiffened. Once again he turned to the king. "I should like to see this so-called Stone of Bran, Your Majesty."

"See it?" Arthur was deadpan. "What on earth for?"

"Word has it that the thing is demonic. I should like to ascertain that for myself."

"You can tell by merely looking at it?"

Serenely Gildas replied, "I can."

Without saying a word, Arthur sighed, got to his feet and gestured that they all should follow him. He led them into his private den. A guard was on duty there. In an enormous glass-fronted wooden cabinet were Arthur's treasures—the crown jewels, the sword Excalibur and, at a central place in the display, a gleaming crystal skull.

"There," Arthur said. "The Stone."

John asked, "Can you see Satan's fingerprints on it?"

Gildas glared at him, then stooped to examine the skull more closely. "Legend has it," Merlin said helpfully, "that it was carved by the god Bran himself. Some people even believe it is the god's own skull."

Gildas leaned even closer to the glass. "May I hold it?"

"You may not." Arthur put a hand on his shoulder and pulled him back from the cabinet. "The palace jewelers have polished it to a high gloss. I don't want anyone smudging it up."

"But, Your Majesty—"

"That is enough. You wanted to see it and you have. What is your opinion?"

"My opinion," the bishop announced importantly, "is that Morgan is right. For the wrong reasons, as usual, but the

Stone must be replaced where it was found. Its presence here—"

"Among all these tempting jewels and all this valuable gold," John said.

But Gildas ignored him and went on. "Its presence here is blasphemous. The Most High is displeased. Return it, and the plague will end."

This left Merlin reeling. "You are not serious, are you? You and Morgan—actually agreeing on something? On a religious matter?"

Serenely Gildas announced, "Even a blind pig can find an acorn."

John snorted at him, doing a perfect imitation of a pig. "You are referring to yourself, aren't you, Bishop?"

Gildas faced the king. "The Lord has spoken. Camelot must be freed from the baleful influence of this pagan thing. England must be rid of it."

"You are serious." Merlin had had a moment to reflect. "You are really serious. You believe this preposterous skull caused plague to erupt in Dover?"

"Great is the power of the Lord."

"Of course."

"Well. That settles it." Arthur looked grave. "It is clear what we must do. Both Morgan and Gildas say so. I don't understand it, Merlin. I doubt if even Gildas, here, does. But it is clear this stone has brought a curse down upon England."

"From which god or gods, precisely?"

"Stop it, Merlin. I will have Simon prepare a travel party. Perceval will come along; we will need him to show us the exact spot where he found the skull." To Merlin and John he added, "And I will want the two of you to accompany us."

"No, Arthur." Merlin spoke firmly. "I should remain here, to coordinate the fight against the plague. Even now, my assistant Colin is drafting instructions for burying the plague dead. They must be buried outside city walls, where they will be less likely to spread the disease."

"That is all well and good, Merlin." Arthur put on a formal smile. In his heartiest manner he patted Merlin on the back. "As usual, you render excellent service to the country. But Colin may remain here to continue that work. I want you to come on this journey."

"Colin is not a trained physician. He can hardly—"

"Enough. I want you along, and that is that." He pointed a finger at John. "You, too. Please don't be difficult."

"Yes, Your Majesty. I'll come along and hold your hand. It is only fitting that I come, after all. Merlin is right—this is a fool's errand."

Merlin laughed. Arthur frowned. Gildas persisted. "You are certain I am not to be permitted to examine this evil thing more closely?"

"Quite certain." He forced a slight smile onto his lips. "You will come along, also?"

"It is not my habit to travel with court jesters. But if Your Majesty wishes it . . ."

"I do."

"Then of course it will be my honor to travel alongside you, Sire. But now, if you will excuse me, other duties call. It is almost time for Vespers." He bowed slightly.

John started to make another snide remark, but Arthur cut him off. "Of course you may go. I am most grateful for your counsel. England is a finer land for your presence here."

Merlin rolled his eyes skyward at this. John laughed. And Gildas, ignoring them, bowed again and left. As he was going, John called after him, "My regards to your dress-maker."

Gildas paused slightly, then sped up his pace. In a moment he was gone.

Arthur turned to face the boy. "Now you go, too."

"But Arthur, I thought you wanted me at your side."

"Go and eat your dinner or something."

"Yes, sir." And he followed the bishop.

As soon as the boy was out of earshot, Merlin, frowning, confronted Arthur. "He is one of your bastards. There is no other reason you would put up with him."

"My—! What the devil do you mean?"

"The devil is precisely what you've gotten up to, far too many times. Exactly how many of them have you sired? The two who died last year, and this one, and—how many more?"

"I don't know what you're talking about. Go back to your tower, Merlin. Read a book, or write one. I'm in no mood for this."

"Look me in the eye and tell me that obnoxious boy is not one of your illegitimate sons."

"I have to meet Sir Bedivere in the courtyard." He started to go.

But Merlin caught him by the sleeve. "Arthur, I know it is a king's privilege. But do you not think you have over-done it? It must have occurred to you that keeping them secret will only lead to more unpleasantness. Does it not occur to you that this may be what drove Guenevere to her various rebellions?"

"I was faithful to her. Right up to the day she—"

"Of course. Arthur, how many are there? Have you ever met a pretty country girl you didn't rut with? Keeping all these sons secret can only lead to unpleasantness. You must be aware of that. Even you, with your dogged determination to avoid inconvenient facts till they smack you in the eye."

"John is a good boy. A bright boy." Arthur raised a finger and pointed at Merlin. "Even you must have seen that."

"Granted, Arthur, but—"

"Of all of them—and no, I don't know the number—of all of them that I know of, he is the brightest."

"And so you have made him your fool." Merlin's disapproval could not have been plainer.

"He has a gift for sarcasm," Arthur said weakly. Then a bright thought occurred to him. "Like you."

"Do not attempt to change the subject." Suddenly he had a revelatory thought. "All this talk of yours about finding a successor—!"

"Merlin, don't."

"That is what is at the bottom of this. But Arthur, you cannot possibly think that making him court fool now will make it easier for everyone to accept him as king when the time comes. You have sabotaged the boy and your own plans for him."

"He—he—"

"Yes, Arthur?"

"I like him. He likes me. Do you have any idea how rare that is between a father and son?"

"I do. But Arthur—"

"There were others. The two boys Mark killed. You remember them. I loved them. I loved their mother. Surely you would not deny me the simple joys of love, Merlin?"

"No, of course not. But love in royal families is the exception, not the rule. You love this one?"

"Yes, unlikely as it seems."

"Then why have you put him in a place that is certain to make everyone in Camelot loathe him?"

Arthur froze; this was a new thought to him. After a moment's thought he said, "I will simply have to keep him close to me, that's all."

"How long have you known him? Do you know him, really, at all?"

"I will not let any harm come to him."

"Can he fight? Can he defend himself, if it comes to that? No, not if, *when.*"

"I will keep him safe, Merlin. I will."

"I hope so, Arthur. I do not mind telling you I am beginning to like the boy."

"Good. I want you to like him."

"But he has spent his life raising geese. He is hardly prepared for court life. I only hope that you have not turned him from a goose farmer into a sitting duck."

Camelot was abuzz with the news that Arthur would be making a pilgrimage to rebury the Stone of Bran. Simon of York was busy preparing the entourage. John and—against his wishes—Merlin were to go along on the journey. Various functionaries would accompany them, as well as a retinue of knights and squires. Gildas was to go along, but Arthur wanted Morgan to remain at Camelot; she bristled at this and insisted that at the very least she should return to her own castle, but Arthur was quite firm. And of course there would be enough servants to tend everyone. It was a large undertaking to be planned impromptu, and Simon was in his glory, fussing over details and complaining about everything.

Arthur hinted that he had come up with a strategy to ensure the party's safety as it progressed through the territories of possibly hostile barons. Britomart disliked the plan—she said it was far too risky and wanted to go on the journey herself. But Arthur was adamant. "With Merlin gone, you should be here to keep a careful eye on the plague and all the problems it may cause. You will have absolute authority to deal with it any way you see fit."

Brit was unhappy, but acquiesced to the king's will.

When Merlin returned to his study that evening he found one of Marian's twin sons waiting for him. The boy seemed anxious; his hair was unkempt, his clothes disheveled. "Please, sir, I want to go with you."

"With me? Where?"

"Please, sir, on this journey to Wales. Everyone has heard about it. I want to go."

Merlin peered at him. "First, tell me who you are."

"Who I am?" The boy seemed puzzled. "I am Marian's son. You remember."

"Yes, I do. But which one?"

"Oh. Oh, that. I am Robert. I'm afraid I forget that my brother and I look alike."

"You are twins."

"Wayne loves having a double. I hate it. I always have."

"I see. And how does your mother feel about it?"

"She loves having twin sons. She encourages us to dress alike, talk alike, do everything as similarly as we can. I have always disliked it. Very much."

"Then?"

"Mother is a strong-willed woman. She wears me down. Wayne sides with her. But I have never liked being one of identical sons. I never will. That is why I want to come on this journey. It will get me away from them, at least for a time. And for that time I can be myself. I don't get many opportunities for that. I want to be Robert, not part of a set."

Merlin sighed. "I see. Families. My own was no bed of roses. Still—how would your mother feel about this?"

The boy stiffened. "Does that matter?"

"Possibly to her."

"I'm old enough to be on my own."

"Yes." A faint smile crossed Merlin's lips; Robert was not certain what it might mean. "I suppose you are."

"Please, sir. I can be your valet. I make a good personal servant. You won't be sorry."

"My valet." Merlin turned the thought over in his mind. "Yes. I deserve a bit of pampering."

Eagerly Robert said, "I'll pamper you. I'll see to your every wish."

Merlin ruminated briefly. "Yes, you may accompany us."

The boy beamed. "Oh, thank you, sir."

"You can thank me by being a good valet."

"I will, sir."

"First, I want you to go and find Simon."

"Simon of York?"

"Exactly. He is probably over in the King's Tower. He clings to Arthur like a barnacle to a ship. Tell him you'll be coming along. And find out when, exactly, we will be leaving. Then come back here and let me know."

"Yes, sir." Robert jumped to his feet. "I can't wait to have this time away from Mother and Wayne. Thank you so very much." He dashed out of the room, leaving Merlin to wonder what life would be like with a personal servant.

Later, he told Nimue about it. "I have never had a valet before. It will be an interesting experience. I only hope he does not cling to me too fussily."

Nimue was wry. "Does he know what he's in for? Does he know what a curmudgeon you are? Does he know how foolish you think this journey is, and how irritable that will make you? Within two days, he'll avoid you like the—" She caught herself.

"The plague?" Merlin smiled ruefully. "If only avoiding the plague was that easy. Now if you will excuse me, I want to get some sleep. This journey is likely to be long and frustrating. If I am not rested, I will never survive it."

An hour later, Merlin crawled into bed. The night was chilly, and he always slept with his windows open so his birds could get in and out, so he pulled a fur coverlet over himself and curled up for what he hoped would be a good night's rest.

But almost at once there came a knock at his door. He sat up wearily. "Yes?"

The door opened and Robert looked in. "Excuse me, sir. I was sent to fetch you."

"Sent? By whom?"

"By Simon of York, sir. You are wanted—by the king."

"By Arthur? What the devil does he want? If he has been drinking again—"

"I don't know, sir. I was told to say please excuse the late hour, but you must come at once."

"In the name of everything human!" He climbed out from under the cover. "Hand me my clothes. And fire up the boiler for my lift. Do you know how to do that?"

"No, sir, I'm afraid not."

"Drat. I will have Petronus show you, as soon as possible."

Ten minutes later, assisted by Robert, Merlin climbed the spiral stairs to the King's Tower. Halfway up, they encountered Simon.

"Merlin." The majordomo smiled too widely for it to be genuine. "And his new valet. How nice to see you."

"How did you know I'd taken a valet, Simon? It only just happened tonight."

"It is my job to know everything that occurs in Camelot." He smiled again, pleased with himself. "The boy came to me and told me he'd be accompanying you on the journey. He said you sent him. I questioned him at length."

"You sound awfully smug about being a busybody."

"In the service of the king." Simon lowered his eyes in mock humility.

"Anyway, what on earth does Arthur want at this hour?"

"There is a visitor."

"What?! You got me out of bed for that?"

"It is Peter of Darrowfield."

"Oh." Merlin turned to Robert. "Give me your hand. We ought to get up there quickly. Good night, Simon."

Moments later he was at the door of Arthur's study. He told Robert to wait outside, arranged his clothing so it looked neat, not disheveled, and went in. Peter was there, with the king, still dressed for travel and covered with dust from the road. They both smiled when they saw Merlin, and Peter stood.

"Peter. How wonderful to see you here. Does this mean you have found Lord Darrowfield's murderer?"

"I regret not. No, Merlin. I came because I have not received any communications from you for more than a week."

"I have written every day."

"So His Majesty tells me."

Arthur rubbed his hands together and poured goblets of wine. "We have just been discussing the situation. Apparently someone has been interfering with our couriers."

"I see. And whoever it is must be the killer."

"I thought so." Peter took his wine and drank deeply. "Naturally I thought you should know. I'm afraid my inquiries have gone nowhere. But if we can find out who's been doing this . . ." He left the sentence unfinished and took another drink.

"And who is protecting the village and the castle while you are here?"

"I have two deputies. I have trained them quite thoroughly. Darrowfield is in good hands."

"I see. How is Lady Darrowfield?"

"Wracked by grief. More for her sons than for her husband, but even so . . . She is not too mournful to work at consolidating her position as Lord Darrowfield's heir."

"She wants the fiefdom for herself?" A look of concern crossed Merlin's face.

Peter nodded.

"I have just been telling Peter about this journey we're making." Arthur drained his cup and poured himself more. "We won't have time to get a full report from him. There is too much for him to tell. The murders, whatever has been happening to our envoys . . . I've suggested that Peter come along with us. He can ride in your carriage and give you all the information you require. Unless you'd rather wait till we get back for Peter's report."

"No, no, it will be fine, of course. It has come as a surprise, that is all."

"Government is always a matter of surprises, Merlin." Arthur drained another cup.

"Please do not remind me. Or, if you must, at least try not to sound so hearty about it."

"Stop grumping at me."

"Well, it is late, and I need my rest. I will see you both in the courtyard tomorrow morning, then." He found Robert and went back to the Wizard's Tower and bed.


And so the next morning, well before dawn, the party assembled in Camelot's main court. Dozens of people—squires, knights, servants—were there, forming up in a rough line, some to accompany the king, some to see him off.

A score of Camelot's knights, dressed to the teeth in their armor, though no one anticipated much danger, strutted about, jockeying for position; each of them wanted to ride as close to the king as possible. Arthur had solved the problem of their constant bickering within Camelot by adopting his famous circular table. But once they were outside the castle, it was a free-for-all. Perceval was there of course, to guide them to the place where he had found the Stone. And Bors, Gawain, Kay, Agravaine, Accolon, Lionel . . . they squabbled like old women after succulent fruit in the marketplace. Merlin watched them with detached amusement.

Simon of York was there, fussily overseeing last-minute preparations, dressed in his finest clothing as if he thought it might impress someone. He went from person to person and from group to group issuing orders, which they promptly ignored.

Bedivere and Britomart, neither of whom was leaving on the journey with Arthur, emerged from the castle and approached him. The king greeted them with robust heartiness. "Do you have it clear what I want you to do, Bed?"

"Yes, Arthur, but—"

"Do it, then, and don't bicker. You are to follow us one day later. If we have any trouble, you will come along and fix it."

"If it is still fixable. I hardly have to tell you how much can go wrong in a day. This idea of you making your progress with only forty armed men—"

"How many times do we have to go over this? We were up half the night, arguing about it. The country is in turmoil. If I travel with a sizeable force, it will give the appearance of tyranny or, worse, that I want to start the civil wars again. I will not try and explain to you still again how catastrophic that could be. If we—"

"Would you rather have them think the king who was victorious in those wars is a fool?" Bedivere was offhand.

Arthur worked to maintain patience. "Look, you know how tenuous our position is. Half the barons in England would start fighting again on the least pretext. More than half. Look at John's father, Marmaduke of Paintonbury. He'd go back to war against us gleefully. We can't afford— I can't afford—to give him that pretext."

"That does not make what you want to do sensible, Arthur," Brit protested. "I beg you to reconsider this foolish plan. Or at least take more knights with you now. We have no idea what dangers may—"

"That is quite enough, both of you. I have decided on this, and that's that. It is the royal will."

"But strategically this is—"

"Enough, Brit! I have decided, and that's that."

She glared at him. "This is what comes of listening to Merlin on military matters instead of your military staff."

"Merlin does not enter into it. You know I never consult him on things touching the army."

"Be serious, Arthur. You can't expect us to believe that."

Arthur made a quick survey to see that the preparations were proceeding. Then, still talking, still bickering, the three of them went back inside the castle.

A large carriage had been readied for Merlin; he had made it clear to Arthur and to Simon that he had no intention of suffering a journey of this length on horseback. And there was also a second carriage, solely to carry the Stone of Bran in its silver shrine, along with two guards.

Robert met Merlin beside the carriages. "Good morning, sir."

"Good morning, Robert."

"This is all rather exciting, isn't it?"

"That is not the adjective I would use."

"I beg your pardon, sir?"

"Nonsensical would be the correct word."

"I don't follow you, sir."

"Never mind. You have packed all my things, as I instructed?"

"Yes, sir."

"My medical kit?"

The boy nodded. "It is all in the carriage. I was up before dawn getting it all ready." He grinned, pleased with himself. "Are we—is there really any chance we'll encounter the plague, sir?"

A squire pushed past them, nearly knocking Merlin off balance. He glared at the young man. "I certainly hope so. If there is any justice in England."

"You shouldn't joke about a thing like that."

"What makes you think I am joking?"

Nimue joined them. Merlin went over last-minute instructions with her. "I shall want daily reports on the disease's progress. Send the most reliable riders you can find. Someone's been interfering with communications between Camelot and Darrowfield. We can't let that happen to us. Write more often than daily, if you think it warranted."

"Yes, Merlin."

"And you must keep in careful contact with the mayors of all the important cities. Tell them what you must, to avoid panic. Invent, if need be."

"We've been over all this, Merlin. Three times."

"This is not a situation we can take chances with," he grumped. "Have you met Robert?"

She smiled at the valet. "Yes, of course. At Darrowfield."

"Of course. I had forgotten. As I told you last evening, Robert is to be my new valet. Oh—and do not let Petronus fall behind in his lessons. You know how lazy he can be."

"Yes, Merlin."

"I wish the king did not want me on this foolish trip."

"Yes, Merlin."

He narrowed his eyes. "Do I detect a note of patient condescension?"

"Yes, Merlin." She turned to Robert. "How long do you think it will take you to get used to this?"

"Believe me, compared to my mother, Merlin is the soul of calm reason." He smiled, first at Nimue, then at Merlin.

Simon came past again, consulting a sheaf of papers in his hand and barking orders at everyone, quite ineffectually. Merlin could not resist goading him. "And do you have any instructions for the plague dead, Simon?"

Simon glared at him and kept moving.

"Don't go." Merlin didn't want to give up his little game so easily. Simon turned and faced him again, not trying to disguise how unhappy he was.

"What do you want, Merlin?"

"Do you know what the king was talking to Brit and Bed about? It seemed like a tense little conference."

Simon shrugged. "They are worried about the king's safety."

"And well they should be. This plan of his—"

"He has gone back inside. He said he wanted to fetch that supercilious jester of his. No one has seen the boy all morning." He looked around impatiently. "Arthur should be out here, helping to impose some order on all this. But you know how he likes to make a dramatic entrance."

"Honestly, Simon. You act as if he has never traveled before. How much order is needed? How many of these journeys has he made?"

Simon shrugged. "The king loves his country." He glanced up at the sky. "He should be joining us shortly. Along with that rude young man of his."

"John."

"Precisely. Oh dear, some of the knights are squabbling." He rushed off to try to calm them.

A group of musicians emerged from the castle, playing a fanfare. Merlin turned in their direction, expecting to see Arthur. But instead, Morgan le Fay swept out into the courtyard, her black robes swirling magnificently. A few paces behind her was her son Mordred, looking even paler and more sickly than usual in the morning light.

Simon crossed to her, rather anxiously it appeared. They exchanged a few words; before long, neither of them looked happy. Merlin decided it would be wise to get between them.

Approaching them with a smile, he asked, "Is there some problem? Good morning, Morgan, Mordred."

"There is a problem indeed. This fool"—she indicated Simon—"refuses to obey my instructions."

Simon stiffened. "I am the majordomo of Camelot. I answer to no one but the king."

"Now, now, Simon." Merlin was all conciliatory unction. He turned to Morgan and asked her what she required.

"A carriage. I have no intention of letting this expedition proceed without me."

"I see." Merlin made a show of rubbing his chin pensively. "I was not aware you were planning to come along. Did Arthur not order you to remain here?"

"Of course I will come. If only to make certain that fool Gildas remembers his place."

"I see." Scanning the crowd, he asked Simon, "Where is

Gildas, anyway? The good bishop does not seem to be in evidence."

Simon shrugged. "The king only mentioned two carriages, one for the Stone and its shrine, one for yourself and your new valet." He wrinkled his nose at Robert.

Morgan smiled a political smile. "Perhaps we might ride along with you, Merlin."

Alarmed, Merlin said that there was likely to be much more room in the Stone's transport. "Besides, the king's orders . . ."

Morgan stiffened slightly. "I see. Very well, then." She gestured to Mordred that he should get into the coach; he did so glumly.

Simon put a hand on the boy's arm, to stop him.

But she was not finished. Looking from Merlin to Simon she said sternly, "It would behoove the two of you to remember who I am. Who *we* are."

"Morgan, we know." Merlin was in no mood to be lectured. Why did she not simply go back inside the castle and let the matter rest? What could she possibly hope to accomplish by needling everyone?

"I am a member of England's royal house. If something should happen to my brother, I stand next in line to the throne."

"I would not be too smug about saying so."

She ignored this. "Even if the barons should bristle at the thought of a woman on the throne . . ."

"Yes, Morgan?"

"Even so, Arthur has no heir. My son Mordred would then inherit the crown."

"Such a heavy crown for such a frail boy." Merlin was suddenly amused at her morbid seriousness.

She glared at him, angry at his insouciance. Simon pointedly stood between the two of them and the carriage door. Morgan tried to push Mordred into the carriage but

Simon quite effectively blocked his way. Morgan glared and put a hand on Mordred's shoulder. "Come. We will discuss this with your uncle." In a moment they were lost in the press of people.

As they left, Merlin whispered to Simon, "She has a point, you know. Despite all her pretentious balderdash, she *is* next in line for the throne. You would do well to show her a bit more deference."

"The way you do?" Simon scanned the crowd, watchful for more trouble.

"I have known Morgan almost as long as I have known Arthur. I know her moods and her caprices; I know just how far I can taunt her. And I know that hiding behind my titles would be useless, if she was really angry at me."

Simon stared at him blankly. "What are you saying, exactly?"

"Only this: When handling a venomous serpent, it is best to use a light touch. And Morgan has more venom than any serpent I know of."

Peter of Darrowfield came out of the castle, carrying a pack. He joined Merlin and Robert. After bidding them good morning he asked, "Where are our horses?"

"Horses?" Merlin laughed. "With my poor back? I have ridden enough horses to last me till doomsday. We will be riding in this carriage."

"Ah, I see. If you don't mind, I'll get in now. I'm afraid I didn't sleep well."

"Please. Make yourself comfortable."

More musicians appeared, playing still another fanfare, this one slow and regal in tone. Arthur emerged from the castle, dressed in his best battle armor and accompanied by Bishop Gildas, who looked more self-satisfied than Merlin had ever seen him, and John of Paintonbury, who looked quite out of his depth.

They walked slowly, deliberately, in accord with the music. Arthur looked neither to his left nor right, but kept his gaze magnificently forward; no Byzantine emperor could have looked more regally aloof.

But it quickly became apparent that something was wrong. John was tottering as he walked; and he was mumbling something to himself. Arthur and Gildas seemed not to notice.

John stumbled but caught himself and kept walking. His complexion flushed. He coughed violently. Then he started waving his arms about wildly and shouting, "The dragons! Keep them way from me!" The sound of his distressed voice carried clearly over the music.

Merlin rushed forward to help the boy. "John! John, what is it? Tell me what is wrong."

John fell into his arms, and Merlin eased him to the ground. The boy was hot, feverish. Red-black blotches began to appear on his skin. "The dragons!" he cried. "Their fires are devouring me!"

His body gave an enormous shudder and was still. Merlin checked for a pulse and breathing, then looked at Arthur. "He is dead." His voice held a trace of astonishment.

Arthur's face was a mask; it might have been made of wax. Slowly, in a tone so low it was barely audible, he asked, "Is it—?"

But before Merlin could respond, someone in the crowd cried out, "Plague! The plague is here!"

People scattered. People rushed about madly, as if mere activity might protect them. Up in Merlin's tower a dozen ravens took to the air, squawking shrilly. Yet nothing seemed to offset the awful stillness of John's body.

# SIX

The mere suggestion of plague seemed almost to have a magical power, or at any rate a superstitious one. People fled into the castle or to the various wooden buildings surrounding it, as if to be in an enclosed space with the plague-infected might be safer than being out of doors with them. In only moments, most of the crowd in the courtyard had vanished; the only ones left were Arthur, Merlin, Nimue, Robert, Peter, Gildas, Morgan and Mordred in the carriage, and a few knights. Peter of Darrowfield stood apart, evidently uncertain whether he should be so forward as to join the king's inner circle.

Merlin watched the panic with a sort of detached alarm. "This should not be happening," he said softly.

Arthur's face was stone. "And so the plague comes to Camelot."

"No one touch the body." Merlin spoke much more forcefully than usual for him, even though no one had made a move to touch John's corpse. "I must conduct an examination as soon as possible."

"To what point?" Arthur sounded more annoyed than puzzled. "We know what killed him."

"Even so."

Morgan smiled out the window of the carriage. "And so, brother, this Cloud-Cuckoo-Land of yours, this nation of justice and brotherhood, comes to its end." She laughed, long and heartily. "King Arthur."

"The only thing that has come to an end," Merlin interjected strongly, "is the life of poor John of Paintonbury."

"And you think this plague will stop with just him?" She could barely suppress her glee.

"Why do you sound so smug, Morgan? Do you suppose," Merlin asked her, "the plague will confine itself to obliterating only those people you disapprove of?"

"The plague," Morgan pronounced, opening the carriage door and stepping down, "was sent by the Good Goddess to punish the sins of Camelot."

"No!" Bishop Gildas was more vehement than Merlin had ever seen him. "The disease is a punishment for the veneration of a pagan symbol."

"Stop it, both of you!" Arthur's voice rang in the near-empty courtyard. "This is no time for your bickering. Merlin, take John's body away and examine it. Do whatever you think you must. But be quick about it. We must leave as soon as possible."

"Excellent idea, Arthur. We must be certain what killed him."

"Surely we know that, at least." Gildas had not stopped glaring at Morgan.

"When you have finished your examination," Arthur said, looking from one person to the next as if daring them to stir up trouble, "come back here."

"You still mean to make this journey, Arthur?"

"Of course. Now more than ever."

"With only a small armed force?"

"Don't start."

Merlin sighed deeply, then instructed Nimue to find servants and a litter for the body. "There is that cloth treated with wax—you know, the material I have been experimenting with. You will find it in my workshop. Wrap the body in that, and the disease should be contained."

Nimue ran off to follow his orders.

Arthur looked numb; the morning's events were beginning to wear him down, and it showed. "You think you can contain the plague with cloth?"

"If it is plague that did him in, I cannot say. But we must not be hasty in our conclusions."

"You've described the plague to me time and again. John showed all the symptoms, the red marks, the fever, the hallucinations . . ."

"Yes." Merlin fell silent and would say no more.

"Where is Simon?"

"Your majordomo fled like a frightened hare." Morgan did not try to disguise her pleasure at this. "He was the first to take to his heels."

"Why don't you go back inside the castle, Sister, and stop trying to annoy everyone?" Suddenly her presence there struck him. "You are not to come with us on this journey, Morgan. You have too many partisans out there in the hinterland. I want you here at Camelot, where I can keep you under surveillance."

Morgan laughed at him. "I should go, anyway. With the plague threatening us, I should go to my sanctuary and pray. For England."

"You are to remain here at Camelot."

She smiled. "Of course. Whatever the king wishes."

Mordred followed her out of the carriage, and the two of them headed back inside the castle.

Peter finally found the resolve to join the others. "Merlin, may I assist you in your examination? The chance to work with you—to learn more about your methods—would mean so much to me."

"This will be only a cursory examination. There is hardly

time for a full postmortem. But I would be glad to have you along."

Nimue returned from the castle carrying a bolt of waxed cloth and accompanied by two servants, neither of whom tried to disguise his fear.

Merlin took an end of the cloth and wrapped it around John's body, being careful not to touch any exposed areas. "Take it up to my tower. There is an empty room—you know the one—two levels below my quarters." He turned to young Robert. "Go along and help them. Then I want you to stay behind to assist Colin. He will need assistance, with all this happening."

"But, sir—"

"Do it."

He frowned. "Yes, sir. But—but—"

"Yes?"

"If I am to be your servant, sir, I should be with you. You may need someone to help you."

Merlin sighed. "Oh, very well. You probably have a point. But go and assist Colin now."

"Yes, sir." The boy beamed.

Merlin followed them into the castle.

Arthur waved to one of the knights, Accolon, who was loitering at the entrance to the castle, beckoning him to join him. "Go inside and see if you can find Simon. We'll be leaving soon, and I need him to organize things."

"Surely everyone essential is here, Majesty."

Arthur looked around. "Except most of the knights, plus the functionaries and the servants. They have all scattered. I will need Simon to arrange to get them back here or arrange for some new ones, so we can get under way."

"Yes, Majesty."

Merlin's lift mechanism had been shut down; he was expected to be gone for days, after all. So he made his way slowly up the tower steps to the unused storeroom where the body had been taken; Peter helped him. Merlin took the opportunity to ask him about the status of the investigation into the death of Lord Darrowfield. "You must certainly have some idea by now who did the murders."

"None, I'm afraid, Merlin. Lady Darrowfield seems to have had the best motive, for her husband's death, if not their sons', but there are half a dozen servants who saw her safely in her room the whole night."

"And are those servants reliable witnesses?"

"I'm not certain what you're suggesting. They are trusted retainers."

"Simply this: If Lady Darrowfield was responsible for the killings, she could hardly have done them alone. Moving the bodies and lashing them to the stone would have been work. And if Darrowfield and his sons fought back . . ."

"I see what you mean."

"It is the sort of duty only a 'trusted retainer' could be called upon to do. Surely that has occurred to you before now."

"Yes, but it seems so unlikely she'd have murdered her own sons."

"You know the myth of Medea. But you know the lady much better than I do."

Nimue was waiting for them in the examination room. "I got medical instruments from your quarters and brought them." She held out a brown leather bag.

"Excellent. But fetch some lamps, will you, and some magnifying lenses? Peter, will you go along and lend him a hand?"

They went. The two servants who had helped carry the body had vanished as soon as they had placed it in the room. Merlin sent Robert also to assist "Colin" in whatever way he could.

Merlin found himself alone with the corpse. The room was filled with an eerie stillness. Softly he whispered, "Why do I feel so uncertain what killed you? Everyone else seems positive enough."

When Nimue, Robert and Peter were back, the examination began. Merlin inspected the entire body with his lenses. And everything was consistent with death by plague. The red blotches on the body were darkening to a near-black. And there were no other marks, nothing that might have suggested an unnatural death.

When they were finished, Nimue asked, "Well, are you satisfied?"

"I do not know, Colin. Something is nagging at me, but I am not able to pin it down with certainty."

"Something that would not show, even under your magnifiers?"

"Perhaps. But you have been following the dispatches from the countryside. There have been no reports of plague appearing anywhere close to Camelot. It seems so unlikely that it should crop up here, in this spectacular fashion, just at this moment."

"Would you prefer a whole wave of disease to strike us?"

"In a way, yes, I would. At least that would conform to the way we know the plague spreads. But this." He made a vague gesture at the corpse. "This seems so very unlikely."

Peter asked him, "Do you mean unlikely or unnatural?"

Merlin furrowed his brow. "I do not know. I wish there was some way to be certain. But I cannot shake the feeling that the court jester is laughing at me in death, just as he did so often in life."


By the time they rejoined Arthur in the courtyard, the sky had clouded over with a thick layer of ominous black clouds. There was distant lightning. Simon had returned from wherever he had fled to and was busily overseeing a new group of servants as they made ready for the journey. They grumbled. Robert stowed all of Merlin's things in the carriage.

"So our majordomo is back on the job." Merlin did not try to hide his disdain for Simon.

But Arthur wanted to be conciliatory. "Simon keeps everything running efficiently. You should have a bit of respect for his office, at least, if not for the man himself."

Merlin ignored this. "It is going to rain."

Arthur scowled at him. "Would a bit of peace cost you so much?"

"If it rains much, the roads to the west may become impassable."

"Merlin, please. If you are determined to be difficult, at least do it in an amusing way. Better yet, tell me what you found in your examination of John's body."

Merlin hesitated for a moment. "All signs indicate that he died from the plague, as everyone had assumed. But—"

"Yes?"

"I am not satisfied. I do not know why, but something about his death is nagging at me, as if there were something obvious I have overlooked and I cannot remember what."

"It will come to you. Sooner or later, you think of everything. As does Simon." He added this pointedly.

"You have the mind of a bulldog, Arthur."

"A *British* bulldog. I will take that as a compliment."

"But since you have mentioned Simon again, you must instruct him to cremate John's body as soon as possible."

"I was planning on carrying him home, so that his family could bury him. We should be passing near Paintonbury on our journey."

"That would be unwise, Arthur. You remember his father. He was one of your fiercest opponents. Avoiding Paintonbury would be wise. Besides, assuming he really did die of the plague, his corpse could possibly infect everyone who comes near it. You could be helping to spread the disease to another part of the country."

"You honestly think so?"

"I do not know. And that is the problem. There is so little we know. Why has only John been stricken, of all the people here? And why him, at all? He came to us from the west. The plague is raging in the east.

"At the very least, I would like to return to Dover to interview some of the people who have been ill with it but recovered. We could learn so much that way. As things stand, we have no idea how it is transmitted from one person to the next. By touch? Through the air, like malaria? It would be so helpful if we could know."

Arthur paused. "You think this journey is foolish, don't you?"

"There are so many ways that we know diseases are transmitted. And none of them involve crystalline skulls. There are times I fear I will never persuade you to reject all these superstitions and approach the nation's problems with reason. If it actually is the plague that killed John, his corpse could potentially spread the contagion to every town it passes through."

"If you don't know how the disease is spread, Merlin, how can you be so certain it has nothing to do with the Stone of Bran?"

Merlin threw his hands up to show his exasperation. "Fine, Arthur. We will go to Wales and bury your rock. Then, when we return, you and I can go over all the reports of mounting deaths in the meantime."

"Don't be morbid. This may work. It is the only concrete idea anyone's come up with. The fact that two of my advisors have proposed it gives it force enough, in my mind."

"I'm through arguing, Arthur. Let us get this journey over with as quickly as possible. I will leave instructions for the cremation of John's body with my assistant Colin. Please see that Simon will cooperate with him."

"Yes, of course." Arthur's mood changed suddenly. "Merlin, I have lost another of my sons."

"The lot of kings and princes . . ."

"I know. I hoped it would be different."

"It never is, Arthur. Nothing human ever is."

The first drops of rain fell. There was a quick shower, then it passed. Arthur glanced up at the sky disapprovingly. "Simon, give the signal that we are ready to start. Have everyone form into a proper train."

Simon was about to do so when someone appeared from inside Camelot, shouting loudly, "Dragons! He said there were dragons!" It took Merlin a moment to recognize the shouter. It was mad old King Pellenore.

Merlin sighed, exasperated. To Arthur he said, "It appears your permanent guest has news for us."

Pellenore rushed across the courtyard to Arthur's side. "They told me that awful boy jester of yours has died."

"Sadly, yes. But there is no time to discuss it now, Pellenore. As you can see, we are about to leave."

"He said there were dragons devouring him. Attacking him. Their flames burned him to death."

Arthur looked to Merlin. "Say something."

Merlin laughed. "What would you suggest?"

"Dragons!" Pellenore shouted the alarm so everyone could hear. People began to break their formation, confused. To Arthur and Merlin, Pellenore said, "You see? I've been telling you for years they are here. And they pose a very real danger to us all."

"Pellenore." Arthur made his voice firm. "Listen to me. John died of the plague. The first case this far inland. Dragons had nothing to do with it."

"The servants ran into the castle to hide." The old man was terribly worked up. "They said he was screaming about dragons. He knew what killed him, all right."

A streak of lightning crossed the sky and more rain began to fall.

"You see?" Pellenore could not have been more distressed. "Their fire is inflaming the very sky!"

"Enough of this." Arthur was usually patient with the

mad king whose castle he had stolen. But he was at the end
of his patience. "Pellenore, we have to go. This rain will
slow our progress. I promise you we will be on guard for
any dragons that may attack us."

Pellenore started to reply, but Arthur made a signal and
the column departed on its progress across the countryside.


The journey was easy enough, or would have been. The
rain never turned heavy, and as a result the roads remained
easily passable. There were relatively few other travelers,
so the column would have made good time except for a
persistent mist. It snaked its way in streamers among the
trees. It billowed in translucent banks, at times blinding the
riders. Arthur ordered the knights with the best vision to
lead the way. For three days their progress grew slower and
slower.

At night the mist developed into fog. Thick walls of it
welled up in the road, slowing progress even more. Worse
yet, it made hunting difficult. Simon had ordered sufficient
provisions for the journey, but there was an expectation that
they would be complimented by freshly caught game. Instead of that, the party relied on stocks of dried venison and
salt pork; it was not long before the knights began to grumble.

Villages along the way were fogbound. There was no
more fresh meat to be obtained in them than there was in
the forest. Inns were low on food. Most of them could not
accommodate so large a number of guests anyway. Arthur
and his close advisors got rooms. Everyone else was left to
camp out.

Late the third night at one inn, over a meager supper of
soup and bread, Arthur muttered, "I wish the gods would
give us decent weather for this."

Gildas jumped at the opening he had given him. "Perhaps the One is angry at your repeated blasphemies."

"Let him send us some fresh beef, then, and the blasphemies will stop." Merlin grinned.

Arthur got between them and ordered them to stop their bickering.

"I was not bickering," Merlin said emphatically. "Merely making an idle comment about the weather is enough to get *him* started." He pointed at Gildas with his spoon.

"Stop it, both of you." Arthur used his best command voice. "If you have to engage in this kind of nonsense, do it outside where it won't bother anyone else."

Suddenly a young man rushed into the room. Merlin recognized him as one of the knights' squires; he was not certain which one. The squire bowed deeply to Arthur. "Your Majesty, I am Philip of Manchester, squire to Sir Accolon."

Arthur stopped eating. "Yes, Philip. What is on your mind?"

"Accolon sent me to report to you, Sire. We have a crisis."

"Crisis? We're in the middle of a forest. What kind of crisis can there be?"

"The knights, Your Majesty . . ."

Arthur wanted to get back to his dinner, such as it was. "Well, what about them?"

"Someone is bothering them, Sire."

"Bothering them?"

"Throwing things."

Merlin broke out laughing. "Someone is throwing things at the knights? And that is your idea of a crisis?"

Arthur brushed this aside. "What is being thrown?"

"Stones, sir. And handfuls of mud."

Again Merlin laughed. "Which knights have been spattered with mud?"

Philip started to answer but Arthur cut him off. "Try and hide your amusement, Merlin. Philip, who is doing this?"

"No one knows, Your Majesty. He throws his missiles,

then disappears into the forest." He looked abashed but added, "The undergrowth is especially thick here."

"This is all well and good." Merlin sipped his soup. "But in the name of everything human, what do you want us to do about it?"

Philip blushed. "The knights and the other squires sent me to ask you for instructions. How are we to deal with this?"

"Surely," Merlin said gravely, "Camelot's finest knights can mange to catch a trickster."

"But is it merely a trickster?" Arthur directed the question at no one in particular. "We are moving into unfriendly territory. The local kings and barons here have never really reconciled themselves to the idea of a central government under one man's rule."

"Excellent point, Arthur. But if our knights cannot capture one mud-throwing hooligan, what chance will they stand against an armed force led by a determined ruler?"

Arthur sighed heavily. "There are times when I think I should never have made myself king."

Merlin put on his best schoolteacherly manner. "Nevertheless you did it."

"Yes," the king said, a bit sadly. "I suppose I did. All those wars I fought. *We* fought. All that bloodshed." Then he found his resolve again. To Philip he said, "Tell the knights to redouble their efforts at catching this . . . whoever it is."

"They won't like hearing that, Sire."

"Well, what the devil do they want to hear? I can't very well go out and capture this imp for them."

"Yes, Your Majesty." Philip bowed and left. Arthur bit into a piece of bread more fiercely than seemed quite necessary. Merlin held his tongue and ate, too.

The next morning Accolon, rested and looking fit except for a cut over his eye, approached Merlin.

"Accolon. You are looking quite fine. Travel agrees with you."

"Thank you, Merlin. I wish I were as well rested as you think I look."

"Troubled sleep?" He chuckled. "What is bothering your conscience?"

"Spare me your sarcasm, Merlin." Accolon had been in England since Arthur took the throne. His English was only mildly inflected with a French accent. "I'd like you to have a word with the king."

"Why not talk to him yourself? You are as close to him as any of the knights."

Accolon sighed deeply. "What I have to say to him, he doesn't want to hear."

"Oh. And what do you have to say?"

"It's about this pest that's dogging us. Throwing things." He reached up and rubbed his brow. "That is how I got this cut."

"I see."

"No, I don't think you do. I'm far from the only member of the party who's suffered an injury. Most of them are minor, granted, but the number of them . . . Arthur has to do something."

"If you can't catch whoever is doing this, how do you expect Arthur to?"

Peter of Darrowfield was standing nearby, eavesdropping. He joined them. "How hard can it be to run down one prankster?"

"We don't know that it's only one," Accolon grumped. "Stones, twigs, blobs of mud, leaves chewed up and soaking with spittle—they seem to come at us from every direction."

Merlin clucked his tongue in sympathy and shook his head. "So you think this may be a band of random pranksters?"

Accolon scowled at the dig. "We don't know what to

think, Merlin. The barons in this territory are not friendly to Arthur. This may be their way of letting us know we're not welcome."

"I see."

"Still," Peter went on, "there can't be that many of them or you'd have caught a glimpse of them by now. Perhaps you should redouble your efforts."

Accolon brushed this aside. "Arthur told Bors this morning that he thinks this is probably just a matter of mischievous boys. He doesn't want us using too much force."

"That's quite sensible." Peter was not about to be left out of the conversation. "If they really are just boys, being too hard on them would only antagonize their fathers. That would be the last thing Arthur wants."

Again Accolon ignored him. "We don't want to impale them or behead them or anything. We only want to use a bit more force and tenacity hunting them down—and making them stop this puerile behavior. By whatever means."

Merlin rubbed his brow thoughtfully. "Fine. I'll have a word with the king. But let us wait until he is in a generous mood."

"When will that be, in this god-awful country?"

"Patience, Accolon. I will do what I can."

And in due course, he did so. Later that night, Arthur was rested and seemingly at peace with himself and the world. Merlin broached the subject. "They are insisting that something be done. You have told them to try and capture the culprit or culprits, but not to hurt him. The knights say that makes no sense. They want action. As usual, they want *bloody* action."

Arthur was breezy. "What do they want me to do?"

"Give them permission to use force."

"I don't believe that would be advisable, Merlin. This attacker, whoever he is, might well be injured. Or worse."

"You know I dislike violent conflict, Arthur. But for

goodness' sake, so a few bumpkins get their ears boxed. What of it?"

"I am the king of all Britain's people, bumpkins as well as knights. How can I authorize such a thing?"

Merlin sighed. "I am the one who is supposed to persuade you to use reason. You are turning the tables on me."

"Relax, Merlin. You can't always be reasonable. No one is, not even you."

"I—"

"I've seen that contraption you use to go up into your tower. There is nothing even remotely reasonable about risking your neck to save a few steps."

"Stop it, Arthur."

"We'll be out of this country in another day or two. Suppose our villain-in-hiding is the son of one of the local barons? One whose loyalty to me is shaky? And suppose the knights present the boy's head to me on a pole? Do you realize how much trouble that could cause?"

Again Merlin sighed. "I suppose I see your point. But your knights are restive. If they decide to take this matter into their own hands . . . Well, you could find yourself with more than one disloyal vassal."

"Merlin, I know it."

"Good. If only you'd been persuaded to bring a larger force . . . There has to be some way out of this."

"I can't think what. Let us trust time to correct the situation."

And so the journey continued, with the knights grumbling more and more about the indignities these "guerrillas" were subjecting them to. From time to time one of them would get stung by a flying stone or spattered with chewed leaves. At one point Sir Kay was hit in the face with a huge blob of mud. Then Kay went, furious, from one of his comrades to the next, demanding that this affront to the dignity of the Knights of the Round Table be avenged. But most of the others merely laughed in his muddied face. He found his squire Jumonet and had him clean it for him.

Livid, so angry he was almost foaming at the mouth, Kay rode along the column to Arthur. But Arthur held his ground. There was to be no violent retaliation.

The weather worsened; there were storms. Progress was slow. Roads were soaked with rain, which fell relentlessly. Forests were more and more heavily fog shrouded. Merlin's carriage got mired repeatedly and the knights, already grumbling, made no secret that they were unhappy at having to free it.

Merlin watched the expedition's mood turn darker and darker. The "guerrillas" threw more and more rocks, sticks, blobs of mud. The knights were talking openly about turning back to Camelot, despite the king's wishes. Then one evening, at a place between two towns, over bread and venison at the fireside, Merlin broached the subject with Arthur.

"Returning the Stone to Wales may be more of a challenge than you anticipated."

Arthur was concerned only mildly. "Soldiers always grumble, Merlin. You know that. Wait till the weather warms up and dries out. Wait till we're able to hunt for game. Wait till we reach a place with a strong, friendly overlord. The knights will be singing a different tune then."

Peter was dining with them in the king's tent. He seemed more concerned than either of them. "But in the meanwhile, Your Majesty . . ."

"Yes?"

"Suppose we have to rely on these men while they are still so disgruntled?"

"Fair point." Arthur called for a tankard of ale. "But my knights are made of better stuff than you think. They will go on complaining about this and that. That is their nature.

But when it comes to a crisis, you will see them to be loyal."

"Grudgingly loyal," Merlin added, "but loyal. In a way, this rock-throwing pest is a blessing."

Peter was lost. "How do you mean, exactly?"

"Our 'guerrilla' will have the full force of their anger directed at him. Their unhappiness with whatever Arthur does will be secondary."

"Still, it would be better if Britomart was here, or Bedivere. To help keep them in line."

"Bedivere has his orders. He—"

Just then, there was a commotion outside the inn. Men were shouting raucously. In the middle of it could be heard cheers; from the sound of them they were of victory. Arthur got up and went to the door; Merlin followed. "Can you see what is going on, Arthur?"

"It's the knights. Naturally."

"Naturally."

"They've . . . they've . . . Let's go and see."

Peter followed them, and they went out to where the ruckus was happening. Arthur carried a joint of venison and chewed it as they went.

The knights had formed into a loose circle. In the center of it, bound hand and foot and kneeling in the mud, was a young man, not much more than a boy really, in his late teens. His head was bent down; Merlin heard sobs. The first knight they came to was Accolon. Merlin asked him, "One of the guerrillas?"

"*The* guerrilla, more like. The one we've caught, at any rate."

"There was only one?" Arthur sounded astonished. "All that mischief was done by only one man?"

"Apparently, Sire."

Arthur pushed his way through the press and came to Sir Kay, who stood imperiously over the prisoner. Just as Arthur reached him, he kicked the young man viciously. "Rocks, is it? Mud, is it? We'll teach you better than to trifle with the Knights of the Round Table." Again he kicked the young man, who cried out, louder than before.

"Stop it, Accolon." Arthur used his sternest command voice. "He's harmless enough now. There's no glory in maltreating a helpless boy."

The knights stepped back from the young man. Slowly he looked up. And he was indeed not much of a man, barely eighteen or so. He was dressed in homespun. His hair was dirty blond and he had blue eyes and freckles. When he saw Arthur a look of alarmed recognition crossed his face and vanished quickly.

Merlin looked him up and down with evident amusement. "So this is our dangerous subversive. Very impressive."

"He's only one of them." Accolon was insistent. "There must be more, still in the woods."

Merlin took a step toward the boy. "Is that so? Are there more of you?"

The boy looked away diffidently. "No. I'm alone."

Accolon took hold of his arm and began twisting. "Tell the truth, you little fiend, or I'll—"

The boy screamed. "I am telling you the truth. There's only me."

Accolon twisted his arm again, and again he cried out.

"I think you can stop that now." Merlin took Accolon's hand and moved it firmly away. "If he has allies, where are they? Do you think they would stand by and let you torture him?"

The knight shrugged. "Who knows what these villains would do? Let's find out." He moved to take the boy's arm again.

But Arthur got between them. "Not now, Accolon. Let's give Merlin a chance to interrogate him. You can always use more forceful methods later, if need be."

Accolon took a step back. A number of the other knights grumbled. Sir Kay stepped forward and caught the young prisoner by his hair. "So it's mud, is it? You think spattering people with mud is good sport, do you?"

The boy struggled to get free of him. "Let me go! The mud wasn't meant for you."

"Then your aim is mighty poor, boy."

"Let me go!" He fought valiantly, but his captors were too strong for him. Struggling to get free, he bit Kay's hand and kicked Merlin in the shin. "Get off me, damn you all! Wait till my brother hears about this."

Sir Accolon joined the fray. "So you're going to tell your big brother on us, are you?" Gleefully he boxed the boy's ears.

"Stop it now! All of you!" Arthur's voice rang. "This won't get us anywhere. Peter, escort the boy to my tent. Merlin and I will interrogate him there. If we don't learn what we want to . . . well, there are other ways of extracting information from prisoners."

Accolon looked at the boy and grinned. "More emphatic ways."

Peter took hold of the young prisoner's collar and escorted him to the king's tent. Merlin followed, bending to rub his shin as he walked.

"Did he hurt you that badly?" The king walked just behind him.

"Yes, blast him." They paused outside the tent and Merlin leaned on one of the poles. "But is he the one I should be questioning?"

Arthur's eyes narrowed. "What the devil do you mean?"

"He knows you. It showed. How?"

"I don't know what you're talking about, Merlin."

Merlin's eyes pierced Arthur. "He's another one, is he not?"

"Another what? I wish you'd get to the point."

"And I wish you would. Tell me the truth, Arthur."

"I don't know what you mean."

"I think you do. He's another one of your damned innumerable bastards. Admit it. Do you ever keep your trousers buttoned up?"

Arthur sighed, muttered something incomprehensible and stomped into the pavilion.

The boy had been left alone in a small, sparsely furnished corner. He was seated on a three-legged stool. And he was beginning to look alarmed. Before Arthur could speak, his prisoner said, "You're the king, aren't you? King Arthur?"

Arthur glared at him "If you know I'm the king, then you should know enough to stand in my presence till I give you permission to do otherwise."

"Sorry, Your Majesty." The boy got to his feet. As he did so, a slingshot fell out of his pocket and onto the floor.

Arthur bent and picked it up. "I take it that is the fearsome weapon with which you've been harassing my knights?"

Merlin approached, followed by Peter of Darrowfield. Peter stepped discreetly aside. Merlin, seeing the slingshot in Arthur's hand, glared at the boy. "Oh, this bloody arthritis."

The boy said, "Sorry, sir. It's only a toy."

Arthur advanced on the boy. "Never mind that. Tell us who you are and why you've been hectoring my men."

"Bruce, my lord. I'm called Bruce."

"Address the king," Merlin told the boy, "as Your Majesty, not your lord."

"Sorry, sir. Your Majesty."

The king glanced at Merlin, indicating he should go on with the questioning. Merlin wasn't sure what would work best, authoritative menace or kindly, grandfatherly understanding. The boy didn't seem especially dangerous, so he decided on the latter. "Now, then, Bruce. His Majesty wants to know what you have been up to, and why."

"I said, sir. I'm looking for my brother."

"Of course." Merlin glanced at Arthur, but the king's face was impassive. "And you are not looking for the king, here? Whom you know?"

"Know?" Bewilderment showed in Bruce's features. "I've heard his name often enough, yes. And heard him described. But know him?"

"Tell me the truth, boy."

"I am, sir. I've never seen the k—His Majesty before."

"Never?"

"No, sir."

"You have been in touch with him by letter, then."

"No, sir." The boy was quite lost, and it showed. "Never."

Merlin looked skeptical, or perhaps unhappy. He turned to Arthur, who was smiling smugly.

"And why," Arthur asked the boy, "have you been following us and shooting things?"

"Like I said, sir—Your Majesty—my brother. I thought he might be traveling with you. I knew, or rather I had heard, that this was a royal party. I was hoping he might be with you."

Arthur's face was a blank. "Your brother."

"Yes, Your Majesty. John."

"John?"

"John of Paintonbury, Your Majesty."

For the first time, Arthur registered something like emotion—genuine surprise. "You are the brother of John of Paintonbury?"

"Yes, Your Majesty."

"I see."

"When he left home, he told me you had invited him to join your court. In some important position, he said. Father was furious. So when I heard you were making a progress through our land, I—"

"Your land?!" Merlin almost shouted it. "Who are you? I mean, who are your people?"

The boy averted his eyes. "Our father is baron of these lands, sir. Marmaduke of Paintonbury."

Arthur looked at Merlin and said in a lowered voice, "One of the more troublesome barons."

"Arthur, I remember." He turned back to Bruce. "Young man, I am afraid I have bad news for you." He found a skin of wine and poured a cup. "Here. You will need this."

Uncertainly, Bruce took the cup. "Bad news, sir?"

"I regret to tell you that your brother is dead. He died of the plague, just as we were setting out from Camelot."

"Dead, sir?" Bruce took a long drink. "The plague?"

Arthur told him, "I'm afraid so."

"But—"

"He was a fine young man," Arthur went on. "With a good mind. In time he would have been a valued member of our retinue. But—but if it was John you were looking for, why were you harassing the rest of us?"

"I'm sorry about that, sir. I mistook the others for him. The fog, you see. John and I had always . . . Well, we had always teased each other. Playfully, you understand. I didn't realize he was . . ." The boy's face was twisted; he had obviously loved his brother. He took up the wine cup and drained it. "I was only playing."

Peter had listened to all of this in silence. Finally he spoke up. "You must return to your father now, young man. We are on a quest."

"Please, Your Majesty, may I not join you? I could take John's place. Our father is . . ." He let the sentence die unfinished. "Please, may I join you?"

"I'll have to think about that. You may spend the night here in our camp. I'll have some of the servants make a bath for you. You're covered with mud."

"Thank you, Your Majesty. I know I can be of service to you. Especially if all the knights I hit are typical of your forces."

Merlin suppressed a chuckle. "You are John's brother, all right."

"Peter, will you take Bruce off to the servants?" Arthur looked mildly nonplussed by the boy's presence. "And Bruce,

I would suggest that you keep a low profile for the night. You will find many of the knights are humorless and less than forgiving."

"Yes, Your Majesty. And thank you."

"Go along now and get scrubbed up."

"Can I . . . May I have my slingshot back"

"No."

"But I— Very well, Your Majesty. But . . ."

"Yes?"

"Might I stay with you? Join you? Return to Camelot with you?"

Arthur rubbed his chin. "I'm not sure that would be a good idea. For either of us."

"But—"

"I promise to give it some thought. Now go and sleep."

Pouting slightly, the boy left.

Merlin stared pointedly at Arthur. And Arthur knew immediately what was on his mind. "I told you, Merlin, he is not mine."

Merlin was skeptical, and it showed. "His brother, but not him?"

"You have grasped it."

"Arthur—"

"You remember Marmaduke of Paintonbury, surely."

"Well, I recall the name. And of course there was John. But I am afraid the details—"

"Fat man. Coarse man. During the wars that brought me to the throne, he was one of our bitterest enemies. You must remember that."

"Something comes back to me. Not much."

"Why do you think he hated me so ferociously?"

Merlin narrowed his eyes. "His wife?"

"Exactly. John was the product of our . . . union. But it only happened the once. Bruce is Marmaduke's, all Marmaduke's."

Merlin sighed. "If there are any gods, I pray they will rescue England from its noblemen. There can't be a more irresponsible class of people anywhere."

At this, Arthur laughed. "Just point anyplace on the map of Europe. You'll find them. Nobles are human beings, Merlin." ·

"I wish you would not remind me."

"We do what everyone else does. But we do it more . . . vigorously. Power and wealth make that possible."

"Of course."

"What concerns me at the moment is that we seem to have drifted into Marmaduke's territory. All this bloody fog . . . We must have missed a turning or a fork in the road. We need to move on as quickly as this weather will permit."

"Let us hope Marmaduke has learned to show more temperance than you showed him back in the day. You should post guards on the boy."

"Why, for heaven's sake? Now that he knows John is dead, he would have no reason to—"

"Can we trust him? He is Marmaduke's son. His story might be . . ."

"I see your point."

"And of course he will need protecting from our own men."

Arthur frowned. "I wish you wouldn't always take such a dark view of things."

Merlin shrugged. "The facts of human nature—"

"That's enough. No guards. If only so I can prove you wrong, for once."


Late in the night, Merlin was awakened by shouts. A moment later, Arthur woke, too.

They stared at each other across the tent. Merlin said, "Do you suppose . . . ?"

Arthur jumped up and began to dress. "Marmaduke's men. It must be."

A moment later, still half undressed, they were outside. There was confusion; knights and servants were running about, carrying torches against the forest blackness, plainly not knowing where the shouts came from. An instant later Accolon's voice cut through it all. "Here! Over here!"

They took torches and rushed to see what was happening there.

Next to his bedroll, Bruce of Paintonbury was lying on the ground, bleeding horribly. "Help! Murder! Help me! Please!" He was sobbing horribly.

Merlin took charge at once. He ordered men to carry the boy to the king's tent. Then he rushed to his carriage and got his medical supplies.

Bruce's arm was nearly severed. Merlin dressed the wound as well as he could and gave the boy a drink of strong wine to help dull the pain. When he was calmer, Merlin asked him, "Who did this? Tell me."

"A knight. It must have been a knight. I couldn't really see well, what with the night and the fog, but it must have been a knight."

Merlin looked skeptical. "Must have been."

"Yes, sir."

"Might it not have been one of your father's men? You are consorting with his enemy, after all."

"No, sir. They don't know I'm here."

"They might have some inkling. Your brother—"

"They don't know I'm here. Besides, they're more brutal than that. My head would be lying in the mud. Only Camelot's knights are so humane as to do this." With his good arm he gestured at the bandages.

"You are John's brother, all right . . ."

"You keep saying that."

Merlin put a hand on his good arm. "You should try and get some sleep now. That will hurt terribly in the morning."

"I'm used to pain, sir. It's the way we were raised. Father saw to that."

"Not like this. Sleep."

A few moments later Merlin was alone again with Arthur. "The boy thinks it must have been one of our knights."

Arthur rubbed his chin thoughtfully. "They were furious at his little . . . should we call them pranks? And they did swear to punish whoever was doing it."

"Yes, but Arthur, an attack this brutal . . . Our men had him. He would be brought to justice by you. They know that. I can't help but suspect it was one of Marmaduke's men."

"Perhaps they thought I would be too lenient. But why this sudden faith in the integrity of our knights? And would Marmaduke's men try to kill their own baron's son?"

"If I remember the character of these outlying tribes, yes, they would do that in a minute."

"Is it possible the boy did this himself? To give us a reason to keep him with us?"

"Arthur, his arm was nearly off."

"Of course." He frowned. "But our men . . . I don't want to believe it."

"The knights would be glad to hear you say so."

The king sighed. "Stay here with him, will you? Keep an eye on him." He lowered his voice. "He was my son's brother, after all. I . . . I wouldn't want to see him follow John to the grave."

"He's not as much a brat as John was. There is that, at least."

"Stop it, Merlin. Stay with him tonight."

In the morning, the forest fog was even more dense. Thick clouds of it surged among the trees. The road, such as it was, was all but invisible. Arthur cursed the autumn weather.

Merlin, as always, was wry. "This is England. The weather is the same in springtime—miserable."

"I know it. I wish we didn't have to rebury the Stone." Merlin started to speak, but Arthur cut him off. "And don't say *I told you so*. We have a long way to go yet. Clearly, the fog has led us off our course. Let us hope we don't actually have to deal with Marmaduke."

"Marmaduke is hardly the only baron who bristles at your rule."

"How is young Bruce this morning?"

Merlin shrugged. "I wish I could tell. He slept fairly quietly. But this morning he has no appetite. I can't even persuade him to take a bit of soup. Some blood has seeped through the bandages. And he says he can't feel his arm at all."

"That is not good."

"No. It is early yet. The attack only happened last night. But I am afraid the signs are not good."

"Keep an eye on him, will you? I don't want him to—" He cut off whatever he was going to say. "He can ride in your carriage. Will that be all right?"

"Of course, Arthur. I was going to suggest the same thing. The seat opposite mine is wide enough for him to lie and sleep. Peter and I can ride side by side."

"That's good."

And so they set forth again. Except for the presence of Bruce, everything was as it had been before. Knights grumbled while their servants did the work. Arthur commanded, breezily ignoring the complaints in the ranks. Merlin chatted with Peter or passed the time by reading.

The one thing that did change, for the worse, was the weather. There was constant fog, all day long. Dense banks of it clogged the forest. Thicker streamers of it coiled among the trees. It was impossible to see very far along the road in front of them. A constant drizzle began to fall.

Bruce slept in Merlin's carriage, but only fitfully. He kept waking every few minutes, complaining of pain in his shoulder. Merlin applied a painkilling salve to his wounds as often as necessary, but it helped only so much. When the carriage hit a bump in the road Bruce would cry out, softly if he was asleep, more loudly if he was awake. His arm was still quite numb.

Merlin and Peter avoided talking about anything too alarming when the boy could hear. But when he was asleep, or when they thought he was asleep, they let their guard down.

"How much worse can this get?" Peter asked, staring out the window.

"This is England, Peter." Merlin was sanguine. "Our one claim to distinction on the world stage is our atrocious weather."

"A fine distinction."

"A humble thing, but our own." Merlin was wry.

"What worries me most is security. There could be anyone or anything out there in the fog, and we'd never know it till it was too late. Half the Byzantine Empire could be out there, sharpening their spears."

"Just for us. But do you really think we have to worry so much about external threats?"

Peter scowled. "You mean whoever tried to kill our young companion, here."

"Precisely. With a murderer—attempted murderer—in our midst, why fret about imaginary armies?"

"His father's men—"

"Do you really think so? Would not Marmaduke's men be more likely to try and assassinate Arthur? Why would they go after their own leader's son?"

"It's been known to happen, Merlin."

Slowly, groggily, Bruce opened his eyes. Weakly he announced, "My father's men hate me. At least the ones who want to take his place. All of them hate me."

Peter, mildly startled at this, asked him, "Why would they hate a boy like you?"

"I'm next. It's no more complicated than that." He closed

his eyes again and, to appearances, fell instantly asleep.

Peter looked at Merlin. "Does he mean next in line for leadership, or next to die, do you think?"

Merlin shrugged. "I am a scholar, not a mind reader."

"To hear people tell it, you're both."

Merlin ignored this and looked out at the fog-shrouded landscape. The world was a blank gray. After a few moments, Peter fell asleep, too, lulled by the motion of the carriage. Merlin became lost in his thoughts.

Then suddenly, quite abruptly with a jolt, the carriage stopped. Merlin craned his head out the window to see what the holdup might be. But the fog made it impossible for him to see more than a few mounted riders ahead.

But then a rider appeared out of the fog. It was Sir Kay, driving his horse to gallop back along the line. "Merlin! Merlin, come quickly!"

Merlin opened the carriage door and began to climb down. "I cannot do much of anything quickly, Kay. Blame this bloody arthritis."

"Come! Let me help you up onto my horse."

"What is the problem?"

"My squire, Jumonet. He's been hit."

Merlin let the knight pull him up just behind him on the mount. "Hit? What on earth do you mean?"

"Hit." The knight said nothing else but spurred his horse back to a gallop. Merlin held on tightly and watched the puzzled faces as they flew past the rest of the party.

In a short time they were near the front of the line. Kay slowed the horse and turned to the left, and they headed into the woods.

"Will you please tell me what happened? And where we are going?"

"Not far."

Through the fog a group of men appeared, clustered around something or someone on the ground. Merlin squinted but could not make out much more than that Arthur and Peter were among them. He sniffed the air. "We must be close to a town or a village. There is smoke mixed with the fog."

"That is what we thought. We sent out scouts to see. Jumonet was one of them."

They reached the group, and Kay reined the horse to a standstill. "Here we are."

"Give me a hand down, will you please?"

With difficulty, even with Kay's assistance, Merlin dismounted. He stretched to work kinks out of his back. Then he advanced to where the men were clustered. Peter appeared, on foot and out of breath.

On the ground in the center of their circle was a young man. Dark hair, pale white skin. His eyes were closed tightly; he was evidently in pain. Arthur was on one knee beside him, cradling his head. Through the boy's throat was an arrow. Blood cascaded onto the ground. Arthur tried to staunch it with a piece of cloth, but there was too much.

The king looked up at Merlin helplessly. Weakly he said, "Someone shot him."

"So I see."

Kay stepped to Merlin's side. "We think it's another prankster, like that little fiend in your carriage."

Merlin bent down and touched the arrow lightly. "This is hardly what I would call a prank."

"Even so." Kay stamped the ground.

Suddenly another arrow came out of the fog. This one lodged itself in a tree trunk with an unpleasant *thwunk* sound. Kay scowled at Merlin as if to say *I told you so*.

Jumonet was still bleeding horribly. His body heaved and shuddered, as if the pain was too much to bear. Merlin told Peter to run back to the carriage and get his medical kit. "No—*ride*. Take one of the horses. And tear up some cloth for bandages."

Peter ran off. Merlin looked up at Kay. "I am not sure there is any hope. If we try to pull the arrow out, we may only do more damage. Even to stop the bleeding may be beyond my ability."

Kay scowled. "You have to do something. Jumonet is the best squire I've ever had. Bright, loyal, attentive . . ."

Jumonet opened his eyes and looked up at the knight. "Thank you, Sir Kay. I have always tried to do my best." The last few words were not much more than a gurgle in his throat.

"You have, Jumonet."

The squire heaved an enormous sigh. "Now all of you, please leave me alone here."

"Alone?" Kay's face registered puzzlement and alarm. "But—"

"Alone." The squire said it forcefully. It brought on a fit of coughing and another heave of his body. When it subsided he added, "Please. Merlin understands."

Merlin looked up at Kay. "Yes, I think I do. If you give it a moment's thought, you will, too."

But Kay's expression turned fierce. "No!" He got down on his knees beside his stricken squire. "I've always taught you to fight. Don't give up, boy. Fight. Fight harder than you ever have before."

Weakly Jumonet said, "There is no use. Fighting the facts . . ." His voice trailed off and his eyes closed. Then a moment later he managed to open them again. "Please." It was no more than a whisper.

Peter returned with Merlin's medical things and a handful of strips of white cloth.

Suddenly Jumonet cried out loudly, "All of you, please go!" He caught hold of Merlin's arm. "Please, Merlin, make them go away."

Merlin got slowly to his feet, looked around and gestured to everyone, indicating they should move off and leave the young man, as he wished. Arthur had stood silently through all this. He raised a hand, seconding Merlin's gesture. And slowly everyone began to move off. Merlin and Kay stood over the squire for a moment, watching him wordlessly.

Jumonet whispered faintly, "I can't see. I've lost my sight. Go away from me."

Merlin put a hand on Kay's shoulder and they moved off and joined the others.

When a few moments later, the two of them went back to the squire, he was dead. Kay was plainly shaken by it. Merlin tried to console him. "He died bravely. He was brave enough to want to die alone and not require any of us to watch it. We should all have such fortitude."

But Kay was not consoled. "He was so young. My nephew, you know. I don't know how I'll tell my sister."

Before Merlin could say anything more, another arrow whizzed by his head, barely missing him, and planted itself in the ground beyond him. It was followed by another, and another, and then even more. They whizzed through the air like large evil insects.

Kay put an arm around Merlin's shoulder protectively and steered him toward the main party. By that point arrows were coming in a rain. Arthur and his best knights immediately armed themselves with their own bows and shields and began firing back. But through the fog they could barely see who or what they were shooting at. Dim figures moved through the mist around them, but none was distinct enough to make a good target.

It became apparent almost at once that they were surrounded. The hail of arrows kept coming, from all directions, and kept growing thicker.

"What kind of fools would attack with bows and arrows in a fog like this?" Arthur seemed genuinely baffled. "They can't possibly see what they're shooting at."

Merlin shrugged. "Warriors . . . With so many of them shooting, some of them are bound to hit . . . something."

"Take cover!" Arthur shouted. "Protect yourselves. Don't give them good targets to aim at!" He himself ducked under the second carriage, the one that carried the Stone. "But keep fighting!"

Merlin and Kay joined him there. Merlin said simply, "Marmaduke's men."

"Perhaps." Arthur sent off another arrow. "Perhaps not. If word has gotten round about the mission we're on . . ."

An arrow landed three feet in front of Merlin. He ignored it. "You are suggesting that someone else may want the Stone of Bran?"

Arthur nodded and kept firing.

"You may have a point. These petty warlords are even more superstitious than our people at Camelot."

Arthur scowled at him.

From out of the fog a warrior ran, screaming a battle cry as he came. He was dressed in furs and was wielding a sword in one hand and a mace in the other. Kay ran forward to meet him. The mace crashed down onto Kay's head, making an awful crunching sound. But Kay, perhaps angered by the slaughter of his squire, kept fighting. His sword plunged into the man's stomach. Guts spilled, and the man fell to earth.

More and more of them came out of the fog, screaming and killing as they went. There were scores of them, easily three times the number of Arthur's men. In short order nearly a dozen members of the king's party lay dead, knights, squires, servants.

It was clear the royal party was greatly outnumbered. Arthur called for his men to stop fighting.

"Surrender?" Sir Kay was appalled. "Never!"

"We can't win, Kay. If we stop fighting, they will. At least we can hope they will. They can hardly want to kill every last one of us. Bedivere and his men will be here before—"

"They must be bogged down in this fog the same as we are. If we'd had any warning . . . If we'd had time to form all the horses and wagons into a circle, instead of being strung out like sitting ducks . . ."

"'If' is a game for scholars, Kay. What if fairies danced on specks of dust? Leave that kind of thinking to Merlin."

Merlin bristled at this but held his tongue.

And so Arthur stepped forward from under the wagon, hands raised. Seeing him, the rest of his men surrendered as well. In a moment, they were completely surrounded by mounted warriors in fur and rags, arrows and swords pointed at them. More warriors, on foot, augmented their numbers.

One of the mounted warriors rode forward. He focused immediately on Arthur. "You are Arthur Pendragon, self-styled King of the Britons?"

"I am." Arthur's face was granite.

The mounted man clapped his hands, and a dozen of his warriors came forward and bound Arthur and his immediate circle, including Merlin and Peter, in chains. The man on horseback, who was clearly the party leader, clapped again, and the entire army started moving forward, with all their prisoners on foot.

Kay muttered, "Surrender, hah! We are knights of Camelot."

"Bedivere will be here. He must. Would you rather have kept fighting, and be dead knights of Camelot?"

"There is no honor in surrender."

"Nor in death, Kay."

Merlin, weighted down by his chains, was having trouble keeping pace with the others. He kept stumbling, and he was stooped by the heavy weight. "Stop complaining, Kay. If anyone here has reason to complain, it is I."

But Kay was not about to be swayed. "The fact that the king's chief counselor is here among us, and is so infirm, is one more reason why we should never have given in."

The lead warrior reined his horse and waited for the captives to catch up to him. "What is all this mumbling?"

"Mumbling. Nothing more." Arthur tried to use a reasonable tone. "Did you expect us to sing happy songs?"

"Well, stop it."

"Yes, sir. Uh . . . may we know who you are?"

The man seemed lost in thought for a moment, as if he was unsure whether to answer this—as if it might be giving something away. Finally he answered, "Robin of Paintonbury. Chief lieutenant to Lord Marmaduke of Paintonbury."

"I see. It is not quite a pleasure to meet you, Robin."

Robin laughed, then spit on the ground. "King of the Britons."

"Tell me, does your master know what he's bitten off by attacking my party and taking me prisoner?"

"I suppose it makes him King of the Britons, or would if he was enough of a megalomaniac."

Arthur laughed at this. "My advisor, here, Merlin, is quite infirm. Might you arrange for him to ride, somehow?"

Robin narrowed his eyes. "Merlin? The famous magician?"

Calmly, Arthur said, "The same. I would suggest you not anger him."

"The man who erected the rocks at Stonehenge with his magic?"

"You have it."

Merlin was looking less and less comfortable with this. Finally he said, "Arthur, stop."

Robin laughed. "He doesn't look like much of a magician to me."

"If truth be told," Merlin said to him, "I am not one."

Skepticism showed in Robin's face. "Of course not. I would advise you not to try any of your spells while you're in this territory. We know how to deal with sorcerers here."

"I am not a—"

"There is no place in Paintonbury for the black arts. Except those of our own priestess."

"Of course not." Merlin raised his shackled arms and clanked his chains.

"Let's get moving. Marmaduke is expecting us."

# SEVEN

The party set out at once but made slow progress. The muddy roads—not much more than wide footpaths, really—ensured that. Robin's men drove the two carriages; Merlin and the others went on foot, which only served to slow things even more. One of Robin's soldiers discovered Bruce, sleeping in Merlin's carriage, and rode up to report to Robin. "You had best come and see this, sir."

Robin went with him and returned a few minutes later to confront Arthur. "Marmaduke's son has been made your prisoner?"

Arthur nodded. "Not prisoner. Not exactly. He was wounded, and not by any of our people."

"By who, then?"

Arthur shrugged. "One of yours, I suppose."

Robin scowled; he could not have looked less happy. He urged his horse to a gallop and sped up to the front of the column.

Merlin whispered to Arthur, "Bruce may be our trump card."

"How do you mean?"

"He is Marmaduke's son. We saved his life. That must count for something with our captors."

"Don't count on it, Merlin."

Another of Robin's men came speeding past them, spurring his horse to a full gallop. Arthur watched, puzzled. "What on earth can that be about?" He looked over his shoulder, back along the road.

"I think I saw him looking into the other carriage. He must have found the Stone, or at least that gaudy shrine you keep it in."

Arthur sighed. "I'm beginning to think you were right, Merlin, and we should never have made this journey."

"I never cease to marvel at how quickly you catch on to things. At the very least, we should never have relied on this plan of yours to separate our forces."

"Be quiet."

"We are prisoners of your enemy, and you want quiet."

"I told you to stop it. We will survive this. Bedivere will be here. My plan—"

"Plans have gone wrong before now, Arthur. Even your plans."

"This one won't."


The party set forth. Four of the raiders surrounded the carriage that carried the Stone, as if they knew they were guarding something precious. Bruce was placed on a makeshift litter, as if it might be dangerous to let him occupy one of the carriages. He slept almost continually, and his sleep was interrupted by moans and crying. Peter was herded into line with the knights. Gildas was hustled into the procession well back of Arthur and Merlin. This pleased Merlin considerably, though he was careful not to say so or let it show. All of Arthur's people were watched over carefully by Robin's men.

The train of soldiers and their captives moved quickly, bogged down occasionally by the muddy roads, but generally making good time. Robin kept a careful eye on everything.

Two hours later they arrived at Paintonbury. It was not much of a town, not really much more than a large hamlet. Everywhere was mud. A small stream, not much more than a rivulet, flowed along one side of the town; it was dark brown with mud. Houses were made of mud and wattles. There was only one larger building, built of wood, at the far end of the road. Merlin asked one of his guards what the building was. "Marmaduke lives there," was all the man would say.

"That is the palace here?"

No response. They kept moving.

A few children, naked or near naked despite the cold damp weather, played in the town's one road. Most of them were covered with mud. Scrawny, emaciated dogs roamed the street. Hens scratched at the mud. Crows perched in the surrounding trees, keeping a careful watch for anything that might be dropped or discarded. There was not much for them.

Merlin noted that there were no adults in view. He commented on it to Arthur. But just as he finished speaking, a woman ran out of a hut, grabbed two children off the street and pulled them indoors. The children went along numbly, as if they had no spirit to resist. More and more adults, presumably parents, appeared and pulled their children indoors as the raiding party and their prisoners progressed though Paintonbury.

Along the side of the road were men in wooden cages, some of them plainly weak, some dying, some dead. The cages were barely large enough to hold their occupants; there was not even room in them to sit or lie. Under his breath Merlin muttered, "Marmaduke's justice?"

"I'm afraid so." Arthur looked away from the nearest cages. "There are times when I look at the human race and despair."

"You are not Marmaduke, Arthur. You have made such strides toward true justice in Britain."

Arthur made a vague gesture in the direction of the caged men. "Have I? Just look, Merlin."

At length one adult did appear who showed no interest in the children but kept his gaze fixed squarely on the approaching party. A man in his late fifties or early sixties, he walked out of a large mud-brick structure and planted himself squarely in the center of the road in front of the warriors. And he was the fattest man Merlin had ever seen. He was wrapped in furs; he had a thick, scraggly beard. On his head was a horned helmet, like the ones Viking warriors wore. A stench came from him. Merlin winced and held his nose. After a moment two more men emerged and planted themselves on either side of him.

Merlin whispered to Arthur, "Who on earth can that be? He must weigh four hundred pounds."

"Don't you recognize him? No, he was nowhere near so fat when you saw him last. But he is unmistakable. That," said Arthur, "is Marmaduke of Paintonbury."

"You're joking. I can't recall ever seeing him at all, with any certainty. How could that lump be lord over a society of vigorous warriors?"

"Nevertheless, that is Marmaduke."

Merlin gaped. "I have only a faint memory of seeing him once before, and I am not certain that memory is reliable. But he was nowhere near so heavy."

Arthur shrugged. "These things happen to leaders. Have you ever seen the Pope?"

"Not this one. They keep changing. But the Pope is—"

Before Merlin could say any more, Marmaduke raised a hand and bellowed, "Stop!" The voice, unlike the body from which it emanated, was vigorous and impressive.

Obligingly, the party stopped. Robin trotted his horse to Marmaduke's side and they shared a brief, whispered conversation. Even whispering, Marmaduke's voice was loud enough to carry, though the specific words were lost.

Finally Marmaduke looked directly at his prisoners and bellowed, "Arthur!" He laughed a bit too heartily for the situation. "*King* Arthur!"

Arthur kept his face and his voice carefully neutral. "Yes, Marmaduke?"

Marmaduke laughed, and the sound roared through the street. "King of the Britons." The derision was impossibly loud. "My prisoner. The prisoner of humble Marmaduke of Paintonbury."

If Arthur bristled at this, he didn't let it show. "Prisoner? I thought I was your honored guest."

Again Marmaduke roared with laughter. "And so you are. Exactly like these other honored guests." He gestured at the cages lining the road.

Loudly Robin said, "Arthur is not the only prize we have taken this day. Look."

From under his cape Robin produced a parcel wrapped in black cloth. With a flourish he removed the cloth and let it fall to the ground. High aloft he held the crystal skull, the Stone of Bran. It gleamed.

Marmaduke eyed it avariciously, as if it might be a huge diamond. "Give me that."

He took it from Robin's hands greedily. Carefully he inspected it, running his fingers over it, feeling its contours. Then he looked at Arthur again. "This is your famous Stone of Bran? The one all England heard about when you found it two years ago?"

Arthur was granite-faced. "It is the Stone of Bran, yes. Handle it carefully."

Marmaduke tested its heft, then tossed it from hand to hand. "Pretty thing. How can it be so evil?"

Merlin spoke up. "Evil? What on earth do you mean?"

Marmaduke glared at him, then narrowed his eyes and peered. "You are Merlin, the magician?"

"I am Merlin, yes."

"Then you know perfectly well what I mean."

"No, I do not."

Marmaduke laughed again, more loudly than before. It was not clear why.

A small child, a girl, ran out of one of the huts toward him. Without missing a beat he drew his sword and pointed it at the child's neck. "Go back to your mother."

The child stopped in her tracks. Looking confused and vaguely hurt, she turned and walked back to the hut. When she was inside again, Marmaduke turned back to his prisoners. "One of my children," he said. "One of my true children, not one of the bastards that were foisted on me by my late lady wife."

Arthur could not keep the alarm out of his voice. "Margaret is dead?"

More laughter from Marmaduke. "She died." The irony in his voice left no doubt that her death had not been natural.

Merlin decided he had nothing to lose. "What happened? Did she suffocate while you were making love to her?"

For an instant Marmaduke glared. Then he calmed himself and turned to Robin. "This little crystal skull is most valuable. The priestesses will want to know we have it. They will notify the Great Queen.

"Take our two honored guests to their 'quarters.' Send the rest of their men to the field west of town. But keep close guard on them. Make sure they understand that any attempt to rescue Arthur will result in his death."

Robin bowed his head slightly. "You want us to keep both Arthur and Merlin?"

Marmaduke nodded. "Disarm the rest of them and hold them in a little camp where they can rest themselves and lick their wounds. Keep careful guard over them. But they won't make any trouble as long as we've got their king."

"And what shall we do about him?" Robin pointed to the litter that carried Bruce.

Marmaduke squinted, then took a few steps toward it. Unhappy at what he was seeing, he muttered, "I'll have to think. Disarm the rest of them. Keep them all in one place, and make sure there are enough of our men guarding them so they won't try anything." He grinned. "Not that they would, while we hold their king."

He held the Stone of Bran at arm's length and inspected it, beaming. He tried polishing it with a sleeve, but that served only to smear it with mud. Then he turned and stomped off toward his wooden "palace." His feet made repulsive squishing sounds in the mud.

It was nearly dusk. Soldiers armed with spears and broadswords led Merlin and the king off to a place where empty cages, of the kind that lined the road into town, were waiting. Each of them was forced into a cage at sword point. The cages were made of wood and were barely large enough to hold one man apiece. They were apart from the other ones; the nearest were ten yards away.

Then peasants, from the look of them, under the supervision of Robin, hauled the cages to a place at the side of the main road, in the center of town. Once they were in place, Marmaduke reappeared, carrying a torch against the fading afternoon light, plainly ready to gloat. "Arthur, King of the united Britain." He spat. The saliva dribbled down his beard and the front of his clothing but he seemed not to notice, or not to care. "England was better off divided."

"You mean that you were better off." Arthur remained calm and self-possessed. "With no constraints on what you wanted to do. It must have been quite luxurious for you back then. You were able to treat anyone just exactly as you pleased. The rule of law—"

"I still can." Marmaduke roared with laughter again. "That

must have dawned on you by now. Besides, that's an odd thing to hear from a man who runs around the country impregnating other men's wives."

"Marmaduke." Arthur forced himself to speak calmly. "You must not do this thing to us."

"Thing? What thing?" Marmaduke did not understand what Arthur was getting at, and it showed.

"You must not make us your prisoners. You will regret it."

More loud laughter. "Regret it? When, Arthur? When will that happen?"

"Sooner than you think."

Marmaduke stopped laughing and turned to Merlin. "And you, Wizard. You must have known better than to let Arthur do what he's done. Bringing the plague to a peaceful land."

So that was it. Marmaduke believed Arthur had somehow caused the plague. Merlin wondered whether Paintonbury had actually been touched by the disease, or whether Morgan's and Gildas's nonsense about the Stone of Bran had reached this far west. Taking his cue from Arthur, he spoke calmly. "Plague? What are you talking about?"

"Don't try to bluff me, old man. Everybody knows the plague has struck the southeast. Dover is dead. Canterbury is dying. And everybody knows it was Arthur, digging up that crystal skull, that brought it on."

Merlin turned to Arthur and mouthed the name, "Morgan." Then to Marmaduke he said, "But we are on our way back to Wales to rebury the Stone. The god Bran will be placated. You do not wish to impede that, do you?"

"Oh." He furrowed his brow. New thoughts were plainly difficult for him. He scratched his stomach. "I don't know. I'll have to think. I'll have to ask the witch what to do."

"There is a witch?"

Marmaduke nodded gravely. "Placed here by Morgan le Fay herself."

Arthur smiled. "It's nice that you have some respect for my family."

"The Paintonbury witch knows and understands all that happens here."

"Oh. Of course." Merlin smirked. "Ask her, by all means."

Arthur added, "And while you're at it, ask her what happens to petty warlords who harm the duly recognized king."

Again, this was a new and difficult thought for him. "She lives a few miles away. It will take a while."

Merlin laughed. "Then why is she called the witch of Paintonbury?"

Marmaduke ignored this. "Meantime, Wizard, don't try any of your magic here. Understand?"

"I would not dream of such a thing."

"See that you don't." He stomped away, evidently confident that he'd told them a thing or two.

Merlin tried the bars of his cage halfheartedly, then turned to the king. "So we have your sister to thank for this."

"No. Marmaduke."

"He is her pawn. I have often suspected she is behind half the rebellious barons in England. The ones who are not devoted to your wife, that is. Royal families. You will be the death of us all."

"If death means I won't have to listen to you complaining all the time, I hope it comes soon. Why don't you try and think of a way out of this?"

"I have already done that. I advised you not to make this journey in the first place."

"Be quiet, Merlin."

But he was not about to. "And I advised you that this 'strategy' of yours was foolish. So did Britomart and Bedivere. If you are not going to listen to your own advisors—"

"For once in your life, Merlin, be still. My plan will work. Why do you think I'm not panicking?"

"Let us hope it works while we are still alive to benefit from it."

"It will."

Just then, another group of workers appeared, seemingly

from nowhere, dragging another cage into place beside the others. This one was slightly smaller than the ones Arthur and Merlin were in. Arthur asked them, "Who is that for?"

They ignored him and kept working. Once the cage was in place, they tested its bars for solidity. Then they went back to wherever they'd come from.

Merlin had watched them, his curiosity aroused. "Who the devil can that be for? Marmaduke seemed content to let all the rest of our party remain free but unarmed."

Arthur shrugged. "We'll know soon enough."

And they did. A few minutes later several of Marmaduke's warriors, swords drawn, approached. Two of them were carrying someone. When they drew near, it became clear who. It was Bruce, Marmaduke's son.

The boy was half unconscious, and his wounded shoulder was dripping blood. They pushed him into a cage ten feet away from Arthur and Merlin. Like the others, it was not large enough for him to lie down. He held on to the bars to support himself. Drops of blood ran down his arm and dripped onto the ground.

Merlin turned to Arthur. "We are in the hands of barbarians."

"Englishmen. We have civilized a great part of the country. We can do it here, too."

"From these cages?"

"We will not be in these cages forever, Merlin."

Merlin tried to throw up his hands in exasperation, but the cage was too small to allow it.

Marmaduke appeared. He walked to the cage where his son was imprisoned and tried the bars. Evidently they were strong enough to suit him. He smiled and turned his attention to Arthur and Merlin.

"That boy is in serious trouble. His arm was nearly severed." Merlin's face was grave. "If you force him to remain in that cage, he will surely die."

Marmaduke laughed loudly. "What is that to me?"

"He's your son, for God's sake." Arthur found Marmaduke more and more appalling.

"My son? Hah!" Marmaduke had not stopped his roaring laughter. "My late wife's son, yes. But mine? No more than that other one, that rat who scuttled off to join your court. Why should I care whether a bastard lives or dies?"

"Your wife came to me, Marmaduke, not the other way around. And that was . . . John was . . . This boy is not my son."

"A convenient lie. He went off to join you. He knew."

Merlin decided to try to inject something more substantial than allegations into this. But he realized there was not much he might say that Marmaduke would believe. "He came looking for his brother. There was no more to it than that. He was hectoring our knights. They wanted him dead."

"They will get their wish." Marmaduke turned and stomped away. His stench receded with him.

Merlin turned to Arthur. "You see what your rampant coupling leads to? Even this innocent boy will—"

"I know you disapprove of me, Merlin. Of that part of me, at least. Do not lecture me. These deaths have been . . . will be . . . *have been* terrible enough." He lowered his head. "We will get out of this, somehow. One of the knights will creep in and free us in the night. Or Bedivere will . . . I don't know. But we have not come this far, we have not begun to build our new, just nation, only to die in the mud of Paintonbury."

Merlin closed his eyes and tried to nod off.

A light rain began to fall and they both slept.


A shriek pierced the night. "Help! Help me! Monsters are devouring me!"

The sound of footsteps receded into the darkness.

Merlin woke with a start. Marmaduke's men had built huge bonfires. The rain was slowly, inexorably, putting them out.

Arthur stirred in his cage. He yawned. "Damn. Why couldn't they give me a prison large enough for me to stretch my arms?"

"Marmaduke will stretch your neck soon enough. Will that make up for it?"

"Someday your sarcasm will go too far, Merlin." Arthur snorted in frustration and turned to see Bruce's cage. Bruce was slumped, crumpled in the bottom half of his cage, in an awkward heap. Blood from his shoulder had stained the front of his tunic; the flow had stopped, but moist blood still glistened in the light from the fires.

Merlin squinted to see better. There was a small wound in the boy's throat, and more blood had flowed from it, then dried.

"Look at him." Merlin could not keep the sadness out of his voice. "Look at him. That wound on his neck is new. It was not there before. When I think what Marmaduke must have done to him . . ."

Arthur could not take his gaze off the boy. Softly, in a low voice, he asked, "Is he dead, then, do you think?"

"It is not possible to tell from this distance. It appears so. If he were alive, blood would still be flowing."

"Perhaps there is not enough left to flow." In a loud whisper Arthur called, "Bruce."

The boy did not stir.

More loudly, "Bruce!"

"It is no use, Arthur. Even if we could wake him, we can do nothing to help him. Not from these cages."

Arthur bellowed, "Marmaduke! Robin!"

No one responded, and he called again. A few men looked idly in his direction, then went on with what they were doing. "Come here! Quickly! It's not for me. It's for Bruce of Paintonbury. He needs help."

Slowly, Marmaduke emerged from his house, stopped to warm himself by one of the bonfires, then walked toward them. A handful of his men followed him, carrying torches, looking grim. Marmaduke stopped midway between Arthur's cage and Bruce's. "What is the problem?"

"For God's sake, man, look. You son is dead, or dying."

Marmaduke spat on the ground, then ambled casually to Bruce's cage. "Let me have a torch."

One of his men handed one to him. He leaned down and inspected Bruce's crumpled from. "For love of all that's holy."

He stood upright and took a step toward Arthur, smiling a tight smile. "You did this. You are the cause of it. England is damned."

"What the devil are you talking about?"

Merlin asked, "The boy is dead, then?"

Marmaduke's face turned to stone. "I loved him. Or I used to. But when I realized . . . when I knew that he . . ." He could not make himself finish the thought. Instead, he returned to the cage holding Bruce's body and moved his torch close to the dead boy's face. It was covered with red-black blotches.

"You brought this, Arthur. My son or yours, he is dead, and you are the cause of it. The Great Queen Morgan warned us years ago that you would be the end of England." He opened Bruce's cage and eased the body out. "We are all dead men. It is your doing."

Merlin spoke up, loudly and, he hoped, forcefully. "There are no reports of plague this far west, Marmaduke. No one in our party has any signs of it. Plague is not what caused his death. It must have been something else."

"Rot. Look at him."

He placed the boy's body back in its cage and turned to one of his men. "Build a pyre." Then he turned and glared at Arthur and Merlin in their cages. "My boy is not the only one who will burn on it."

Another of this lieutenants said in alarm, "We have a rat by the tail, Marmaduke. Provoke it and it will bite. Their men will try to rescue them."

"If they do, you are to kill them at once. I will make sure their men understand that."

"What difference will that make? If they are going to be executed anyway, what will their soldiers have to lose by trying to save them? You are only giving them more reason to try."

In the torchlight it was clear that this was a new thought for Marmaduke. The effort of thinking showed in his features. Finally he barked, "Don't confuse me," and began to stomp off back to the main part of the camp.

"What shall we do with the boy, Marmaduke?" one of his men called.

He turned and exhaled deeply. "Leave him here for now. The pyre will be ready soon enough."

Merlin called after him, "If it really is the plague that killed the boy, you are most unwise to leave his body in the open."

Marmaduke halted for an instant, turned and looked back at them and muttered, "What difference does that make? We are all dead men. All England will die." He kept walking.

Merlin looked at Arthur. "Everyone says you are a military genius. Even Britomart endorses that view. Just look what your genius has brought us to."

"Be quiet. I'm thinking." Arthur barked the words impatiently.

"Like Marmaduke? Perhaps the two of you could get together and compare notes on the way intelligent leaders behave."

"Merlin, if you don't stop needling me, I'll—"

"You will what? Come, Arthur, make your best threat. What will you do? Burn me alive on Bruce's pyre? Arrangements for that are already being made."

"Stop it, will you?" Arthur lapsed into silence for a moment, then said, "If only Bedivere—"

"Yes, if only Bedivere."

Arthur glanced at the distant end of the camp, where there was a large clearing. His men were being held there. For the briefest moment he thought they might break loose and come to his rescue. But they were badly outnumbered— and unarmed. For them to try anything would be tantamount to suicide.

Half an hour later, amid considerable fuss, a small carriage pulled into the camp. It was jet-black, pulled by four black horses. It glistened in the torchlight. And it was riding low, as if it was carrying something very heavy. A small contingent of lightly armed guards accompanied it on horseback, all dressed in black. The two caged prisoners watched it, more than curious. Arthur said, "My sister. I should have known she wouldn't stay at Camelot."

"Morgan? I think not. That carriage is too small for her taste. So is the guard. She likes things extravagant."

"It is she. It must be. She will not permit them to harm us."

"No, of course not. She would never permit anything that might result in her taking the throne."

"Stop it, Merlin. She is my sister."

"Exactly the point." With more than a little distaste he muttered, "Nobility. Besides, look at that carriage. It is riding low. It must be burdened with some enormous weight."

"Morgan—"

"It cannot be Morgan, Arthur."

The carriage pulled to a stop just at the entrance to Marmaduke's "palace." Its guards lined up ceremonially outside it. Slowly the door opened. Something large and black appeared at the door, then stopped.

"What on earth—?" Merlin strained to see.

It soon became apparent to him that what he was seeing was a woman, a terribly fat one. She tried to exit the carriage, but the door was too narrow for her. Two of her soldiers took her by the hands and pulled, and finally she managed to squeeze her way out of the coach. Heavily she descended. She was wrapped in black robes. On a slimmer woman they would have swirled and billowed, as Morgan's always did. On this woman, they were as tight as anything.

Merlin turned to look at Arthur. "Morgan, is it?"

"Be quiet. I've never seen a human being so heavy. She makes Marmaduke look petite. Who on earth can she be?"

"There was mention of a witch of Paintonbury. At a guess, I would venture that is she."

"Witch." Arthur turned the thought over in his mind. "No, that cannot be."

"In the name of everything human, why?"

"Look at her, Merlin. She's fatter than Marmaduke. Witches, they say, fly on their broomsticks, but no broomstick ever made could support a burden like that. How much good black cloth must go into her robes?"

Merlin chuckled and watched the woman as she took a few ponderous steps toward Marmaduke's palace. But she was spared having to walk too far. Marmaduke came out and walked to meet her. Compared with her ponderous movements he seemed almost sprightly.

When he reached her, Marmaduke extended his arms to embrace her. She did likewise. But they were too large to be able to hug each other. Instead they bumped stomachs lightly, rubbed each other's arms, then stepped quickly apart.

They exchanged a few words, and Marmaduke pointed to his two caged prisoners. The woman looked and frowned. One of Marmaduke's men brought out the Stone of Bran. She inspected it, nodded in approval, and the man took it back inside.

Then the two of them walked toward the cages. Slowly.

Arthur gaped. "Is it possible they hold such a creature in reverence here?"

"Once you have trained people to accept the fantastic without evidence, you can make them accept anything. Religion. Superstition." Merlin watched them as they approached. At one point the woman became stuck in the mud and had to be pulled free. "On some of the Greek islands they dig up ancient statuettes of the fertility goddess. You should see her. She makes even this creature look dainty."

Marmaduke and his companion approached the cages. He said to her, "Here they are. Arthur and his advisor Merlin. The gods have been kind enough to deliver them into my hands."

Slowly the woman spoke. She seemed to have trouble digesting what Marmaduke had said. Her voice, when it emerged from among her multiple chins, was deeper than his. "Kill them at once."

Marmaduke seemed shocked at this. "Surely not. Not now. We must wait until dawn and sacrifice them to the rising sun and the god whose soul it reflects."

She squinted; she thought. "You are right, Marmaduke. The gods would be angered by an improper sacrifice."

"Who wouldn't?"

Merlin found his voice. He peered at the woman and asked, "Who are you?"

Casually, unfazed, she told him, "I am Lulua. I am known as the witch of Paintonbury."

"And may I ask," he went on in an equally casual tone, "how many hens it takes to feed you each morning?"

"Merlin!" Arthur tried to make his tone stern, but he couldn't resist chuckling. "You must be polite to this woman. Even if she does want us dead."

Merlin chuckled. "You be polite to her, then, Arthur. I do not have enough politeness in me for such copious amounts of flesh."

Marmaduke ignored this. He told Lulua, "They have brought plague with them. My son Bruce has died of it."

Slowly, as if thinking was an effort, she responded, "Plague. The Great Queen has sent us word of it in the south. This is the first I've heard of it reaching this far into the heartland."

"Would you care to examine the body?"

She shuddered. Sympathetic vibrations set in, and her entire anatomy became animated. "That is a job for an undertaker, not a priestess. The body must be burned."

"Yes, Lulua. My men are making the pyre even now. We're planning to burn him at dawn."

She narrowed her eyes. She was thinking again, and the struggle showed. Finally she said, "Burn these two on the pyre as well. England will be well off without them."

"That was our plan."

"If they carry the plague . . ." She shrugged. Again thought came with difficulty. "If they carry the plague, they will have to be burned anyway, eventually. The sooner, the better."

"Yes, Lulua. What about their men? And their servants? There are more than fifty of them."

She frowned. Once again, thinking seemed to come with difficulty for her. Finally she pronounced, "They must all be killed. See that they are guarded most carefully. If one plague-infected man should escape . . ."

"Yes, Lulua."

Arthur had listened to this exchange with mounting alarm. "Obviously, you don't know who you're dealing with here."

Marmaduke laughed. "With two fools in cages. You will be surprised at how quickly the wood burns, and with what heat."

Arthur was not about to be intimidated, not to let it show. "Do you forget who my companion and advisor is? He is not just any petty courtier. He is Merlin, the greatest sorcerer in Europe."

"Arthur! I am no—" Merlin began to protest.

But Arthur cut him off. "This is no time for false modesty, Merlin. Be quiet." He turned back to Marmaduke and Lulua. "You know the stories. You know his reputation. This man, who has permitted himself and me to be made your prisoners, is the man who made the stones march down from Ireland and form themselves into the monument at Stonehenge. The man who brought life back to my dead squire, to unmask the boy's killer. You are dealing with a greater power than you know."

Marmaduke seemed taken aback by this. But Lulua only smiled. "Let him make his cage dissolve, then."

Arthur kept up his bluff. "He will. And your copious flesh along with it."

"Bid him do it soon, then. Before dawn, if he's to do it at all." She laughed. Her body vibrated. "Whatever power he possesses cannot be a match for the power of the Good Goddess."

She turned and walked off. Marmaduke followed in glum, confused silence. As they were leaving, Merlin heard her say, "I want you to prepare a nice, big breakfast for me. Beef. Eggs."

Arthur whispered to Merlin, "There cannot be enough hens in Paintonbury."

Merlin chuckled. "Have you ever seen anyone fatter? But Arthur, did you have to bring up my supposed magical powers? That was foolish."

"If we can't prey on their superstition, we are lost, Merlin. What other weapons do we have?"

"It ill becomes me to tell a king 'I told you so,' Arthur, but you were warned about the dangers of traveling this way. By Bedivere, by Britomart, by nearly everyone. What would you suggest we do now?"

"Don't nag, Merlin. You have fooled people with a show of sorcery before. You must do it again."

"Would you care to suggest how, precisely? When I have done it in the past, it has involved what my old friend, the actor Samuel Gall, calls showmanship. Props. Lighting. Elaborate preparation. There is not much I can do in this cage."

"You must do what you can."

"I am not a real magician, Arthur. I cannot make something out of nothing."

Arthur looked away from him. "If only Bedivere would get here with the army. He could dispatch these bumpkins with no trouble at all."

Merlin fell silent for a moment. Then he said softly, "Arthur, we may die when the sun rises. I am ready for it. At my age, how could I not be?" He hesitated, then asked, "Are you?"

"Don't be absurd, Merlin. Bedivere will come." Arthur's tone made it clear this was not something he wanted to think about.

"I merely ask the question."

"You always ask the inconvenient ones. That's what makes you such a valuable advisor, damn you. But look at me. I have Morgan le Fay for a sister. I have been married to Guenevere for more than a decade. I fought ten years of civil wars, with half the barons in England after my blood. After all that, how could I not be ready for death? I've lived with it all my life. Now try and get some sleep, will you? I have to think what we're going to do to get out of this."

Merlin leaned back and let his head rest against the bars. "I was not involved much in the wars. Not on the military side, at any rate. You know that. But I do know that you emerged from that horrible period with a reputation as a brilliant military strategist. What has happened? How could you let us end this way?"

"We will not end. Bedivere will get here in time."

"Of course."

"Go to sleep, Merlin."

Merlin closed his eyes. "The fog is thickening. Even if

Bedivere is en route, what makes you think he will be able to find us in this?"

"Be quiet."

They both fell silent. Soon enough, despite everything, they were asleep again. Exhaustion had taken its toll on them.


Morning light woke Merlin—what there was of it. While he and Arthur were sleeping fitfully, uncomfortably in their cages, the fog had built even more thickly than before. It was almost perfectly opaque. Torchlight reflected back from it, as it would from a blank wall. Dawn only brought a kind of half-light; it might almost not have been daybreak. At least the rain had stopped. Fires burned brightly throughout Paintonbury.

Merlin opened his eyes slowly. The damp air, and the fact that he had had to sleep standing upright in his cage, had made his entire body ache. When he realized that, despite the absence of light, it was morning, he whispered softly to himself, "Damn this arthritis. Damn my old age."

Arthur roused himself. Slowly, groggily, he asked, "What? Did you say something?"

"Nothing that matters. I have been thinking."

"In your sleep?"

"Our unconscious minds often tell us things that do not occur to our conscious minds."

Arthur started to yawn, but the cage was too small to permit him to stretch. His body shuddered. "What insight has the god of dreams brought you?"

"My mind," Merlin said pointedly, "has examined our situation. It occurs to me that if we can sow the seeds of mistrust between Marmaduke and Lulua, set them to doubting one another, it may give us more time to wait for Bedivere." He smiled a mordant smile. "Assuming that he and his men haven't perished in a swamp somewhere."

"Don't be absurd."

"We read of an entire Persian army that was swallowed by the Sahara Desert. They were—"

"Spare me the pedantry, Merlin. I happily cede the lamp of learning to you. Just tell me what you've come up with."

"Our plump friends think they are on the same side. We must get them to realize they are not."

It took Arthur an instant to digest this. "I see what you're suggesting. And how would you propose we do that?"

"They will be coming for us soon. Just follow my lead."

"Yes, Merlin. You are the strategist now. Dazzle me."

"You are in your late thirties, Arthur. Too old to be a brat. You should have more kingly dignity."

Arthur shrugged. "What can I say? I had a good teacher." He glanced up at the sky. It was slowly lightening but not by much. "If something doesn't happen soon, we'll all be dead of the plague."

"You still think the plague is what did those boys in? What kind of plague is it that only attacks individuals, not populations? And very specific individuals, at that?"

"I've never heard a corpse ask how it got that way."

"No, of course not, Arthur. It is for us, the living, to ask that question. And to find the answer."

"If you have to ask questions, Merlin, ask into the deaths of Lord Darrowfield and his sons. Those killings were—"

Merlin cut him off impatiently. "I have a growing suspicion those murders were related to these. Somehow, I don't know how. Not yet."

Dawn was showing itself more and more, or what passed for dawn in those conditions. The world was still dark, but the first faint traces of morning light were beginning to show. Banks of fog kept rolling in, thicker and thicker. Daylight illuminated them; the whole world seemed bathed in a dull gray, opalescent light. Scattered fires throughout the hamlet provided the only real contrast; everything else was matted to the same dull, dark, but brightening gray.

And the fog was so thick Merlin and Arthur could hardly see a thing. Merlin kept scanning the landscape.

Through the blinding fog, he noticed that more and more torches were being lit in the town. No people were visible through the pervasive fog, only their lights. Softly he said, "They will be coming for us anytime now."

He had hardly finished the sentence when the various torches and the men carrying them formed into a procession and headed in the direction of the caged prisoners. But also through the fog he thought he saw another light, a more distant one. It flared into existence, then vanished, presumably quickly extinguished. Were Bedivere and his soldiers here at last, then?

The marchers and their lights approached. Slowly the forms of Marmaduke, Lulua and Robin became visible through the mist, more and more distinctly as they came nearer and nearer. They were walking with unnatural rapidity. Marmaduke led them all, and he was grinning like a naughty schoolboy who had just pulled a prank. Lulua was plainly struggling to keep up with the others. She puffed, and her breath added a bit to the mist in the air.

Marmaduke stopped six feet in front of the cages, and a moment later Lulua took her place at his right side. "Well," he said heartily, "good morning. I am sorry there is no sun for you. This would have been the last sunrise you'll ever know."

Arthur glared and said nothing. Merlin, seemingly at ease with himself and the situation, smiled and said, "We have had our last midnight. That is enough."

Marmaduke laughed more loudly than seemed appropriate. "You're in a pleasant mood, Wizard, for a man facing his end."

Merlin shrugged. "Philosophy teaches us nothing if not how to face death. I am facing the two of you. Socrates himself would envy me."

Marmaduke was unsure whether he was being ridiculed,

and it showed. His grin vanished and he stopped laughing. "Arthur, do you have nothing to say?"

Before Arthur could respond, Lulua spoke up. She pointed a finger at Merlin. "Some sorcerer you are. Spending the night trapped in a cage. Hah!"

It was the opening Merlin had been waiting for. He ignored her and faced the warlord. "You want to be King of all England, not just Paintonbury, Marmaduke, to take Arthur's place. Do you really think killing us this way will accomplish that?"

Marmaduke seemed taken aback, not by the question itself, but by the fact it was being asked. "When you are out of the way," he said slowly, as if he was thinking at the same time and it was an effort, "when all of this nonsense about peace and love and brotherhood is gone, too, then England can get back to warfare. That is the way it's always been. It's what we know. All we have ever known. I was a man then, a true warrior, a leader. I was respected and feared. Those were better times."

Suddenly, loudly, Lulua belched. Her chins quivered.

Merlin looked to her. "And you. You have promised Marmaduke your support, of course?"

She held a fingertip up to her mouth and pressed it to her lips. "The blood of kings carries special properties. Magical ones. When Arthur is dead, we will know if he truly was a king, and meant to rule."

"And what about Marmaduke's blood? When will you test that—after Morgan le Fay is on the throne of England?"

Marmaduke glanced at her. Plain suspicion showed in his face. But Arthur had caught Merlin's drift, and before either the witch or the warlord could answer, he spoke up. "If you want the throne, Marmaduke, handing it to this woman is an odd way of getting it."

Marmaduke's brow furrowed. "What do you mean?"

Arthur smiled an indulgent smile, like a schoolteacher

lecturing a slow pupil. "Think, for goodness' sake. Why would you assume her loyalty is to you?"

He was wrestling with the thought. It showed. "She's the witch of Paintonbury. Who else would she be loyal to?"

Slowly, still smiling serenely, Arthur intoned, "To my sister."

And Merlin added quickly, "Yes, to Morgan le Fay."

Marmaduke glared at Lulua. Suspicion was growing, and that was what the prisoners wanted. "You told me—"

"It's a lie!" Lulua screeched the words. "Can't you see what they're trying to do? Think."

"These women," Merlin went on quite calmly, "these witches, used to reign virtually supreme in England by claiming they had the ear of the gods. Their word was law, their will went unchallenged. By anyone, not the strongest baron. The civil wars and Arthur's ascent put an end to that."

Lulua started to object, but Arthur took up the game. "My sister has hardly made it a secret that she wants the throne. As high priestess of the witches and their religion— as the 'Great Queen,' as she styles herself—she thinks it is her right. But men rule here now. If you kill us—if you kill us at the behest of this *woman*"—he snarled the word—"you will be handing it back to them."

"No!" Lulua's alarm was growing. Her face, like Marmaduke's, was a book where all her thoughts could be read. "I serve Paintonbury. I serve you, Marmaduke!"

But the seeds of doubt had been planted. Marmaduke furrowed his brow, like a slow dog trying to figure out how to get a bone. "Lulua, we have to talk about this."

"There is nothing to talk about. They are lying, trying to set us against each other. Can't you see that?"

"Follow me. We have to talk." He turned on his heel and began to stalk away. Lulua glared at the prisoners, then started to follow.

Arthur called after them. "I'd talk quickly, if I were you. With the light of dawn, Merlin's power increases."

Over his shoulder Marmaduke said, "Power? What power? He can't get out of a wooden cage."

"You'll see, Marmaduke."

The warlord and the witch kept walking. After a moment they were far enough away for a private conversation. Each in turn gesticulated wildly and raised his voice, obviously threatening, however mildly. Watching them, Merlin said to Arthur, "Playing for time is never very hard with these types. I wonder England has lasted as long as it has, with people like these running things. But I thought I had dissuaded you from dredging up this wizard nonsense."

"It's useful." Arthur was sanguine. "Have you not seen what is growing around us, out there in the fog?"

"I have. What is the point of—"

"Be quiet. They're coming back."

"But Arthur, you can't see any more through this fog than I can. Suppose these aren't our men. Suppose they are more of Marmaduke's? Or a raiding party from some other warlord?"

"Be quiet, I said."

The sky was lightening more and more. The world was still that dull gray, not light yet but not exactly dark. Merlin watched the surrounding fog and saw more and more glints of armor and weaponry. Then he glanced at the nearby mud where Bruce's body was slumped.

Marmaduke stopped ten feet away. "This," he said firmly, indicating the poor object that had been his son, "will be burned. My men have nearly finished building the pyre. You," he added, pointing from Arthur to Merlin, "will be burned with it."

Arthur, keeping a close watch on the surrounding fog, intoned loudly, "You are making a great mistake, Marmaduke. Merlin is the greatest wizard in the world. He can summon armies out of the air," Arthur threatened. "All the forces known to the wisest philosophers are at his command."

Marmaduke spat. "Let him get out of his cage, then."

Lulua added, "All the most powerful magicians are women. Witches. Merlin does not qualify."

Marmaduke laughed, more heartily than seemed appropriate. "If he's going to summon an army, he'd better do it quickly." He gestured to a few of his men, who surrounded the cages, poised to open them and pull the prisoners out. Two more of them lifted Bruce's body.

Merlin watched them. "If he really did die of the plague, your men would be most unwise to handle his body."

"Why?" Marmaduke narrowed his eyes. "He's dead. What harm can be done?"

"In the name of everything human, it is the plague. Plagues spread. It is what they do. That is what makes them plagues and not ordinary diseases. You must let me examine Bruce's body."

Marmaduke thought for a moment, then brushed this aside. "Nonsense. My men are strong and vigorous."

"Good for them. But—"

"I'd concentrate on making that army appear, if I were you."

Marmaduke raised his hand, and at that signal the group of his men surrounding the two cages drew their swords. One of them unlatched the cages, then stepped back and drew his own sword. With it he gestured that Merlin and Arthur were to step out.

The king and the pseudo-wizard exchanged resigned glances and started slowly to march toward the village center. As they did so, Marmaduke told them, "Be happy I didn't leave you to die in those. The carrion birds around here are having a lean season."

"Again, you should tread carefully, Marmaduke." Arthur spoke the words solemnly. "Merlin speaks the language of birds."

Marmaduke laughed. "Let him tweet up a few thousand of them to rescue you, then." He nodded to his men.

Soldiers prodded the prisoners with their sword tips, two of them carried Bruce's body, and the entire party continued to move in the direction of the town's center. Merlin looked around furtively; yes, there were dim figures moving in the fog.

At the center of town a wooden funeral pyre had been erected. Four torches burned brightly at its corners. Other lights in the town were being extinguished gradually, one by one, as the morning light grew.

The pyre was a good ten feet tall. Two boys were atop it, pouring oil over it. When the party reached it, the men carrying Bruce's body took it to where a pair of wooden ladders rested side by side against it and slowly, awkwardly, carried the corpse to its resting place on top. The two oil boys, their task finished, jumped down to the ground.

Arthur whispered to Merlin, "Now is the time. Summon your army."

Merlin shot him a disapproving glance. "My feet hurt. This bloody arthritis—"

"Do it!"

The two soldiers climbed down from the pyre and took places at Marmaduke's side. Lulua, at a signal from Marmaduke, raised her hands high over her head. "O Bran," she intoned, "mightiest of the gods of England—"

But Merlin interrupted her. He raised his hands even higher in the air and chanted in Latin. "*Caveat emptor. Cum grano salis. Et tu Brute. Omnes Gallia in tres partes divisa est. E pluribus unum.*"

"Stop that!" Lulua barked.

But Merlin chanted on, intoning over and over, "*Caveat emptor. Cum grano salis . . .*"

Arthur pointed a finger at Lulua. "Do not interrupt, woman. He is summoning all the dark forces of the universe."

Marmaduke, visibly unhappy, told the men at his sides, "Light it. Now!"

The two men took up two of the torches and lit the pyre. Thanks to the oil, it took fire quickly; the flames burned bright and hot, and they spread quickly. In a matter of moments the entire thing would be consumed.

"*Omnes Gallia in tres partes divisa est.*"

Marmaduke snapped his fingers at the two pyre men. "Get them up there. At once."

The men drew their swords and began prodding Arthur and Merlin toward the ladders. Merlin, still chanting his Latin, stumbled, and a soldier prodded him with his sword point. Merlin drew himself up to his full height and shouted, "*Nunc, Bediverus!*"

Arthur echoed him. "Now, Bedivere!"

From somewhere deep in the surrounding fog, a trumpet sounded, playing a military charge. Marmaduke looked around, alarmed.

Lulua did likewise. "This isn't possible. He could never—"

"He has done it, Witch." Marmaduke called to his men, "All of you, draw your weapons! We are under attack!"

The men looked around, confused.

From the fog, a second trumpet sounded.

Then the first of Arthur's soldiers, led by Bedivere, appeared clearly from out of the mist. They were on horseback, swords and spears drawn, charging at full gallop. They shouted a battle cry. More and more of them followed. Marmaduke's men panicked, some bracing themselves for the fight, but most scattering. The pyre burned more and more brightly. A third battle call issued from the unseen trumpet.

Amid the confusion, Lulua remained calm. She looked around for her carriage and began slinking toward it, or what passed for slinking in a woman so heavy. Arthur, noticing her, caught her by the back of her robe. "No, you don't, Witch."

She struggled. "Let go of me, pretender."

"Be careful, Witch. I once saw a hog mired in mud. It was stuck for days. The same is apt to happen to you."

She swiped at him. "Let go of me!"

Arthur extended a leg and tripped her. She fell, and the muddy ground made an unpleasant sucking sound as she hit it. She called out for her attendants, but they were in the process of mounting the carriage and speeding away in it. Arthur laughed at her. "Root around, while you're down there. You might find some truffles." He turned to Merlin. "Come over here and deal with this harridan. You and she talk the same language."

Merlin stiffened. "I most certainly do not speak the—"

"You both deal in the same mystical flimflam. Come over here and take her in charge."

Most of Marmaduke's men had vanished into the mist by now, in the opposite direction from where Bedivere's men were still charging. Marmaduke kept shouting encouragement to the ones who remained. "Fight! Fight for your wives and children! Fight for Paintonbury!" He made for Merlin, plainly intending to slaughter him.

But Arthur took a sword from one of the fallen men and followed him, thwacking him across the buttocks repeatedly.

"Stop that," the flustered warlord ordered him.

But Arthur only laughed and kept spanking him. "Surrender, lump. Why let any more of your men be killed?"

"My men will fight on to the last."

"Surrender, for God's sake. Use your wits, for once."

"Never."

But Bedivere's men had them outnumbered four to one. The fighting ended quickly. Individual warriors surrendered. The ground was littered with their fallen comrades and dropped swords.

Then, when it was apparent he had lost, Marmaduke dropped his own sword. Puffing heavily he said, "You win.

Again. Arthur, King of England." He made an ironic little bow, then spat.

"Why, Marmaduke, how nice of you to acknowledge my kingship—once more."

The warlord sulked and said nothing more.

But Arthur was not finished gloating. "Remind me, Marmaduke. My memory is failing me, I'm afraid. Was it this simple to best you, back in the civil war?"

The pyre was roaring with flames by now. Marmaduke fixed his gaze on it and remained silent.

"Come, now, Marmaduke, it was twenty years ago. Not so long, really. Longer for me than for you, at any rate. I have had the burden of government on my shoulders all that time. You have had . . . what? Mud? You might at least have had a bath sometime in twenty years."

"You damned, self-styled aristocrats. You romp around the country violating men's wives and then have the gall to complain to us. 'Oh, how hard my royal life is. Pity me.'" He spat again.

Arthur smiled indulgently, in a way he hoped would be conciliatory. "It was only the once, Marmaduke. And she wanted it. They tell me I was quite a handsome young man."

"'They tell me I was a handsome young man,'" the warlord mimicked. "You make me sick, Arthur. All of you, you're all alike. Your father was just as bad, in his day. But at least he was content with his own little kingdom. You wanted all of England, and all the women in it."

Something the fat man said made Merlin's ears prick up. He stared at Marmaduke fixedly and did not move a muscle.

"What is that about Uther?" he asked.

But before Marmaduke could answer, Lulua, trying to rub the mud off her robes, said to Merlin, "Well? Are you coming for me or not?"

"Be quiet, woman. I am talking to Marmaduke."

"No, you're not. Look."

Two of Bedivere's men prodded Marmaduke with spears and led him away.

Bedivere approached. Arthur glared at him. "Where the devil have you been?"

The knight was out of breath and puffing. "I've been trying to impose some order on this scene, while you stood here taunting that fat idiot Marmaduke."

Cowed, Arthur said nothing.

"The men who were with you, Arthur—they haven't been fed since they were captured."

Arthur rubbed his stomach. "Neither have I, for that matter. Find out where Marmaduke keeps his provisions, and feed us all."

"And one of the knights has taken sick. Maybe it was the lack of food. That can't have helped him, at any rate."

"Which one?"

"Accolon."

A look of grave concern crossed Arthur's face, then vanished. He called, "Merlin, come over here."

Merlin joined them. Arthur asked Bedivere to repeat what he'd said.

"Accolon?" Merlin turned thoughtful. "He is one of—" He caught himself. "He is one of the younger knights. What is wrong with him?"

Bedivere looked away. "Well, Merlin, it looks like . . . That is, we think it might be . . ."

"Say it."

Bedivere looked directly into his eyes, then into Arthur's. "The plague."

# EIGHT

By early afternoon, calm was beginning to emerge out of the morning's chaos. Most of Marmaduke's men had either fled or surrendered, those that weren't wounded or dead. Bedivere took charge of seeing that all of Arthur's knights who had been held prisoner were fed.

The fog was finally beginning to dissipate; after so long, it seemed a miracle. But the winds that scattered the mist were cold; they carried the first breath of winter. And though they dissipated the mist, they brought heavy gray storm clouds.

Arthur kept a careful eye on the sky, fearing snow. "The last thing we need," he whispered to Bedivere. "Our going has been heavy enough already. With an early snowfall . . . This chill breeze will be hard enough on us. I can taste the ice on it."

"We've brought cloaks and blankets," Bedivere offered. "And there are trees for firewood. We'll be fine, Arthur."

"That isn't what frightens me."

"Then . . ."

"Do you suppose there really are gods? Do you suppose Lulua could be right?"

Bedivere put a hand on his shoulder. "You haven't eaten. Come on." As they were walking to the cook-fires he added, "Besides, if it gets cold enough for the ground to freeze, it will speed up our progress. Perhaps *that* is the gods' gift."

"Why is everything they do so ambiguous?"

"There is nothing ambiguous about winter, Arthur."


People whispered that the wind must be Merlin's doing, and when the rumors reached his ears he grew irritable.

But he dutifully tended to the wounded, cleaning stab wounds, dressing cuts and bruises, applying salves where he thought they would help. One of the squires had a broken leg, and he set the bone and applied splints. Peter assisted him, as best he could, and Merlin instructed Robert in ways to treat the simpler, more routine cases. Neither of them had any real medical training but they both learned quickly. A good many of the knights refused their ministrations, claiming to be men enough to brave out the healing process. Merlin was amused and thought them foolish but said nothing.

Once all of Arthur's men and their retainers had been cared for, he turned his attention to the remainder of Marmaduke's people. At one point Arthur asked him how it was going.

"If it is any comfort to you, Arthur, their wounds and injuries are, for the most part, worse than ours. I suppose that is a testament to the skill of Camelot's fighting men. One or two of them will almost certainly die."

"But how many of our men are fit to fight?"

"Nearly all of them. Ninety percent of them, at least."

Arthur dealt personally with Lulua and Marmaduke. He interrogated them as thoroughly as he could, trying to find

out whether his sister Morgan was up to something nefarious. The cross-examination proved inconclusive. Lulua refused to say much of anything except to make veiled—and
not-so-veiled—threats against Arthur's kingship. When it
was clear they would tell him nothing useful, he ordered
Bedivere to have them taken to Camelot under armed guard,
to await trial for treason. The most badly wounded of Arthur's men were to go with them.

"Put Kay in charge of them. It will do him good to get
home. Half a dozen mounted knights should be sufficient to
guard our corpulent prisoners. I doubt either of them has
much fight left."

"Yes, but we will have to protect our own people against
possible hostility."

Arthur frowned. "You're right. Consult with Kay, and
send whoever you think you need to."

Bedivere gave a cursory glance at the two prisoners.
"We have some of those large packhorses from Scotland.
They'll have to ride those. Ordinary mounts would buckle
under their weight in no time."

"Why burden unsuspecting horses with all that flesh?
Let them walk."

"All the way? Arthur, they'll never make it."

He smiled. "I think they will. The exercise will take
weight off them. And if they succumb . . ." He shrugged.
"Leave them to rot in the nearest ditch. But why punish the
horses?"

The party left for Camelot soon after.


Of Arthur's men, the one in the worst condition was Accolon, the young French knight. His skin was covered in
bloodred blotches, the largest of which were slowly turning
black, and he had a raging fever. Merlin checked on his
condition hourly. He was not worsening but not improving
either.

Merlin ordered him removed to Marmaduke's house. "All this cold dampness cannot be good for him. Carry him gently."

The servants he gave these orders to balked at them. "He has the plague!" one of them cried out. "We'll catch it and die."

"Nonsense. You must be careful not to touch him, that is all. The contagion may be spread through bodily contact."

"And it may not be," said another of them. "Plagues are divine visitations."

"Divine or not, if Accolon was spreading disease, we would all be ill by now. Take him, and be careful."

The servants were plainly unhappy. They sulked and appealed to other leaders, ultimately even to the king himself. And at every stage they were told to do as Merlin ordered. Finally, glumly, and facing the threat of a whipping for disobedience, they wrapped Accolon in sheets of coarse fabric and carried him off to the little wooden building Marmaduke had called his palace.

Merlin had not eaten since the battle and his capture. Once he had seen to all the wounded, he made his way to Bedivere's command station. Three cook-fires were blazing. Knights, squires, servants huddled round them. Arthur was there.

"Merlin." Arthur was having a goblet of wine. "Is everything ready? All the men treated who need it?"

Merlin nodded. "I smell meat. I have had nothing since we were captured. I am hungry enough to eat Lulua."

"I thought you said you want meat. Lulua is pure fat."

Bedivere offered him a plate loaded with meat and fruit. "Here. Eat your fill—there's plenty more. One thing Marmaduke did was to keep plenty of good food on hand. This roast beef is the best I've had in ages."

Merlin gaped at the plate. "So much. Not even I could finish it all."

"A minute ago you were famished." Arthur laughed. "Eat

up. Our host is gone, but we can still enjoy his hospitality. I had forgotten how pleasant warfare can be."

"Not to mention gluttony. Go easy on that wine, Arthur."

"Nonsense. We have a victory to celebrate. You should have some yourself."

Merlin ate pensively. "I need sleep. I got none in that bloody cage. When I'm finished eating, I mean to take a good nap. Have someone wake me in an hour. I want to keep an eye on Accolon."

Arthur took a long swallow of wine. "How bad is he?"

"I do not know yet. If he has the plague—"

"He has. What else could it be?"

"If he has the plague," Merlin repeated with emphasis, "he should be watched carefully. This will be my first opportunity to study the disease's progress."

"He will die. Another one."

Merlin looked into his eyes. There was no need for him to speak. They both knew what the king was thinking, and there was nothing he could say.

Bedivere asked Merlin if he wanted more venison.

"No. No, thank you, Bed. Just find me a nice, warm blanket so I can curl up somewhere and get some rest."

"We're building fresh fires. All of Marmaduke's have burned too low to be of any use."

"Good. We will need them." He looked up at the deepening cloud cover. "At least this cold will staunch the plague." He added, "If plague this is."


Merlin napped, and an hour later he woke to Bedivere shaking him. The air had grown still colder; a stiff breeze blew from the north. Merlin had wrapped himself in a blanket, but he had kicked it off in his sleep. He was shivering with the cold.

"What on earth—?"

"You wanted to be wakened, remember?"

"Since when do you care what I want?"

"Don't be disagreeable, Merlin. You have to check on Accolon. Have a cup of wine and go see to him."

Slowly, stiffly, Merlin got to his feet. "Oh, this bloody arthritis. If there are any gods, they must hate humanity or they would never have devised winter."

"You complain like a soldier."

"Do not be rude, Bedivere."

He spent a few minutes warming himself by the largest of the cook-fires with a cup of spiced wine. Then, accompanied by a servant and leaning heavily on his cane, he headed off to the "palace."

As Bedivere had predicted, the muddy ground was freezing. The morning's battle had left it rough, uneven. Merlin found the footing difficult. The roads in the heart of Paintonbury were not quite frozen yet; the mud was thick and viscous. He found it even more unpleasant. Most of the residents had fled. Only the elderly and a few children were left. Small as it was, the village had the saddest appearance.

Two torches blazed brilliantly at either side of the entrance to the "palace." One was too close to the wall; the wood was charring. As Merlin approached, an elderly man came out of the building and bowed to him. "Ralph of Paintonbury, at your service, sir."

Merlin pointed to the charring wood. "You had better do something about that. This place will go up in smoke."

"Would that matter, sir?"

"Possibly to the people inside." He introduced himself. "You were in service to Marmaduke?"

"Yes, sir. I am his majordomo."

Merlin laughed. "A majordomo, here. This is not much of a domo to be major of, is it?"

"When I was a young man, I was a warrior, in service to Marmaduke's father."

Merlin ignored this. "I sent a sick man to be tended here. Where is he? Take me to him."

Ralph made a slight bow. "This way, sir. One of your men is with him, sir."

"Peter, yes. But what is that awful smell?"

Just at that moment, Peter appeared in the doorway. "Merlin. I was just coming to look for you. I need fresh air. I'm not certain keeping Accolon here is a good idea."

Merlin waved Ralph away and began to walk past Peter into the building. "Why not? We have to keep him warm and dry if he is to—"

"The poor man has to breathe. Can you not smell the awful odor?"

Merlin stopped in his tracks. "Good heavens. What an awful stench. It smells like—"

"I'm afraid that is exactly what it is. Rotting garbage mixed with—well. Let's just say that Marmaduke was an even worse pig than we thought. Are you certain you want to come in?"

"I have to check on Accolon, stench or no stench."

The interior of the palace, such as it was, was lit by torches. They were set too far apart to do much good against the gloom. But more than the darkness, Merlin was struck by an increasingly strong, increasingly unpleasant odor.

"It's over there," Peter indicated. "There is an entire room full of it. Apparently the concept of sanitation had not penetrated with Marmaduke. There are open pits dug in the floor where they—well, you understand."

"A full room? You are joking."

"I'm afraid not, Merlin. Would you care to see it? Aside from the foul stuff itself, there are worms, centipedes, rats . . . I've seen to it that Accolon is as far away from it as possible."

"Very wise." He sighed. "At least Marmaduke confined it to only one room. Which way?" He held up his fingers and pinched his nose. "You are right. Marmaduke is a pig in more ways than we realized."

Peter led him along a hall to the rear of the palace.

Torches flickered; room after room opened up as they passed along the corridor. The awful odor abated somewhat, but it was always there.

In a room with no windows, lit by three torches, lay Accolon. Merlin did a quick examination. "He seems no worse than before. But we must move him. Find a room with windows, take him there and let him get fresh air."

"Windows? As far as I've found, there are none. The entire building is as close as this room."

Again Merlin heaved a sigh. "Let us get him out of here. Breathing air this foul cannot be good for him. Find servants to carry him."

Peter went; Merlin followed him to the entrance. Old Ralph was waiting there, leaning casually against the front of the building.

"What a horrible man your master was. Did he ever bathe or clean himself? Did anyone, at his court?"

Ralph ignored the question and spat on the ground.

"Answer me, old man."

Ralph laughed. "Who are you to make sneering references to anyone's age?"

Merlin took him by the collar. "We have a seriously ill man inside."

Unruffled, Ralph spit again. "I thought it was odd, you bringing him here."

"We did not know what a sty your overlord occupied. There must be other buildings here. Cleaner ones."

"If there are, I've never noticed them."

Merlin released him. "An entire village of swine. What about the fat witch, Lulua? She did not live in this foul hamlet. Where was her residence?"

Ralph reached up and removed Merlin's hand from his collar. "Lulua occupied a big old mill a mile and a half from here." He smiled and pointed to the muddy rivulet. "Downstream."

"Where? Which way is it?"

Ralph pointed casually to the muddy brook. "Just follow that stream."

"That . . . that tiny trickle of mud?"

Ralph leaned back against the lintel of the palace door. "That rivulet floods every time it rains. You'd be surprised how much fury it can unleash. I'm surprised it hasn't left its banks already, with all the rain we've had. Besides, it joins a larger stream."

Just then a servant approached with a message from Arthur. "A messenger from Camelot has finally made it to us. There is a letter for you."

Merlin focused on Ralph. "Two miles downstream, you say?"

Ralph spit again, then nodded. Merlin turned to the servant. "Let us get back to the king."

There was indeed a courier from Camelot. Arthur was walking briskly about the camp, overseeing everything. Bedivere was at his side. Most of the wounded were fit for travel; a few required more time for healing and rest. Everyone had been fed amply. A crew of servants was digging trenches for latrines.

Arthur scratched his head. "No one can seem to find any sanitary facilities, so we have to make our own. What did the residents do, I wonder."

"Trust me, Arthur," Merlin said in a low voice. "It is not something you want to inquire into."

"Tell me, what have you learned?"

"No, Arthur, I really—"

"Tell me!"

So Merlin described the interior of Marmaduke's palace. "I have had Accolon taken there. He needs to be kept out of the elements. But that place cannot be healthy. I am told

Lulua occupied a large old mill a few miles upriver. We should take him there, along with any other wounded men who may need more care."

"Excellent. Before you go, though, there is this." He produced a letter. "From Colin at Camelot."

Merlin took the letter and unsealed it. It was in Nimue's hand and was headed *Confidential. Only for Merlin.*

*Merlin,*

*Reports from around the country have slowed due to these awful autumn rains. But the state of affairs, as near as I can determine, is this:*

*Cooler weather seems to have slowed the plague's progress, as you expected it would. The area around Dover has been hardest hit, naturally, and the nearby towns have all reported outbreaks. There have been a few cases reported as far west as London. We have received no news of plague farther west than that.*

*Camelot, except for the death of John, has been spared. Not one more case has erupted here. Perhaps that is because we were quite prompt and diligent in cremating John's body and having the ashes buried, not scattered.*

*There are reports that in some sections of the country social standards are breaking down. Large numbers of people are drinking much more heavily than is usual, and even larger numbers are engaging in orgiastic sexual abandon. (We have had tentative news that the same thing is happening across Europe, wherever this plague has erupted.) But with the plague on the wane, that will stop in time. And if it does not, it will be a problem for local authorities. In due course order will return, as it has already begun to do.*

> *It may be premature to be optimistic, but it appears that the worst of this crisis is behind us.*
>
> *Nimue*

Merlin folded the letter carefully and placed it in his pocket. When he was finished reading he noticed that Perceval had joined Arthur and Bedivere. The three were conferring, presumably about how best to reach the spot where the Stone of Bran had been buried.

Perceval was saying, "I'm not certain how we should proceed. We were more lost in that bloody fog than we realized."

Arthur told him, "We have maps with us. It should not be too difficult to find our bearings and decide how to proceed."

Merlin interrupted their discussion. "Let me see who else should be removed to Lulua's mill. There should not be many, I do not imagine. Marmaduke's warriors were . . . less than skillful. Thankfully."

"I think we should spend a day or two here before we move on." Arthur told Perceval to go and check the maps, then turned back to Merlin. "A good rest will do us all good. Can't you treat Accolon and the others here?"

"They should be kept warm, indoors. And the buildings in this awful hamlet are pigsties. It will be easier to keep them warm and tend to their needs in the mill. Assuming Lulua was more fastidious than Marmaduke, that is."

"She would almost have to be, from what you've told me. I want to go and inspect Marmaduke's little castle myself."

Merlin looked at him inquiringly.

"Call it morbid curiosity."

"Of course. But before you do it, Arthur, might I suggest that you get out of those tattered clothes? You look a good deal less than kingly."

Arthur grinned. "There were times during the civil wars when I looked considerably less kingly than this. But you're right, Merlin. I need to bathe and change. I don't suppose you saw anything resembling a bathtub in the palace?"

"Hardly. A bathtub for a man as fat as Marmaduke would be the size of a small pond."

"I'll look around. There must be something I can use. Meanwhile, go and tend to the wounded and make whatever arrangements you need for their transport."

"I'll see to it right away, Arthur. Oh, and I'm told this foul little stream we are using joins a larger, cleaner one not far from here."

"Good."

Arthur began pulling his tunic off. Merlin saw that there was a huge gash in his left side. "In the name of everything human, Arthur. That wound!"

"It isn't very painful. Marmaduke himself struck the blow."

"Were you going to keep it a secret? What would be the point? You must let me clean it. I have some healing salve that will help it. And after you have had your bath—if that is possible—you must let me dress it with a bandage."

"Don't fuss, Merlin."

"It is my duty, remember? We can hardly have King Arthur die because his wound went untended. We read that several Roman generals—"

"Spare me the history lecture." The king sighed. "Very well, if you must. But go see to the others first, all right?"

And Merlin sighed in return. "If you insist. But do not think I will forget about it."

"Your relentlessness is part of what makes you so valuable to me. Go, now."

There were three more men whose needs could be better tended in the makeshift infirmary Merlin planned to set up in Lulua's mill. He arranged for them to be transported there in the two carriages. The Stone of Bran was to remain with Arthur at Paintonbury for safekeeping. When Merlin had seen to all the necessary arrangements, he went back to Arthur to tend his wound. "You have put me off long enough, *Your Majesty*." He leaned on the title with irony. Arthur grumbled but let him do what he needed to.

"When we are ready to move on, Arthur, I would suggest that you ride in a carriage for a few days, just to be certain there are no complications from this. It is not terribly serious, but it is close to your heart. If something should happen to tear it open . . ." He made a gesture as if to say, *There would be very little I could do.*

Arthur scowled. "If I listened to you, I'd be wearing an apron and hiding in Camelot's kitchen all the time."

"Hiding among the women did Achilles no harm." He grinned. "Perhaps you should take a lesson from that noble hero."

"I have a country to run. Achilles had nothing to do but tend to his concubines and fight. When you get to Lulua's mill, if any of her people are still there, I want you to interrogate them. If Lulua was in league with my sister to make trouble, they will know about it. See what you can learn. I will stop there tomorrow to see how things are progressing."

The road out of Paintonbury went northwest, paralleling the creek. About a mile out of town it joined with a much larger stream to make a small river. Merlin and Peter rode on horseback, side by side. The carriages followed.

"I do not recall this river on any of the maps, Peter. I am beginning to fear we may be more lost than Arthur realizes."

"We don't have good maps? I had the impression—"

"The ones we are using date from the civil wars, nearly two decades ago. Arthur has never seen a need to have the

whole country surveyed and accurate maps made. I will
have to have a word with him."

"It does seem like a great deal of effort. Perhaps—"

"If we are ever to make England a truly unified nation,
good charts are essential. How can we hope to unify it when
we do not really know what is here? No, I think Arthur will
have to make it a priority."

The new creek was much larger and much clearer than
Paintonbury's one. When the two met, the muddy water from
Paintonbury made what looked like a huge brown smudge
in the new, larger stream. But after a few yards it was lost in
the clearer water. Merlin's eyes took it all in. "This is good.
We will have fresh water. I was quite concerned we—and our
wounded—would have to continue drinking that foul stuff."

After another mile, the mill came into view. The first
thing in sight was its thatched roof, then more and more of
it appeared. It was much larger than Merlin had expected,
and in surprisingly good condition. The roof was thatched
with what appeared to be fresh straw. Either the place was
new or Lulua had kept it in excellent repair. The one sign of
ill repair was a loud, low moaning sound made by the waterwheel. It carried clearly to Peter and Merlin three fourths
of a mile up the road. The ground sloped gently downward;
the wheel turned briskly.

Peter made a show of covering his ears. "Horrible sound."

"It will be worse when we actually reach the mill."

"Whatever can be causing it?"

"I have heard its like once before, on my travels through
Egypt. There are ancient waterwheels at a place called Me-
dinet El-Fayyum. After long millennia they are still turning,
still providing power and still making a deafening wail.
The residents call their moaning the crying of the gods."

"Splendid. I don't suppose there's any chance these
'gods' might be silent for a while?"

"I am afraid not. But you will find that you get used to it
rather quickly."

Peter wrinkled his features. "Horrible sound. It sounds as if the earth itself is in pain."

"It is a fit place for a hospital, then."

"Seriously, Merlin, can't we simply make a camp somewhere nearby and keep our patients warm with fires?"

"We are here, Peter. Let us make the best of it."

The patients had slept more or less soundly on the entire journey. All of them but Accolon, that was. He kept waking from his slumber, ranting incoherently about fantastic beasts devouring him. At one point, just as they reached the mill, he cried, "The dead! The dead are leaving their tombs and attacking me! They are living skeletons, and they claw at me with their sharp, bony fingers!" At times his rant was a shout; at others it was not much more than a whisper, barely audible above the moaning of the waterwheel.

Merlin tried to comfort him, but for the longest time it was no use. Then finally he fell back into sleep.

When they reached the mill, Robert and the other servants carried the patients inside. Merlin followed and was pleasantly surprised to see that the place was clean and well kept. Of Lulua's servants there was no sign. Presumably they had received word of the way the battle had gone, and they had fled.

Merlin and Peter followed the servants. Once they were certain the patients had weathered the trip well, they went to explore the mill. There were a great many small rooms. They were tall, dark and shadowy, right up to the thatched roof. "This is not at all what I was hoping for. But I suppose it is what I should have expected, given that Lulua lived here." Merlin noted that all the windows were glazed, though there were not enough of them to cut the darkness very much. But he was quite pleased to find stores of food and even wine.

The one exception to the mill's general gloominess was the kitchen. There were a half dozen windows. And there were three ovens, two of which were still giving off heat.

Peter found a small pantry with a great many bottles of wine. "At least the wine will keep us warm tonight. We can heat it up. And there are spices for it. Lulua has an herb garden outside. Nothing cuts the cold like good mulled wine."

In the one large room the two huge millstones turned slowly, driven by the waterwheel outside. Their friction against each other made a low grinding noise; it was all but drowned out by the sound of the waterwheel. There was no sign of any grain for them to mill; there was no sign that there had been any for years. Peter observed it disapprovingly. "It seems such a waste. This place could feed the whole countryside."

"Indeed." Merlin inspected the mechanism that turned them, fascinated. "Look at this assemblage of gears. I was wondering how a relatively small stream could turn such large stones. But these gears must improve the mechanical advantage. I must make sketches of them. I would like to use something similar to improve my lift mechanism at Camelot."

Everywhere, the loud groan of the waterwheel penetrated. When they went outside to inspect it, Merlin was quite startled to see that the axle on which the wheel turned was made of metal. "I have seen such wheels in Africa and in a few of the eastern stretches of Europe. Never in England."

"How could Lulua have obtained this, then?"

"We do not know that she was actually responsible for the building of the mill. She may simply have . . . appropriated it. The question that vexes me is how she—or anyone else—could have afforded such a thing as a metal axle for the wheel."

"Priests and priestesses grow wealthy. They find money wherever it is." Peter smiled and squatted down to inspect the wheel more closely. "It is a law of nature, like swine hunting for truffles."

Merlin chuckled. "Still, importing this—and importing an

engineer to devise those gears inside—would have been quite a considerable extravagance. Lulua was more than wealthy enough to grow as fat as she is. She must be even wealthier still."

"Or the sorority of witches is." Peter stood again. "That groaning will drive me mad. How can you stand it, Merlin?"

He shrugged. "I have arthritis in my knees and hips. When you learn to withstand the pain, you are able to withstand most anything."

Peter squinted and stared at him. "You take drugs to kill the pain."

"Let us go back inside, Peter."

As they were heading back indoors, Peter commented that he found the whole place ominous. "It is too dark, too gloomy. And there is that awful noise from the wheel. I would like to go back and rejoin Arthur."

Merlin shook his head. "You are valuable. I need you."

"Something terrible is going to happen here, Merlin. I feel it."

"Nonsense."

Robert and the other servants had done everything they could to make the mill comfortable for the patients. As Merlin and Peter went back inside, there was a minor hubbub. Robert had found a young man hiding there. "He was hiding in one of the pantries, sir. What shall we do with him?"

Merlin peered at the man; he was not much more than a boy. "What is your name?"

"George, sir." The boy had a thick shock of black hair and bright blue eyes. He was Robert's age, or perhaps a year or two older. He was slender and quite pale. "George o' the Mill."

"They call you that?"

"Yes, sir. That, or George the Miller. And sometimes George Cook."

"Well, George o' the Mill, what are you doing here?" He smiled. "You were in the pantry. Was Lulua going to eat you?"

"I live here, sir. I always have. In service to the witch of Paintonbury."

"The others seem to have run away. Why did you not go with them? Where are your parents?"

The boy looked from Merlin to Peter to Robert, then to Merlin again. A trace of fear showed in his face. "Please, sir. They said my mistress had been captured—taken prisoner. By whom, sir?"

"By Arthur, the rightful King of England. Your true lord and master."

The boy's face was a complete blank. "Who?"

"Never mind. You are now a prisoner, too."

For the first time his face registered emotion. His fear was obvious. "Are you—are you going to kill me, sir?"

"I have not decided." Peter noticed the twinkle in Merlin's eye.

George clearly did not. "Please, sir, spare me. I will do anything."

Merlin furrowed his brow and stroked his chin, to make a show of thinking. "I shall have to ponder that awhile. Meantime . . . can you cook?"

Timorously the boy nodded. "I always cooked for my mistress."

"A large job, no doubt."

"Yes, sir." He beamed with pride.

"Well, you shall cook for us now. We have four men with us who are quite ill. They will need good soup for the time being. And there are a dozen more of us."

"Uh, yes, sir. I made delicious soup for my mistress. She always said so."

This took Merlin aback. "Are you telling us that she grew that fat on soup?!"

George mistook his surprise for menace. "N-no sir. She ate everything. Everything. I was always busy."

"I believe it. The pantry is well stocked."

He nodded. "Shall I make soup, then, sir?"

"Soup for our patients. Bread and meat for the rest of us. Make cakes for our dessert. Robert, go with this young man and keep a careful eye one him."

Robert snapped to attention. "Yes, Merlin."

The two boys left. Merlin turned to Peter. "At least we will have a good lunch, albeit a late one."

And a good lunch it was. The venison was succulent, the bread fresh and aromatic, the cakes delicious. Robert brought a cask of fine wine from the pantry. The patients were glad of George's soup, all but Accolon, who was only half conscious and muttering in his sleep about living corpses and dragons.

Merlin whispered to Peter that he might take George back to Camelot to be his personal cook. "Then I would never have to leave my tower. With Colin and young George, I might never again have to leave my books and my laboratories." He smiled, plainly finding the thought pleasant.

"You lead too insular a life already, Merlin." Peter chewed his venison enthusiastically. "You should get out and about more."

"That is what Arthur tells me. But I am content in my tower, when I am able to stay there. With Plotinus and Aristotle for company, what do I need with anyone else?"

"I envy you your misanthropy."

"It is hardly misanthropy, Peter. I do not hate my fellow human beings. But I find life so much more restful when I do not have to deal with them."

"You can hardly detect crime from your tower, Merlin."

He shrugged. "You are the sheriff, not I. Besides, crime happens whether I am cloistered in my tower or not. And criminals . . . I find I have seen enough of them. And of humankind in general. I should like nothing better than to retire to Egypt, under the protection of my old friend Germanicus, and live an even more isolated existence."

Peter sipped his wine and said wryly, "I understand they have crime there, too."

"Yes, but in a much more lovely setting. And with much better weather."


Just after sunset a ferocious wind blew up. Trees trembled in it; the waters of the stream were roiled wildly and even sprayed up onto the banks. The roar of the wind was loud enough even to drown out the incessant moaning on the waterwheel at times. Bits of the mill's thatched roof tore free and blew away; the wind gushed into several rooms. But George prepared a meal for the party, and it was every bit as good as Merlin hoped.

"You are quite an excellent cook," he told the boy.

"My mother taught me." He seemed abashed by the compliment. "She was really good. You should have known her."

"Where is she?"

"She died six years ago, sir. Lulua took me in, or I would have . . . I don't know."

There was a tiny barn adjacent to the mill, and Merlin ordered that the mounts and the pack animals be moved there for shelter from the driving wind.

Peter oversaw this. Then he reported to Merlin, who was standing beside the stream, watching the waves, "The building is quite small. The horses are unhappy at being so crowded."

Merlin's robes were blowing wildly, to the point where they almost knocked him off balance. "They would be unhappier still if they had to stay out in this horrible storm. At least, that dreadful groaning will be less loud there. It cannot be pleasant for them." He raised an arm to protect his face from some blowing leaves, then glanced up at the sky. "Let us hope this wind does not bring rain. Or worse yet, snow."

Robert came out and joined them. "Please, Merlin, the sick men are all asleep. And they are right in the main part of the mill. Should we leave them there?"

"Find another room large enough to quarter them—and myself. I shall sleep in that same room, so that I might keep an eye on them."

"What about the room where the millstones turn? It's the biggest in the mill. It should be more than big enough."

"If you can find no other place for us, that will be fine. I only hope the turning of the stones does not disturb their rest."

"If the damned sound of the waterwheel does not keep them awake, nothing could." Peter raised an arm to protect himself from the wind. But a twig blew and hit his cheek. There was a trickle of blood. "Of all the horrible places for a hospital."

Robert had not moved. "If you please, sir, that boy—"

"George?"

"Yes, sir. He has eaten and rested, as you ordered. You wanted to know, so that you could question him."

"Yes. Thank you, Robert."

"You . . . you want to know about the witch?"

He nodded. "Arthur requires intelligence. And while I am at it, I may ask the boy for his recipes, just in case he does not want to return with us. Dinner was delicious. Go and place the boy in the mill room. I will join you there shortly."

"Yes, sir." Covering his face for protection from the wind, Robert ran back inside.

Peter stared fixedly at Merlin. "Wizard, you are a fraud."

This caught Merlin off guard. "I never claim to be a wizard. There is no fraud. Do not be disagreeable, Peter."

"That isn't what I mean."

A particularly ferocious gust caught Merlin's robes and nearly knocked him off balance again; Peter caught him by the arm and steadied him. "Thank you, Peter. But what on earth are you talking about?"

They began to move toward the door of the mill. "I am talking about you. You preach a life of reason, of the mind, of austerity. Yet when a good chef comes your way, you all but leap at him. You are as much devoted to the senses as any Roman emperor."

Merlin's hat started to blow off and he raised a hand to steady it on his head. "Pleasure is essential to life, Peter. The things that give me the most pleasure are not the usual ones, though. I derive more pleasure from a good book than from any woman I have ever known. Besides, I have lived longer than the typical Roman emperor." He smiled. "Much longer."

They stepped inside the mill and Peter pushed the door shut against the wind.

Merlin shrugged. "I never claim to be an ascetic, and I certainly never suggest that anyone else should live a life without gratification. I am merely . . . different in my choice of pleasures, that is all."

"Different indeed. And does unmasking murderers give you pleasure, then?"

"Let us say *satisfaction*. More satisfaction than I can say."

"Have you ever not found a murderer you were pursuing?"

Merlin brushed bits of dead leaves and twigs from his robes. "Young George will be waiting. Come. I want my new cook in good spirits."

"Sybarite."

"Cynic."

In the mill room the great stones turned more quickly than they had earlier, driven by the furious water in the furious wind. They made a constant grinding sound. Merlin wished there was some way to brake them, but the mechanism offered no such option. A fire roared in a huge open hearth not far from the stones.

George was waiting there, pacing and looking nervous.

Robert was standing off in a corner, trying to look unobtrusive but clearly keeping an eye on George.

When Merlin entered, he waved Robert away. "Thank you, Robert. You may go and get some rest."

"I don't think I could rest with that horrible groaning. I'd really like to stay."

"Go, I said."

Robert pouted. "You need protection, Merlin. And I am in your service."

"Do you think George, here, is going to assault me with a bowl of soup? Go and sleep."

"Yes, Merlin." Sullenly he went.

Merlin found a stool for himself, then turned his attention to George. The boy was looking anxious, and Merlin smiled to reassure him.

"That Robert fellow doesn't trust me." The expression on George's face was part apprehension, part bewilderment. "Why?"

"You are Lulua's servant." He tried to make his voice calming.

"What of that, sir?"

"Well . . ." Merlin chuckled. "She does fancy herself a witch, after all."

"She's more like a priestess to all of the local tribes. Not a witch like a mean old woman."

Merlin gave the boy a brief summary of what had nearly happened to Arthur and himself at the hands of Marmaduke and Lulua. "So you see, Robert wonders if you can be trusted. You serve the woman who wanted me dead."

"But you said she is a prisoner now. She can't hurt you. Can I sit down, please?"

"Of course."

George looked around for another stool. Not finding one, he sat on the floor five feet in front of Merlin. "Lulua has taken care of me since my mother died. I owe her a lot."

"That is the first good thing I have heard anyone say

about her. Besides, your cooking made her fat—or kept her that way. I would say you had repaid your debt to her more than sufficiently."

The boy lowered his eyes. "I feel like I owe her a lot more."

"Feed her much more than you have, George, and she may explode. But tell me, what happened to your mother?"

"She died, sir."

"Yes, but how? What happened to her?"

"She just . . . stopped living, that's all."

"And where did this happen?"

"Paintonbury, sir. She was Marmaduke's cook. She taught me."

"I see. So your family has made a tradition of fattening up villains." Merlin's bench wobbled. Irritably he got to his feet. "Now, tell me about Morgan."

George's face turned blank. "Who?"

"Morgan le Fay. The king's sister."

It registered. "Oh—the Great Queen."

"She calls herself that?"

"Everyone calls her that. She is the rightful ruler of England." He paused uncertainly. "Isn't she?"

"Her brother Arthur is King of all the Britons. You would do well to remember that."

"Yes, sir. But—but the Grea—but Morgan le Fay hasn't been here for months. Why are you asking me about her?"

Merlin sighed and sat down again. The stool wobbled, and he got quickly to his feet. "Is there no decent furniture is this mill? What did Lulua sit on?" But before George could answer, Merlin held up a hand. "No. That is not a thing I want to know." He moved to the door. "Robert!"

A moment later the door opened and Robert put his head in. "You need something, Merlin?"

"A good chair. Find one."

"Yes, Merlin." He closed the door behind him.

Merlin turned back to George. "The matriarchs effectively ruled England for centuries and styled themselves queens like, apparently, Morgan. Boadicea was the most famous of them. They invoked their gods, cast their so-called spells, worked their supposedly magical charms, did everything they could to cow warlords and common people alike into obeying them. And they had armies. Then they were displaced, first by Arthur's father, Uther Pendragon, who went a long way toward unifying the country, then by Arthur himself. But you must know all that."

"I do. Some of it at least. I was taught. But my lessons were never couched in language like yours, Merlin."

"Of course not, no. But the witches—"

"I was always taught to call them priestesses, sir."

"Priestesses, then. Under their Great Queen. They want their power back. They have been conspiring against the king. You must tell me what you know of their clandestine affairs."

The boy looked lost. "I'm afraid I don't know much, sir. Sometimes the Great Queen would come here to confer with Lulua. Sometimes other priestesses would. But I never knew what they talked about."

"No, of course not." Merlin was annoyed but worked to keep it from showing. "But anything you can remember may be of use. Scraps of conversation you overheard when you were serving them, perhaps."

The boy paused for a long moment. "I'm sorry, Merlin, really I am, but I never heard a thing."

Merlin sighed a resigned sigh. "No, of course you did not. But try and think back. Try. Anything that comes to mind—"

"It is important, isn't it?"

"Where is Robert with that chair?" He pulled the door open. Robert was on his knees just outside. He had obviously been eavesdropping. He jumped to his feet. "Here is your chair, Merlin."

"Thank you. Now go and join the others and get some sleep."

"Will you be needing anything else, sir?"

"Go, I said!"

Robert turned his back and left. Merlin watched him go, suspicious of him for the first time. Why had the boy been listening? What did he hope to hear? Then he dragged the chair into place and turned back to George. The boy seemed honest enough. He decided to trust him. "You must not repeat what I am about to tell you. Do you understand that? Not to anyone."

"Yes, sir."

"There have been deaths. A series of them. Of people who were close to Arthur." He lowered his voice. "Potential heirs." He leaned back in the chair. "These deaths give every appearance of being natural, but I am having more and more doubts. Do you follow me?"

"Yes, Merlin."

"That knight who is ill, Accolon—"

"That poor Frenchman?"

"Exactly. I am suspicious of his illness."

"He is related to the king?" The boy whistled softly.

Merlin avoided the question. "And my valet, Robert, the one who was just here, he may be at risk as well." Softly, almost as if in a reverie, he added, "If he is the ille—" He caught himself. "Listen, shortly the wounded men, including Accolon, will be brought to this room for the night. I will sleep here as well. And I want you to, also. Be alert for anything unusual that may occur."

"Yes, Merlin." The boy lowered his eyes. "Is this . . . is this a test?"

"Let us say it is a challenge. Watch everyone."

"Yes, sir. I will. Trust me, sir." The boy hesitated, then went on. "Merlin, something you said . . ."

"Yes?"

"Do you really mean to say that the wi—the priestesses do not have any magical abilities?"

"That is precisely what I mean to say."

George fell silent. This was obviously a new thought for him.

A moment later servants appeared, under Peter's supervision, carrying the wounded on litters. Accolon was muttering in his sleep. Two of the others were awake and evidently amused at being treated like invalids. The third of them, to appearances, was sleeping soundly. Peter was clearly in charge, telling the servants where to lay them. "Make certain they all have blankets. And bank the fire as high as you can. The night will be cold."

Robert also entered the room, carrying a large bowl. He smiled at Merlin. "I've had a bowl of spiced wine heated. I thought, with this frigid wind blowing—"

"Very good, Robert. Pour cups for all our patients. And one for me. And for Peter, of course."

"And for me?" George smiled eagerly.

Merlin looked at him doubtfully, then said, "All right, but only a small cup."

Once all the patients were made comfortable, Peter saw that beds were made up for Merlin and the boy. Servants extinguished all the lamps in the room but one. Merlin drank his wine, and it was delicious. Soon he grew drowsy. He climbed onto his pallet and wrapped the blanket around himself. Soon the one remaining lamp burned itself out, and there was nothing but the light from the fireplace.

The wind outside howled and blew wildly. Once or twice the mill actually shook in it, but it was built solidly enough to withstand the storm. The great millstones turned and made their constant grinding sound.

After a few moments everyone in the darkened room found the stones' sound comforting, reassuring. It lulled them to sleep.


Merlin slept, and his sleep was troubled. He dreamed about Arthur's sons. One by one they were being devoured by the

dragons of their imaginings, and he stood watching, powerless to stop it. He would wake in the huge dark room lit
only by the fire in the hearth, to the sound of the millstones
turning, disoriented. When, after a moment, he remembered
where he was, he would close his eyes again, only to have
more dreams. Each time, the fire burned lower.

In his dreams he saw Darrowfield and his sons, bound
to the altar stone at Stonehenge, screaming for their lives,
a faceless villain cutting them, blood streaming from their
throats.

All these deaths were connected somehow, but how? The
murdering dragons laughed at him.

There were sounds in the night, muffled, agonized screams.
More dreams came.

And again he would dream of the plague ravishing the
English countryside. Fevers raged, red-black spots erupted,
populations expired. Then came gentle snows and the plague
stopped. He stood in a snowbound landscape wondering
again and again, *Where are the winds that will save Arthur's
sons?*

Merlin awoke to an agonized scream. He sat up and rubbed
his eyes. As it had every time he had wakened through the
night, it took him a moment to remember where he was.
The fire in the hearth was nearly gone; a few wisps of low,
dying flame danced there and embers glowed, but their light
was not much help against the night. The great room was
growing cold and his arthritic hip was aching. "Peter!
Robert!"

In the night there was nothing but the sound of the turning stones. Slowly he stood and strained his eyes trying to
see what was happening in the room. "Robert! We want
light!"

Slowly he regained his bearings. The sound of the millstones reminded him where he was, and why.

"George?"

Nothing. No sound but the stones.

More loudly he called, "George!"

A soft groan came from the direction of the millstones.

"George?"

The door opened and Peter entered, carrying a lamp. "You called, Merlin?"

"Get more lights in here. Something is wrong."

"You should never have used a room this large for your infirmary. It's so cold in here." He looked around. "Let me put more logs on the fire."

"Do it quickly. Then get lamps."

From the shadows near the millstones came another groan.

"George?"

No answer.

To Peter, Merlin said, "Get your lamp close to the stones. Something is wrong. I feel it."

Peter finished arranging the logs in the hearth and took his lamp to the stones.

And there was George. He was between the stones, and they were turning inexorably. The entire left side of his body was crushed and bleeding. The stones moved on in their circular path. George was barely conscious. He turned his head feebly, looked to Merlin and moaned again. Softly, almost inaudibly, he mouthed the words, *Help me*.

"In the name of everything human!" Merlin jumped to his feet and rushed to the boy. "George, how did this happen? Who did this?" He took George's good hand.

"Help me, sir. Please." It was not much more than a whisper.

"Lift him out, Peter. Quickly!"

Peter handed the lamp to Merlin and slid his arms carefully under the boy's crushed body. George cried, "No! It hurts!"

"Pull him out, Peter. We can't leave him there. Quick, before the stones come around again."

Peter pulled George out from the stones' path. George screamed quite horribly.

Robert appeared in the doorway, carrying two more lamps.

George's cries had wakened the other patients, all but Accolon, who was still seemingly asleep. Merlin took a few steps toward them and had to steady himself against a table. From behind him, from George's side, Peter said, "This boy is dead."

Merlin closed his eyes. It was as if he was still dreaming, still in that nameless, featureless place ruled by monsters. Still feeling off balance, he gripped the edge of a table and told Peter, "Leave him there, then, and check the others."

Peter took his lamp to the patients and inspected them one by one. The pupils of their eyes were dilated, and they said they were feeling vertigo. But they seemed to be all right otherwise, wounds still healing, no new complaints.

"My head is spinning also." Merlin tried to take a few more steps but had to stop and steady himself once more.

Peter moved to the side of the pallet where Accolon lay. After a quick examination he turned to Merlin. "This man was another of the king's sons?"

Merlin nodded. "So it has always been whispered."

"Merlin, he is dead."

Merlin put a hand on the wall to steady himself. He closed his eyes. "No. That cannot be."

"Come see for yourself."

He took a step toward Peter. The room spun around him and he fell to the floor. Peter rushed to his side. "Are you all right?"

Groggily he replied, "Yes."

"No bones broken?"

"No."

"No other damage?"

"Peter, just help me to my feet, will you? If the room would stop whirling about me, I would be perfectly fine."

Peter helped him up. Merlin leaned on him quite heavily. "Let me get you back to your bed, Merlin. You need more rest."

"With all this death around me? You think I could sleep?"

"You are unsteady. It shows. Just exactly how much did you drink last night?"

"This is *not* the result of too much wine. I have not felt the aftereffects of too much drink since I was a boy. Help me to Accolon's pallet. I want to examine him."

Slowly they made their way to the dead knight's side. Merlin bent down and examined the body, and it was like the corpses of all the other plague victims.

"Are you satisfied?" Peter took his arm to help him up again. "It is the plague that took him."

"And was it the plague the killed young George, there? In the name of all that is human, Peter, cover up his body. It is quite indecent to leave him like that."

After he had Merlin securely back at his own pallet, Peter found a large drop cloth and covered George's mangled corpse with it. When he returned to Merlin's side he said, "The boy was drinking last night, like all of us. He must have stumbled and fallen between the stones. A terrible accident, but an accident nonetheless."

Merlin gaped at him. "I heard him cry out, Peter. He was begging for help. I thought it was a dream." He glanced at the cloth covering the boy. "Someone did this to him. It was no accident."

"Of course it was. A boy that age, drinking wine. He could never have handled it."

Again Merlin closed his eyes. "I cannot seem to wake up."

"Sleep, then, Merlin. I'll see to it that the bodies are disposed of properly."

Groggily Merlin told him, "We have been drugged. All of us in this room. That wine last night . . ."

"Nonsense. You've just let these events overwhelm you, that's all. Get some sleep. Have you been outside yet?"

"Of course not." He yawned.

"It's snowing. The world has turned magically white overnight."

Merlin's drowsiness overcame him completely. Again he fell into sleep.

And woke to Peter shaking him. "Merlin, get up. The king is here."

Slowly he opened his eyes. An enormous yawn overtook him. "What did you say?"

"King Arthur is approaching. With a band of knights."

Another yawn. "Where is Geo— Never mind. My head is aching quite ferociously."

"So is mine. So is everyone's."

"Our surviving patients, too?"

Peter nodded.

For a moment Merlin fell silent, obviously lost in thought. Then he looked at Peter, filled with sudden resolve. "Help me to my feet. We must go and greet the king."

"Do you want to check on the other wounded men?"

"Later. They are all doing well enough." He clasped his hands to his head and glanced at his patients. They were all asleep. "I hope their heads are not ringing the way mine is. Sleep is merciful." For a third time he yawned, much more widely than before. "The world would be a much finer place if we would all sleep all the time. There would be no crimes then."

Peter placed a hand under his arm to steady him. "Except the ones in our dreams."

Merlin looked at him as if the statement startled him. "Yes, there are always those. Come. Arthur will be expecting us to meet him."

There was very little activity in the mill. A fire roared in the main hearth, and its flames made almost the only motion. Word of the night's events had spread. The two deaths seemed to cast a pall over everything and everyone.

From the kitchen came aromas of cooking food. Merlin started to react without thinking. "That smells quite wonderful. There is nothing like fresh-baked bread in the morning. Arthur will be pleased. He will want to thank young Geo—" He caught himself. "He will want to thank whoever is doing the baking."

Outside the world had indeed turned white and the temperature had grown bitterly cold. Snow was falling heavily. Three inches of it covered everything. Trees were lacy white marvels. A strong, steady wind blew; snowflakes danced in it. Patches of ice were forming on the surface of the stream.

Softly, at the bottom of his breath, Merlin muttered, "Winter. And there are people who believe in benevolent gods."

The king's party could be seen in the middle distance through the falling snow. They were riding slowly, wrapped in heavy, dull-colored cloaks. Under his, Arthur wore his ceremonial armor, and it gleamed in the white landscape.

"It is too cold, Peter. This wind— Run inside and fetch me a cloak."

Peter vanished into the mill. Two of the servants emerged and placed themselves just behind Merlin, in case he should need anything else. He leaned on their arms to steady himself.

Arthur's band arrived. Bedivere and Sagramore were among his companions. The king jumped heartily down from his horse. "Merlin! I trust everything is well here. How are you? More to the point, how are my knights?"

"Things are not well, Arthur."

Peter emerged from the mill with a cloak and placed it around Merlin's shoulders. A sudden, particularly fierce gust of wind blew up, and he pulled the cloak tight around himself. "In the name of all that is human, Arthur, let us go inside before we freeze to death."

Inside, servants were busily placing more logs on the fires in all the rooms. Merlin, the king and his men arranged themselves around the main fireplace and warmed themselves eagerly. Merlin asked a servant to bring wine. "Not the remnants of the wine from last night. Open new bottles."

Then he turned to Arthur. "Somewhere in this mill is my valet, Robert. You must send men to find him and arrest him."

"Good heavens, Merlin, why?"

Merlin told him about the night's events and the deaths of George and Accolon. "The boy died a horrible death. But none of us could help him. We were all quite insensible. Robert gave us wine laced with some narcotic."

Two knights got to their feet and made ready to leave.

Merlin told them, "If he is not in the mill, then he has run away. That would not surprise me. You will see his footprints in the snow. Find him if you can."

He turned to Arthur. "You must send him back to Camelot under heavy guard. And send word to Simon to have his mother and brother arrested as well."

Bedivere sipped his wine. "Camelot's jailors will have a busy winter."

Merlin ignored this. "His mother is one of your cooks, Arthur. She has access to the castle's herb garden. I can only imagine what she must be growing there. Something to make us sleep. And something that can simulate symptoms of the plague." A thought struck him. "Belladonna, perhaps."

"But—but your valet?" Arthur was having trouble digesting it all.

Merlin took a large cup of wine. "Perhaps this will clear my head. My ears are ringing. Robert gave us all drugged wine last night."

"He tried to kill all of you? Why, for goodness' sake?"

"At the very least, he wanted to render us unconscious. As to motive, at this point I can only speculate." He glared at

Arthur accusingly. "Perhaps you know better than I could."

Arthur squirmed. "Enough of that."

Bedivere, too, seemed to be having trouble understanding. "But—but—a pastry cook and two serving boys. Why would they—?"

"As I said," Merlin told him, "I can only speculate as to what motivated them. I will know more when I have had the chance to interrogate them. But they have been present so often when death has occurred. Even at Darrowfield Castle. You sent them there, remember, Arthur? The murders at Stonehenge would have been most difficult for one man alone to have committed. One killer, three victims. Most improbable. But three killers, or even merely two, if the boys did it without their mother's assistance . . ."

"But—but—why would they have killed Darrowfield and his sons? What possible reason could they have?"

Calmly Merlin pronounced, "We shall know that soon enough."

A moment later the two knights reappeared, dragging Robert between them. His face showed fear and confusion, and he was struggling, but the knights were much too strong for him.

"No!" he cried. "Why are you doing this?"

The knights ignored his cries and pulled him toward the king and Merlin.

"Merlin, help me!" Robert pled. "Why have they taken me? I haven't done anything."

When they reached Merlin and the king, the two of them exchanged glances. Then Merlin turned to the boy. "You know perfectly well."

"No!"

"What was in the wine you gave us last night?"

"Nothing." The bewilderment in Robert's face was plain to see. "Nothing. I swear it."

Merlin looked to the king again and nodded. Arthur said to the knights, "Get two more knights from our main column. Take him back to Camelot. Guard him carefully. We will want to question him more thoroughly when we get back."

He went on. "You will almost certainly overtake the party that has Marmaduke and Lulua under guard. I can't imagine they're making very good time, not with those lumps. See to it that they're all placed in very secure cells in the dungeon."

The knights saluted and turned to go. Robert was still pleading with Merlin, protesting his innocence, as they dragged him off and shackled him. The boy fought, and one of the knights struck him. After that he was quiet.

Only minutes later they were ready to leave on their return to Camelot. Arthur and Merlin watched them depart and quickly disappear behind a curtain of falling snow. Arthur had an air of self-congratulation. "I knew you'd get to the bottom of the killings. You always do. But tell me. Why do you think he did it? What could have possessed him?"

Merlin looked away from him. "Can you really not guess? We have discussed it often enough."

"Don't be cryptic, Merlin. I want to know."

Merlin heaved an enormous sigh. "You want an heir. You have sired a great many potential ones. More, even, than is usual for a nobleman in this country. Does it really surprise you that some of them should resort to murder in hopes of gaining the throne?"

"Heirs? I—no!" Arthur caught him by the arm.

"I make no judgment, Arthur. But it must have occurred to you at some point that so many children, in or out of wedlock, would lead to many problems."

"That boy is not mine. He cannot be!"

Merlin shrugged. "I cannot imagine you keep track of all the women you have bedded. Robert's mother, Marian, is one of your servants. You must have had many opportunities to—"

"No! Merlin, I tell you, he is not mine. He and his

brother—don't you think I'd know it if I had fathered twins?"

"Then tell me, Arthur, what other motive could they have had for all this death? Darrowfield and his sons, John and Bruce, Accolon . . . Even if they were not all your bastards, people thought they were. And what about daughters? How many of them have you sired?"

"Darrowfield was twenty years older than me. There is no way he could possibly be my son. Not even with the help of a sorcerer. No, there must be some other explanation. I want you to find it."

"I can think of no other. But if *Your Majesty* wishes it—"

"Don't be sarcastic, Merlin. Morgan, Marmaduke, Marian and her sons . . . When I think about it my head spins."

Merlin turned pensive. "Marmaduke."

"What about him? You think that *he*—?"

"No, it is not that, Arthur. There was something he said. Something that resonated with me. But I cannot remember what."

"You will. You always do."

"If I could only remember." He looked at the king. "But for once I think you may be correct about these crimes, Arthur. I fear this is not over yet."

# NINE

The weather grew worse and worse. Waves of snow and wind alternated with driving rain. The air turned warmer, then cold again. Roads froze and thawed. Arthur's party made slow progress on its way to rebury the Stone, then slower, then a bit more rapid. Cloaks were not sufficient against the cold. Every few hours progress halted completely and the men built fires to warm themselves.

Merlin and Peter rode in their carriage, wrapped in blankets. The other carriage, carrying the Stone of Bran, followed just behind them. Since it was lighter, it gained less traction on muddy or icy roads and frequently had to be pushed or pulled past some difficult patch.

For a time a flock of ravens followed the party. Men took it as a bad omen, but when Arthur reminded them of Merlin's pets, they relaxed somewhat. When Merlin tried calling to the birds, they did not respond. "These are not my birds," he told Arthur. "They do not respond to the language I use with Roc and the others."

"Sorcerer."

Merlin ignored this. "Ravens are naturally scavengers. They are following us for the bits of food we leave behind us." But after two days, the ravens disappeared.

The journey passed through one tiny village after another. The sight of an approaching army, even a small one, invariably alarmed the residents. They expected to be conquered, pillaged, perhaps put to death. Assurances from Arthur and Bedivere helped calm these fears, but the people never really relaxed till the royal party passed on.

None of them seemed to have any clear idea who Arthur was. Bedivere would explain patiently that he was Arthur, King of all England, but the information meant nothing to them. The concept of England as a unified nation was alien. In a few hamlets the elders had heard of Arthur; in most they had not. Bedivere made certain the men in the party behaved decorously, foraged for their own food, left the women and boys alone.

From time to time Arthur joined Merlin in the carriage. Peter would discreetly exit and find a horse for the short time he needed it.

Merlin's arthritis was, inevitably, bothering him. "We really must talk to our people about installing more comfortable seats in these conveyances, Arthur."

Arthur's eyes twinkled. "Would you rather be riding a horse?"

Merlin snorted. "That is hardly the point." He paused. "How much farther is it to—what is the name of the place? Grosfalcon? I want to see the Stone reburied and get back to Camelot and comfort."

"Patience is a virtue, Merlin."

"Do not needle me, Arthur. I am in pain enough."

"About those coins we're having minted . . ."

The sudden shift of subject made Merlin's ears prick up. "Yes?"

"Do you see, now, why I think they're so important?

Why they are not simply a product of royal vanity? Most of the people in England seem to have no idea who their king is. Or that they have a king at all. The coins will help change that, build awareness that England is a nation now, not merely a collection of feuding fiefdoms."

"Yes, fine, Arthur, but—"

"And the people will know who their king is. A unified system of coinage will help us in our work. When we have to deal with other nations—when we treat with the Byzantine Empire, for instance—we will present a strong, united face. And when in time I name an heir, everyone in England will know him."

"Of course, Arthur. But how will you persuade the nation to use your coins? Can you imagine Marmaduke, for instance, requiring his subjects to convert to this new monetary system?"

"Marmaduke is on his way to jail."

"But how many other Marmadukes are there, in how many corners of Britain? How many of them will follow your dictum to use coins with your portrait?"

"They will, in time. You're my policy advisor, for heaven's sake. You're supposed to find ways to implement my policies, not find reasons why they won't work."

Merlin shrugged. He wanted to point out that Arthur's potential heirs were dying at an alarming rate, but it seemed wiser not to raise the issue.

Another messenger from Camelot caught up with the party. Among other missives, he had another letter for Merlin. But this one, surprisingly, was not from Nimue. It was from Merlin's other assistant, Petronus.

*Merlin,*

*I am writing because I know that you wanted to be informed of events at Camelot. Colin asked me to send you this letter. He wanted me to assure you that ev-*

*erything is under control here and that the news from
the surrounding countryside continues favorable.*

*Ships putting in at our ports carry rumors that this
plague has been deliberately spread by the Byzantines. Whether that is true or whether people are being unduly suspicious, we have no way of knowing.*

*Colin is not writing himself because he is ill. He
has developed a severe cold and has spent the last
two days in bed. But please do not worry. It is only a
cold, nothing more. And Marian of Bath and her son
Wayne are tending him.*

> *Your student and assistant,*
> *Petronus*

Merlin grew immediately alarmed. He took pen and pa-
per and wrote a response.

*Petronus,*

*Do not under any circumstances permit Marian and
Wayne anywhere near Colin. Another messenger is
on his way to Camelot with instructions to arrest
them on suspicion of murder. If by chance this should
reach you before that other messenger does, take this
note to Simon at once and see that they are arrested.*

> *Merlin*

He had the note countersigned by Arthur himself, so that
Simon could not question its authority, then sent it off, with
instructions to the rider to rest as little as humanly possible
and reach Camelot as rapidly as he could.

Arthur was puzzled by the urgency. "Why should you be
so concerned about Colin? No one thinks *he* is one of my
sons."

"With so many of your . . . possible successors eliminated, you may have to look elsewhere for the next . . . ruler. Colin is bright, educated, thoughtful, perceptive. You could do much worse than to name him."

"I hardly know the boy."

"That is not the point. It is not merely your bloodline that is under attack. It is the very concept of English stability and continuity. How well did you know John of Paintonbury?"

"Point taken. But—"

"I am not suggesting that you actually should adopt Colin as your heir, mind you. There would be too many . . . complications. But you have littered the country with children, Arthur. Whether you did it to spite Guenevere or simply because you are a robust young man is irrelevant. Colin has reached a position of some authority at Camelot. He is being trained by me—by your chief advisor—and has assumed a great deal of responsibility. How could anyone not suspect . . ." He let the thought trail off, unfinished. Nimue had become like a daughter to him. The thought that Arthur's indiscretions might have put her life at risk was too awful for him to think about. "Let us hope one or the other of our messengers reaches home before anything terrible happens."

Arthur fell silent. After a moment of quiet thought, he uttered softly one word. "Daughters."

"I beg your pardon, Arthur?"

"Nothing. Just a passing thought. I ought to get back to my horse and the head of the column. The knights there are carrying banners that announce me. I ought to be there." And he left the carriage quickly.

But the next afternoon he picked up the theme again.

A ferocious wind had been blowing, but at least the constant rain and snow had let up. Arthur and Bedivere rode side by side at the front of the column. Suddenly out of some bushes ran a young woman. She was in her late teens or perhaps her early twenties. She had blond hair and flashing blue eyes. And she was completely naked. On seeing the approaching knights, she darted back into the underbrush.

Arthur shouted, "After her!" Two men detached themselves from the column and spurred their horses into the dense brush. A moment later they returned, holding her between them. She was fighting like a cornered bobcat.

Seeing how many knights there were, she quieted. Staring directly at Arthur she asked, "Which one?"

Arthur had no idea what she meant. "I beg your pardon, young woman? I am Arthur, King of all England."

Unexpectedly she stood up tall and proud. "Never mind all that. Which one of you wants me first?"

Arthur and Bedivere exchanged puzzled glances. Bedivere told her, "You are under some misapprehension, miss. We are not here as raiders or conquerors. This man is your king."

She laughed. "I want you, too. All of you, or as many as it takes to wear me out. Come on. Let's get at it. There are enough of you that this will take all day and all night." She turned back to the bushes where they had taken her. "Tom, come on out. There are a lot of them, and from the looks of them some of them will want you, not me."

A young man, about her age and blond like her, stuck his head out timidly.

"Come on, Tom, hop to it. There are some nice ones, too."

Tom stepped forward out of the bushes. He was her age or perhaps a bit older. Like his companion he was quite naked.

Arthur turned to the nearest of his servants. "Get them some blankets and some boots. It is far too cold for . . . for that state." He turned to the woman. "Who are you? What are you called?"

"Gillian."

"And what place is this, Gillian?"

"It is called Treasel."

He exchanged glances with Bedivere. "Those damned old maps of ours." To Gillian he said, "We are seeking a place called Grosfalcon. Is it nearby?"

"About ten miles. Just past Smalfalcon. Come on, what are you waiting for? Get that armor off and let's get to it."

"I'm afraid that is out of the question. I am—suppose there should be a child?"

"None of us will live that long. The plague is coming."

"But—"

"We will be dead soon enough. Are we going to get down to some lovemaking or aren't we?"

"No, we are not."

"Then let us go, so we can get back to it. It's your loss, King."

The man Tom had been standing just behind her. He pulled the blanket more tightly around himself. "We were making love."

"So we gathered. In this awful weather? You'll catch pneumonia or worse."

Tom shrugged. "It doesn't make any difference, does it?"

Puzzled, Arthur told him, "No, I suppose it doesn't. You say this road will take us to Grosfalcon?"

Gillian nodded. "Just stay on it. If you don't want me—" She winked at Tom. "If you don't want us, there will be plenty of others there."

Arthur was more and more bewildered by their manner. "We have told you, we're not a conquering force. We—"

Tom pushed his hand inside Gillian's blanket and began to fondle her. She laughed and they both ran off into the undergrowth.

One of the knights made to follow them but Arthur told him to leave them alone. The column resumed its forward progress. "At least we know we're on the right road." He called for Perceval to join them. "Does any of this territory look familiar?"

"No, Majesty. I approached it from the south when I found the Stone. But I did hear of a nearby town called Smalfalcon."

Bedivere was working with the maps. "There doesn't seem to be any indication of it."

"Grosfalcon isn't much of a place. Smalfalcon must be even smaller."

"Excellent deduction."

Perceval kept an eye on the bushes, hoping for another glimpse of the lovers. But there was no sign of them. "It can't be much more than a few old farms. Grosfalcon is not much bigger than that."

Once the party was moving again, Arthur rejoined Merlin in his carriage. "You heard about that young couple we found?"

Merlin smiled. "The copulating couple, yes. Word filtered back along the column before they were out of sight."

"Strange thing. She was a good-looking girl. Downright pretty. The type of woman I've always found attractive. And her invitation could not have been much bolder. But I had no sexual thoughts at all."

"Perhaps you could become a Christian monk."

"Stop it. All I kept thinking was, 'My bastard children—I've made too many of them already.'"

"Perhaps there would not have been a child, Arthur. These country women are very good at that sort of thing."

"There was no temptation at all, Merlin. None." He seemed astonished to hear himself saying it.

"You are getting old, Arthur. Or growing wise, which is not always the same thing."

"Something you said yesterday has been haunting me. Daughters."

Merlin looked at him quizzically. "You said it, not I."

"I must have some. I mean, if only by chance, some of the children I've fathered would be—"

"You are wondering where they are? And what they are like?"

"Exactly, Merlin." He looked at the old man. "Tell me, do you ever regret not marrying?"

"No, never. I could never give a wife the attention she deserves. Half of my life is inside my head. I could never be fair to her."

"But . . . but a daughter. To help you? To take care of you? Even a stoic like you would have to find comfort in that."

Merlin grew uncharacteristically dreamy. For a moment his eyes had a faraway, hazy look. "A daughter, yes." Then he snapped out of it. "I hope our messenger reaches Camelot quickly."

"Your talent for changing the subject amazes me at times."

"I have not changed it."

"Don't get cryptic on me, Merlin. Here." He had a wineskin hanging at his side. "Have a drink of this. It will warm you."

"No, thank you, Arthur."

"Another blanket, then, to help cover you."

"I am fine. Winter is the truth."

"If I lose you to pneumonia . . ."

Merlin laughed. "I am made of heartier stuff."

"If you had a daughter . . ."

"Arthur, go and lead your knights."


Progress continued at a slow pace. The skies remained fair but the cold, driving wind never let up. The terrain changed from thick forest to low, sparsely treed hills.

Here and there along the way they spotted more love-makers. Couples, groups, some naked, some fully or partially clothed, some mature, some young, some not much more than children in the first flower of adolescence. Many of them seemed to be drunk in the bargain. None of them seemed to mind being spotted.

Along the column there was more and more talk about it, some disapproving, some not. Gildas lectured everyone who would listen about sin; most of his target audience laughed at him. But everyone was as fascinated as he by these brazen copulating people.

In time they reached Smalfalcon. It was not much more than a widening of the road, with a few small houses and a barn or two. Dogs, pigs, chickens ran loose in the street. Naked children chased them happily.

A mature man in rags, his arms around a bare-breasted woman young enough to be his granddaughter, waved and approached. "Hello. If you've come here to plunder, go right ahead. Take anything you want. Take any*one* you want. There is no need for any violence." He held up a cup. "Have some wine. Enjoy life, as we've learned to." He kissed his young woman and she kissed him back. They became lost in their embrace, oblivious to anything else.

Bedivere spoke to shake them out of it. "What is this place? Is this really Smalfalcon?"

The woman looked at him and laughed.

"Your children and your livestock are running unattended."

Her companion joined her laughter. "They already know how to enjoy themselves. It is we adults who have to relearn."

Slowly other residents of the hamlet were appearing. Most were quite naked. Most were drinking. Most stared at the column of knights with frank indifference. Here and there couples engaged in sexual play. Merlin left his coach and joined Arthur at the head of the column.

Finally Arthur spoke, in his best command voice. "What kind of town is this? Where are the elders? Who is in charge?"

The man who had approached them originally spoke up. "I suppose I am. I am the mayor. Why do you care?" His female companion left his side, tore off her clothes happily and joined a trio of revelers.

Bedivere told the man who Arthur was. "You should display more decorum before your king."

"Decorum? All that is over with. We're dead men."

"The air is frigid. Why is everyone unclothed?"

"Why should the dead bother with clothing?"

Arthur watched the woman and her new companions. "That's mighty lively activity for corpses."

"Have you not heard? There's plague in England. It's going to take all of us." He took a hearty drink.

Arthur looked back along the column. A few of his men had dismounted and seemed to be joining the more forward of Smalfalcon's residents. Sir Sagramore was in the process of removing his armor. A handful of squires and servants, already half undressed, were romping with the locals, kissing, fondling . . .

Bishop Gildas shouted an order to them to stop. They ignored him. He rushed to Arthur's side. "Arthur, sire, we must put a stop to this rampant immorality."

Arthur was equally concerned at the breakdown in discipline but amused at Gildas's intensity. "How, would you suggest?"

"*Order* them to stop, that is how."

"Gildas, you are a man of the world. You're an Italian, for that matter. Surely you must realize that no order known to mankind can stop hormones from flowing." He looked back along the line of men. "And frankly, I'd say they aren't simply flowing but beginning to gush."

Gildas frowned. "But this kind of carnal lust—"

"I'll see what I can do, all right?"

The bishop, mollified but sullen, went back to his place.

Arthur conferred quickly with Bedivere and Merlin. "I hate to admit it, but Gildas is right. We can't permit this."

"They are knights, yes, Arthur, but they are men, too." Bedivere was eyeing a red-haired young man wistfully.

"I would suggest," Merlin offered, "that we simply move on. Quickly, before this takes hold of more of our men. It will be hard enough to stop it now. If we let it get further out of hand . . ."

Arthur sighed heavily. "I suppose you're right. Bed, give the order to form up. We'll move out at once. It does seem a pity to waste all these willing young women, though."

"The young men seem equally willing. Not to mention the old ones." Bedivere was getting caught up in the carnal atmosphere. "Look at that trio over there." He pointed. "Not one of them can be under sixty."

The trinity of merrymakers disappeared behind a cottage. Merlin scowled at the place where they'd been. "At their age."

"There are times," Arthur goaded, "when you sound more like Bishop Gildas than either of you would like to admit."

"Do not be rude, Arthur. Let us get moving and complete our mission as quickly as we can, so we can get back to Camelot. We have a 'sacred relic' to bury, remember? Or is it a blasphemous pagan idol?"

Arthur scowled. "Look at what the plague is doing. And it hasn't even struck here yet. We have to do what we can to stop it. Come on, Bed, let's get the men back in order and move on."

And so with some difficulty Bedivere got everyone back into the column. There was grumbling. Many of the men considered him a spoilsport anyway; this only confirmed that opinion. But Bedivere pointed to Arthur in his gleaming battle armor to remind them of their duty. And the column moved on.

Away from the hamlet, the people and their carnal activities were less in evidence. Here and there among the trees a couple or a group would be seen, copulating gleefully. Those of them that saw the line of soldiers waved. Gildas registered more displeasure with each incident.

At one point the trees thinned out and a small lea appeared. In it was a man cavorting with a sheep. Gildas spurred his horse to Arthur's side and sputtered. "This . . . must . . . be . . . stopped."

Arthur was amused. "We're in the country, Gildas. Even in normal times—"

"It is a violation of God's law!"

"Then I suggest we leave it to God to punish it."

"But—but—"

"What's wrong?" Bedivere was laughing openly at the bishop's fervor. "Can't we trust your God to enforce his own laws?"

Gildas sulked, fell silent and returned to his place in the column.

In his carriage Merlin was only vaguely aware of everything that was happening. But he could see how unhappy Gildas was, and it pleased him. Every time he looked out of the carriage and saw the frowning bishop, he chuckled.

"Do you really think you should ridicule him so openly?" Peter asked.

"Gildas is a fool." Merlin laughed. "As if there was some way to persuade people to stop enjoying themselves."

"But . . . but a sheep! Really, Merlin."

"I would not worry, Peter. There is no danger the sheep will get pregnant."

"That isn't the issue, and you know it."

"What I know," Merlin told him calmly, "is that anything that annoys that man cannot be all bad."

"His religion has moral standards. Is that such a bad thing?"

Merlin switched to his schoolteacherly demeanor. "The greatest 'Christian' power in the world is Justinian's Byzantine Empire. Or 'Roman Empire' as they so grandly call themselves." He wrinkled his nose. "Most of its grandees could not find Rome on a good map."

Peter watched the industrious shepherd. "What has that to do with Gildas and that sheep-loving fool out there?"

"There have been whispers that the Byzantines may have sent this plague to decimate us. It seems unlikely to me, but they have been known to spread disease among their enemies in the past." He was rueful. "And for better or worse, they seem to count us among their enemies. Or at least as a people to be conquered."

The carriage had moved on past the little meadow. "But a man with a sheep, Merlin!"

"Do you not know the stories they tell about Justinian's wife, the Most Christian Empress Theodora?"

"No, I suppose I don't. What about her?"

"She came from lowly origins. She was a slave. And she used to perform in the arena." Merlin gazed directly at him. "Doing things with wild beasts. Donkeys, oxen, *sheep*. Even apes and worse."

"But that was in the past, before Justinian fell in love with her and elevated her to the throne."

"Nevertheless. The Byzantines were Christians even then. The fact that they would countenance that kind of entertainment, much less revere a woman who took part in it . . ." He shrugged, then peered at Peter. "You are not a Christian, are you?"

"No, of course not. But—"

"There are more ways to be human than Gildas's worldview could ever permit."

"I know that, Merlin. But—"

"We must never be too hasty to condemn other people for their humanity. Your energy would be better channeled into finding Lord Darrowfield's killer."

"Was the killer not 'being human,' too?"

"He—or she—took a life. No society can countenance such a thing."

"Of course not, Merlin. But if you know how much like Gildas you sound—"

"Rubbish."

"You both want moral strictures. You simply disagree about where the boundary should be set."

"No, we disagree about why the boundary is necessary at all. If I ever become as prudish as Gildas, you may call me on it."

Peter laughed at him. "Bishop Merlin."

"Stop it."

It took a moment for Peter's laughter to die down. Then he rode in silence, leaving Merlin to his thoughts. But Merlin found himself wondering, for the first time, about Peter's soundness.

Just before dusk the party approached Grosfalcon. The wind had calmed, but a light, gentle snow was falling. The terrain was more and more hilly; in the far distance, the Welsh mountains could be glimpsed through the snow. In the middle distance the village itself loomed. And it was ablaze with light.

Arthur commented on it to Bedivere. "It looks as if they're having a festival. They must have a thousand torches burning."

"It is winter." Bed shrugged. "People need light and heat."

"At my father's court, we used to celebrate Bran's birthday with lights and music. And at my mother's court we celebrated feasts in honor of the Morrigan, the goddess of death. But I can't recall either place being lit up as brightly as this little backwater village. What do you suppose can be behind it?"

Again Bedivere shrugged. "Bumpkins."

But it soon became apparent that the lights were spreading out from Grosfalcon into the surrounding forest. Before long, torchbearers reached Arthur's column. There were dozens of people, waving torches about wildly, reveling, singing, dancing, making love. Some were dressed, some not, some only partially. Musicians played loud, frolicsome airs. Boys carrying wineskins accompanied them, pouring libations for any and all who wanted to drink. Dogs followed them all, happily snapping up scraps of food that they dropped. Some of the torches set fire to low-hanging tree branches. A group of merrymakers, most of them only partly dressed, set fire to a thick bush, then danced around it in a circle, as if it was a perverse kind of maypole. The falling snow, plus the snow already lying on the trees, made the fires sputter out quickly.

Arthur summoned Perceval to his side. "Well, we're here. Now, where is this barn where you found the Stone?"

Perceval held up a hand to shield his eyes. "There is a hill just east of the village, a little one but steep. The barn is on the far side of it."

Gildas followed Perceval to the front of the column. "Arthur, look at all this glee. You must order these people to stop at once."

"You think," Arthur said with amusement, "the most powerful king on earth could order a stop to all this? Honestly, Gildas, there are times when I think Merlin is right—your view of the world is so terribly naïve."

"The social order is breaking down, Arthur. Look at them. Morality itself is breaking down. Order must be restored."

The king chuckled. "What would you suggest?"

"Arrest them. Use the whip and the sword."

Bedivere spoke up. "Small as this village is, there are more people here than we have knights. Arresting them all is a practical impossibility."

"One of them, then. Is it beyond your power to make an example of one of them?"

Arthur heaved a deep sigh. "For heaven's sake, Gildas, look around you. It's not as if this was only a matter of a few intransigents. It's the entire countryside. We've been seeing this for miles. We'll be lucky to keep our own men under control, much less the general population. Bed, go and fetch Merlin. I want to hear what he makes of all this."

Bedivere spurred his horse and rode back to the carriage. Gildas snorted.

A band of young women approached and began flirting outrageously with the knights. Arthur shouted an order to maintain discipline. But it was apparent the knights were tempted. They would not maintain their self-control very long.

Bedivere returned a moment later with Merlin. Arthur briefly explained the situation. "Gildas here wants me to arrest everyone in sight. What do you think?"

Gildas glared at Merlin as if daring him to disagree. But Merlin was not about to be cowed. "The snow is beginning to fall more heavily. It will put an end to all this . . . what would you call it? Celebration?"

"Order must be restored!" The bishop bellowed it.

"It is a simple matter, then, Gildas. All you have to do is roar a few orders at the citizens and they will stop." Merlin paused to give Gildas an opening, but the bishop grumped and stayed silent. Merlin turned to Arthur. "In the name of everything human, Arthur, let us get the bloody Stone buried and get back to Camelot before winter descends on us with its full force."

Arthur brushed a snowflake from his eyelash. "Gildas does have a point, Merlin. We do have to restore order."

"It might be more useful for you to restore clothing."

Arthur ignored the comment. "Look around. You can hardly deny it. The question is how to do it."

Merlin sighed. "Arthur, think. For once, winter will be a blessing. Cold weather is already ending the plague in the southwest. It will put an end to this revelry soon enough, as well. Nature will correct itself. The natural order will reassert itself. You will see.

"When we return to Camelot, you must send heralds to

every corner of the country with the news that the plague
has died. It is fear of the plague that engenders this kind of
ribaldry. The end of the disease will bring an end to this,
too. When the people realize that death is not at hand—that
they must scramble to keep themselves and their families
alive, just as they always have . . ." He left the thought unfinished.

"Perhaps you're right." Arthur turned pensive, at the
same time eyeing an attractive young woman.

"Arthur!" Merlin was shocked to see it. "Have you forgotten everything we've talked about?"

"No, of course not. But—"

"Remember what happened to Ulysses' men in the land
of the lotus-eaters."

Gildas snorted at this. "Pagan rot."

"You think there is only one ancient book that contains
any wisdom?"

But Arthur had listened to enough. "Stop it, both of you.
I need to think. Let us ride on. We still have a way to go
before we reach that barn of Perceval's. By the way, where
is Perceval?"

He looked around. Perceval, along with half a dozen
other knights, had dismounted and was talking to a young
woman. Some of the lesser knights were already locked in
embrace with locals. Several were kissing and fondling.

Arthur was shocked at the lack of modesty—and discipline. "Bed, get them back into line. We have a mission to
complete."

Bedivere and a few of the older knights bellowed orders
and managed, slowly, to restore order and discipline. Arthur
muttered, "Lotus-eaters, indeed." After a few minutes the column was ready to move on.

Arthur was expecting Grosfalcon to be abandoned. But the
town was populated, albeit sparsely. Children played in the

streets, unattended. Some were crying, looking about futilely, even desperately, for their parents. Elderly citizens shuffled about, evidently trying to maintain some semblance of life as usual. A few parties in the prime of life reeled drunkenly, oblivious to what was happening around them, or perhaps merely ignoring it.

Merlin joined the king and Bedivere as they surveyed still another part of the realm that had seemingly abandoned any sense of order. Seeing the concern in Arthur's face, he tried to be reassuring. "Winter will do its work, Arthur."

"I don't want winter, I want England."

"Unfortunately that isn't your choice."

Arthur ignored this and stopped an old woman. "Who are you?" he asked.

She glared. "Who are *you*?"

Bedivere explained who Arthur was, but the woman seemed unimpressed. "King of the Britons? Don't make me laugh. You think anyone here cares about a king? Especially one who lives at the far end of the country?"

"Arthur is king. He rules here."

The woman spat. "Let's see him stop this plague, then."

Merlin started explaining in his best teacherly voice that the cold weather would bring an end to the plague. But Arthur interrupted this. "Who rules here, woman? Who represents order? Where is the local baron?"

"Are you trying to be funny?" She glared at him, then at Merlin. "And who are you?"

Merlin introduced himself.

And unexpectedly the woman smiled. "The wizard? I've heard of *you*."

"I assure you, I am not a—"

Another woman, slightly younger, joined her. "You are looking for Lord Tambour?"

"Tambour?" Bedivere consulted one of his maps. "As near as I can recall, the warlord here was named Timothy." He lowered his voice and told Arthur, "You remember him,

Arthur? He fought side by side with Marmaduke." He made a sour face. "He was never much of a warrior, as I recall."

"No, I don't remember him at all."

"He was that kind of baron. I suspect he gained power here because no one else could be bothered. Look at this place. It's almost as forlorn as Paintonbury."

The younger woman said loudly, "Tambour seized power three years ago."

"Why was Camelot not informed?"

Her older companion laughed. "You *are* trying to be funny."

Arthur ignored this. "Where is Tambour now?"

"Who knows?" The younger of the two shrugged. "He ran off with the group of catamites who have always surrounded him. The plague—"

"The plague is dying. No one here is threatened. The world will soon be itself again."

"So the men here can start drinking and fighting among themselves for power? Now all they do is drink. My husband ran off with Tambour. Honestly, death by plague would be a blessing."

Bedivere nudged Arthur. "Look."

At the far end of the street stood a figure in swirling black robes. A woman. She slowly raised her arms as if she was trying to cast a spell, or at least as if she wanted to appear so.

Softly Arthur whispered, "Morgan." Then, in his best command voice, he called, "Sister!"

Morgan nodded slightly but said nothing in response.

Arthur thanked the two women for their information and spurred his horse to meet Morgan. The rest of the column followed.

"Morgan. How interesting to find you here. What the devil do you want?"

She was serene. "I am the high priestess of England, remember? I have business everywhere in the realm."

Gildas left his place in the column and moved to a spot just behind the king. In a whisper he said, "Ask her about Marmaduke and Lulua. She must have been a party to their treason."

But before Arthur could say anything, Morgan intoned, "I am seeking my disciple in these parts. A fine priestess called Lulua. But she seems to have vanished. I don't suppose you've had any intelligence of her, Brother?"

Gildas could not restrain himself. "Your disciple is under arrest for treason." He smiled a smug little smile. "Along with your minion Marmaduke."

Morgan frowned deeply. Ignoring Gildas she asked, "Is this true, Brother?"

Arthur shrugged. "They tried to have me killed. I hope you don't mind that I survived them."

"Lulua is a good woman, a loyal servant of the crown of England."

"Perhaps so, Morgan, but she hardly seems to know who wears that crown."

Merlin joined the conversation. "How peculiar that you have shown up here, in the midst of their treachery. You are not a part of it, by any chance?"

Morgan glared. "Are you going to permit your servants to continue addressing me in this churlish manner, Arthur? Respect for the royal bloodline would dictate—"

"Respect for the royal bloodline would dictate that subjects not plot against their king, Morgan. Or do you suppose that yours is the only royal blood that matters?"

"How did you get here ahead of us?" Merlin asked her.

Serenely she replied, "I control the elements. The gods—"

"It is not possible that other rebel barons and their, er, priestesses provided you with safe passage, is it?"

She stiffened. "You are here to rebury the most sacred object in the kingdom. As high priestess, it is most fitting that I be here. It was most impious of you to leave me behind." A faint smile appeared. "Or to try to."

Arthur sighed. "Then let us get on with the burying. But I warn you, Morgan, I am going to get to the bottom of all this. If I find evidence that you were complicit with Lulua and Marmaduke—"

"You will not."

He put on a tight grin. "Time will tell, I suppose. I recall instructing you to remain at Camelot. Yet you are here."

Morgan shrugged.

"We will take that up later. Meanwhile, let's find this barn and bury the bloody Stone. I can't tell you how sorry I am I ever set my knights to find the damned thing."

Gildas sensed an opening. "The plague, Your Majesty, is—"

"In the name of everything human, Gildas, not now." Merlin was tired and impatient. He turned to the king. "Another cold wind is kicking up, Arthur. Let us get this done with and get back to Camelot."


The citizens of Grosfalcon displayed little curiosity as the column proceeded through their village. They went on about their own business, which in most cases appeared to be pleasure. Drinking, gorging themselves with food, lovemaking . . . Nothing the knights might have done, short of actual violence, could have distracted them from their hedonistic pursuits.

The sight of it made Arthur glum. "So this is what plague does to society. We have never experienced one before, not in my lifetime. There are histories of course, but—"

"Be grateful they aren't offering any resistance to us." Bedivere spoke like a military man.

"Seeing any semblance of social-order breakdown is hardly a thing to be grateful for, Bed."

"Not meeting hostility *is*."

A black stallion had been found for Morgan. It was grazing in a field just outside the town, and it had apparently been broken. Or nearly so. Every now and then it snorted and bolted. Morgan, unruffled, manage to calm the animal every time. Arthur had the impression she was whispering something to it. A sidesaddle was found and the mount prepared for her.

But she was unhappy at having to ride. "I am a member of the royal house. I merit a carriage."

Arthur was sanguine. "When the king himself is riding horseback, it ill becomes his sister to demand any more than that."

"That fool advisor of yours is in a carriage. I deserve no less."

"Merlin is old and infirm, Morgan. You know that. Don't be disagreeable."

"You should tell that to him. He is not too 'old and infirm' to make snide comments." She scowled and mounted her horse.

In his carriage, Merlin was restless. He complained to Peter. "What on earth is she doing here? How did she get here so rapidly?"

Peter made a slight shrug. "Perhaps she really is a witch."

Merlin ignored this. "She has a larger network of supporters than we ever realized. Or at any rate a more efficient one."

"More and more of her people seem to be defecting to this new religion." Peter seemed amused by it. "I mean, Gildas does seem an improbable leader, but he is making headway in England. Even Lord Darrowfield—"

"Gildas is hardly alone. More and more of his 'monks,' as they call themselves, keep showing up in various parts of the country. But the Christians are Morgan's problem."

"Then—?"

"I am concerned about Morgan's connection to Lulua and Marmaduke. If she has been complicit in their treason . . . If her whole vast network is treasonous . . ."

"I see what you mean."

"Arthur's . . . what shall I call them? . . . potential heirs are being eliminated, one by one. Morgan has every reason in the world to want to see that happen. She wants the throne herself, after all. Having Marmaduke and Lulua eliminate her brother for her would have . . ." He made a vague gesture. "I am getting old, Peter. This is too much for my poor old mind. Lord Darrowfield . . ."

"Your mind is as sharp as a razor, and you know it. You can quote enormous passages from Plotinus and Plato. You're the smartest man I've ever known."

He sighed. "Thank you, I suppose. But if I am so smart, why can I not understand all these murders? Why can I not find the connection?"

Peter fell pointedly silent and glanced out of the carriage. Morgan was complaining about something, gesticulating wildly at the king, who was ignoring her. Finally he said, "You're too suspicious, Merlin. Maybe the seeming plague deaths really are deaths from the plague."

"Nothing human is ever that simple. Or that innocent. That poor boy who died at the mill can hardly have been a victim of the plague. But if he was working for the interests of Morgan and Lulua . . . and if they were concerned he might not keep silent about it . . ."

"*If* is a game for idle scholars, Merlin."

"Since you only a moment ago told me that is what I am, what is your point?"

Peter laughed. "You are anything but idle. Your mind is more agile than any I have ever known. But I give up. Yes, the plague deaths were not really plague deaths. Does that satisfy you?"

"I have not been satisfied since I became an adult, Peter."

Peter glanced outside again. In the distance he could see a huge, rambling ruin of a barn. He was grateful of it. "It appears we've reached our destination."

Merlin looked, saw the barn, smiled. "Finally. We can be done with this fool's errand and get back home."

"But . . . I thought Perceval said this area was abandoned. There are people."

Merlin sighed. "Another complication, I suppose."

All day the weather had stayed sunny and dry. But more and more clouds built up, so gradually that Arthur was barely aware of them. Then the wind kicked up. He wrapped his cloak about himself as tightly as he could and glanced up at the sky. "Look, Bed. The world never stops working its mischief."

"We'll have more rain, Arthur. Or snow, more likely."

"We have reached our goal. We can bury the Stone soon, then we can get back to Camelot. Back home."

"You think it won't be winter there?"

"Be quiet."

They rounded the base of a low hill, keeping the barn in sight. It was huge, and in ruins. Planks were missing from the walls; the thatched roof was in tatters. Before and around it was a wheat field, or what had been one. The crop had not been harvested; it had all gone to seed. Weeds grew everywhere. At the far side of the barn and stretching off into the distance was what appeared to be a graveyard. Painted wooden grave markers were toppled or listing badly.

Arthur shaded his eyes to see better. "That must be it. It's larger than I expected. Larger than any barn I've ever seen. It could make a good, small castle."

"With its own cemetery."

"Get Perceval."

Bedivere pulled his horse out of the column and headed back. A few moments later he returned with Sir Perceval beside him. They all consulted; Perceval assured them that, yes, this was the ruined barn where he had found the Stone. "The locals call it the Barn of Bran." He wrinkled his nose. "Peasants."

Morgan rode to the head of the column. "Well, Arthur, we

have arrived. You are prepared to do your sacred duty?"

Just behind her came Gildas. "It appears this is the blasphemous spot, Arthur. Are we ready to rebury the profane stone?"

Arthur looked from one of them to the other, smirking. "We are prepared to rebury it, whether it be sacred or profane. But first it appears we must pass through a local festival of some kind." He gestured vaguely.

There were in fact a half dozen people in the field between the cemetery and the barn. They had set up kiosks and were selling things. Little flags and banners that waved in the wind, little pictures of the god Bran, miniature skulls carved out of local stone, strings of prayer beads. Two of the stands were vending food and beverages.

Merlin took it all in. "What the devil can this be?"

Arthur was equally puzzled. He dismounted and approached one of the kiosks and signaled Bed to follow. It was manned by a stout, middle-aged fellow dressed in peasant homespun. Seeing Arthur approaching, he smiled. "Afternoon, guv'nor."

Bedivere stiffened. "This personage is no mere governor, my good man. He is Arthur, your king."

The man laughed. "As you say. What can I do for you?"

"First, you can tell us who you are."

"Duck. Richard Duck. At your service, sirs. What can I do for you?" He gestured at his goods. "Little soapstone replicas of the authentic skull of the god Bran? Guaranteed genuine, sirs. And blessed by the god himself."

Arthur glanced around. Nearly everyone in sight had stopped moving and was watching these armored newcomers. He turned to Richard. "For a beginning, you can tell us what's going on here. Is this some sort of fair?"

"No, sir. This is business as always."

"Business?"

Richard seemed mildly astonished. "Do you not know

where you are, sirs? This is one of the holiest places in all England."

"I had heard rumors to that effect, yes. But surely the Stone of Bran has been dug up and taken to Camelot. There are no relics here."

"The ground itself is holy, sir, made so by the Stone of Bran. Or at least that's what people want to believe. They come from all over the country to see this place. It is more productive for us than farming crops." He lowered his voice to a confidential whisper. "This is how we make our living. Ever since that knight dug up the Stone here—"

"Sir Perceval."

"Yes, him. Ever since he dug up the stone, living here has become quite lucrative. I, for instance, have all these relics of the Great God Bran." He gestured at several tables in his stand. They were covered with tiny polished stones, pictures of the god and various other objects not easily identifiable. "You want to buy one, don't you?" Undisguised avarice showed in his face. "You and all your men?"

Bedivere spoke up. "We do not. How recently did you manufacture these 'relics'?"

Richard feigned shock. "'Manufacture'? These articles are genuine, sir. I swear it. It is all these others"—he made a sweeping gesture to take in the other kiosks—"who counterfeit the holy objects they sell."

"Of course."

The other vendors were slowly getting over their shock at the arrival of this small army, or over their fear that the knights meant trouble. One by one they left their kiosks. Carrying goods, they approached the men. It was clear from their manner they smelled sales. Some of the knights met them with interest; others tried their best to ignore them.

Morgan, seeing it all, stiffened. "Bedivere, tell these people who I am."

Bedivere looked to Arthur, who nodded. Bed announced, "This lady is Morgan le Fay, the high priestess of England."

Richard smiled a wide smile. "Then you would certainly like to buy a holy relic, wouldn't you, ma'am?"

"I would not. How dare you all profane this holy place with"—she wrinkled her nose—"commerce."

"Profane, ma'am? This is our living. People come from miles around to see the barn where the god's skull was interred. We're planning to renovate it, you spruce it up a bit, so we can charge people a fee to go inside. Do you think he gave us this gift only to take it away?"

"This is the resting place of the god." Morgan made herself sound ominous and imposing.

Gildas could not resist. "Or a part of him."

Morgan glared at him.

Richard went on as if she'd said nothing. "Do you think Bran wants us to starve?"

The three of them started bickering, with Morgan arguing for the sacred nature of the place, Gildas arguing the opposite and Richard interjecting occasional comments about his livelihood.

Arthur was enjoying it, but after a few moments he ordered them all to be silent and sent Bedivere back along the column to disperse the other Bran merchants.

Just then the first few drops of rain fell. Arthur glanced at the sky. "Perceval, what is that barn like? Is there enough of a roof to keep us dry?"

Perceval shrugged. "A few of us, I suppose, Sire."

"Then let's get moving. I'm not in a mood for more rain."

The vendors watched glumly as their prospects reformed their column and made for the barn.

Inside, the Barn of Bran was cavernous. Shafts of light penetrated through holes in the roof, but the place was gloomy nonetheless; Arthur ordered torches. There were wooden stalls for horses or other livestock; much of the wood was rotten, and there was no sign any animals had been kept there for years. A broken wagon wheel leaned against one wall. Coils of rope, all of them badly frayed, filled the corners. Rotting wooden planks made up the floor; many of them were missing, and dirt, or mud, showed. Everything was in ruins, and it was all covered in a thick layer of dust. Rainwater dripped through the holes in the roof.

There was room enough for Arthur, Merlin, Peter, Gildas, Morgan and the most important knights. The lesser knights, the squires and the servants were to camp outside, in the overgrown field. Bedivere offered to stay outside with them.

Once inside, Gildas made a comment to the effect that a sacred place should be more presentable, Morgan started to argue with him, and Arthur hushed them both. Then he called Perceval. "Is this place as you remember it?"

"Yes, Arthur. Perhaps a bit more run-down, but quite recognizable."

"Whatever possessed you to dig for the Stone in a place like this?"

The knight shrugged. "I had tried dozens of places that were more promising. I was on the verge of giving up my quest and going back to Camelot when I heard tell of the Barn of Bran, and so . . ." He shrugged again.

"And where was it buried?"

Perceval pointed. "Back there, in the last stall."

Merlin chimed in. "The Great God Bran has rather odd architectural taste, hasn't he? You should see the tombs of the gods in Egypt. Magnificent structures. Limestone and rose-red granite. They tower above—"

"That's enough, Merlin. Perceval, get to work reburying the thing, will you? Let us hope it brings an end to the plague."

"Let us hope," Merlin said to Peter at the bottom of his breath, rubbing his arthritic shoulder, "that it brings an end to this damn fool mission. I want to get home to Camelot and my ravens and my soft dry bed."

Morgan insisted that there had to be a ceremony for the reinterment. Gildas countered that there should be none but an exorcism of the demons he was certain were lurking. When Arthur asked Merlin for his opinion on the matter, he complained about the leaking roof. The king finally decided that any benefit a ceremony might confer would be more than offset by the constant bickering. He forbade Morgan to pray over the stone skull or Gildas to celebrate its disposal.

After everyone had eaten dinner, after dark, Arthur summoned Morgan to his presence. Merlin was at his side. Torches brightened the barn's gloom. Morgan was in a pleasant humor. "I'm glad you've come to your senses, Brother. The Stone of Bran is too important not to be prayed over by the king and the high priestess when it is reburied."

"That is already done, Morgan." Merlin offered the news cheerfully. "The Stone is in the ground."

"I beg your pardon? Arthur, is this true?"

The king nodded.

"But . . . but it is sacred. I naturally assumed you would come to your senses and there would be a formal ceremony to reinter it. With appropriate prayers—led by myself, not by that fool who calls himself—what is it? Bishop?"

"Morgan, it is done."

"But, Brother—"

"That isn't what I want you for." He was offhand. "I've had Perceval and the others bury the Stone six feet deep, exactly as if it was a real burial. Let us hope that, one way or another, it ends this plague. But Morgan, I doubt if your prayers could reach it."

"Then—?" She scowled.

Merlin took up the conversation. Looking as stern as he could manage, he told her, "I'm afraid it is a delicate matter, Morgan. His Majesty wants to know what you are doing here."

For a moment Morgan was off guard. Then, "It was at my urging that you made this journey. Have you forgotten?"

"Indeed he has not." Merlin pressed on, unruffled by her manner. "Your urging and Gildas's. But His Majesty specifically instructed you to remain at Camelot."

"I have duties. The high priestess of England can hardly—"

"Morgan." Arthur cut her off. "I want to know about your priestess Lulua. And about Marmaduke of Paintonbury. What is your connection to them?"

She was serene. "Lulua is a good and faithful servant to the gods."

"And the fat warlord Marmaduke?"

She made herself smile, a politician's smile. "Surely his corpulence is testament to the bounty of your rule, Arthur."

Merlin was in no mood for her evasions. He glanced at the king, who nodded faintly. "His Majesty wishes to know whether you were aware of their treason. And whether you were involved in it, however slightly."

She stiffened. "Treason? How dare you make such an accusation."

"They collaborated in an attempt to murder Arthur." He added, almost as if it was an afterthought, "And myself."

"No! That is not possible!"

"It is not only possible, Sister, it happened." Arthur's manner was calm. With a kind of detached amusement he asked her, "Were you involved?"

"Arthur!"

"Spare me the mock outrage, Morgan, and answer the question."

"If what you are charging is true, it certainly happened without my knowledge or collusion."

Merlin seemed pleased to hear it. "You will testify to that effect at their trial, then?"

"Trial?"

He repressed a smile. "As Gildas told you so cheerfully, they are on their way back to Camelot under heavy guard. With luck they are already there. They will be kept under lock and key, tried and, if found guilty, executed." He was happy about this, and it showed. "I will conduct the prosecution myself."

Morgan was angry but worked to control it. "Lulua is a priestess. She is beyond secular authority."

"Even so. Her status as a priestess hardly gives her license to kill the king. Clerical treason is still treason."

She collected herself and said calmly, "The people of England will not stand by idly while the representatives of the gods are ill-treated."

Arthur laughed at this. "Do you really think you help your case by making more threats against me?"

Almost casually she replied, "My case is the case of the gods themselves."

But Merlin ignored this and went on. "Of course, if their testimony conflicts with your own, you may ultimately be charged, too." He smiled beatifically. "But I am quite certain it will not come to that. We do have your word, after all. You insist you knew nothing of their nefarious actions?"

Before she could respond, Arthur went on. "You are to return to Camelot with us and remain there till the trial is over." He smiled solicitously. "As our guest. You don't mind, do you?"

"It is my intention to return to my own castle. There are numerous affairs pressing on me."

"You may have your secretaries or Mordred bring the paperwork to Camelot."

"But—"

"That is all, Morgan. You may leave the royal presence."

She fumed; it showed. But she got stiffly to her feet and stood before them, tall and imperious. "It is as you wish, of course, Brother. But you will find that imprisoning the high priestess will have repercussions."

"Only if the high priestess herself stirs them up." Merlin beamed at her. "Surely you would never do that, would you, Morgan? In the middle of a treason trial?"

She turned without saying a word and stalked off.

Arthur turned to Merlin. "Will she make trouble, do you think?"

"Not while she is in our custody. Not even Morgan could be that dull."

"She *is* the high priestess, Merlin. She does have followers."

"She may have followers, but we most certainly have her. I think she will behave."

Arthur yawned. "This journey has been more exhausting than it should have been. Let's get some sleep."

"And hope the roof doesn't collapse on us."

"Why is your view of everything so rosy, Merlin? I always sleep well in rainy weather. Let's hope tonight is no exception. Good night, Merlin." He yawned and stretched. "Thank heaven there's still some hay left in here."


Lights were extinguished; Arthur and his men prepared to sleep. There were no dry spots on the barn floor. A few of the more enterprising knights climbed up to the hayloft and made to prepare their bedrolls there. But when the wood began to creak ominously they came back down and slept on the damp floor with the others.

The sound of dripping rainwater made an oddly calming sound. Most of the party were lulled gently to sleep by it. But Merlin slept fitfully. The dampness aggravated his arthritis. He wakened more than once with pain in his hip and had to readjust himself to ease the pressure on it. The fact that most of the others seemed to be sleeping soundly irritated him. Somewhere in a far part of the barn one of them was snoring, and the sound reverberated. Under his breath he muttered, "Knights."

Then in the small hours, just before purple dawn, there was the sound of someone moving, followed by a cry in the dark. A dozen men woke and looked around, groggily trying to orient themselves.

Merlin was barely asleep. He sat up. "What is that? Who is crying out?" No one answered, but as his mind cleared he realized it had been the king's voice. "Arthur?"

More sounds. Another cry, a gurgling sound and what appeared to be someone rushing about in the dark.

"Arthur?"

The king did not answer.

Merlin called out, "Lights! We need lights!" He scrambled awkwardly to his feet, groped for his cane and took a few steps toward the place where Arthur had been sleeping. "Someone get a torch or a lantern!"

One of the squires managed to strike a flint. In an instant a torch was blazing.

"Here!" Merlin called. "Bring it here!"

In a moment he had the torch in his hand. Leaning heavily on his cane with the other hand, he limped toward the spot where Arthur had been.

The king lay soaked in blood. A dagger stuck out of his chest. He was unconscious. Merlin gasped. "In the name of everything human! Arthur, no!"

Peter appeared out of the darkness behind him.

"Run and get my medical kit. Quickly!"

Peter ran.

Bedivere, hearing the commotion, rushed into the barn. "What has happened?" Then he saw Arthur and cried, "No! No! This cannot be!"

Peter returned with Merlin's medical things. He quickly

got down on his knees—as quickly as his arthritis would let him—and examined the king. After a moment he looked to Bedivere. "Fortunately, this is not too deep. The assassin missed his heart."

Bedivere thanked the gods.

"Thank our good luck. I should be able to dress this wound as soon as the bleeding slows." He fell to cleaning it. Then a thought occurred. "Bed, I told you this is not a deep wound."

"What of that? We're fortunate. Arthur is. He's always had good luck."

"That is not what I mean."

"Then—?"

"The wound is shallow." He paused, then said, "Almost as if it had been struck by a woman."

"A woman? But we—"

"Where is Morgan?"

More lights were being lit, but the cavernous interior of the barn was still only dimly lit. Bedivere glanced around. "Morgan! Morgan le Fay!"

There was no reply. The other men looked around. There was no sign of her.

Bedivere returned to Merlin's side. "Is he all right? Will he recover?"

"He will have to rest for a few days. He will have to ride in a carriage on our return journey. Thankfully the one that brought the Stone is empty now. Bring me Morgan. I want to question her."

"Merlin . . ." He hesitated and looked around the barn one more time. "Merlin, she is gone."

# TEN

Camelot came into view just after dawn on the first sunny morning Merlin had seen in weeks. It stood on its hilltop, its stones gleaming in the early light. Its windows beamed with lights that had not yet been extinguished; but they were blinking out one by one.

Arthur's wounds had been healing well but slowly. Merlin, backed up by Bedivere, insisted that Arthur ride in a carriage instead of on horseback at the head of the column. Merlin, seeing the beautiful prospect before them, woke him gently. "Arthur, wake up. This is something you ought to see."

Groggily the king asked, "What? What could there possibly be?"

"Home. Camelot. I have never seen it look so beautiful."

Arthur sat up and rubbed his eyes. "I've seen Camelot before, thank you. Why don't you let me sleep?"

"Don't be difficult. Just look."

He looked. There was the castle, its two great towers soaring into the sky, its stones illuminated brilliantly by the sun.

"Look at it, Arthur. After all the horrors on our journey, we are home. And it must be the most welcoming place in the world."

"Are you turning into a poet? You certainly don't sound like the cold-eyed scholar you always pretend to be."

"Even a cold-eyed scholar can be glad of hearth and home. Paintonbury and Grosfalcon are behind us. I have hope that we have seen the last of the killings."

"And now you've become an optimist." Arthur smirked at him. "And they say old people lose the ability to grow."

"Go ahead, Arthur. Enjoy yourself. You are king and you have the right. Spoil this beautiful moment for me."

Arthur fell silent and looked out at the castle again. "We'll be there in another hour. You're right, Merlin. It is a beautiful place. A fitting symbol of everything we've tried to accomplish in England, you and I."

"And we will have our first good, full English breakfast since we left on this fool's errand."

Arthur's face lit up. "With honey cakes."

Merlin was not certain whether to say it; he did not want to dampen Arthur's mood. But he could not restrain himself. "You forget, Arthur. The woman who bakes those cakes is in jail now, along with her sons."

"Oh. That's right, isn't it?" His smile vanished. "Now that is the voice of the Merlin I know."

"I am not a poet after all?"

"Don't be absurd. But . . . but surely we can release Marian and her boys now. We know that Morgan was behind it all."

"Do we?"

Arthur rubbed the bandage on his chest. "Is this my imagination, then?"

"You have always been so reluctant to confront Morgan. What will you do now? Send out parties of knights to find and arrest her?"

"It's too early to think. I need that good breakfast you mentioned."

When the party moved through the gate and into Camelot's courtyard, Simon of York was waiting to greet them with a sheaf of papers in his hand. Behind him stood Petronus, holding still more paperwork. Various other functionaries were scattered about the yard waiting to press their business with the returning monarch and his chief advisor. Merlin stared at the scene and muttered, "Home. So much for that."

Bedivere dismounted and approached the carriage to help Arthur out.

And Arthur grumped. "I wish you'd all stop fussing over me. I'm over the damage Morgan did to me."

"You are our king. The nation's welfare depends on you."

Arthur took a few steps and brushed some dust off himself. "The nation runs itself. Crops grow or fail, the weather turns fair or foul, people get on with their lives, and there's nothing I can do about it. Even the government goes on its merry way without me." He took a deep breath, seeming to relish the cold morning air. "It's good to be home."

Simon had listened to his little speech with mild alarm. "Welcome, Your Majesty."

"Good day, Simon. How is the bureaucracy this morning?"

"Everything is functioning well."

Arthur turned to Bedivere. "See what I mean? I could spend a month by the sea at Brighton and it would hardly make a difference."

Merlin stepped down from the carriage. His hip ached and he stumbled. Petronus rushed to his side to steady him. "Welcome back, sir."

"It is good to be home, Petronus, and it is good to see you. But tell me, how is Colin?"

"Quite well, sir, and getting better every day." He lowered his voice to a confidential whisper. "She'll be so happy to see you."

"That is good. When I got your message, I was so concerned. You see—" He realized what the boy had said. "What was that?"

"She'll be happy to see you, sir."

"She?" He put on his best neutral manner. "I am asking about Colin."

"Nimue, sir. She raved in her fever. I know the truth about 'him' now."

Merlin sighed. It was bound to happen sooner or later. "We will discuss it later. But when I learned that Marian and Wayne were tending her, I—"

"Why did you have them arrested, sir? They were taking such good care of her."

"Later, Petronus."

Britomart strode out of the castle, beaming. "Arthur!"

"Good morning, Brit."

She glanced at his bandages. "Still smarting from your brilliant military strategy, are you?"

Arthur scowled at her but said nothing.

Merlin, hearing this, crossed to join them. "Arthur's wounds are from another war entirely. We will tell you all about it over breakfast."

"Good. Shall I assemble all our advisors, then? And Prince Mordred?"

Merlin reached out and caught her arm. "Mordred is here?"

Confused by his reaction, Brit nodded. She looked at Arthur. "You did tell him to stay here, remember?"

"I told his mother to remain, too. But she left almost as soon as we did. How did she get away?"

Brit smirked. " 'As rare and lovely things oft do, she vanished in the night.' "

Merlin interjected, "You might have sent us word."

"Why?" Brit seemed genuinely puzzled. "She is the king's

sister. Arthur always says he trusts her. Is there a problem about her?" She looked to Arthur.

"Over breakfast, Brit. I'm famished."

Everyone moved toward the castle. But Merlin and Petronus lingered slightly behind. "Go and fire up the boiler for my lifting mechanism, Petronus. I do not feel well enough to tackle the steps to my tower."

"Yes, Merlin."

"Then come and join us for breakfast."

The boy grinned. "With pleasure."


The meal was huge and sumptuous, a fitting welcome home for the king. He took his place at the head table in the hall, surrounded by his advisors. Knights crowded the other tables. Mordred, apparently unaware that he and his mother were under clouds, took a seat close to Merlin. Peter took an unobtrusive seat at one end of the table and kept silent and listened to the conversation with careful attention. Petronus, having started the fire for Merlin's lifting device, arrived late and sat at a rear table with the squires.

Merlin took the conversational lead. "So, how are our prisoners?"

Brit smiled. "They are still imprisoned. What else do you need to know?"

"It might be helpful if one of them confessed."

"Confessed to what, Merlin? To starting the plague? Most of Europe thinks the Byzantines spread it deliberately. I'll show you the intelligence reports after breakfast."

"But I am not at all certain that—never mind. Have Marmaduke and Lulua said anything?"

"About—"

"About anything at all related to their attempt to do Arthur and me in. About who might have been behind it."

Brit was lost. "Do you think creatures like them need to be urged to commit evil?"

Arthur spoke up. "What Merlin wants to know, Brit, is whether they have given any indication that my sister might have been behind their treason."

Mordred exclaimed, "My mother?! Why would she—? I mean, why wouldn't she, but really, why would she? Eliminating Uncle Arthur would undermine her own position in England. The barons would never—"

"Let us say," Merlin interrupted, "that there are grounds for suspicion if nothing more."

"But—"

"Later, Mordred." Arthur smiled a patient smile.

Merlin pressed on. "What about Marian of Bath and her sons? Has any of them said anything?"

"Not a word that might incriminate them, if that's what you mean. They seem more puzzled and outraged than anything else." Brit took a long swallow of mead. "This is supposed to be a celebration of your return, Arthur. Do you really want to let Merlin turn it into an inquiry?"

"If Morgan is behind what has been happening, the situation is more serious than I would have believed. Or would have wanted to believe. But she has made a grave tactical blunder." Bedivere started to say something, but Arthur anticipated him and cut him off. "Almost as grave as the tactical blunder I made when we were planning the journey."

Everyone looked at Mordred. The young man blushed and tried to go on eating as if he didn't understand. But it was clear to everyone there: Morgan had left her son and heir in Arthur's hands—a bad move for a potential traitor.

"But—but—" Mordred felt compelled to say something but wasn't sure what would be appropriate. "But—would she have done that if she was really a traitor?"

Merlin stroked his beard thoughtfully. "I wonder."

"But—but you can't suspect me, Uncle. I've never—"

"You are your mother's son. You must know as much about poisons and such as she does, or nearly so. I must ask that you remain here in, shall we say, protective custody, until this matter is resolved."

"Yes, Uncle. But I give you my word, I don't want to leave. You know that Mother and I have never—"

"I am afraid," Merlin cut him off, "that the word of the son of a suspected traitor carries very little weight."

Arthur smiled indulgently. "It's only for a short time, Mordred. I'm sure we'll get to the bottom of it all fairly soon."

Peter approached Merlin, smiling. "It is time for me to get back to Darrowfield. I've been away much longer than I'd planned. Our journey together was so very . . . interesting."

"I will miss you, Peter. Having you along to give me support was quite invaluable. With none of my usual aides to help me . . ."

"Believe me, Merlin, it was my pleasure. The chance to see you in action, even if that action was inconclusive, meant the world to me."

"When will you leave?"

"As soon as I can make the necessary arrangements. Before noon, with luck."

Merlin took his hand. "Until we meet again, then. Be well. And be certain to keep me posted on the murder investigation at Darrowfield. The crown wants to know who murdered our baron."

"I'll be sure to do so. And of course I'll send whatever plague news I can."

"Let us hope there will be none."

Peter grinned and shook his hand again. "Well, I'm off to the stables to make my arrangements. As you said, till we meet again." He made a slight bow and a little salute, then turned and headed off toward the stables.


A sudden surge of bitterly cold air swept across England that morning. There was, thankfully, no more snow or rain, but the temperature turned frigid. In the sunlight particles of ice could be seen dancing in the air, stirred by the slightest breeze.

Merlin began to feel the cold in every joint in his body. His limbs grew stiff and sore, even more than they were usually. Every now and again the pain would become so severe that he would wince and curse the weather and his own body silently.

He sent a messenger to catch Peter in the stables. The note he sent read, "Be certain to take blankets and cloaks. Winter is upon us and shows signs of being merciless."

Then it was time to return to his tower. Petronus scrambled up the steps to make certain the lift mechanism was operating properly. Then Merlin took his seat in the sling and began his mechanical ascent, more grateful than ever that he had built the thing.

"Merlin!" Nimue jumped up from her sick bed and impulsively threw her arms around him. "It's so wonderful to have you back! And alive!"

He permitted her embrace for a moment, then pulled free and kissed her cheek lightly. "Alive? Exactly how old do you think I am?"

She laughed. "As old as the stones at Stonehenge, if not older. You look tired. The journey was hard on you."

"So kind of you to say so." The raven Roc flew in through the window, perched on Merlin's shoulder and nuzzled his cheek. He raised a hand to pet it. "But you are right. I have traveled much too much lately. Dover, Darrowfield, Grosfalcon . . . A true scholar does not need to travel."

She cocked her head at him, puzzled.

"I mean it. A scholar may just as well stay where the gods put him, and dig."

Petronus was standing behind him, watching and listening. "You don't believe in the gods. You say so often enough."

"Do not be difficult, Petronus."

"It's so wonderful to have you back and safe. May I . . . may I . . ."

"Yes?"

Instead of finishing his thought the boy rushed forward and threw his arms around Merlin. "The scant reports we had about your journey had us so worried."

"All this hugging." Merlin feigned distaste. "It is so unseemly."

Nimue laughed at him. "You are a fraud, Merlin. You're as glad to be home as we are to have you here."

"Perhaps so." He was giving nothing away. He found his favorite chair and sat. "But tell me about your bout with the plague. What were the symptoms? Why do you think you recovered instead of . . . ?"

"Plague? The report you received must not have been complete." Nimue glanced at Petronus and scowled. "It was not plague. I had a severe case of the ague. Petronus says the French call it influenza. Fever, chills, stomachache, congestion . . . Several people in the castle have had it. How did you get the notion it was plague?"

"At first I thought it was only a cold. But then I grew fearful that it might be something far worse. It was foolish of me. I know better than to make unwarranted assumptions. But Marian of Bath and her son Wayne—"

"They were wonderful, Merlin. They fussed over me like anxious nursemaids. They said they wanted to allay your suspicions about them." She hesitated. "What suspicions? And why? Why on earth did you have them arrested?"

He ignored the question. "They gave you no drugs? Nothing that might have—?"

"Nothing, no. You're being mysterious." It was an accusation.

"I am trying to make sense of everything that has happened. Did they ever give you any reason to think they might be loyal to Morgan?"

"Morgan le Fay? No, none. Not for a moment."

He turned to Petronus. "And you. Did you ever hear either of them say anything of the sort?"

Petronus shook his head. He was plainly lost.

Suddenly Merlin got to his feet. "I think it is time for me to interview them. Which dungeon are they in?"

"The north one. It is rather full down there. You kept sending back prisoners."

"And one of them, at least, is guilty. But we do not yet know the full extent of the guilt."

"You mustn't go till you've told us all about the journey. We want to know everything."

"The fact that *I* want to know everything is why I must go know. I promise I will give you a full account later."

"You're infuriating."

He smiled beatifically. "It is my job. Till later." He made a little salute. "Come, Petronus. Operate the lift for me."

Nimue wanted to go with Merlin. He wanted her to stay in bed till she was fully recovered, but she insisted she felt fine. So while Petronus operated the lift for Merlin, she descended the stairs and met him at the bottom. They headed down to the dungeons.

"So, Petronus has discovered your secret."

"Yes. I wish he hadn't." She shrugged. "But I was sick. He wanted to undress me, to help make me more comfortable. The only way I could think to stop him was to tell him the truth."

"And what about Marian? And her son? Do they know?"

Nimue shook her head. "I don't think so, no. I don't see how they could."

"Petronus . . ." His tone was offhand.

"No, Petronus is quite thrilled to be in on the secret. He is excited by the thought of a woman dressing as a man."

Merlin laughed. "Precocious boy. So, at least for the time

being, and as far as anyone in Camelot knows, you are still Colin. Excellent."

"What do you mean, 'for the time being'?"

"Secrets have a way of leaking out, whether we want them to or not." They had reached the lowest level of the castle. "As I hope will be the case when we interview our unwilling guests."

There were guards posted in the dungeon, of course. Nimue asked Merlin if they should perhaps take one with them as they interrogated the prisoners.

"No. I do not think that would be productive." He smiled. "Besides, the cells are so small, and Marmaduke and Lulua are so large."

"What about the others?"

"There will be five of us in one cell. That is more than crowded enough."

Marian had been confined in a little cell in Camelot's basement. Each of her sons had his own cell as well. Merlin ordered that both of the boys be brought to her cell. As he sat and waited for the jailors to bring them, he questioned Marian.

"You know Colin."

"Yes, of course." Marian was made of ice. "He is the rat who gave you some pretext to arrest us."

"That is not so. Colin is here to make notes, nothing more. I hope you do not mind."

She laughed at him. "And if I do?"

Merlin brushed that aside. "You were at Darrowfield. Tell me what happened there after my party left."

"I've told everyone who's asked." Marian paused to glare at "Colin," then went on. "Nothing in particular happened there. We helped the lord's servants make ready for the feast he was planning." She seemed uncertain whether she should be saying this, or whether Merlin would believe her. Her manner was hesitant. But she went on. "I even gave them the recipe for my honey cakes. Then word came that the lord and his sons had been—had been—"

"Slaughtered." Merlin smiled faintly. "Like sheep. Where were you and your sons when the murder occurred?"

She narrowed her eyes. "You suspect us? So that explains this imprisonment. But we—"

The guards entered with Robert and Wayne. Merlin gestured that they should take seats beside their mother. "Go on with what you were saying, Marian."

She ignored this and told her sons, "Merlin appears to think we murdered Lord Darrowfield and his boys."

"What?!" One of the twins jumped to his feet, plainly angry at this. "Why would we? What was that old fool to us?" The other boy remained seated, his features passive. Merlin was uncertain which of them was which. But he took a guess.

"And you, Robert, you gave us drugged wine that night at Lulua's mill."

"No!" The more agitated of the twins began to wave his arms. "I did not! It was Lulua's wine, the wine that was there."

"Why would Lulua have drugged wine in her house?"

"How do I know? She was a witch."

"Point taken. But Robert, who gave you the wine? Who told you to serve that particular wine to everyone?"

The boy paused. "I don't remember. Someone on your staff, I think it was."

"One of us asked to be drugged?"

"I told you I don't remember."

Merlin changed tack. "Lulua had an herb garden at the mill. You had access to it. What grew there?"

Robert stared at him and said nothing. But his brother spoke up. "So there was a garden. What of that? There are herb gardens everywhere. Lady Darrowfield had one at that castle of theirs. There is a large one here at Camelot."

Merlin looked at Marian. "You are a cook. You know herbs."

"Yes."

"Which ones did Lady Darrowfield grow?"

"I can't remember that. I never really used the herb garden, just the stores of honey they had. They had spices already stored in the kitchen. There was no need."

"Were there any poisons?"

"I tell you I don't know."

"No. Of course not. But Marian, there is something else I must ask you. Something that may be . . . awkward. I am not certain it is a thing I should ask you with your sons here. Shall I have them taken back to their cells?"

"You've only just had them brought here."

"Even so. I—"

"I do not keep secrets from my boys. Whatever you want to know, you can ask with them here."

Her manner was more than slightly assertive, and it caught him off guard. After a moment's pause he went on. "Very well, then. Marian, I must ask you—"

"Yes?"

"Who is the father of your sons?"

The question seemed to surprise her. "The—? Why would you ask such a thing? What can that possibly have to do with—?"

"I need to know. A great deal depends on your answer." He lowered his voice slightly. "Perhaps even your lives."

"Our lives!" Wayne jumped to his feet. "Why are you threatening us? You can't possibly think we've done anything."

Merlin ignored his outburst. "Marian?"

She remained silent.

"I ask you again: Who is the father of these boys?"

Still she said nothing.

Softly he went on. "Come, now, you can tell me." Even more softly, almost as an afterthought, he asked her, "Is it the king?"

Marian's eyes widened. "The king? Is that what this is about? Half the court says you're a fool, Merlin, and they are right."

More vehemently he repeated his question. "Is it the king?"

Marian was working to calm herself, and it showed. Finally she uttered one word. "No."

"Then who—?"

"I was young. I was an attractive young woman, though years of working in Camelot's kitchen have ended that. I had a great many lovers in those days. Knights, squires, courtiers." She added with force, "But not Arthur. Not the king. Never him."

Slowly Merlin got to his feet. "Very well, then. If you are telling me the truth—"

"I am!"

"Then that ends this inquiry."

The three of them were clearly puzzled by this. Robert asked, "Then you will release us?"

"In time. There are still a great many unanswered questions."

"When?"

"In time, I said. For the moment you will be returned to your cells. I thank you for answering my questions."

"But you don't believe us!" Wayne could not contain his anger.

"I have not said so."

"We nursed this fool back to health." He pointed at Nimue. "How much clearer could it be that we're not villains? Let us loose!"

"In time. That is all I can tell you. In time."

He left the cell, with Nimue just behind him, gave instructions to the guards and headed for the wing of the dungeon that held Lulua and Marmaduke.


The cot in Lulua's cell was tiny. As they entered, she was lying on it. Or trying to. Parts of her hung over the edge. Seeing Merlin enter, she sat up, with some difficulty.

"Good morning, Lulua. I trust you slept well." His manner was magisterial. "You are losing weight. Prison food must agree with you."

"Don't be sarcastic, Wizard."

"I am not. I am never sarcastic. I was merely expressing friendly concern. This is my assistant Colin. He will be taking notes on our . . . conversation."

Lulua snorted, then laughed out loud. "Conversation."

But Merlin was not about to be distracted. He sat and said to her offhandedly, "I would like to know what instructions you had from Morgan le Fay pertaining to Arthur and myself."

Serenely she closed her eyes and said, "None."

"So your treason was entirely your own." He smiled. "You were not acting on orders from a superior."

"I am a priestess. I have no superiors."

"Interesting viewpoint. But clinging to that argument will hardly benefit you in your trial."

Lulua struggled to her feet and began pacing. "Try me. Go ahead. What I did I did for England. That is hardly treason."

"A jury of twelve men may think otherwise." He turned to Nimue. "Note that she insists she was acting on her own." Then he looked back to Lulua. "And I suppose Marmaduke was likewise acting solely on his own initiative?"

"Ask him."

"I intend to, believe me."

Heavily she sat down again. "Arthur Pendragon seized England by force of arms. His kingship is an outrage to every principle of justice."

"It is refreshing to hear you speak with such candor. But you must realize that you are not doing yourself any good. That amounts to an admission of treason. English justice—"

Lulua laughed. "Justice? From an ambitious warlord like Arthur? Why don't you go away and prepare for my execution? I am prepared for the goddess to take me to her bosom."

"Of course you are." Merlin nodded to Nimue and they both got to their feet. "As you wish, Lulua. If you decide that you would like to tell me something that might mitigate your offence, have the guards summon me." He stepped toward the cell door. "Oh—one more thing."

"What?"

"Why did you keep drugged wine at your mill?"

She laughed. The cot creaked under her. "Are you serious? Why would I do that?"

"Drugged with narcotics from your herb garden."

"You think I grew belladonna to use on myself?"

"Belladonna." The clouds in his mind seemed to part. He froze for an instant.

Nimue asked him what was wrong.

"Nothing." He recovered himself quickly and smiled a wide smile at her. "What other poisons did you grow, Lulua?"

"Go away. I want to sleep. And have the guards bring me some food."

"You can eat in your sleep?"

"Go away, Wizard."


Outside the cell, Merlin paused for a moment, evidently lost in thought.

Nimue asked if anything was wrong.

"No, of course not. But she grew belladonna. In the name of everything human, I wonder if—"

"Belladonna is a poison, Merlin. Why would anyone grow it?"

He shrugged. "Morgan does, I suspect. Are you certain you've recovered from your illness?"

The change of topic left her reeling for a moment. "My— Yes, of course. But why do you ask?"

"If you are quite over your ailment—"

"Yes?" She was suspicious. What could be on his mind?

"If you are quite recovered, I will want you to go on a little mission for me."

"A mission." She was deadpan.

"Yes. To Darrowfield."

"To—! Merlin, this doesn't make any sense. Are we investigating treason, or—?"

"I want you to inspect Lady Darrowfield's herb garden. I need to know whether she is growing belladonna, like Lulua."

"Belladonna?" Nimue leaned casually against the wall, grinning. "I thought we were investigating treason, trying to get to the bottom of it. What has belladonna—?"

"Belladonna, as you said, is a poison." He smiled like a fox.

"I'm quite aware of that, Merlin. But—"

"The symptoms of belladonna poisoning are quite similar to the symptoms of the plague."

"Oh." It was almost a whisper. "Oh." Then the surprise wore off. "But there really is a plague. Or has been. We're all so grateful it's ending with the cold weather. But—"

"Let us go and interview Marmaduke."

"Merlin, will you please tell me what you have on your mind? Are you suggesting that the plague deaths were . . . ? I don't even know what to ask you. Please, tell me what you're thinking."

His smile had not diminished. "The thought is only half formed. I could not articulate it in a coherent manner. Not yet. But I have had a suspicion all along that all the awful things that were happening were somehow related. The murders at Stonehenge. The deaths of John, Bruce and Accolon, and poor George . . ."

"Then how—?"

"Let us move on. Lord Marmaduke is waiting."

He moved briskly toward the traitor's cell, with Nimue just behind. The jailor, seeing their approach, got his keys from his pocket and made ready to unlock the door.

Just as they reached it, Merlin stopped. "I should warn you. Marmaduke . . . How shall I put it? . . . The air in his cell is apt not to be fresh."

"I wish you'd stop talking to me in riddles."

"You will see, soon enough. Or rather, you will smell."


The jailor's key clanked in the lock and the cell door swung open. Instantly Marmaduke's stench wafted out. Nimue reflexively covered her nose. "Good grief!"

"Exactly. And his entire palace reeks in that way."

Marmaduke had been resting on the floor, curled into something like a fetal position, or as close to one as a man of his bulk could manage. The sound of the door opening wakened him. He sat up and rubbed his eyes. "Wizard. What the devil do you want?"

Merlin stood at the threshold and made no move to enter the cell. "Your trial will be starting soon." He smiled and added, "Your trial for treason."

"I should have killed you both at once, when I had the chance. The mistake I made was waiting."

"The mistake you made was thinking you could attempt regicide and get away with it."

Nimue leaned casually against the doorpost. "Regicide and wizard-cide," she added, grinning.

Marmaduke struggled heavily to his feet and took a step unobtrusively toward the door. "You're going to put me on trial and kill me. Our positions are reversed. That is war."

"No, that is justice." Merlin arranged his robes.

"Justice?" Marmaduke was growing angry and it showed. His eyes widened and his face flushed. "Robbing a man of his territory? Defiling his wife?"

"It is hardly possible to 'defile' a woman who is quite willing."

Marmaduke glared.

"And even if it was possible, it is hardly a crime in the same league as what you planned. But all of this is beside the point. I want to know about Morgan le Fay."

Puzzlement showed through the anger in Marmaduke's face.

Merlin pressed. "How was she involved? What were her instructions to you? Were they given through Lulua? Did she give similar orders to other barons?"

Suddenly Marmaduke let out a roar. He lunged and in an instant his hands were around Merlin's throat. "I'll finish it now, Wizard."

Nimue let out a scream, jumped onto Marmaduke and began trying to pry his fingers loose. But he was much too strong for her. Merlin was gasping for breath. His face turned red.

The guard, hearing her scream, came running. He instantly realized what was happening and joined Nimue's efforts to pull Marmaduke off his victim. The color in Merlin's face went from red to purple.

More guards from other parts of the dungeon heard the commotion and came running. In a trice three of them were on Marmaduke. With great difficulty they pulled him off Merlin, forced him back into his cell and slammed and locked the door.

Merlin stood, gasping for breath, one arm on the wall for balance. Slowly his natural coloration returned.

Just then Simon of York entered the dungeon. "Merlin! What on earth happened?"

Nimue explained. Simon took a moment to digest it all. "Are you all right now? Is everything under control?"

Still gasping for breath, Merlin said, "Asked like a true bureaucrat."

Nimue broke into a grin. "I think he will be all right. He's well enough for his usual sarcasm." Suddenly the unexpected oddness of Simon's presence struck her. "What are you doing down here?"

"I heard someone was strangling Merlin and came to watch the fun."

Merlin had recovered sufficiently to say, "Nonsense. What do you want here, Simon?"

Simon couldn't stop smiling. "You are wanted above. In the king's tower."

"What is wrong?"

He paused for dramatic effect, then said, "The king is dead."

The shock of hearing this brought Merlin to himself once and for all. "Arthur, dead? Then why have you been standing here, grinning like an ass?"

Simon grinned even more widely. "Not Arthur. The old king."

"Pellenore?"

"No, I'm afraid we're not that fortunate. The king who has died is Uther Pendragon."

"Oh."

"Yes." Simon smiled. "Oh."

Merlin turned to Nimue. "Get to Darrowfield. Leave as soon as you can. Examine the lady's garden. If she is growing belladonna, try and bring me a sample. Leaves, berries and roots. There are different strains of the plant and they produce different effects."

Nimue repeated her instructions to be sure she understood them.

"I will arrange with Brit for a military escort for you. I think a dozen soldiers should be enough."

"I can travel faster and less obtrusively alone, Merlin."

"Did I say that I want you to be unobtrusive?"

"But—"

"Take soldiers. Make a show of yourself."

"But— Merlin, what are you thinking?"

"I am more and more certain that the solution to this—to all of this—lies there."

"In Lady Darrowfield's herb garden?"

"Possibly. Possibly not. At any rate, I do not wish to see a repeat of the mistake Arthur made on the journey to Grosfalcon. There are traitors loose in England—or at least one. I will have you take no needless chances with your safety." A sudden draft swept through the dungeon. Merlin shuddered. "And make certain to take plenty of blankets and heavy cloaks. I wish I had thought to send you along with Peter." With emphasis he added, "Bring back that plant."

"I'll be fine, Merlin." Impulsively she hugged him, then turned and left.

Simon was puzzled by the exchange. "What was that about?"

"I am collecting specimens for my botany collection. Let us go and comfort the king on his father's death."

"Congratulate him, you mean."

"Either way, Simon, let us go."

Arthur was pacing. When Merlin entered the study he stopped and glared at him. Before Merlin could speak, Arthur barked, "Well, what do I do about this?"

Merlin stayed calm despite the king's obvious agitation. "There is not a great deal that can be done about death."

"Don't be sarcastic. I need counsel. Counsel me."

Merlin arranged his robes and sat. "I am not at all certain I see the problem. Obviously you must attend the funeral. Uther had a great many friends and allies. It would hardly do to offend them. Will he be buried in Cumbria?"

Arthur nodded. "There is a little graveyard near his castle. I always found it appropriate." He looked Merlin in the eye. "I loathed the old viper. He loathed me. You know that."

"Still, Arthur, there are certain proprieties to be observed. If you were to let him go to his rest with no family present . . ." He sniffled. "I had a handkerchief, but I seem to have forgotten it. Send one of the servants for one, will you?"

Arthur ignored this. "Morgan will be there. The two of them were always close. Would you get into bed with a viper just because she happened to share your blood?"

Merlin paused. "Perhaps you should take Mordred with you. Not as a hostage, of course. Nothing official. But the mere show of having him with you may deter her from . . . from whatever villainy she may be planning. I would suggest taking as large a party as possible. Surround yourself with a great many people. As the Romans used to say, there is safety in numbers." He lowered his voice a bit. "Do not let her get near you."

"Pellenore and Uther were friends. He will want to go." Arthur turned pensive. "And a few of my knights, the older ones, were originally part of his army. And . . ."

"Do not make the mistake you made on that journey to Wales. Take plenty of people. Knights." Suddenly, violently, Merlin sneezed.

Arthur narrowed his eyes. "You aren't coming down with the ague that's been having its way with our people, are you?"

"No, Arthur. It was nothing more than a sneeze."

He looked doubtful. "At any rate, the journey to Cumbria will be a lot less eventful. It is a much more civilized part of the country."

"Yet it comes fully equipped with 'old vipers.' "

The king sighed. "Point taken. I'll get Simon and Bed to work preparing the party right away. You are coming, of course."

"Me?! No! I mean, I've only just—I—I—Arthur, I need a spell of rest."

"You can rest in the carriage. The roads are good. The ride will be smooth." Suddenly something occurred to him. He snapped his fingers. "Old Fedora!"

"I beg your pardon, Arthur?"

"Fedora, the midwife. She was at Uther's court before she came here. She always says she feels a certain loyalty to me." He turned shamefaced. "She delivered me, you know."

"I had always assumed as much. So she oversaw your mother Igraine's confinement. At Uther's court."

Arthur nodded. "Ancient history."

Again Merlin sniffled. "And was your mother still married to Gorlois, or had she and Uther made their union official by that time?"

"I don't wish to dig up the past." Arthur glared. "And so help me, if you say, 'Like father, like son,' I'll toss you down the steps."

"I do not speak in clichés." He sighed. "But please, Arthur, do not make me go along on this trip."

Arthur waited for him to go on.

"The journey to Grosfalcon was hard on me. You know that. And now this spell of frigid weather. Every joint in my body is aching like the devil."

"But—"

"Another long trip would do me no good at all. Please, Arthur. It is only a funeral. You can hardly need me."

Arthur scowled. "Very well, I suppose you're right. There is nothing you can do." He broke into a grin. "Unless you can work a spell to bring the old reprobate back to life."

"You have been spending too much time with Bishop Gildas."

Arthur left the following morning, accompanied by one hundred knights, plus squires and attendants of various kinds. It was a three days' ride to Cumbria. If the weather stayed dry, they could travel quickly and be back at Camelot within a week.

Merlin went to the courtyard to see them off. His nose was runny and he carried a kerchief, and he had another one in his pocket. He took the king by the sleeve and led him aside. "It occurs to me that there is another good reason why you should attend this funeral."

Arthur was in a good mood, smiling and energetic. "And what would that be?"

Merlin lowered his voice. "Your patrimony."

"Are you serious? I have all of England."

"Even so. Think, Arthur. Uther was widely respected in his day, marital indiscretions or no. You are his heir. Claiming your inheritance rights will only help to bolster your claim to the throne."

"But I already—"

"Equally to the point, you must make certain that Morgan has no chance to make herself Uther's heir."

"I see your point." He seemed to lose energy. "But—but—"

"Hm?"

"Whatever people may think about the legitimacy of my parents' marriage, I am the eldest. Morgan is arguably even less legitimate than I am. Her mother was—"

"Do you think the technical points of genealogy will matter if she gets the barons to support her?"

Arthur whistled. "I had best get moving. No use giving her more time to subvert my loyal subjects."

"I thought you would see it that way. Travel well, Arthur. Send messages as things develop."

Fifteen minutes later the party left. Merlin remained standing alone in the courtyard, looking after them, not moving. Suddenly he was overcome by a fit of coughing. One of the sentries approached him. "Is anything wrong, sir?"

"I hope not." He put a hand on the man's shoulder. "I hope not."

Roc flew down out of the sky and perched on his shoulder. He stroked the bird's head and went back inside Camelot.


By sundown Merlin was quite ill—feverish, achy, congested. He took to his bed and slept. Roc and the other ravens seemed puzzled. They lingered by his bedside for a few minutes, then when he did not respond they left. Petronus watched over him as best he could with his limited medical knowledge.

Nimue returned from Darrowfield the next day, having made the journey there and back again in very good time. She realized that Merlin had contracted the same influenza she had just recovered from. She brought him soup from the kitchen and kept monitoring his condition carefully. Petronus wanted to help, but she warned him to stay away lest he fall victim to the disease, too.

For days he remained unconscious, waking only to eat and even then not seeming aware of his surroundings. In his sleep he muttered, vague but alarming words about murder near the crown, traitors striking near the very heart of England. At times he raved quite deliriously.

The infection spread in the castle. It struck knights, squires, servants with varying degrees of severity. Even Simon of York fell victim to it. No one was certain what to do, since to nurse the sick could only serve to spread the disease to the ones doing the nursing. The only one in the castle with substantial medical knowledge and experience was Merlin, and he was out of commission. Nimue did her best to present a confident front and to manage all the efforts to contain the disease; but it was only a front, and she felt inadequate.

When she was not tending to the outbreak, she did her best to keep current on all the reports that were coming in from local officials about the plague. Cold weather did indeed seem to be halting its spread. There were still occasional riots, especially for food, but those could be safely left in the hands of local authorities.

Then on the fourth day Merlin's fever broke. He awoke, sat up in bed, looked around and barked at Nimue, "I'm hungry. Why hasn't Simon sent my breakfast?"

Nimue watched him with a smile. "So you're finally up."

"What do you mean, finally? I'm hungry."

"You've been asleep for four days, Merlin. And it's nearly sundown, not time for breakfast." She crossed the room to him and put a hand on his forehead. "Your fever's finally broken."

Realization began to dawn. "I have had the influenza?"

"You and several dozen others. I'll send for some porridge."

"Porridge? I need my strength. Send for some beef."

"Yes, Merlin." Amused by his ferocity, she went to the door and called for a servant. When the boy was gone, she turned back to Merlin. "You've been missing the fun. Simon has been sick, too. They say he's been complaining like an old woman."

"Well, what can you expect? That is what he is." He sat up. "What word have we had from Arthur?"

"None at all."

"Blast. And how widespread is this awful infection?" He narrowed his eyes. "You are the one who gave it to me."

"A few dozen people are ill. The knights are grumbling about a disease that does not respect their rank."

"They would. How serious do things look?"

"Two people have died. Two elderly servants. So I was worried about you."

"I am *not* elderly."

She laughed at him. "No, only your hips are. Anyway, other than those two, people seem to recover and show no signs of being the worse for wear."

"That is good. But tell me, what did you find in Darrowfield?"

She shook her head. "Nothing of any real interest. Lady Darrowfield was not cultivating belladonna. Peter helped me inspect her garden. There was nothing suspicious."

"Peter." Merlin sat on the edge of his bed. His voice betrayed his misgivings.

"Why that tone? Do you suddenly distrust him? He was a great help to you on the trip to Grosfalcon. You said so yourself."

"Yes, of course. Only . . ."

"Yes?"

"Sometimes when we are asleep our minds function with special clarity. Peter was present when each of the murders occurred. John, Bruce, Accolon, little George, even the attempt on Arthur . . ."

She did not try to hide her skepticism. "You were delirious, Merlin. Can you really make an accusation like that based on fever dreams? Why would he have done all those awful things? What could he have gained?"

"Then it must have been Morgan. Get me my slippers." He yawned. "I suppose we should be grateful so few have succumbed to this awful disease. No more deaths here, then."

"Only the very young and the very old seem to be affected in dire ways." She added pointedly, "The very, very old."

"Spare me your sarcasm. I am hungry."

"They say old Fedora is quite unwell. You know—that horrible old midwife. If she goes, I doubt anyone will care much."

"Fedora!"

"Yes. The most venomous old crone in Camelot."

"She must not die! I must go to her at once!" He got to his feet and looked around for his cane.

"I thought you were hungry."

"For the truth, Nimue. Go and fire up my lifting device. I must get to Fedora at once."

The lift creaked ominously as Merlin descended, and the chains that held his chair swayed. He had to force himself not to look down the full height of the tower.

Nimue, having started the mechanism, raced down the steps to meet him at the bottom. "You're going to kill yourself on that thing someday. You really ought to have Simon arrange for a suite of rooms down here among the people."

He got to his feet, leaning heavily on his cane. "Perish the thought. If I had to live every day surrounded by knights, serving girls and Simon of York, I would certainly go mad."

"There are people who think that the fact that you trust this absurd mechanism is a sign of madness."

"Be quiet, Colin. We must get to Fedora as quickly as possible."


There were three old women sitting in the hallway outside Fedora's room, praying over candles, wailing like forlorn banshees, apparently mourning the imminent demise of their friend.

Merlin, accompanied by Nimue, made his way slowly along the corridor. None of the women showed the least sign of noticing them. They gazed into the candle flames and wailed their orisons, to all appearances aware of nothing else.

They even seemed quite unaware of an overpowering stench that filled the hallway. Nimue covered her mouth and nose with her hand. "Goodness, can that actually be from Fedora?"

"The dissolution of the human body is never agreeable, Colin." Merlin paused for a beat, then moved on. To the first of the women he encountered, he said, "You should not have those candles burning unsheltered. There is too much that could take fire. Tapestries, wood . . ."

The woman interrupted her show of mourning. "Stone does not burn." She went immediately back into her wail.

"Camelot is more wood than stone. Every castle is. You could start a blaze that would endanger us all."

She wailed.

Merlin nudged her with the tip of his boot. "What is that awful smell? How can you stand it? How can you leave Fedora here?"

She looked up at him. "We are following her instructions. We have sacrificed nine black puppies to the Good Goddess for her."

"In the name of everything human, woman, what good can you possibly think that will do?"

"It is standard practice, Merlin," Nimue whispered in his ear. "Morgan used to do it whenever someone in her household was seriously ill. She bred black dogs against the eventuality."

"Fools!" He bellowed it. "Superstitious dolts!"

He pushed past them, moving more quickly than before. Fedora's room was pitch-dark. The awful odor seemed to billow out of it. He stared into the blackness for a moment and listened. Faintly, very faintly, he could hear breathing. Except for that, the room was pervaded with the eerie stillness of death. Then softly came the sound of her coughing.

He went back to the hall, took one of the candles and went back inside. Then quietly came Fedora's voice. "No, young man, you may not have my hand."

Gently, almost whispering, he said, "Fedora, it is I, Merlin."

"All you lovely young men. I know what you want. But you may not have it."

He moved to the bedside and put a hand on her arm. "Fedora, it is Merlin."

"Merlin?" His voice seemed to register with her. "No. Not Merlin. Not at all."

Her mind had regressed to her far-off youth. It took him a moment to realize. "Tell me about your young men, Fedora."

"No!" It was almost a hiss. The sharpness of the expletive made her cough again.

"Fedora," he whispered, "I have come to make love to you."

"No, not you. Not any of you. My love is for the women here."

"Yes." He stroked her arm. "Yes, Fedora. I love you."

He moved the candle close to her. She was soaked in sweat. Her skin was pale as the candle wax, and her breath smelled of imminent decay. There was blood on her lips; she had coughed it up. Merlin took his kerchief and wiped it away.

Like a serpent gifted with speech she hissed, "None of you! Not one of you! I have seen what you do to your women. You will not defile me. It is them I care for, them I tend." Suddenly, quite abruptly, she shouted, "Uther Pendragon! All your women! All your sons! What will they benefit you now?"

The stench in the room was growing stronger, or Merlin was succumbing to it. It was coming from under the bed. He looked, and by dim candlelight he saw the bodies of the young dogs, arranged in circle, in a basket. The corpses glistened with moisture. Decay was taking them quickly. He called for Nimue.

She stepped into the room and stood just inside the doorway, outlined faintly by light from the hall, and held her hand over her nose. "Merlin, how can you stand this?"

He gestured under the bed. "Remove them."

She bent and took the basket, then glanced at Fedora. "She isn't—is she—?"

"Not yet." He looked at the dying woman and said almost tenderly, "She told me once that she knows secret things. Let us hope she remembers them in her death throes. And will speak them."

Nimue looked doubtful. She bent and took the basket with the dogs with one hand. Covering her nose with the other, she left quickly.

Merlin lowered his voice. In a whisper he said, "Fedora, it is I, Uther. I need you."

"Again?" Eyes closed, she chuckled. "Another one? You are insatiable."

"You know who the woman is. Who the son is. Tell me their names."

Fedora opened her eyes wide and without warning spit in his face. She coughed up more blood. "Men! Kings! Your women deserve better than you give them."

"I know it."

"You treat them like swine."

"I know it. I know it. But tell me, Fedora, who is this one? What is her name? What is the name of the child?"

Her hand caught his and squeezed. All the life seemed to leave her body.

Agitatedly he shook her. She must not die. She must not, not till she talked. "Fedora! Wake up! Speak to me."

Feebly, her eyelids parted. The candle flame seemed not to reflect in them. They were black, dying.

"My new son, Fedora." He shook her. He whispered. "What is his name?"

So faintly it was almost not a sound but a breath she said the word, "Darrowfield."

"Darrowfield? Old Lord Darrowfield's son was really Uther's?"

Her eyes closed. She repeated the word. "Darrowfield." There was a violent spasm of coughing, and a great deal more blood came up. It soaked her bed gown and the sheets. And she was still.

Merlin sat staring at her for a long moment. From the hallway came the sound of the women mourning, wailing, as if somehow they knew Fedora had passed on.

So young Lord Darrowfield, his father's heir, was really the son of Uther, as had long been rumored. He was no mere lord. He was Arthur's brother. Or had been.

But what did that tell about all the deaths, all the kill-ings?

Then it dawned on him.


In the hallway the women were mourning, wailing, crying. Merlin paused to watch and listen. He had intended to tell them to make arrangement for Fedora's burial. But it was no use, not in their state. He would tend to it himself.

He saw Nimue returning, at the far end of the hall. They met, and he told her, "Let us go to the refectory. I have not eaten a proper meal in days."

"How can you eat after . . . ?"

"It might have been me, Nimue. Fedora was twenty years older than I, but it might have been me. One day it will be. A full stomach will remind me that I am still alive."

They walked to the dining hall without saying much more. It was past dinnertime; there were not many other people. Merlin had a plate of beef and vegetables. Nimue had already eaten, but she sat with him and sipped a goblet of wine. "Did she tell you what you needed to know?"

"I believe so."

"What was it?"

"She talked about Uther's sons. The late Lord Darrow-field, the one who died so horribly at Stonehenge, was Ar-thur's brother."

She drank her wine. "That has always been rumored. I mean, I had heard he was a bastard. But Uther . . . !"

"Yes, Uther. I should have realized long ago that Ar-thur's pursuit of women was not unique to him. It was Marmaduke, of all people, who reminded me of that."

Nimue was wry. "It's nice to realize that Marmaduke knew anything at all."

"Yes. But I think Fedora was trying to tell me something else. I think I understand what, but I cannot be certain. Unless . . ."

"Unless?"

"Nothing, Nim—Colin. Do you have any idea where Petronus is?"

She finished the wine and put the cup down. "Off at school, I think. The schoolmasters missed several of their classes because of the influenza."

"We weathered the plague. We can weather this."

"Yes, but the plague never really struck here, remember."

"Except for poor John. If it was plague that killed him. Let me have a swallow of your wine."

She turned the cup upside down to show him it was empty. "I'll go and get you some."

"A small cup, please."

She went. Merlin sat alone, brooding. What he was thinking was too unpleasant to contemplate.

In a moment she was back. Merlin thanked her, and she said she wanted to go back to her room. "It has been a draining time. Worrying about you, I mean. I need some rest."

"Fine. Go back to our tower. Oh, and start the steam engine for my lift. I certainly do not have the energy for all those stairs."

"I'll be sure to."

Merlin finished his meal and his wine and began making his way back to the Wizard's Tower. But just after leaving the refectory he encountered Simon. Simon, fussy as usual, was carrying a thick sheaf of papers and having trouble holding on to them. When one dropped, Merlin picked it up and handed it to him. He felt a twinge of pain in his back and rubbed it.

"Thank you, Merlin. I was just coming to find you. I was afraid you might still be under the weather."

"There is always weather to be under. What is it you want?"

Simon riffled through his papers, dropping several more.

"We've had a message from the king. I must have left it behind."

Suddenly Merlin sneezed. More of Simon's papers scattered and he scrambled to retrieve them.

"Does it not occur to you that you might carry those in a pouch of some sort?"

"In a pouch or out of one, the king's message is not here."

"Yes, of course. What does he say?"

"He is en route back to Camelot. The funeral was uneventful. Morgan never showed up."

"That is hardly surprising, I suppose. Now if you will excuse me, I need to return to my tower and get some rest. Oh—have you heard that old Fedora died a while ago?"

"Fedora?" Simon scowled. "I wish I had visited her. She delivered me, you know."

"Who among us is without sin?"

Simon made a sour face, commented on Merlin's sarcasm and left. Merlin went on his way, back to his tower.

His chair lift was waiting for him at the foot of it. He could hear the steam engine chugging steadily far above. Glancing up, he saw small, periodic puffs of steam from it, a hundred feet above. Looking up the tower always made him dizzy. The vast cylindrical shape, the staircase spiraling along the wall . . . He leaned against the wall momentarily to steady himself.

The seat was swaying slightly, he presumed in a draft. It added a bit more to his vertigo. He reached out and steadied it. Then gingerly he took his place in it, pulled the chain to start the mechanism, and began his ascent up the height of the tower.

It was slow. The lift always took three minutes or more to travel the full height of the tower. He watched as the stones moved downward past his field of vision. The staircase spiraled around him. The slow upward movement, the gentle swaying of the seat, lulled him to a state of complete relaxation. The seat moved twenty feet up, thirty, forty. He closed his eyes.

Then suddenly there was a huge jolt. The seat swung violently, almost striking the wall. Merlin gripped the chain and held tightly. Somehow the chain must have slipped, missed a cog. He leaned back in his seat, holding tight the chain, and glanced up. Everything was as usual. Everything was as it should be. The wild swaying gradually stopped, the gears reengaged and the ascent continued.

He was sixty feet above the ground. He could hear the gears as they turned, the engine as it hummed, the clanking of the chains.

Then there was another violent jolt and the lift swung wildly again. Merlin gripped the chain for dear life and looked up again.

There was someone at the landing on the top level, partway onto the wooden landing stage there. It was a man, and he was holding a long pike. He stretched it out and poked the top of the chain with it, and the lift swung wildly a third time. The man looked down at Merlin and cried, "Fall, damn you!"

Merlin recognized him. "Peter!"

As the seat rose closer to the top, the arc of its swing grew smaller. But Merlin was now eighty feet above the stone floor of Camelot. If he slipped, if the lift jerked too violently, he would fall to a certain death.

Peter stepped farther onto the landing platform and prodded the chain again. "Go on and fall!"

"If I die, Peter, it will be with the knowledge of what you are."

"When you sent that boy to Darrowfield, I knew that you were onto me." He pushed the tip of his pike into the gear assembly. With another jolt, the seat stopped its ascent.

Merlin was far above the castle's floor now. The seat

was still swaying. But he realized that if he could keep Peter talking, there would be no opportunity for him to pull his pike out of the gears and start prodding the seat again.

"I sent Colin there to flush you out. You had to realize I suspected you by that time."

"You are a good actor, Merlin. When did you first suspect? How could you possibly have guessed?" He twisted the tip of his pike and the seat rocked slightly.

Merlin tightened his grip on the chain. He had to force himself not to look down. "I found it odd when you showed up here at Camelot, abandoning your investigation into the murder of Darrowfield and his boys. And gradually it dawned on me that you were present when all of the killings were done. You were the only one. You are quite a good actor yourself, Peter. Or should I say 'Prince Peter'?"

"I was Father's favorite. He always hated Arthur. But I . . . He loved me."

"And not Darrowfield? Not his eldest son?"

"Darrowfield was a fool. You met him. You must have realized. Uther wanted me on the throne of England, not him."

"And so that is what he was doing at Darrowfield Castle? Plotting his eldest son's death with you?" He paused slightly. "With you . . . and Morgan?"

"Morgan despises Arthur, too. That is no secret."

"And you let her manipulate you into doing her murders for her. It was you who attacked Arthur at Grosfalcon, not her."

Peter nodded. "But she was concerned. After I killed Darrowfield and those two clots he called sons, she and Uther persuaded me to use, let us say, less direct methods. The plague was a gift to us. She had her own strain of belladonna. And she mixed it with some other poison from her stockpile. It made the deaths look like plague casualties."

"Even where there was no plague. That was the other thing that made me suspicious. But then, why not simply poison that poor boy at the mill? Why crush him between the mill-stones?"

Peter shrugged. "He caught me as I was administering the belladonna to Accolon. What else could I do?"

"You are a fool, Peter. You cannot possibly think Morgan would have let you rule. She is ambitious for herself and for her son."

"No. She is my sister."

"Arthur is your brother. Did that stop you from plotting his death? Morgan wants herself on the throne, or her son Mordred, not you."

Peter hesitated. This was obviously something he had not thought of before.

There was someone else on the landing, moving in the shadows behind him. Merlin realized it must be Nimue. He had to keep Peter talking. "So the three of you met in Darrowfield's own castle to plot his death. Yes, that sounds callous enough for Morgan, all right."

"The four of us. Darrowfield was a fool. He was in on our scheme from the beginning. But it never occurred to him that he might be our first victim. Why do you think he let me get close enough to kill him at Stonehenge?"

"This has gone on long enough, Peter. You cannot keep me dangling here forever. Let me finish my ascent. Surrender."

Peter laughed at him.

"There is no use going on with this, Peter. Do you think I have kept my suspicions to myself? My assistant Colin knows. I had to explain to him when I sent him to Darrowfield. I wanted him on his guard against you." He told the lie smoothly. Then he raised his voice slightly. "I did not want him to grapple with you. You are the larger man. He would not have had a chance against you."

"I can keep you dangling there till I get another pike to prod you off of that absurd seat of yours. I have one waiting here for just that purpose." He twisted the point of the pike farther into the gears, and the seat began rocking again.

"And Arthur knows as well," he lied. "You will be hunted down, arrested and put to death."

"Then I will join you in Hades."

Suddenly Nimue stepped into sight. She was carrying a pike, the second one Peter had brought with him. She prodded Peter with the tip. "I would suggest you surrender now and peacefully."

Startled, Peter went off balance and staggered to the edge of the platform. He reached out and grasped the end of the pike to steady himself. But Nimue was not about to let him regain his equilibrium. She let the pike go. Peter lost his balance and tumbled off the platform and fell down the hundred feet of the tower. His screams echoed. He hit the floor with a horrible sound.

Nimue stepped onto the platform and pulled the first pike loose from the gears. For a moment nothing happened. Then slowly the lift continued its ascent. When it reached the top she helped Merlin onto the platform. Grateful to be on something solid again, he put an arm around her. "Thank you, Colin. You are a good man."

The season's first heavy, sustained snow fell on the English countryside. Trees were airy white lace. Flakes danced in the air.

It was just after sunset, now and then the clouds parted and there was a large moon. Arthur and Merlin strolled side by side on the castle rooftop. The snow was three inches deep but neither of them seemed to mind. Except for the falling snow the world was still, and they walked in silence as if infected by it. At length they came to the rear of the castle and stood looking over the white landscape. In the distance was Camelot's graveyard. Headstones were capped with snow.

At length Arthur spoke. "I hope Fedora is resting peacefully."

Merlin kept his eyes on the cemetery, not the king. "There is no other way for mortal remains to rest."

"Always the romantic, aren't you? I wish just once you'd let your human side show."

Merlin paused, uncertain whether to go on. "Self-revelation never comes to me easily, Arthur. You know that. When I found that poor boy crushed to death between the millstones, my feelings were human enough. But it was also human feeling that led me to trust his killer." He turned to the king. "I was a fool to let my feeling of friendship for him cloud my judgment. He flattered me only too successfully."

"As always, you are too hard on yourself."

"I have never apologized for the harsh tone I took with you when we were Marmaduke's prisoners."

"We thought we were going to die, Merlin. No apology is necessary."

"I think one is due. I like to think of myself as a philosopher. At least a minor one. Prepared for death. I acted like a spoiled boy."

This made Arthur uncomfortable. A snowflake clung to his eyelash and he brushed it off. "We will never know what other secrets Fedora took with her to the grave. I suppose, in a way, we should be grateful for that."

"Secrets are the essence of humanity, Arthur. Or at any rate of human society, human interaction. What is hidden is what keeps us going."

"That seems an odd sentiment for a detective."

"It is the truth. To know, to actually *know* another human being is impossible, for all that we pretend otherwise. For all you know, I might be planning your assassination right now."

Arthur laughed. "As always, you are being overdramatic. I

have known you since I was a boy, Merlin. Why would you wait till this moment to use the knife in the dark?"

"Ripeness is all, Arthur." He ran his fingers through the snow on a battlement. "When Peter told me his messages to me were being interfered with, I had no reason to doubt him. Now I understand the lie.

"When he showed up here unbidden, just before John died, I should have realized. He was there when every murder was committed."

Arthur stared up at the moon. "Are you ready for the trial of Lulua and Marmaduke?"

He nodded. "We have already selected twelve knights to form the jury. I do not think making the case against them will be difficult. There were dozens of witnesses."

The king kept his eyes on the moon. Merlin had the impression he was trying to read something in its face. Finally he said, "That is all good, Merlin. But . . ."

"Yes?"

"What do we do about my sister?"

Merlin heaved a deep sigh. "I am not certain there is anything we can do. If we find her and arrest her, we could never put her on trial. The only concrete evidence against her is Peter's confession, and Peter is . . . Our England is concerned with justice. We cannot expect a jury to convict her on no evidence."

"So she remains at large, remains free to keep plotting against me." He looked directly into Merlin's eyes. "Against *us*."

"I fear so. The best we can do is to watch her very carefully."

Arthur looked from Merlin back to the moon. "It is too much for me. I need to have some wine and go to bed."

Softly, "Good night, then, Arthur. Sleep well."

"Aren't you coming in? The wind is starting to pick up."

"No. I need to be alone with my thoughts for a while."

The king left. Merlin stood alone on the rooftop. The wind gusted, and clouds filled the sky.

The raven Roc flew to Merlin's shoulder and nuzzled his ear. He reached up and stroked it. He whispered, "Roc, there is nothing human about you. There is not the least trace of my species." Lightly he kissed the bird's head. "That is why I love you."

**E**nter the rich world of historical romance with Berkley Books.

Lynn Kurland

Patricia Potter

Betina Krahn

Jodi Thomas

Anne Gracie

*Love is timeless.*
**penguin.com**